THE PSYCHOPATH WHO NEARLY LOST HIS ARM

LOVE-BOMB. DEVALUE. DISCARD.

JULIETTE A H CAVENDISH

The Psychopath Who Nearly Lost His Arm.

Love-Bomb. Devalue. Discard. A Novel.

Copyright January 2021 by Juliette A H Cavendish

This novel is a work of fiction. The names, characters and incidents portrayed in it are the work of the author's imagination. Any resemblance to actual persons, living or dead, events or localities is entirely coincidental. Adult readers recommended only, due to the mature nature of the content.

Cover Design by London Red Publishing 2021.

ISBN Paperback: 9780648853084

ISBN Ebook: 9780648853008

www.juliettecavendish.com.au

www.ziforah.com

A,

Forever Remembered

Children live in wars, when there is peace outside
and tiny souls are shaped by fires of
burning rage,
floods of despair,
and endless silence.

They search for love, which, appearing veiled
sneaks through light then dark
cleverly disguised,
mask elusive,
then gone, again.

Tiny soul, tiny hope
wanting, needing
arms that wrap, adorned with safe
trusting instead,
impenetrable walls
of hit, of rage, of loss.

Unloveable is not, was not,
forever my child,
but you never heard,
your burden heavy
encasing, smothering, then carnage.

Death stepped forward
to take, perhaps kindly,
what you had carried
with such courage
and for time that had appeared,
in clever disguise.

Fly free now.
Our love, funny, silly, ageing, now yours to take.
Find your place amongst the vast
and be at last,
the shining star
having found your infinite belonging.

forever
and always
xxx

TO BE OR NOT TO BE...

THAT IS NOT THE WHOLE QUESTION, FOR THERE MAY BE A THIRD WAY OF BEING, ONCE YOUR TRUTH IS UNCOVERED AND SPOKEN. STAND IN YOUR POWER AND SPEAK IT WITH CONFIDENCE, FOR IT IS YOURS TO SPEAK AND YOURS ONLY. THE EVIL IN OTHERS, AND THAT IN CIRCUMSTANCE MUST NEVER CLOUD THE RIGHT FOR ANOTHER TO LIVE WITHIN THE CERTAINTY OF THEIR OWN SELF.

..... Pippa O'Shea

NOTE TO SELF: IT WON'T MAKE SENSE
IF THEY DON'T KNOW WHO HAMLET
IS.

CONTENTS

1

———

THE BIT BEFORE THE START
I FEEL LIKE SHIT

Day 1.

Pardon this opening, but I feel somewhat like shit. Not even a whole turd kind of feeling. Hard to describe, but something akin to being a long, streaming, endless cascade of complete and utter crap. There, I have started this standing squarely in raw and eloquent honesty. Okay… not eloquent, but indeed honest, even if bordering on unwholesome imagery. I was going to start this by being witty and intellectual and then write sentences consisting of beautifully crafted adjectives, like a real writer. Someone who knows how to sculpt and polish words into literary masterpieces. Then I thought, why not try the raw truth instead? So, giving away any notion of literary prestige in the future, I've chosen sailors, butt holes, amputation, zips, pig wrestling and other unsavoury stuff, because to be honest, that's more indicative of real-life with my family and suitors.

So if you're after a Mr Darcy story, told as elegantly as Jane managed to, then I think your adventure awaits you somewhere in the romantic pleasantry section in your local library. This story will instead be found under the counter, wrapped in plain brown paper and authored by someone who grew up on a Tasmanian alpaca farm. You'll need to whisper 'Pippa… the psycho book,' to even lay eyes on it. To clarify, this tale does have sprinkles of funny bits, but then it changes, as love always does for me. Be prepared for a ride with a psychopath, and recounts of getting down and dirty with family-pig wrestling No, not real pigs. That's just how it feels when I attend family get-togethers. It's all grunts and mud where I come from, along with the occasional fisticuffs thrown in for fun.

After the instances of love-bombing, the sudden death in my family and all that muck-filled wrestling, this story ain't pretty. By then, neither am I.

Day 2.

To cut a long story short, for those naughty readers who turn to the last page, first, I was searching for love one day and stumbled across an innocuous-looking predator. A man who turned out to be an actual genuine and certified psychopath in fact. My intention in engaging with him was to love and have a good time. His was to find a victim to mock, shame, demean and hurt. I put my hand up and volunteered for the experience. Blind, oblivious, naive and stupid to the danger awaiting me, he then did hurt me. Significantly, in mind, body and soul. Since then, I'm supposed to have moved on, healed and be out there again, trying someone else on for size. I haven't moved at all, trapped amongst endless emotional flash-backs, and still shocked at how cruel, human beings can be to each other. It's a lonely time, as people only give you a couple of weeks to get over grief before they tire of your neediness.

You know how it works. You get one sentence of acknowledgement, and then people forget. They tell you that they are sorry for your 'mistake… dud… loss,' as if you are absent-minded and might have misplaced the missing person. In reality, no-one gets over someone that they thought they loved that deeply in that time. The process of discard, in reality, is long and lonely. The first two weeks of afterwards merely allows for the shock to wear off. By the time you are ready to start processing, everyone else has long since fled the scene. Anyway, when you try to explain how it unfolded, some people just don't get it and run in the other direction. Stories like mine seem too bizarre to be true. Maybe it is best to suffer this sort of loss in silence, squeezed between sheets of journal paper?

Day 3.

I pretend to have bounced back at work, not that anyone asks any more. I'm just a bouncing ball of positivity and utterer of motivational platitudes. It's only when I get home, and no-one is looking that my genuine grief is allowed to surface. It's not really very exciting either. I'm not wailing into empty spaces or rocking on the floor. It's more a kind of lethargy that shrouds everything in slow and bleak, with silent tears, self-doubt and endless ruminations. Nights filled with intrusive thoughts and a heart that beats too quickly on occasion.

After he had spat his last word at me and had stormed off in his cloud of self-righteous indignation, I wondered who was left standing there, not wholly recognising the remnants of myself. Being discarded was akin to having witnessed his mask being lowered, but instead of seeing him, I had seen into the eyes of a monster. I thought I knew who I was until my psychopath told me that he had figured me out better. In his eyes, I was unequivocally pathetic, a failure as a human being and completely unloveable. Luckily, to soften the impact, I was raised in a family of narcissists, so I already had a hunch I was unloveable, given the numerous discards I'd already gone through. He just sealed the deal. It's official. In amongst the billions on this planet, I am apparently destined to walk alone. I did search for a way back but saw nothing ahead of me. I surmise that perhaps he also took my path away when he left, because he could.

Day 4.

I've had some lovely post-break-up suggestions from well-meaning people. One told me to 'go eat more bananas.' Someone else suggested I try Tinder and swipe right for everyone, including the guys holding long, dead fish. Another told me to cease dating altogether. I've been told to cut my hair, grow my hair, colour my hair, change my wardrobe, drink more local beer (?) and find a higher consciousness. As if somehow any of that will help. My heart got broken, dudes. My soul was shredded, and my trust obliterated. Whilst bananas are good for potassium, they aren't going to fix what is now wrong with me.

Day 5.

I wonder if growing up inside a house of dysfunction, twisted meaning and burning rage, has wired me wrong? In hindsight, I'm beginning to see that falling in love with a psychopath isn't normal. The fact that I persisted trying, in such a gigantic mess of a relationship, believing it was the right one, says so much about how brain wiring can get messed up when dysfunctional parenting and family interactions are all you have known. I wanted to help him, and he knew that. Nothing wrong with that until you donate your soul to the cause as well. The more dysfunctional he became, the more of me I gave. Then one day there wasn't anything left of me to give. He had taken all of it. He blamed me then for my nothingness, seeing it as weakness, and blatant failure as a human being. Then he shat on my memory, verbally abused my oxygen supply, obliterated my hope, and walked off, feigning injury as the victim.

Day 6.

I don't like writing in journals.

Day 7.

INCLUDE MOUNDS OF SALT, SLESSOR, GET SERIOUS CHAPTER SIX, FLUFF! BEES, RATS, BUTT HOLES.

mother-fucker-pink-shorts

PARIS. ALPACAS, TOILET WATER, POX.

fluff chapters then story gets heavy. No drugs and alcohol to be consumed.

2

———

TO BEE OR NOT TO BEE

THERE'S A SQUATTER IN MY HEAD

'He's claiming squatters' rights,' I said to my life-coach, Brad, my eyes still too wide for normal.

My regular life coaching sessions were mostly held at the same cafe, known for its exotic coffee bean blends. It was a small, cosy cafe, filled with urgent chatter. Hessian coffee bags draped onto white-washed crates, provided a place to park yourself to divulge whatever needed sharing. Down one end, where I was sitting with Brad, you could plug your laptop into the distressed timber tables and stay to savour the coffee. The other end was for quicks shots and fast talkers - people who needed to be somewhere else. After an hour at my end, they sounded your table bell and then it was buy another coffee or have a nice day.

'Sorry, what squatter?' Brad looked up at me, somewhat blankly from his laptop.

'The squatter dude in my head. He's interfering with my everything.'

'Are we talking voices, tent zips, the smell of wood fire?'

'Brad, be serious.'

'Sorry. It's a bit early for humour I'm presuming?' He shut the lid of his laptop and offered himself as fully available. 'Okay, emails done, all yours. Let's have it. Start at the very beginning.'

'The guy let himself in without asking, is creating havoc amongst my neural networks, and now apparently refuses to leave. I'm sick of him. I need his memory out, and I need to get these flashbacks under control. I miss feeling like… me.'

'So, this isn't a family member I'm assuming?' Brad leaned over and plugged his laptop into the table charge.

'My family, do squatting? They do a detonation type of thing and then run as it blows.' As if on cue, the cafe bell sounded.

'So this is psychopath dude, I'm guessing, who has pitched a tent in your head? We can work with this. Your family, though? I'd need specialised training to deal with them. Preferably in bomb disposal with six months of therapy thrown in and a new identity that includes relocation.' Brad smiled, pleased with his apt description. His upturned mouth managed to disengage my abdominal muscles from their death twist for the first time in three days.

'Might be safer?' I returned a real smile back, my first for the week.

'We could try for extraction? It depends on where he's pitched himself? You may come out quite badly if he's squatting in your brainstem. Could get rather messy.' Brad gulped the last of his coffee. 'You done? Want another, or have you had enough caffeine for one day? You look like you might have snuck in a few before I arrived? We can walk and talk or order another?'

'I never say no to coffee Brad. I'll try that new blend, from Tanzania is it?' I squinted, trying to read the small but arty chalk writing on the menu, perched above the counter.

'It says it's dark and brooding,' he offered, helping me out. 'Keep it simple? Flat white?'

'Yeah, thanks. Dark and brooding? Seems appropriate,' I sighed.

'Look, I shouldn't be so flippant,' he said, returning with two steaming white, chunky, mugs. 'How are you doing? Really?'

'Being honest? Not that great. It's like he left me in pieces and I'm supposed to reinvent myself as a mosaic. When people say they feel shattered? I get that now. I also feel foolish, like I should have known better or something. In hindsight, I can't understand why I stayed. None of it makes much sense in hindsight.' I shook my head. 'I make no sense.' In hindsight, it was true. Then again, hindsight can only be gained *after* the event I reasoned.

'You certainly met the real deal, from what you have told me,' Brad said, his tone softening. 'Are you still following the self-care plan we worked on?'

'Trying to and working hard not to turn to stuff that would numb it all. It's exhausting, to be honest, all this self-analysis. Drinking and taking pills would be a lot easier,' I added, hopefully. 'A bit of numb to help me ride out the waves of despair?'

'You're doing great Pippa, given what you went through, but pills and alcohol aren't included in the plan. Sorry. You have to ride this out using helpful stuff, not drugs.'

'Boring, but worth a try.' I gazed out of the window at the people hurrying past the cafe on their way to somewhere. I wondered if they had ever met a psychopath too, and had been sucked into a love affair that had taken them to a place where nightmares are crafted and souls destroyed. I surmised that my thoughts were entering into histrionic territory and turned back to reality.

'Here's something that might interest you,' Brad said, trying to lift the mood at the table. 'It turns out that you can't be diagnosed as an actual psychopath. I looked it up in the DSM-5.'

'Really?' I wondered if psychopaths were too dangerous to get close enough to, for a proper diagnosis. They really should keep them in a separate room, just for the safety of those around them.

'Individuals who are psychopaths are labelled as having Antisocial Personality Disorder instead. Psychopaths exist only in the movies, and in art classes, as you discovered.'

'That's lame,' I muttered, sipping the new coffee, my tastebuds dancing from the assault.

'Dark and brooding not good?'

'No. The coffee is great. It's earthy and has a nice edge to it. It can go on the keeper list. The DSM-5, though? It literally takes the 'psycho' out of a psychopath. Describing them as simply antisocial? Makes them sound as if they just don't like social gatherings. Introverts are antisocial. Psychopaths are literally, psychos.' I sighed as memories cascaded into my mind.

'It means suffering soul,' Brad volunteered. 'If that's any consolation.'

'What does?'

'The term that psychopath originally comes from. It's a German term.'

'Suffering soul? As in the person who has to deal with a psychopath? My soul certainly suffered and continues to do so. Besides, psychopaths don't even have souls. His insides were a vacuous cesspit of turds.'

'Charming, Pippa. Isn't that impossible?'

'What?'

'Being vacuous and full of shit at the same time?'

'Nah.' I shook my head. 'Anyway, doesn't having a soul imply human traits such as empathy, guilt, and kindness? All three definitely missing from where I was standing.'

'On the bright side…'

'You actually think there's a bright side to this?' I asked, my tone both incredulous and hopeful at the same time.

'At least he's not a narcissist like everyone else out there. All of my other clients are dealing with narcissists parking themselves in their heads. It's the dysfunction flavour of the year.'

'I've never truly understood how some people can end a relationship and not look over their shoulder, even if it's only to be compassionate. It's negligent, as well as cruel.'

'That insight means you're not a narcissist, Pippa. Congrats.'

'Well, that's a relief. I'll tick that one off my list of current dysfunctions then.' I sipped the coffee, my hands warming around the cup. There was something comforting with the action.

Brad typed into his phone, then turned it. 'There are thousands of books about narcissism online. All with the same broken heart on the cover. I have always thought that smashed avocado would be more appropriate given the mess they leave behind.'

I imagined my own heart, smashed on toast, with a sprig of what was left of my dignity as a garnish. 'People like that,' I said thoughtfully, 'they coax your heart out, so gently and so carefully, promising it love and attention. Then, one day, they suddenly pulverise it. Next? They walk away, leaving someone else to clean up the mess.'

Brad shook his head. 'Lovely imagery there Pippa.'

'Glad to share.' I paused, reflecting some more. 'It's the way they trap you, though. Do you know those Venus flytrap plants? It's similar. You think you've found something good only to find yourself in the clutches of something that wants to kill your spirit, not love it. Only by then, you're kind of trapped. It's weird.'

'That's what a lot of my clients say. This sort of thing is what I deal with the most. People who thought they had found their perfect match, who turned out to be their worst nightmare. Happens a lot, unfortunately.'

'I'm not alone then if that's any consolation. The whole thing with Noah was bizarre. When I first met him, I honestly thought that soul mates were real. At the end? I feel perplexed that I managed to get myself into a mess like that. In the end, I was spun around so much, even if I had wanted to find the exit door, I couldn't have walked out. It's that dichotomy stuff. Intelligent woman… blah, blah, blah. Why didn't she just walk and leave? The door was there. The door was open… and no-one was stopping me.' I shook my head.

Brad jumped in to help me finish my thought. 'Because there's more to it than that. The invisible control boundaries for a start.'

'Yeah… true… all the stuff that he said when no-one else was looking. If I cried because he'd sworn at me, I was crazy. If I was sick, then I had strange illness behaviour. If I missed him, I was neurotic. If I spoke, then I talked too much. It was like everything I did had this negative label attached. Then one day I realised I couldn't move,' I sighed. 'I knew that no matter which way I turned, it would be the wrong way. That no matter what I said, that I would have chosen the wrong words. That's when I knew I was in trouble - especially given how pretend-nice he was to everyone else.'

'There's a term for some of that. It's called gaslighting. If you say you're hurt by a comment they have made, they tell you it was a compliment, and you've misinterpreted it. They provoke, and you respond, and then they tell you it's all in your head. Or they abuse you, then blame you for being weak when you react. It's enough to screw anyone up - not that I'm saying you're screwed up.'

'Thanks. I feel screwed up, to be honest. It's like he had two faces. The first one was kind, and then this other one showed up that was cruel. I miss the nice one and am relieved to be away from the cruel one. It makes no sense. A weird situation that makes for quite a mindfuck. What I do know is that I'm a moron for having stayed in it for so long.' I shook my head, not understanding my own sticking power.

'No, Pippa. You are wired to tolerate his weirdness and idiosyncrasies. He knew that. You are able to love someone whose head spins with polar opposite emotional states.'

'A spinning head?' I looked at him quizzically, imaging a Chucky doll with a head acting as a lighthouse.

'People like that, they meet someone and then test them out. They want to know if they've got a blind spot for weird shit. If they have, it's game-on, and they play with them. That's the point of the relationship for them. They don't want a genuine relationship. They want the game. The rhythm and cycle of love-bombing, devalue and discard. They crave the thrill of the chase and then the high when they discard you. They enjoy it with their own sense of warped self-righteousness.'

'Like, you're saying that they test to see if you will play?'

'Yeah. Did he say something right at the beginning that was odd? Out of place? They usually do to test the water.'

I thought back to the beginning and then remembered something that had seemed out of place. 'This might count as weird?'

'Okay, what did he say?'

'He told me his arm was probably going to have to be amputated.'

'His arm? Gees. What was wrong with his arm?'

'He'd had surgery for a rotator cuff injury and said that the next step was amputation. But his arm seemed to be quite okay, looking back on it. It wasn't just hanging there, lifeless or anything. He was using it reasonably well. Although, I'm not medical,' I clarified.

'So, he tells you that his rotator cuff tear requires a complete amputation of his arm? Not because of cancer or some other terrible disease? Did you question him over it?'

'As discreetly as you can at a dinner table. I wasn't going to interrogate him. I mean, I was assuming that he was honest.'

'So, what did you say at the time?'

'I told him what anyone else would have said. Showed some support, understanding, empathy and was non-judgmental.'

'How many weeks into the relationship was this?'

'That was during our first date. We went to that French restaurant opposite the Opera House. Breathtaking views.' I was back there, sitting at the table, looking out over the harbour that had reflected back such promise for our relationship. Brad interrupted my sugar-coated memory.

'So, hi gorgeous, nice to meet you. By the way, my arm needs to be amputated, even though the injury isn't serious.'

'He didn't put it like that. I'm not stupid, Brad. He was cleverer than that. Somehow, he got me to believe him.' I frowned. 'In hindsight, I can see how absurd it is, but at the time? He had a way of making it all… sound so convincing.'

'Did he say anything else that was out of place?'

I thought back, scanning through the memories of our first date. 'That he liked hurting people.'

'As in physically hurting them?' Brad asked, concerned.

'Again, I didn't ask for clarification. It seemed like a normal comment in context. I think he was talking about how he could be blunt at times, so I assumed that he hurt people by being unintentionally blunt. Brutal honesty, that sort of thing. I didn't assume he meant intentionally or physically at the time. Otherwise, I would have run in the other direction.'

Brad paused. 'Anything else?'

'I don't know. Snippets of small-talk. Like his ex-wife had been withholding sex for eight years or something.'

Brad laughed. 'The blue-balls pity party? Was that on the first date too?'

'Yeah, and he said that he'd gone to this really expensive school. He kept mentioning all these famous people who had been at school with him. That, I did find a bit odd. Kind of like he was name-dropping and trying to impress me. Not that I recognised any of the names.'

'So, you met someone from a rich family, suffering from blue-balls, whose arm was going to be amputated from a relatively minor injury, and who was blunt enough to hurt people?' Brad looked at me, squinting his eyes ever so slightly. 'All of this said to you by a man who was supposedly making a good impression on a first date?'

'Yeah? You make it sound so obvious. It wasn't like that when he said it though. It just seemed like a normal conversation.'

'That's the way people like that test you. They ascertain where your boundaries are - or in your case, aren't. A healthy person would have walked away, sensing that something wasn't quite gelling with them. You saw an opportunity to…'

'Run in and start helping.' I paused, realising my stupidity. 'Oh my God, it's like I've been programmed to help people with problems. Can I be fixed, or do you think I'm a lost cause at this point?'

'Nah, we just need to keep re-wiring you.'

'You make me sound like an AI.'

Brad smiled. 'There's been huge developments in brain plasticity, epigenetics and stuff. You can change,' he said reassuringly. 'You can learn to see red flags, and you can learn to walk away. You're going to have to in a sense if you ever want to find normal.'

'Can you do a brain transplant, maybe? Give me a different life completely? That might be nice.' I started to think about a new identity and a different family.

'No, we have to work on the one you've been living.'

'Bugger. I was afraid you were going to say that.'

'I'M TIRED,' I said, sometime later, as we walked back to the carpark after the session. 'It's like this suffocating world-weariness is getting to me. I've run out of *joie de vivre*. I'm running on empty.'

Brad looked concerned.

'I'm too old to be so easily hurt, aren't I? Hamlet was right to ponder whether to be or not to be. I don't sometimes know if I have the energy to *want* to keep doing the same thing over and over.'

'Hamlet? You reading Shakespeare or something? Seriously though, how bad are you feeling, right now?' Brad asked, sounding concerned.

'I keep trying to find traction, only I get knocked down again and again. I'm down on the floor, gazing up at the red soles of people who are going somewhere. I'm crawling along, sniffing wear and tear on carpets. I sometimes wonder if people like me, who grow up with such shitty families can never make it? What if we are destined to never get it quite right?'

Brad winced at the imagery. 'Are you still taking those meds?'

'Nah. I got letter-boxed. I was too content. Apathetic even. I may as well have been finger painting, drooling and weaving baskets. There has to be a happy medium between living in post-psychopath anguish and living in a world of letter-boxes. Anyway, no pill will ever solve what to do with all of that grief or my family. I'm at the *finding practical solutions stage,* not sedation.'

'How bad are you feeling Pippa?'

'I just want *normal.* Just for once.'

'Get the tattoo of *weirdos, come get me* removed from off your forehead then?'

'Brad!' I laughed. Brad had the ability to inject humour into times where it was needed.

'Look, I have an idea that might help. Writing therapy is good, as it can help clarify things. You have to work through what's in your head to get it out onto the page. It might help you to gain insight as to what you have been through.'

'I tried writing in a journal recently. I lasted six whole days. Even the paper was cringing from what was coming out of my head.'

'I mean a proper recount. Tell your whole story. Maybe start with the sailor you were telling me about.'

'Why the sailor?'

'Because you just need to start somewhere, and that's a good a place to start as any.'

'So, you think if I start with the sailor and then get to the psychopath, that all of this will make better sense? Make me feel better?'

'Yeah, I do, Pippa.'

'Why not just go straight to the psychopath bit?'

'It won't explain how you managed to get yourself into that mess. That's why. People don't just meet psychopaths, fall in love with them, and then stay when there is that much crap flying around. Many small steps are taken before getting to that point, and many reasons why people put up with being treated like you were.'

'You're probably right. There were plenty of times I should have walked, and instead, I hung on more tightly.'

'Write your back story. Then, it all makes sense. Early dysfunction wires the brain in strange ways. It makes you susceptible to more weird.'

'The sailor, though?'

'Yeah, the sailor, that living disco ball, the mounds of salt, and those rubber shoes. All that stuff.'

'I'd like to add the bees and rats too,' I said, thinking carefully about my past.

'What bees and rats?' Brad asked. 'Have I heard about the bees and rats yet?'

'Haven't I told you about the bees and rats? It's a pretty cool story.'

'Does it have any relevance to the rest?'

'Not really… more of a tenuous link, I think? I mean I could make it relevant if I try?'

'I'm not sure about including it then. This is therapy writing, not a novel.'

'Every good story needs a bit of fluff. You can't deny me fluff, Brad, especially if I'm going to have to trawl back through the horrors of my past. It might act as a humorous, literary buffer amongst the bleakness of my life.'

'I suppose not. It's not my story, after all. However, add a warning that an entire chapter is full of fluff, for the sole reason that it's a good story in itself. It *is* a good story then? he asked, clarifying.

'Yeah, totally. So, if I add a disclaimer about how the bees and rats are solely included as literary filler at the beginning?'

'Pippa.' Brad's face went serious. 'I know we're joking around here, but some of the stuff you went through was serious. Have your fluff, yes, but this psychopath you met, as well as your family issues? That stuff is real. Don't minimise it for the sake of a few giggles about bees and rats. Don't use humour to detract from what happened. It's important to tell it as it is. The whole idea with writing therapy is to process what happened, not to do a written stand-up comedy routine.'

'So, tell it all realistically? Okay, how about I start with humour and then allow it to get dark?'

'Just rip the bandaid off and write your story so that the truth can emerge. What was it like to be around narcissists and psychopaths? All this pressure to belong to a happy family? Blow it out of the water.'

'This is for your eyes only, right?'

'Of course. Unless you decided to upload it somewhere public, it's up to you, Pippa.'

'Okay, then. Deal. Fluffy chapters, then serious from say, chapter six?'

'You have five chapters of fluff? Jesus, Pippa. Can you not condense it to say… two?'

'It's just a guesstimate at this stage, but I need to set the scene properly.'

Brad got his car keys out. 'Writing all of this down is going to help you, I promise. Phone me if you need me at any time because you may trigger. If you do, walk away for a bit. The real benefit of this will be to sit in it and find your way out.'

'Find my way out? Like it's my responsibility to do this?'

'Yeah.'

'Hey - what's the title for all of this?'

'You need a title? Okay. What's the weirdest aspect, do you think? Call it that.'

'How about… *The psychopath who nearly lost his arm?*' I called after him.

Brad gave me the thumbs up. 'Yeah, I like that. He never did have it amputated, did he?'

'No.'

'Just checking. If he had, then that would undermine the whole story.'

'I feel inspired,' I called over, arriving at my car. 'So, start with the sailor? Okay, I think I can do this.'

complain to fridge manufacturer

avoid chilli in future

cleaning hack. salt absorbs blood

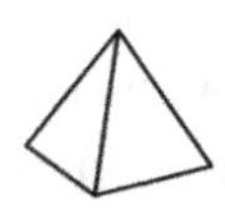

3

LIVING DISCO BALL
SLESSOR

I think I know why I'm starting with the sailor. It was the first time I'd done something verging on independent, knowing that I couldn't get caught and punished for my spontaneity. There was no family to witness the event and report me to my parents and no rod long enough to reel me back in if only to criticise me for my unacceptable behaviour. It was time to let my hair down and do something that might take my breath away. The potential problem with this was my lack of street-smart experiences - usually acquired throughout one's teenage years in the safety of a family unit. You learn by your mistakes. A child like me, so heavily controlled, leaves the nest with no boundaries and no street-smart wisdom. A child of narcissists has no compass about what is expected and what isn't, and indeed no experience with independent action. Right from wrong? No idea. Boundaries? What are those? My early experiences speak for themselves.

I'm just twenty and working in a travel agency, and I've just dialled 'Dine With A Sailor' using one of those old dial phones because that's what my flat came with and everyone loves its antiquity. You needed patience dialling any number larger than a six, as the dial had to return to resting position before you could go again. This nuance of design would have presented itself as an oxymoron for people frantically dialling 000 in an emergency. Jane, who works with me, had passed me a note earlier in the day, with a number scrawled in black. I'd looked over at her quizzically and had shaken my head, not knowing what it was for. She'd mouthed at me 'just call it.' So, I did.

'Hello, you've reached 'Dine With A Sailor.' How can I help you?'

'Sorry?'

'You've called 'Dine With A Sailor'. Would you like to book an evening with a sailor?'

'A sailor?' I asked, surprised that one could even book a sailor. 'An evening for what?' I added curiously.

'The American aircraft carrier Black Eagle will be docking later today. You can organise to meet one of the sailors for a drink and perhaps dinner?'

'Really?'

'Yes. You did just dial the number to make a booking.'

'I'll need to see if I'm… free. I'll call you back.'

'That's fine. Just be aware that we don't have many sailors left for bookings this evening.'

I put the phone down, my heart now thudding to a dangerous and tantalising beat.

I WAITED for Jane in the lunchroom, and took her to one side, into the discreet nook, mostly used for gossip and emergencies, just like this was.

'Are you encouraging me to meet with a random American sailor, and then have sex?' I asked, my eyes wide, full of excited conspiracy. 'Isn't that being a little lackadaisical with my virginity?' I added, just to add some sense of moral overtone to balance things out.

'Pippa. Seriously? No. You just meet them for a drink. Poor buggers have been at sea, too long for normal. They just want a bit of company. You can do other stuff *if* you want, though.' She laughed, 'We're all adults here, Pippa.'

'So, you don't *have* to have sex?'

'No, Pippa. These aircraft carriers have been docking in Sydney for ages. Have you never done this?'

'No, never. Not once. So, do I get to choose the type of sailor I want?'

'Yes. You get a choice when you phone. They ask what you would like. That is unless you've left it too late and you get the last one.'

'What I like? As in, like when I order a pizza?'

'Not following your connection there,' she said, frowning at me.

'As in flavour? Type?'

'Oh, you mean like ordering an all-meat lovers? Yeah, I suppose that's essentially what I've asked for, in hindsight.' She giggled, hope in her laughter and a bounce in her chestnut curls.

I considered ordering a vegetarian, something mild and underwhelming, so as not to get myself into trouble later on.

'Are you definitely doing this then?' I asked, just to be sure. I felt as if my toes were hanging over the edge of a diving board. I just needed one tiny push, and I would be in free-fall.

'Pippa, for God's sake, just call. We'll go to a bar together, the four of us. You'll be perfectly safe. I promise.' She grinned, and I knew at that moment that this was going to spell trouble.

SO, HERE I am, standing in the toilets at some seedy bar in Kings Cross, where music is blaring, and the ladies sign is hazy from the smoke. The outside had welcomed me in with glaring, red flashing lighting. I was met with a vision of old oak wood draped with sweat and bodies talking over tattered paper coasters. A drag queen is now standing next to me, reapplying her lipstick on huge, shimmering, purple lips. She's well over six-five and is dazzling, head to toe, adorned in purple sequins, presenting herself as a living disco ball. This shimmering vision is leaning forward, teeth all smiling at me, anxious to gain my approval for being in the ladies' toilet, a risqué move for such a moment in our social timeline.

Now she's speaking, only I'm silent, lost in my awe because I've never actually met a drag queen before, especially one encased in ten thousand shining sequins, who smiles like a T-Rex might, before feeding. I look from her toes towards her head as if studying some magnificent statue at a museum.

'Isn't this the most fun you've had in ages?' she grins at me, wiggling her flashing tush. I feel the air in the toilets move from the action.

'Yes.' I clam up, not wanting to hint that it's the first time I'd been out socially, in months… years… ever.

'So, loving this bar girl, or what? Yeah? Great atmosphere and fabulous company.' She smiles… too much. I'm not used to someone smiling at me this close-up, and it feels odd.

'Yeah. It's great,' I said to the teeth, which I am now fixated on.

'You got a sailor with you, sweetie?' Her eyes widen a little at me, wanting, needing, *demanding* to know.

'Yes.' I pause. Does she have a sailor as well, I wonder?

'Me too. What's yours like? Did you get a good one? I did this year, thank fucking Jesus. Last time I was given a full ironing board, lordy me. He may as well have been a stiff, and not in the right place, I can tell you. I complained too, asked for a replacement. Can you imagine that?' She giggled at her memory. 'Must get back to mine. This new one? He's promising me *everything*. Can't resist that now, can I?' She smacked her lips together, then stood back to admire herself in the mirror. 'Do I look beautiful darl? Do I? I think I might. Have fun honey, make sure you have *lots* of fun.' She exited, taking her light show with her.

What does one offer when promising *everything* I wondered as I took some time-out in the toilet cubicle. My logical mind kicked into action, wondering how the disco ball would manage to do anything in such a tiny space, in such massive attire. Would she try to heave it all up to pee, and then hope to land fair square on the seat, coming down blind? Or maybe she would stand, hoping to aim and fire in a straight line from under her cloak of purple? Personally, it would be easier to stand, I deduce. She seemed to like me though, and I remember the exchange as the day that a dazzling drag queen shared a few moments of her life with me, smiling with all of those teeth.

SHE ISN'T MY SAILOR, of course, she is just more interesting to discuss than my sailor, who thinks that Jane is far more attractive than me. The problem is that Jane's sailor also thinks that her assets are more delectable than mine. I've spent the evening sitting with them, watching them ogle Jane. Sometimes I try to get noticed by being funny, but they just half-laugh, in my direction, and then face Jane again. I've made several origami birds with stained, cardboard coasters, not that they have wondered about the growing flock on the table. I've also observed the proliferation of several strains of bacteria lurking in the peanuts in our table bowl, acting now as a petri dish. For a night out, this is such fun compared to some of the evenings I've shared at home with my family.

My sailor is called Christopher, pronounced with a southern drawl, 'Crist-ow-fuurrrr' he had articulated to me, but that's as far as the exotic goes. Oh, he did add 'MD in training' only I haven't been able to find out what that means yet. He's short, mousy, skinny, and smokes too much, creating a hazy cloud that sits over all of us. Cigars, Padron, 1964. I'm supposed to be impressed by that, and the MD bit, because he did this considerable pause after saying it all. Not what I ordered earlier in the afternoon, though. Specifically, an order of tall, solid sailor with arms, my hands couldn't fit around. I told the woman to make my order a salami, I'm sure. Instead, they'd given me a rubbery twiggy stick, partially obscured by foul-smelling smoke. I'm sure 'disappointed' has formed on my forehead in beaded sweat.

Jane's sailor is drop-dead gorgeous. An infectious smile, blonde hair and blue eyes, wrapped up in layers of delicious meat. Too beautiful for me, though. I worry in fact that the T-Rex-disco-ball might smell his deliciousness and stalk him later on. I wonder if dinosaurs like twiggy sticks, wondering if I could coax Christ-ow-fuurrrr into its vision. However, Jane loves all of this attention, and the last I saw of the magnificent three, was them walking towards the park to partake in a ménage à trois. I wonder if they'll get caught by a security guard innocently investigating a potential grass fire in the bushes, after smelling smoke?

I wonder if I'll ever be daring enough to be the slice in a sandwich one day? It might be fun to try. One day that is. I put it onto my to-do bucket list, and start to head back home to my flat. I walk towards the quay, mulling over how it might feel to be as beautiful as Jane and realise that I will never feel the same, not with the face I've been born with. I know my face must have issues because I was once dating a guy who was cheating on his girlfriend with me. Not that I knew, until I got an angry phone call from her.

The words spat fast and furiously from recollection were.

'Pippa, he thinks your face is so unattractive that he has to shut his eyes when you guys kiss… and then he thinks of me.'

All said in a lofty tone as well. Like ouchy, you bitch! I gave him back to her for exclusive use after that, return post. I've been told my arse is quite good, but if I put that on my face, I'd be continually talking bull-shit, wouldn't I, and most likely suffer from bad breath?

The ferry docks clumsily, hitting the wobbling chipped and battered pier, and I steady my feet as not to fall. I walk the plank between wharf and boat, choosing a seat outside. It's summer, and the breeze is warm, caressing even, an apt descriptor for a night that was so sexually charged. I wonder if Jane appreciates the warm breeze, too, in the park, as the sailors do what they want with her. I imagine one in front and one behind, one head still in his artificial cloud and apologise silently to Jane for imagining her in such a compromising predicament. I'd like to know how that feels though, to be taken by two men at once, and then wonder if 'taken' implies more abduction than action?

The ferry turns awkwardly, yells out to the city and then gathers speed, slicing through the water, a sound that washes away my disappointment at being less than beautiful, but more than ugly. I watch the gulls swooping and diving in parallel, looking for fish in the ferry lights. It's only when I look to my left, that I see him. *Him.* A man staring, as if lost in his thoughts. Tall, dark hair, late twenties, and dressed in a suit with trousers that are a tad too short. I try to read his mood, but can't because he looks as though he has a mournful resting face. This intrigues me, and now I'm watching the man rather than the gulls. I note that his head is tilted slightly downwards and not facing the unfolding vista of city, now leaving our grasp of reach. He is blind to me, the city and his journey.

He doesn't respond when the ferry blasts out a rude warning to a smaller vessel, and nor does he appreciate the Slessor landscape unfolding in front of him. A canvas of dissolving verticals of light and muted colours, reflected by skyscrapers. As the ferry moves forwards, the bough cuts through this impressionism, parting, dissolving and folding the reflections down into the depths of murky saltwater. Slessor, my favourite poet, now prattles in my mind, as an imprint of ghost might. At dark, his Five Bells ring mutely in my ears as I look for man overboard, swimming forever to get to the safety of the shore, which he never will.

The ferry slows, to meet with the wharf as if gentle might be possible, and the man rises, with his head now changing angle. This man, my ferryman, suddenly turns and looks directly at me, and something weird happens. A sort-of spiritual connection, green eye his, to green eye mine, and I know. I know at that precise moment that I will marry that man. It's a strange thought, I agree. However, it was the right thought. I'll call it a knowing because that makes it sound cool and like it happened and isn't merely a figment of my imagination.

I think of Jane, probably now sticky and sweaty, with American sweet stuff, and then wonder about the nuances of fate. I follow my fiancé as he disembarks at the quiet and creaking wharf, and I'm excited to follow someone because it gives my life a sudden degree of mystery and allure. Usually, I would take the bus up this steep hill, because walking at night for a young woman, alone, is known to be dangerous. I smile at the irony, my person having earlier, been between the ticking potential of drag queen and sailor.

The man walks fast, a striding pace, but his mind is elsewhere, I can tell. He doesn't look around him, either side at the vast mansions perched on the cliff. He strides instead, to a regular beat, breathing heavily, as if working through a difficult scenario in his mind. Then he reaches the place he calls home. A tall block of red-brick flats and I decide to stand behind an oak tree and see which window illuminates from someone's return. Watching him just for a moment, out of burning curiosity is okay, I assume, because no-one is stopping me from doing it, not that anyone else is around. I feel as if I'm extending my notion of dangerous a little more after my earlier courage in the seedy, stained bar.

However, I'm also trying to think ahead, imagining all possibilities, and think of an excuse for tree loitering, in case the police stop me and ask me what I'm doing. Nothing springs to mind, except I'm watching someone I know I'm going to marry. I decide to take the punishment on the chin if one is dealt out. A light goes on, seven floors up and a small, indented aluminium frame glows. Then a shape appears at the window with the same outline as my fiancé. I now know where he lives, although the information seems without context, just yet. He then pulls down a bland blind, and I hug the tree because a gesture of thanks needs to be noted. Oak doesn't respond to my gratitude, remaining stoically still and scratching my skin with a rough and harsh exterior.

4

FERRY

BRAINS, CHILLI AND DICAPRIO

I'M ON the early morning ferry, packed with commuters, and my fiancé is there. It took a few days to bump into him again, on the 7.25, to be exact. The ferry is full of serious suits and way too many briefcases, that sit at ankles like black dogs obeying their masters. Today though, he's annoyed me. Not like a furious annoyance, but more of a niggle, stemming from having had my time, possibly wasted. My fiancé is already having an affair, you see. An act that is too early on in our relationship… right in front of my eyes. He's not even trying to hide it from me.

He's staring at a blonde woman, hard to miss amongst all the black. Straight, ice-maiden hair, cascading, accentuating a tiny waist, perfect face with huge blue eyes, almost like a doll. I can't compete with her ruby butterfly lips or dainty button nose. His eyes are different too. He's having sex with her in his mind, that much I can tell. She pretends not to see him the whole way across the harbour, her eyes glued to the bottom of his seat, listening to her music, and then, just as they are about to get off, I see her look up at him and smile. A real smile that says, you're gorgeous, and I'm lovely, when can we do the deed? I stand next to them, my average invisibility cloak doing its job well, his eyes never moving for a moment, away from her beautiful face.

. . .

THEN SOMETHING HAPPENS. I'm on the night ferry, standing at the front, pitting myself against the sea-breeze, like in Titanic, only without DiCaprio at my rear, which is a shame. Instead, behind me, through the glass front, separating inside from outside, there are tired-looking people, missing the point entirely in catching the commuter ferry home. They sit in rows, their view obscured by glass, smeared with god knows what and the dullness puts them all to sleep. Outside, I'm being buffeted by the wind, and my long hair is lifted into tendrils, my cheeks red from the slap of the squalls. I'm merged into the fabric of the harbour, within the action, part of the action and every sense is invigorated and ready for something. Suddenly, my fiancé is standing next to me. The one in a relationship with the blonde woman, and he speaks, *to me.* It's banal small talk about having turned thirty, his work, and the briskness of the breeze. I reply, saying what is appropriate so that our conversation fits together correctly. He smiles and asks me if I might like to meet him in the city one day after work.

I'm speechless and turn to look for blonde woman, just in case this conversation has been undertaken over my head. I don't see her, though. I'm his second-best, but that doesn't matter, because I'll take what I can get. We dock, and I agree to meet him at a city bar in five days. As an after-thought, I ask him his name as he starts to stride away, back up the hill to his rectangular window. His name is Alan. Alan Parker.

I reflect on this situation because this is now a genuine crisis. This man was involved with blonde woman, who is now gone, possibly fallen overboard I fear, at Slessor's whim. Having sensed her loss and grieved, he's turned his attention onto me. I didn't even think he had noticed me, so it's put me into a state of rumination over-drive. I watch him from behind Oak with a new fervour, determined to gauge some inkling as to what he might be up to. I conclude he wants a companion to watch TV with, as he does little else. I could do that well, I surmise, because that's what my parents trained me to aim for, in marriage. A happy marriage is where you sit and watch television every single night together for decades. I'm a pro in television watching - having been raised on quality programs including topics about Hitler, war documentaries, political stuff, aggressive wildlife documentaries and overseas news stories. I'm a rare expert in all the colours of the old overnight test pattern. I'm everyone's dream Trivial Pursuit team player. Topic? Dry.

Every day, my man, my fiancé, strides up the hill and into the lift, and then his face appears at the rectangle in the wall. His TV is switched on, and the lights dance on the blind, allowing it to vicariously partake in the activity. Then, many hours later, everything goes dark. Not precisely exciting in there, is it? However, being a television partner is better than nothing in this challenging world. I already know what nothing feels like, an identity I have worn many times depending on what I've said, growing up. Words that didn't meet with approval would relegate me to nothing status, a place to be dug out from, where redemption was to be placed back into the fabric of family life.

I go back to the first time our green eyes met when I knew this man would be the one I married. I wonder if the universe has sensed my desperation and that the law of attraction might be real? I wonder if I need help for thinking something so bizarre? Is it wrong to name your fiancé before speaking to them?

Brad interrupts, 'Like um… yeah… Pippa.'

'You can't comment in the journal story.'

'I was the one who told you to write it.'

'So?'

'I don't know? It should give me commenting rights?'

'Maybe.'

'By the way - reading this? I hadn't realised how much you ruminate.'

I DON'T LET my crisis get in the way of meeting Alan, however, and we do, in a trendy harbour bar, a posh place that generally I wouldn't have the courage to go inside. It sits on the edge of the harbour in the middle of the action. Palm trees line the entrance, and red carpet has been placed to give you a sense of importance as you arrive. It's a place where jackets provide company for suitcases and where neckties release their grip. Alan's not what I imagined. He's louder and more confident than his ferry muteness hinted at, and the fact that he speaks with words etched in a distinct London accent, makes him sound incredibly sexy, no matter what comes out of his mouth. He could utter words like dull, bland, nothing and grey, and their precise allocation into time and space with such a posh rhythm, would most likely quiver my atoms. He gesticulates a lot too, and my eyes are always tracking his hands, which at times, wildly flounce around his person, forcing me to duck.

Now we're back on the ferry because he wants to cook *me* dinner. I jumped at the opportunity to see how big his TV is. It's not a euphemism for sex, he reassures me. He honestly is just hungry. I don't ask why we can't eat at the table we are seated at. Others are devouring seafood baskets, oysters are being sculled, and bubbles are inhaled from glasses. Alan must have other ways to impress me, I think, and I get on the ferry with him, so trusting and so naive.

I'm pondering my upcoming donation. My virginity was going to be lost amongst London black lines, red overtones, glossy prints and *that* accent in moments. My stomach forms lumps of excited scared as I follow him into the flat. I stop, though, four steps in. I find myself standing in a giant mess with a small, outdated TV poking its head through as if gasping for breath using a metal snorkel.

Where was the passionate sex on a black countertop, edgy London style with red overtones? Where are the sophisticated glossy prints on the walls? Where is the industrial rawness of masculinity that matches his aftershave? Instead, I see mess. I smell unclean, and I see disorganisation. My libido gets back into the lift and leaves the building to stand behind the safety of the oak tree.

He then gets busy in his small galley kitchen and asks me to sit in a chair, next to the window. I look out, admiring the harbour from this height and watch the ferries weaving their way from dark water to wharf. He presents a plate of pasta with red bits, and I thank him. I wind the pasta politely around the fork, as one does when hoping to create the illusion of sophisticated and then eat it. I begin to die quickly. The burning starts mildly, and I try to be polite by inhaling deeply. Only the burning is now penetrating the mucus membranes of my mouth. My throat begins to constrict, and now I can feel warmth, sweat and my face flushing. I imagine I only have moments left on the planet.

However, I smile towards him, not allowing any flashes of my life to intrude into such a delicate moment, as I don't want to look or sound ungrateful. As soon as he returns into the kitchen for a second helping, I throw the lot, aside from the plate, out of the window. If I'd been standing behind the oak tree, I would have seen something like brains being flung out of the seventh floor only to land with a plop onto the concrete below. I wonder what I might have thought of such a vision?

He doesn't notice the speed at which I have eaten everything, and we talk about life stuff, my mouth remaining burning for some time, and the topic turns out to be quite dull. There is no sex to be had that evening, and then he walks me back home. Four blocks, his flat, straight line to my flat. I'm standing on the doorstep to my yellow brick life, and he leans forward, giving me a sweet kiss on my cheek. My cheek! No, I don't want a soft kiss on my cheek! I want him to push his tongue down my throat and take me on the doormat, but he's already striding back to his flat. I curse the universe in my mind for such restraint, and as if reading my mind, he suddenly turns and walks back to me, and my heart races towards him. Instead of ripping my clothes off and burying his head between my legs, he presses a shiny key into my hand. He tells me I can let myself into his flat whenever I want. Tomorrow, perhaps? He's playing squash in the morning. What? Who does that? He does. Alan Parker does. Who accepts a key on the first date? I do. Pippa O'Shea.

• • •

I GO ALONG with his script, and I am glad to be in his flat the next day, luckily a Saturday where I'm off work. I enter the building, now feeling a privilege that I'm not stuck behind Oak on the outer anymore. I enter the ageing lift, hoping that my libido is still lurking close by and travel to the seventh floor. I feel like I'm starting a new, cool life. I'm disappointed again, however, to be greeted with yesterday's mess. It takes the shine off the illusion that I have concocted in my head for our future together.

This isn't part of the script I have for us, and so I begin to clean. I'm cleaning a stranger's mess. I'm organising a stranger's life for them, and I look out of the window and wonder if someone is watching my face at the rectangle from behind Oak? I figure Alan needs help though. My help specifically, and I don't see an issue with that. Not really, because I've always helped. That was my role. To find the right words to speak and help. I'm trained for this position, and I wonder if he's already sensed that.

I start with his white, rectangle fridge, complete with a freezer down below. I open the top door and see three shrivelled chillies, a litre of milk, a bowl of coagulated pasta and some beef heart. All sit on a shelf which offers an archaeological analysis of what he regularly eats. My first thought was how disgusting the sight was, my second about health, and my third was to clean it all for him. It seemed only fair given I was there, faced with the issue, and he wasn't.

As I'm cleaning the top shelf, I slice my finger open on a sharp bit, right down the entire squishy bit of the finger-tip. I place pressure on it, but the blood won't stop. There's blood going everywhere as if the residual beef in his fridge, is pumping red again. His flat now resembles a crime scene and looks worse than when I started cleaning. I place small mounds of red-absorbing salt on the bloodstain trail, leading from the kitchen to the bathroom, and all of a sudden, his world resembles Cairo, a landscape of exotic, small pyramids in amongst his dull. I organise a taxi to the closest medical centre, and leave his flat with a large tea towel bound around my hand, to stem the flow of my exiting life force. A friendly doctor glues my finger together again, fascinated that sharp bits exist in the confines of fridges, and places a large dressing around it. I walk away, giving everyone the bird finger, inadvertently.

I decided it might be safer to do his washing upon my return, and as I reached over to switch the machine on, with a more polite finger, I felt a sharp pain that ran up my arm and through my chest. I feel like I've been punched in my heart. I look around for clues to this invisible assault and see that rain has blown in from the open window and has wet the socket. I've been electrocuted. I phone for an electrician, rather than an ambulance, feeling a bit embarrassed at my back-to-back medical emergencies, and the electrician measures the voltage on the power socket. It's got a death number of volts, he tells me way too enthusiastically, and I would be dead if I hadn't been wearing my runners.

'You've got a good thick rubber base on those,' he tells me with a tone of admiration.

He gazes almost lustily at my ugly cleaning shoes, which have now saved my life. I limp my battered body back to my flat, with a new appreciation for my life-saving shoes, and sit and gulp down a cup of tea. I pour another. My life has gone weird ever since I dialled the number for the sailor. I reflect that adult life is difficult to negotiate my way around, given I've had no experience in doing it - neither anecdotally nor through living. I'm flying blind out here I deduce and crashing into many obstacles. It's mildly terrifying with a hint of the exotic.

Alan Parker tells me I'm too kind in having cleaned up his flat, despite not knowing what to do with the small, red-salt mounds, that indicate stuff has gone down in his flat. I tell him they are for spilt cordial, and I'll vacuum them up later. I don't tell him how my kind gesture almost killed me, and I made up a story about slicing my finger while preparing dinner. He says he likes my cooking and I can cook for him whenever I want. We then fuck, and it's an excellent first attempt. No bells and whistles, but things went into the right place, and no-one died. I think I'm in love to be honest because he tells me during our interlocking that he wants to marry my pussy, and I beam with happiness. I knew it! Sometimes, you just know that intuition is the real deal. I start planning our wedding the minute I return home, using a piece of pizza cardboard for my white vision board.

WE ARE INSEPARABLE, soul mates for sure, and we make it all official over the next two weeks. I moved in, leaving my little flat on its lonesome, and I cooked for him and cleaned, and we visited every museum and art gallery in the city together, hand in hand. I experience a surreal moment in which everything has fallen into place as if I'm a character in a Truman script. My conversation falls effortlessly into his, and his interests in jaguar cars, cooking and red wine quickly become mine. I morph into his life and am absorbed as quickly as a sugar cube dissolves into a hot cup of coffee.

I am thanking the universe for Alan three months later, clearing my flat for good, when my phone rings. As I'm twirling my engagement ring around on my finger - a dazzling g-grade diamond, set in eighteen-carat gold someone speaks terrible words to me. My happiness fades as a cloud of death passes into vision. Alan is dead the doctor tells me over the phone, searching for more family to call. He's been hit by a car next to Oak, and I realise that our story is over, the chapter redundant, just like that. The hospital tells me that his parents will be flying over to sort out the flat and possessions. I move everything back into my flat and put the engagement ring back into the box. I put the vision board into the bin and re-enter my life before Alan.

LIFE UNRAVELLED after that as if someone had pulled a thread. You know how it happens. You see an innocent, loose bit of thread on a piece of clothing, and being a lazy git and not wanting to find a pair of scissors, you pull, thinking you can get away with it. Whole sections unravel as a result. That's what happened to my life at that moment. Here I am, years later, on the eve of my thirtieth anniversary, holding a ball of thread the size of an inmate's shackle, and it is weighing me down.

Brad's still adamant that this was the place to start, to find my normal.

'See, already there are patterns and reasons for it all,' he says. 'That's why you ended up with a psychopath, wanting to marry him.'

'I think I'll do the fluff bit,' I say, needing respite after the recount of Alan's death.

'So, the rats and bees are next?'

'Almost. A couple of steps back and then pure fluff coming up.'

'Why a couple of steps back?'

'When I read this back, it isn't normal, at all, that's why.'

'See? That's why I'm getting you to do this. By the end, you're going to see why you fell in love with a psychopath and stayed.'

I wonder if I've started too late in the piece because you must also have a clue that something went down, well before I began tree-hugging and watching people from off ferries? Most people don't go in and start cleaning up a stranger's house for fun, do they? That was rhetorical by the way Brad. He's dying to say more right now, but he doesn't need to. I'm sure everyone can see a few issues floating around in these early words, and I promise they will be retrieved, their origin sought, and their meaning explained. Then, when I introduce Noah, my psychopath, you'll understand the dynamic a bit better.

COULD HAVE
CAUGHT BEES
AND STARTED
SMALL HONEY
BUSINESS. LOST
OPPORTUNITY?

if they were sewer
rats, why was the
toilet the only
room they didn't
eat?

5

PLATO, KAREN MACLAREN AND
THE SANDWICH

I tend to ponder a lot if you haven't gathered by now. If I were a man and had been born, say around 300 BC, and had hung out with Plato, I might have been deemed a philosopher. A great thinker of important life stuff. Today, I'm accused of ruminating, my internal mind-chewing being listed in the DSM-5 as an anxiety trait. My musings are assumed to be an illness, whereas Plato's ramblings, for want of a better descriptor, have assumed him, immortal status.

'Are you jealous?' asked Brad.

'Jealous, Brad? What? Of Plato? I'm not jealous. I'm pointing out how human musings are now often deemed to be an indication of anxiety, rather than a deliberate analysis of our reality.'

'Fair enough. I suppose Plato's cave might be seen as a depressed person's thoughts these days.'

'Exactly. I mean people chained to a wall watching shadows all day?'

'Yeah, when you say it like that?'

'So… take this thought I had, for instance. This is hardly a rumination. It's much deeper than that. Imagine that you are inside someone else's head and body. Now, take this a step further and imagine your sense of self inside of them. Are you still 'you' but now with a different life story and physical body? Is the sense of 'you' perfectly translatable between bodies? Tell me that doesn't make you go, *'like yeah.'* Are we all the same sense of self but experiencing different contexts, placed in different human shells?'

'Like yeah,' says Brad, frowning. He went silent. 'I just imagined myself in your head, with your life and thoughts. I feel the need to take a sedative.'

'Haha. Funny Brad. Not.'

This thought experiment can be taken further. When *you* are born, you are entombed into a lineage, not of your choice, and not of your timing. You get what you are given, and the entire process is outstandingly and magnificently unfair. Prince George of Cambridge will live a life of privilege and one day be crowned as a King, whereas Jilka Alora-Nambi from Zambia will struggle, suffer and then die, aged only five, from starvation. As a result of a particular sperm and egg uniting, this disparity of fairness becomes evident at some point in one's life, with a moment signalling that something isn't quite right. It's a moment in which you suddenly realise that there is this thing called a short straw. A straw that you can't quickly put down for your entire life.

For me, it happened when I was eleven. It was a trifecta of small pings. I had a friend called Karen Maclaren… yeah, I know, right? She had a pretty, pink, rectangular lunchbox. At lunch, she would open it ceremoniously, with a full brass fanfare announcing this action. She fully understood that the contents of her lunchbox were a form of status currency. Inside, was usually a white chicken and salad sandwich, cut on the diagonal, most likely using a set square, and wrapped in smooth glad wrap, no creases visible. The cut's perfection was exquisite with none of the insides from the sandwich ever having spilt out during the process, not even a hue of pink from beetroot slices, staining any edges. The bread had no indentation marks from the pressure of fingers either. Her lunch was a piece of art, worthy of the praise it received every day from her fellow small worshippers.

Included with this magnificent centrepiece, was an apple, a yoghurt, a chocolate bar, and a small drink *with* an attached straw. Plenty of obvious tangibility to tell everyone within the luncheon group that Karen was adored and valued by those at home. On the other hand, my lunch, made purely from self-love, was usually found squished at the bottom of my school bag and produced murmurs of concern, rather than any jubilation.

With her elocution accent, Karen, sitting in her throne, would neigh, 'Pippa, what do *you* have in *your* sandwich today?'

All the eyes in the luncheon circle would turn towards me. Me, being me, would say excitedly, 'Tomato sauce on white bread… yum!'

Everyone would then purse their lips in various yuck expressions, and then pity me, as I ate the said sandwich with way too much enthusiasm than it deserved. Ping number one. Karen, by the way, now does un-boxing Youtube videos, and actually does include real brass fanfares, as she gleefully rubs everyone's faces in all the expensive shit she can buy.

Karen Maclaren then invited me over to her house one day and took me into her bedroom, which had everything an eleven-year-old could wish for. She put some music on and started to dance. The music was cool, and so I asked her who the band was?

'Happy Girls.'

'Who?'

Silence.

'You've never heard of Happy Girls?' She stopped dancing and was just staring at me.

'No.'

'So, you've never heard them played on the radio or… ?'

'Oh, we're not allowed to listen to the radio at home.'

'Why not?'

'I don't know,' I replied. I'd never asked why not. I just knew that listening to the radio could result in lots of irritated anger from my parents.

'Wow,' she said, looking deeply concerned. Ping! Moment number two concerning disparity of egg and sperm.

Moment number three was followed closely after when I was invited to Joanne Blandy's house for a sleepover. She lived on an apple farm, and her mother had cheeks as rosy at their red, delicious apples. It was peaceful out on the farm, and I noted how her mother's soothing and consistent voice seemed to blend in with everything else.

'Your family is nice,' I told her thoughtfully, as we were going to sleep.

'Why do you think that?' she asked.

'Your mum is like, serene. She doesn't get angry very easily.'

Joanne laughed. 'Why would my Mum get angry?'

'I'm not sure,' I said, realising a vast difference between my life and Joanne's.

Ping! Ping! Ping! The trifecta was in. See? This family lineage you get born into means everything. It shapes you in ways that seem trivial when isolated, but they become significant as you age. They shape you, without you even knowing. Brad wants to know why I've mentioned three relatively small things and not the big ones. The ones that would smash their way out of white paper, and into your face, changing the pace and tone of the story. I don't have an answer for that just yet. Maybe it's easier to start with the small and work my way up?

SO, ALAN Parker, my fiancé was now dead, and I took the bus into work instead of crossing the water. I didn't want to travel on the ferry anymore, because it reminded me of my unfinished love story and that

Alan Parker was now trapped in a coffin in the ground. I hadn't been close to anyone who had died before, and when the black of the night blinded me, it would throw up images of his body starting to decay. At times, I wanted to dig him up and organise a quick cremation, just so that the images of exploding cells and putrefaction would stop. Then I worried that such thoughts were abnormal, feeling weirder than simple musings. Did other people *suffer* from the process of human decomposition as much as I did? Maybe that was a sign of how my anxiety manifested?

I DATED a string of other men after that, none like Alan Parker. Now that my virginity had been lost, although it was hardly lost, was it? It was with Alan, now dead. I wondered on a metaphysical level, whether that meant my virginity was also now dead? But taken it was, down-under, losing its specialness. I tried on lots of men for size after that, pardon the pun. I dated two drug dealers, a sex addict, a swinger, an exhibitionist, a piece of cardboard, and a single-cell amoeba. I was a walking magnet for the desperate and dateless. All the Alans, nice men with a possibility of marital bliss, had run away from me, fearing being knocked down too, I presume. I got the dregs. The strange thing was that with each new man, I would initially mould myself to be just like them as if I was a shirt hanging in a shop. I would become someone's perfect fit, to ensure that they would take me home with them.

'That's typical,' interjects Brad, as I'm reading from my rough draft at one of our cafe sessions.

'Typical for what?' I ask.

'Growing up with narcissistic parents.'

'How?'

'Well, in order to be loved by them, you had to essentially be reflections of them. Yes?'

'That's deep. What do you mean?'

'Well, to be loved, you had to be someone that fitted in with your parents' expectations, as in, not be yourself. So, translating that into a dating setting, you made yourself appeal to guys so that they would take you home and love you. See themselves in you?'

'That is indeed profound.' I said, mulling it over in my mind.

'It's meant to be,' Brad replied, sounding pleased with himself.

'For a life coach,' I add, taking the piss.

Brad glared at me. 'So, when are these bees coming?'

'Soon. This is the fluff bit coming up now.'

'Tell me why the bees need to be in this again?'

'You'll see. I have my reasons. It's fluff with meaning.'

'If you say so.'

6

BEES, WASPS AND COW UDDERS

CRAZY-MOTHER-FUCKER-PINK-SHORTS

JUST AS I'D recovered from Alan, the universe crapped on me with gigaparsecs of unfairness and fluff, as it had now spied the short straw in my hand. Therefore, I was fair game and deserved and needed a maximum amount of disruption added to what was already a problematic existence, which I haven't explained fully, just yet. I became the main character in a satirical comedy, and those watching, would say things like 'you should write a book, this stuff is so crazy.' It was true, though, my life became a series of unfortunate events, blindsiding me into a state of constant anxiety and chaos. There was no time to feel the regular flow of routine, or set goals which were in any way achievable. Instead, I was hanging on for dear life, just to survive.

TAKE THE DAY, for instance, I went for a simple walk to contemplate my complicated and chaotic life. An innocuous Sunday afternoon - the sun was shining, the birds were singing, and 'crazy-mother-fucker-pink-shorts' was on the loose. A middle-aged skinny guy on a racing bike, wearing pink lycra with his arse in the air. Not looking where he was hurtling along, he managed to mow me down with his racing bike. There I was, walking along one minute, admiring the view, and then the next, flat as a pancake on the pavement with his tyre tread running up my back. He was stupendous too in the after-math. Crying, wailing and being comforted whilst I stared at the small, irregular grains contained within pedestrian concrete. Like, who gets mown down on a Sunday stroll and ends up in rehab for a year? Me. Pippa O'Shea. I do.

The universe then said in a low grumpy voice. 'Pippa, for you to learn essential life lessons and become strong, I feel the need to crap on you some more.'

I must have replied, 'Go for it, you big piece of infinite shit. The first time was simply amazing.'

So, it did, and I hung on, as it emptied it's limitless bowels and sent my way, as much chaos as a human being could endure. My flat got washed away in a pipe flood. My car self-combusted in my driveway, no key in the ignition. My lounge room burned down…

'How?'

'Brad, you're not supposed to interrupt *all* the time.'

'Usually, kitchens burn down, not lounge rooms. I'm interested, that's all.'

'Okay. I was listening to some music and had put a candle onto the top of the stereo. The sub woofer caused the top of the stereo to vibrate. This made the candle move sideways, bit by bit. It eventually fell into a waste paper basket full of recycling paper. It caught fire.'

'Weird.'

'Then it was small stuff, like someone set fire to my replacement car, and wrote it off and the insurance company investigated me. Then, there was this elderly gardener at my block of flats who forgot to wear boxers under his tracksuit pants every single time he randomly knocked on my door.'

'Wait,' says Brad, interrupting again. 'I feel like I need to take a breath, and I'm not the one speaking.'

'Okay. Have you taken one? This is all about rhythm and flow right now, Brad. Hurry up, there's more to tell.'

'Yup. All good to keep going,' he says. 'It's just the image you left me with. The gardener and…'

'You're lucky you didn't have to deal with the real thing. It was like…'

'…Pippa. We don't need the details.'

'Okay.'

The universe decided to up its game. 'Are you ready for this one Pippa O'Shea?' it asked me, in the same deep, resonating voice.

'Hold on,' says Brad. 'Did you actually hear the voice of the universe?'

'What do you think, Brad… seriously? Actually, I did. I met the owner of the voice as well. He was a man with a big white beard, sitting in this big chair with angel wings on it and everything.'

'Just checking.'

THE UNIVERSE THOUGHT rats should be next. Not a bad choice when choosing from off the Big Shit List. Rats overran my next rental. Not normal sized ones. No, these were enormous, giant sewer rats. I once saw them running along the top of my back fence. They looked like a line of special squad, hairy ninjas, serious too, they were, as if on a mission. Their mission? To eat my life away. Why? Why me? What life lesson involves having your life eaten away by sewer rats? These sneaky, hairy-legged rectangles, would only ever eat the back of boxes in my pantry too, so when I would go to pull something out, like a box of cornflakes, I would only find the back of the box with all the contents gone. I ended up living in what amounted to a cardboard facade.

After they had eaten all of my pantry, they started in on my furniture. They were gnawing away from the bottom, to the tops of anything that I owned. I baited them, but these buggers were clever. They never ate the baits or the cheese. I gave up and moved out when I discovered three small turds of rat poo on my face as I woke up one morning. A rat had squatted to take a dump on my face as I slept? What's that life lesson? Seriously?

THE UNIVERSE LAUGHED. However, this time in a kind of slightly hysterical voice. It was having fun. It moved into the bee phase of my life.

'So, we're finally getting to the bees?'

'Yes, Brad. Lots and lots of bees.'

'Get on with it then.'

'You're the one that keeps interrupting.'

'Okay. I'll be quiet.'

'A psychic once told me I had been a 'bee whisperer' in a previous life, you know.'

'What the heck is a bee whisperer? Did you believe her?'

'Why? Do you believe in past lives? I don't.'

THEY CAME at four in the afternoon. A squadron of invaders had perused a million homes in Sydney for a base and had decided that my flat was perfect. Sixty thousand of them, squeezed into my wall cavities, their buzzing making my walls vibrate. But that wasn't the rest of it. No, there was more, as I later found out. The bees had made a beeline into my small abode because my wall cavities, were literally cavities. A million termites had stealth-eaten through the wooden framework of my flat, and the bees had come to eat the termites. I had been living amongst a life cycle in action, only not as beautiful as Attenborough might have depicted.

The following year, precisely on the *same* date, and many thousands of repair dollars later, I saw a bee hovering near my air vent. Then there were two, then three and then ten. I raced outside with newspaper and started frantically tearing the paper up, scrunching up little pieces, and stuffing them into any holes I could see. The bees were onto me, multiplying by the second, competing for the holes. This time I won, my air vent now not acting as an air vent, and the vibrating swarm gave up after several hours and moved on. Both swarms had arrived on November 5th. Guy Fawkes Day. What did that mean?

'Yeah,' said Brad. 'What did it mean?'

'Fucked if I know,' I said. 'Maybe a tenuous link to Alan? He was English, and so was Guy Fawkes.'

'Yeah… maybe? That's kind of lateral though.'

HAVING GOT RID of two lots of bees and having moved yet again, another swarm of bees found me several months later, as they searched for a new home. Mine leapt out at them, naturally, probably because they knew I now had experience. This time, I had lit a fire in my open fireplace, a perk of my new abode. Percy, my cat, had begun licking the wallpaper, an odd action, even for a cat. Investigating, I realised that the sticky substance dripping down the walls in long lines was honey. Then I heard buzzing.

'Buzzing? As in more bees?' asked Brad.

'Yeah. Buzzing.'

They were in the chimney this time, and the smoke from the newly lit fire was smoking them out. The heat was melting their hive and the honey, which had filled the wall cavity, was now dripping down the walls in trickles from the architraves. Percy, the cat, was in heaven.

'I didn't know cats liked honey.'

'Is that relevant right now, Brad?'

Now, there were two ways this could go. Sixty thousand of them could fly down, and into my home or, they could fly up and out into the sky. I raced, stumbling into my kitchen. Grabbing a saucepan, I filled it with water and then splashed it over the smoking kindling. Next, I grabbed the duct tape and black plastic from the cupboard, as if about to commit a murder. Taping the plastic over the fireplace, and stretching it taut, I thought back to physics at school and tried to remember Newton's Laws of Motion. Nope, my brain had been hijacked by stress hormones, and nothing was happening up there. Would a piece of plastic hold thousands of bees at bay? I had no idea.

The bees came down en masse, the entire squadron having been instructed to find me, and I listened to thousands of dull thuds as their tiny bodies tried to infiltrate my space. In the end, realising that I wasn't going to sleep that night with the repetitive thudding sounds, I phoned an apiarist who climbed onto the roof, peered down the chimney, and then announced to my neighbourhood.

'Nope, you had a giant wasp nest in there as well as the bees. I have never seen anything like that before. Co-existing in there, they were. You're just lucky the wasps didn't attack.'

IT HAPPENED *AGAIN* the following year. This time in my ensuite. A small, nondescript space with no termites, no fireplace, no Percy…

'What happened to Percy?' Brad asked.

'He died.'

'How?'

'Old age. He'd been a rescue cat, and he just died in his sleep.'

'Glad it was peaceful. More bees, though? I'm beginning to see why you wanted to include the bees. It's like life was throwing weird at you, on top of the weird you'd already experienced. What's with you and bees, Pippa?'

'My point *exactly*, Brad.'

There was no reason for this invasion, as war had not been declared. None. I asked the apiarist if it were normal for bees to keep finding me, and he said, 'Yes, absolutely, happens to everyone, *all* the time.'

'Really?' I asked. 'Like four times to the same person, different addresses?'

'Yes,' he said adamantly, 'I've heard of people getting bees *every* single year.'

'Even people who move house regularly? I've never met one. Not a single one.' I said.

'I have. *All the time.*' Then he looked at me, defying me to argue with him anymore.

BULL SHIT. No. I've not met anyone who has ever had bees repeatedly find them and invade their homes. In the end, it happened seven times. I have attracted seven swarms of bees into six different homes during my lifetime thus far, and I have yet to hit thirty.

Anyway, that evening, as I was ruminating over the cocky apiarist, comfortable in my new cow pyjamas, my lounge room started glowing red and blue. I heard yelling and peeked out of my curtains. Yellow firefighters were running around, grabbing hoses, outside of *my* window. My flat was on fire! I ran around, completely panicked, trying to find the fire to no avail. I couldn't even smell any smoke. Then there was urgent banging on my front door.

'Fire Brigade! Let us in!'

I opened the door, and they fell in with a long hose urgently pointing at everything. I stood staring, aware that my swaying material udders, supposedly pyjama quirky, looked blatantly bizarre in front of them. They raced around my little space, and then an announcement was made.

'Wrong block of flats! This is number eight, not eleven! Move out!'

Then they were all gone, and I sat down to continue mulling over the apiarist.

'SO, IS that it for the universe crap?' asked Brad, hopefully.

'Not quite.'

'Wow. Okay, I think I'm seeing the relevance to this now.'

Out of desperation and wanting a haven from the entire planet, including bees, rats, firefighters, floods, and drug dealers, I caved in and married a work colleague named Nigel. A man who had begged me for a date for months, promising everything with his nods and winks, but who resembled a piece of cardboard in reality. His personality was dry, without spark or passion. However, I'd given up on finding anyone better in amongst all the small crises that were adding up.

This was not a good premise to start a relationship and led to a banal and short marriage. It wasn't bad, and it wasn't good. We had little in common, no obvious sexual attraction towards one another once we saw each other undressed, and Nigel liked to play computer games too much. Two years into the marriage of the boring, with no children having been successfully produced, he announced he'd been having an affair with a man he'd met at the gym and was leaving right there and then. He did, precisely nine minutes later, dropping a bombshell that he'd had a vasectomy before he'd met me. What the proverbial fuck, fuckitty fuck?

'A VASECTOMY and he hadn't told you? Shit Pippa. I hadn't heard that bit before.'

'Yeah. No wonder I hadn't fallen pregnant. I was organising fertility tests too, only he didn't seem interested.'

'No wonder. Have you heard from him since?'

'No. That's the weird thing. He was there, and then he was gone. Just like that. So was our townhouse after that, our car and all the money from our joint bank accounts.'

'So, although you thought he was like a piece of cardboard and had no sexual attraction to him, you wanted kids with him?'

'Yeah.'

THAT'S HOW how all of this started. A short straw I couldn't let go of, and the universe crapping on me whenever it could. There's only so much the exterior of a human being can take to retain its shape. My shape was being dented and morphed into someone else's shape. A person who was too busy trying to protect themselves from crap situations, than follow some pre-determined, happy life plan. I was just bouncing from one crisis to the next.

It was a friend who suggested that I consider getting a life coach, and recommended Brad. I needed to re-wire my neural pathways, apparently because they had been fashioned into the wrong shape. Years of weird had made me unaware of what was healthy and what wasn't. Not having a great start with my family meant that I was disadvantaged, especially when choosing a healthy romantic partner. For a small fee each week, Brad could become my shadow and shape me into someone who might just find happiness, contentment, the right partner, financial security, and perhaps help me to win the lottery.

'It was never my job to help you win the lottery.'

'That was a joke, Brad.'

'Shame? We could have split it.'

my real
gratitude list

7

F* CK YOU

THANK YOU VERY MUCH

I think Brad, my life coach, was frustrated with me, but I couldn't tell because his face was now frozen from Botox, resulting in a 'WHOA!' kind of expression. His cheeks, pumped to the brim with filler, had made him look like a chipmunk who was tripping out. It was hard to take him seriously when he couldn't look cross or despairing anymore. However, his tone sounded frustrated, which I thought went against the whole point of being a life coach. I thought he was paid to make me feel better, to spur me on with motivational quotes and create a false sense of achievement within me when I had achieved small, insignificant and banal goals.

'You thought I looked like a tripping chipmunk?'

'Brad, you can't comment on the story anymore.'

'Why not?'

'Because I'm writing about you now. You have to allow the story to flow.'

'Oh, okay. What if it's important?'

'Nope.'

'Fine.'

'Don't sulk.'

'I'm not. I just thought the Botox and filler had made me look good.'

'You did look good. Always. An expression of perpetual surprise and happiness. You could have auditioned for The Sound of Music.'

I HAD no idea what a life coach did when I first went to see Brad. He enthusiastically outlined his program, which included heaps on 'goal stuff,' which would help me 'move forward' with my life. A life that a psychologist had explained, rather pedantically I might add, had lost its 'purpose and control.' He had been correct. I'd lost faith in everything because so much shit had landed in my lap, that I now *felt* like shit too.

Brad thought he would start with the notion of 'gratitude,' which, when explained, sounded like total bull shit. There was no way in hell that I was going to be thankful for bees, rats, floods, or Nigel's vasectomy for that matter.

'The idea is that are grateful, Pippa, for where you are *now*.'

'Grateful for what, sorry?' I had asked him, immediately scanning my brain for the good stuff that was hiding from me. I looked around at the trees and bushes in the park, as today, Brad had suggested a walking session, to help explain his mindful gratitude technique.

'For the life you have today.'

'Life? As in the fact that I'm breathing?'

'Precisely,' he said, ignoring my sarcasm. He stopped and then looked at me intently, as if I had realised the answer to a profound secret. 'Breathing is more important than you think,' he added.

'You mean, I'm supposed to be grateful for the *act* of breathing? Isn't everyone who is alive breathing? It's generally an automated process, so I can't take the credit for it.'

'Yes and *no*,' he said, adding dramatic emphasis to the word *no*.

'You mean some people are holding their breaths?' I asked.

'In a way, yes. Do you get it now?'

'No.' I was trying not to scratch one of the chickenpox scabs on my face, one of the hundreds now glued to my body. Life had thrown a plague at me too in recent weeks, designed to pockmark my face as if I were impersonating the moon. I had gone from attractive to lunar in a week.

'You're not still contagious, are you?' he asked, trying not to look alarmed. 'I'm not sure we're supposed to be out and about if you are?'

'No. It's fine, they've all scabbed over now. Most people get chickenpox as a child. I hadn't. Got an adult dose instead, quite late for someone in their twenties. It's been hell.'

'Well, it's time to be grateful for what you have,' he said, steering the conversation back to the notion of gratitude. 'You have your health, for instance.'

'My health?' I said incredulously, having just explained why I looked like a plague victim from the medieval ages. 'Didn't we just discuss…'

'You're still alive and breathing. That's where you have to start.'

'That's dredging the barrel a bit, don't you think, calling that health?'

'Not at all. Look around you, Pippa. See all of this?' He waved his arms around quite wildly. 'Look at the beauty around you. See what's in front of you. Feel the wind, smell the air. Look at the tiny flowers on this plant, for instance. Now, buy a gratitude journal and write down five things that you feel grateful for at the end of each day. Start with breathing.'

'And this gratitude process will make me feel better? Get this pervasive depression from off of me? Such a simple solution. I'm surprised no-one has suggested it to me before now.'

'Yes.'

. . .

'OKAY, I'M sounding like a total wanker in this journal, Pippa. Is that how I put things?'

'You're not supposed to interrupt, Brad. That was the deal.'

'Yeah I know… but seriously. Did I come across like that? I mean you're like saying I looked like a chipmunk and talking about breathing and flower buds like this?'

'Yup.'

'I need to change the gratitude program. It sounds wanky even for life coaching.'

'It was.'

'Gee, thanks, Pippa.'

'Go write down five things you can change about it. You'll feel better.'

'Really, Pippa?'

'Yeah. Seriously. You should try it.'

I BOUGHT a gratitude journal from a stationary supplies store. That in itself was a challenge as there were far too many to choose from. A whole wall of colourful journals begging to be the witness to my unlimited gratitude towards the planet. I chose one with a floral cover, simply because of Brad's reference to the flower buds and opened the cover feeling like a child starting a new project. I creased the page and then hovered my pen above the expansive white. It was easy to start because I already knew that I was grateful for breathing and also thankful for my health, especially the hundreds of scars now on my face and the residual pain still running up and down my legs from being run over by *'crazy-mother-fucker-pink-shorts.'* What else could I be grateful for, I thought, as I perused my flat?

'Being cynical,' I wrote down, before rubbing it out. How about silence? Given there's no-one special in my life anymore? I listened, hearing only the sound of the clock in my kitchen, the only hint that time was indeed being measured.

'I am glad that I don't have to listen to the sound of Nigel shooting people in his computer games.' I wrote down. I needed two more, so as not to fail my optimism-filled life coach.

I scanned the room. Should I feel grateful for my sofa? Some people may not have a sofa, so perhaps I needed to appreciate that? Number five? I thought of Maslow and the hierarchy of needs. I looked up at my ceiling, white, bordered and with a ball of illuminating metal mesh hanging from it. A roof over my head, I wrote. There, now my depression would lift and I'd be given a new family, a new love interest, a new job, and my life would fall into place.

I phoned Brad the next evening, asking him if I could write the same five down again. He told me no. I had to think of a new list. I told him there was only so much furniture in my flat and he had laughed, thinking I was funny. Some days later, after I had listed all of my furniture and belongings, Brad told me that I needed to start finding things about myself that I was grateful for. We arranged for a session-meet the next day. This time, Brad had chosen a bush walk.

'Grateful for what?' I asked, trying not to step onto the milling ants at my ankles.

'Like your hair, for instance.'

'You want me to be grateful for my hair?'

'Yes. It's long, and it's healthy. Is it yours?'

'Why wouldn't this be mine?' I tugged at my chestnut ponytail. 'See, it doesn't come off.'

'Keep your hair on,' he joked, increasing his pace and breathing in deeply. 'This air is so fresh,' he commented, walking fast enough to have been deemed an Olympic potential in the walking race.

'It is,' I said breathlessly, trying to catch him up. I was literally jogging. 'Okay, I am grateful for my hair.'

'Do you feel a bit better?' he then asked hopefully, slowing down a bit. 'Endorphins are released when one exercises. It makes you feel better.'

'Not really. My hair? It's an automated system, like my breathing. I can't take credit for either, I'm afraid.'

'Can you feel the endorphins whizzing around your system though? I can.' He stretched up and then lunged forward to touch his toes. 'Okay then,' he said, returning to straight. 'Find something else. How about your fingernails? They look nice.'

'Brad… they're gel.' I held them out, ten talons of pink.

'You're quite hard on yourself. I wouldn't have known they were gel.'

'I don't mean to be.'

He jogged on the spot. 'There are people worse off than you.'

'I know. There are millions of people worse off than me.'

'Some are even dead.'

'Yes, so I've heard. Apparently, over a hundred billion people have already died on this planet. Some are starving, some in war. I get that.' It was true. However, I was stuck in my head, in my reality, and not theirs. You can't walk in someone else's shoes, not really, no matter how hard you try.

'Walk,' he suggested, mind-reading me. 'Go for a walk every single day. A long walk. It will improve your mood. At least an hour and make it brisk enough so that if you had to hold a conversation, you would find it hard.'

'Do I talk to myself to test my speed?'

'What?' Brad looked confused.

'I can't, anyway. My back isn't strong enough after that racing bike mowed me down. I get stuck. My sacroiliac subluxes.'

'Your what?'

'The joint just here,' I pointed to my back. 'It sort of dislocates at random times, and then I can't move. It happened at the supermarket a couple of months ago. I had to call an ambulance.'

'Ouch. Really? That's a bummer.' He paused, thinking. 'You could sing as an alternative?'

'Sing what? On the walk or after?'

'Just sing. No walking.'

'Brad. Are you making this up as you go along?'

'No.'

'You are. This is life coaching? Telling me to sing?'

'Yes. You need a distraction from yourself, Pippa. Do something that breaks the rumination circuit. I get you've been through shit, but in a way, you have become your own worst enemy. You overthink everything, and because you're on your own, there's no-one to interrupt your thoughts. The answer lies in doing and not thinking.'

'Fine. So, I stop thinking and sing. That's going to make me feel better?'

'Yes.'

SO SINGING WAS going to save me from impersonating Plato. I bought a karaoke machine and started with one-hit songs. After singing those a hundred times, I moved onto loud rock anthems in which I screamed everything I had into the microphone. Then I sang love ballads, tearfully remembering Alan, and then Nigel's vasectomy… those poor little sperm, our potential children, who had been trapped in his testicles.

My neighbour dropped off a note in the morning, asking me to keep the noise down.

'I can hear you having sex through the wall,' I wrote back, in pure, juvenile style.

It was true. Clear as the day when it happened, like someone cranking up an oooh pitch combined with a grunting pig... not that I sat there trying to join in vicariously.

I phoned Brad, quite pleased with myself. 'Okay, Brad. I've done the hits from the seventies, eighties and nineties, and now I just don't recognise any of the music. However, I found a song by Lily Allen called 'Fuck You.' I quite liked that one.'

'Good. You have made progress.'

'How?'

'You said you *liked* something.'

'I did.'

'This is what I call progress.'

'I'm going on a date, by the way.'

'What? Where did that come from?'

'The Fuck You song, actually.'

'Not following?'

'That's what I was singing at the communal washing line. It's where we met. He's from upstairs.'

'You're going to date someone from your flat complex?'

'Yeah. His name is Sam.'

'Wow. Okay. Do you have anything in common?'

'Don't think so. Not at this stage. I'm thinking of going to Paris too, by the way.'

'What? That was a bit left-field, even for you Pippa.'

'Yeah. This goal-setting stuff got me thinking. I've always wanted to go, so I might take some time off work and just do that. You said the answer was in doing.'

'I did. I don't see the harm in that.'

'No, nor do I.'

'By the way.'

'What?'

'Do you like the guy from upstairs?'

'Yeah.'

'That's a good start then. So, when are you aiming to get to Paris?'

'Hopefully, I should get there in three months.'

'Wow. You don't waste time.'

'Thanks to you.'

'Mmmm.'

THOUGHT OF THE DAY

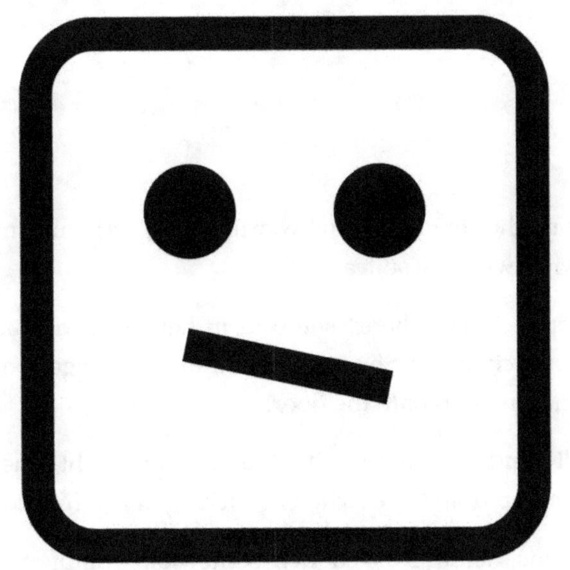

NEVER ENGAGE IN A CONVERSATION ABOUT BUTT HOLES
WITH MOTHER AGAIN

CHANGE TOPIC TO STALIN, DEATH, GALLSTONES, ANY
WAR, SPIDERS, CAKE BAKING, FURNITURE POLISH.

8

HELLO MOTHER

GRAVITY MAKES THE STORY HEAVY

My mother barged in awkwardly to my flat, three months later, with two large suitcases.

'Right, Pippa… finally here,' she said in her thick Irish accent as if I had been expecting her. She staggered into the lounge room and then dropped the suitcases onto the floor.

'I wouldn't mind a cup of tea, after that dreadful flight,' she puffed, her chest leaping up from the exertion of sucking in much-needed air.

'Why are you here?' I asked her, somewhat dumbfounded by her sudden appearance, including the fact that she hadn't knocked, and had opened my front door using my emergency key, the one that was *only* supposed to be used for emergencies. I passed her my cup of Earl Grey and a plate of biscuits that I had just been about to enjoy for afternoon tea.

'Is there an emergency?' I asked, my heart sinking by her sudden appearance. I picked up the biscuit packet, stuffing a whole biscuit into my mouth, my anxiety now rising. I didn't want to know why she here. Something had obviously gone down, and it always spelled trouble when she arrived out of the blue.

'Not that I know of,' she replied, sitting down on my sofa and making herself comfortable. She pedantically sipped my tea and then frowned. 'Too much milk Pippa.'

'I wasn't expecting you. I have plans for…'

'Your father has been googling unsavoury things' she then announced, stoically. 'I took him in his eleven-o'clock tea, and there it was. On the large computer screen too.'

'What was on the screen?'

'It looked like a part of a woman's anatomy Pippa. An unsavoury one. Not even one where a baby might emerge from, or suckle from.' She looked at me, clearly traumatised and as if I was supposed to make everything better for her.

'Okay,' I said slowly, stalling for time. 'Are you sure?' I thought of several other things, more appropriate for my father to be perusing, given his elderly age, like model trains, coffins, adult nappies and lethal injections. I hadn't expected what seemed to be leading to the announcement of buttholes.

'Of course, I'm sure,' she said crossly. 'As sure as God is looking down on me, right now, seeing why I am here in this moment.' She then nibbled on a Tim Tam, as if a mouse, in no hurry.

I wanted to ask her the obvious, like have you actually looked at a butthole, for instance, to know that this image, was indeed a butthole, but I risked her saying yes. I didn't know which was the worst scenario, to be honest. A mother who had previously been looking at buttholes, or a father who had been doing it in private.

'Why?' I finally asked. The only sound in the room having been one of gnawing, as several biscuits had been chewed through.

She pursed her crumbled lips towards me, holding in the obvious answer. 'I've taken copies, for evidence. I've got a disk in my suitcase that I'm going to give you for safekeeping.'

'Sorry?'

'Yes, a disk… one of those finger drives, full of your father's buttholes. There were many Pippa. It turned out it wasn't just one, it was multiples. It's my proof, just in case he tries to divorce me. I could use them.'

I stared at her, trying to catch up. 'Sorry? For what? How do you know how to copy stuff from off his computer? How did you get his password?'

'That's my business, how I got them,' she whispered, as if she were divulging top-secret information.

'So… I'm not following. What will you prove with them again? Who are you going to give them all to?'

'To prove he's an idiot Pippa. He's having an affair, obviously.'

'An affair? Isn't he a bit old to be having an affair? Look, I'll make you another cup of tea, and then we can talk some more.' I quickly walked into the bathroom and phoned Brad.

'Why would I know the reason your father is looking at buttholes, Pippa? Why has your mother travelled all the way from Tasmania to tell you this, bringing a thumb drive with her? Have you even seen this evidence?'

'Good point. She could have phoned, and no, I haven't checked it's even real yet.'

'Does she know you are going to Paris?'

'No, not yet.'

'You need to keep this under control. I don't like the sound of this visit. It sounds odd at best. Be careful.'

'I know. That's why I've employed you to help me navigate the force I call family.'

'I can't protect you from your mother, Pippa. Only you can do that.'

I sighed. 'Yeah, I know. I get that.'

. . .

MY MOTHER started talking about how she had found the buttholes. She set the scene by re-visiting 1954 because the colour of the computer screen border had reminded her of oranges? Or was it the orange peel she'd noted on my father's desk… which had reminded her of oranges that were in someone's garden? Was it her garden? No, perhaps a cousin's garden? The she jumped to 1976, because her Cousin had moved and developed an allergy to pineapples?

'Pippa, sorry for interrupting…'

It was Brad again.

'This next bit. It changes tone quite dramatically. I think you need a trigger warning.'

'A trigger warning?'

'Yeah. Some people might feel a bit uncomfortable reading this stuff.'

'Okay. Trigger warning in place.'

'That's it?'

'Yeah. So, can I get back to the story?'

'Sure.'

MY MOTHER COMPLAINED in her thick Irish accent without taking a breath. She was so involved in her recounting of my father's new hobby that she failed to see me packing my suitcase for Paris. I was used to her self-absorbed interaction, however, and I could have been lying dead on the floor in front of her, impersonating an ironing board, and she would still have kept talking, and possibly ironed on me as well.

'So, your father is having an affair, after all these years of me being faithful.'

'An affair?' I sounded surprised. 'Are you completely certain of this?'

'Dear God, child. Is the Pope a Catholic? I have the evidence for that as well.'

'I know that the Pope is a Catholic.'

She stared at me.

What evidence?' I sighed, bracing myself for another lengthy recount. This time it started in 1982 and a line up of work colleagues, family friends and acquaintances were mentioned, proving what, I wasn't clear on.

'I've been convinced for years that he's been having a relationship with the woman from that bakery. Every morning he goes to the bakery at the same time. The pink one, with the doughnuts on the front, next door to the hairdressers.'

'And?' I interjected, feeling perplexed, and not following her train of thought.

'That woman. The blonde one. The one who bakes the bread.' She nodded at me as if that had been the clincher.

I wondered if it were my blonde woman from the ferry for a fleeting moment. She had possibly fallen from the ferry. I was sure that she remains trying to swim to the edge. Maybe she had made it and started a new career as a baker?

'She's been after your father for years, you know, and now she's got him. I'm sure she was the one to force him to google this depraved content.'

'So, the proof for this affair is?'

'That is *my* proof. Pippa. Can you not be supportive, just for once?'

'Mother, he's seventy-six. I mean, do you truly believe that he's driving down to buy a loaf of bread and popping his… himself into her oven? Really?' I smiled at my witty analogy. My mother did not.

'Yes,' she said, adamantly, nodding and looking me square in the eye.

'He doesn't have time for an affair, with all the responsibility of the alpacas, does he? How many have you got left?'

'Four. We lost Gerry last winter, remember.'

My mother and father had started an alpaca farm in Tasmania after moving from Ireland in their late twenties. They had successfully bred an exotic line, selling raw and carded fibre, a hundred percent alpaca yarn, and felting kits. The business had been moderately successful, and the animals had been good companionship as I was growing up. Most of them were now long-gone.

'Now,' my mother said.

I looked up at her. She was about to change the subject. I knew that tone, all too well. A verbal starter's gun sounded, and she was off.

'When are you going to end it with Sam, Pippa? You know your father and I have never approved of those sorts of men for you. You should end that relationship quickly. It's all out of wedlock and totally against God. Your father has sent me up here, to sort you out. Look, he's compiled a dossier on him.' She got up and searched around in one of the suitcases and then handed me a thick yellow folder, full of paper.

What the proverbial fuck? The conversation had done a one-eighty. Was she serious? I opened the folder and caught my breath. It was the sort of dossier that an ASIO spy would have been proud to have collated.

'What's this? Did I even tell you about Sam?' I was confused. I hadn't spoken about Sam to them at any length. I knew better than to divulge personal information.

'No, someone else did. Someone who is looking out for you, Pippa.'

'Who?' I was bewildered.

'None of your business.'

'Did one of my brothers say something?'

'I'm not saying. It's not my place to say.'

'None of *my* business? Has dad visited Sam's family? Workplace? Friends? Are these notes from actual interviews?' I asked, flicking through pages and pages of transcripts. 'Who transcribed all of this up?' I was dumbfounded.

'Of course not, Pippa. He called in a favour, and one of his old friends did the information collation. How would your father visit all of those people from the farm? He's got so much information about Sam, though. We think he's a paedophile and could have a penchant for minor criminal activity relating to insider trading.'

I sat down. My sense of reality was distorting and entering into my mother's parallel universe. 'Sorry, who thinks Sam is a rock spider? Wait… what criminal activity? Insider trading? Mum… he's an electrician for God's sake.'

'Do not take the Lord's name in vain. You need to break it off at once. You're in danger, Pippa. Father Jones agrees. That's why I'm here. What's a rock spider?'

'A paedo. What danger? That's the reason you're here? Did you speak with Father Jones about my relationship with Sam? I thought you were here about Dad having an affair and googling butt holes?'

'You need to listen for once in your life.' My mother was heading into fight mode.

'Me, listen?' This was not a good recipe for calm. 'Who gave you both permission to delve into my personal life?' I asked, with evident frustration.

'There you go… always shouting at me.' She started to cry. 'You are so abusive Pippa.'

'I'm not shouting. Hang on, you've just said that my boyfriend is a rock spider… a paedophile. What?'

'Yes, and you're always shouting Pippa. The shouting. It has to stop. You need to get help for this aggression. Have you been drinking again?'

'Drinking? What? It's four in the afternoon. Why would I have been drinking?'

'You always get like this when you drink.'

'What? I'm not shouting. I'm confused, and no, I haven't been drinking!'

SHE PHONED MY FATHER. 'Pippa is shouting at me,' she told him in a little girl's voice. 'I'm being abused, Callan. I'm scared. I believe she may have been drinking. What should I do?'

'What? Dad… I'm not abusing Mum!' I called over from a safe distance, 'and I haven't been drinking!'

She upped the crying, now a wail. If I didn't do something, I would lose control of the whole situation. I needed to diffuse things and fast. 'Look, I'll go out for a bit, okay? Give you some time to rest for a couple of hours?'

I walked for a while, meandering aimlessly up and down the streets near my flat, a familiar sick feeling in the pit of my stomach. There was so much going on at once, and I was finding it hard to control my emotions. I could not believe what was transpiring. Invading Sam's work? Speaking to his friends and what was this paedophile, criminal activity? As well as the fact, I was a woman in my twenties, not a fledgling teenager.

When were my parents going to understand the concept of boundaries? It was frustrating, as I'd been to countless psychologists to create 'effective boundaries' with my mother. No amount of 'positive language' and 'standing confidently within my space' had made any difference with the woman or my father, for that matter. They didn't give a dandelion about my boundaries in the first place, let alone abide by any rules relating to them. My parents were boundary crushers, crucifiers of personal space and information.

I returned to the flat after a time I thought appropriate, praying to God that she had calmed down. I quietly let myself in. She was still crying, her face now puffed, red and teary.

'See these?' she cried, holding out her arm.

I looked over at the tablets in her hand.

'I almost took these. I almost committed suicide, Pippa.'

'Really?' I asked, not meaning to sound more surprised than concerned. That seemed a tad melodramatic, even for her.

'I cannot believe the way you just treated me. I've travelled all the way from Tasmania to help sort you out, and look at how ungrateful you are. We are doing this for your own good Pippa.'

'I am very grateful that you are here.' I tried to find the right words. Not the ones that were the truth, rather the words that would extinguish the rage starting to burn deep within her. My opinion about how things were unfolding was irrelevant. I could tell that the flame was growing. A daughter like me, you see, has this special built-in radar.

We *know* when things are going pear-shaped. It starts with *that* feeling. You hold your breath and your ears prick up. You hear the sound of your heart pumping that little bit faster, and then you start noticing everything. Fingers that curl into a fist shape, a foot that might be tapping, and the colour of someone's face. If it's getting flushed, you are getting warmer, and you need to retreat, even if it's only a footstep backwards. A daughter like me will follow eyes, see where they are looking, and how fast they begin to dart. Then we look for what might be within reach. Something that might be used as a weapon, wrapped in rage. A daughter like me will look for an escape, just in case. All of this happens in a split second, time that seems too small for so much to be observed. A daughter like me knows what happens next.

The tears were switched off, and the waif mother, helpless from my defiance, suddenly grew into a witch that wanted revenge for my disobedience. I had not bowed before her, instead, I had appeared as if angered by her control. Then she was all-powerful, looming over me, all-consuming. Her rage was boiling and exploding as she ejected words at me for minutes and then for hours. I wasn't listening, not properly. I was surviving it, watching where her arms flung and carefully following her feet on the carpet as she paced, up and down, side to side. She attacked and attacked, although to achieve what, I wasn't sure. Annihilation of my defiance, perhaps?

My job wasn't to protect me in there but to protect *her*, from herself, as I had done for as long as I could remember. It was a sick dynamic. Golden Child, defined as the protector. Compliant child to be worshipped and now, her lessening grip on a maturing woman, to be hated. There was a knock at the door, twice to ask if she could keep her yelling down. The neighbours were concerned. Then it was someone handing me a large piece of poster-sized paper.

'Awfully sorry. Your mother stuck this up at the bottom of the communal stairs. Thought you might want it back.'

I stared at the poster. Twelve dot-points about me. It was stuck to the wall where everyone could see it. What the...? Who does that?

1. Pippa is a whore.

2. Pippa is ungrateful.

3. Pippa has failed at everything all her life...

'When the hell did you put this up?' I asked my mother, now resting, mainly from emotional exhaustion.

'When you went out. You refused to engage with me... to discuss things properly. It was the only way I could communicate with you! Tell you what you needed to see! For your own good Pippa!'

I wanted to scream and tear it up, however, someone had to be the adult in that space, at that moment, just as always. I rolled the cardboard up, along with any emotional feelings I had, found a wildlife series on television, and made her another cup of tea. She calmed, enjoying the programs and then, after making sure she was tucked up in bed, I retreated to my bedroom.

I was shaking and cold on the inside, as if her anger had drained me of my warmth. I lay in my bed, staring into the blackness, knowing this was not over. She had tasted blood, and it would be my blood that had to be readily spilt before she would be satisfied that her objection to my independence had been heard.

Sam knocked on my front door quietly, and she leapt up to open it. Something was happening… I could hear shouting, and then Sam was calling me, urgently.

'She jumped. I promise… Pippa… I didn't do anything.'

My mother had fallen, head-first, down the stairs and was now lying at the bottom. She was motionless and lying awkwardly. My first thought was that she had broken her neck.

'Shit!' I ran down the stairs to see if she how badly she was injured, calling out her name. Nothing. I was about to phone for an ambulance, when, like some religious miracle, she was resurrected. She got up and looked herself up and down, straightened her clothes and then raced back up the stairs, apparently unhurt. She was back into the flat in seconds, shutting the door forcibly behind her. Sam ran up to his flat and shut his door. I stood on the stairs alone. Christ in heaven, this night still had time to get worse.

I sat on the stairs, doing the right thing which I had promised to the various sets of neighbours who had opened their doors. Most had told me to shut the fuck up, some more politely than others. After an hour, I heard the lock click on the front door. Then the door opened, and she invited me back inside. I half expected her to hit me as I walked past her, but she didn't. I said what she needed to hear. That Sam was terrible to have pushed her down the stairs. That the police would be informed, of course. That I would break the relationship off in the morning. I just wanted her to stop. To sleep. Just to be *silent.*

I lay back in my bed. This wasn't over. Her injuries hadn't been enough in her thwarted stair leap for people to *see* her outrage. Her internal fire was still simmering, and I could feel the intensity of it through the wall. Should I make a run for it? No. I needed to stay because I'd been wired to stay and not leave. If I ran, where would I have gone anyway? It was dark outside and late. I had left once and ended up sleeping rough. It hadn't achieved anything, and she had been just as angry the next morning when I had returned. She might kill herself out of pedantic rage if I left now. I didn't want her blood on my hands, and so I lay there, waiting for her to finish off what she had started.

Yet again, this was my familiar, my world, with strange rules that I had to abide by if a relationship was to be had. Rage, pain, humiliation, and hate being spat from the mouth of my protector. The woman who had birthed me. The woman who loved me. The woman whom *I loved*. This was the twisted love that I was born into. It was the only love that I knew. Some had told me to cut her of my life, which was easier said than done. She always managed to find me again.

Time ticked slowly, trying to stop the inevitable. It happened at around three, dead man's time. My door was flung open, and the light switched flicked. Dark to sudden bright, a figure highlighted. She lurched in, tearing the sheets from off my bed. I hid in a corner, just as her anger lifted the mattress from off of my bed. She hurled it across the room, having found super-power strength from her adrenaline rush.

'You won't be having sex in here, not while I'm here!' she screamed. Her anger was now entirely in control of her, and her mind trapped in an outcome that was already certain. She stormed out and into the kitchen, where she then flung all my saucepans around, smashing them into the granite bench tops. She did this while shouting at me that I was useless and ungrateful. Then she pulled a scrunched-up piece of paper from her dressing gown pocket and threw it into my face.

'All the things we've ever bought you. There. That list has taken me hours to write. The bill comes to twenty-five thousand dollars.'

I stared at it. 'Is this what you've been doing all night?'

'Yes, indeed,' she said, and I wondered if she thought it some sort of achievement.

'This includes food, though.' I said, despair streaming through me.

'Yes. It costs to feed kids. I wish I'd never had the lot of you. I really do. I would have preferred just to have raised alpacas. They're a damned lot more grateful. We did everything for you. Everything, and look at how you repay us.'

'I've thanked you for everything. Do you want me to be grateful for the food as well?'

'Look around you, Pippa. Look how much we helped you when you first moved out of home.'

'I know. I've said thank you. I appreciated it then, and I do now. I'm an adult, though.'

'Well, you don't behave like one. We thought carefully about this whole situation with Sam, and we're doing this for the best. You need to end the relationship, or we'll have to distance ourselves from you.'

'Sorry? Hang on a min, you want me just to end it?' I was stunned. 'Why would I end a perfectly good relationship?'

'We can't keep going on like this Pippa. It's exhausting.'

'What?' I was stunned into silence, confusion and anger.

Blood still needed to be spilt, though. She still hadn't finished because I hadn't relinquished all of my power. On this occasion, I had refused.

I PHONED Brad from the hospital a few hours later, holding an ice pack to my jaw.

'She hit me,' I mumbled.

'What? Why did she hit you?'

'I told her in the middle of all of this, that I had become an atheist a couple of years ago.'

'Jesus, Pippa. Are you okay?'

'Kind of numb. They've done an x-ray, and luckily, it's not broken. I just can't open my mouth very far, though.'

'You're probably in shock.'

'Yeah.'

'Are you going to press charges for assault?'

'Charge my own mother? No, I feel sorry for her.'

'Why?'

'She was crying.'

'She was crying? Were you crying?' Brad sounded confused.

'No.'

'Did you kick her out?'

'No, I asked her to leave, later today.'

'Are you safe to go back?'

'I hope so.'

'Has she said sorry?'

'No. She said I was exaggerating a *small slap*.'

'A small slap that landed you at the hospital?'

'Yeah, she flung her arm back and belted me, using all her weight. I fell over from the impact actually.'

'Can you still fly?'

'Nah. Going to have to postpone Paris. Lucky my ticket is one which is flexible. I'll re-book when I feel better.'

'Pippa…'

'I'm fine… really.' Only, I wasn't. I didn't have the words to express how I was really feeling.

MY MOTHER SAID nothing about the ice pack being held to my face, instead, she pretended nothing had happened after I returned from the hospital.

'Would you like a cup of tea perhaps, Pippa? I've just made one for myself.' She sounded as sweet as the sugar in the sugar bowl.

'No. Not really. Actually, my jaw hurts where you hit me.'

'Oh, don't go on about that. It was just a slap. Why do you always exaggerate Pippa? Falling to the floor like that. You should be given an Oscar for your performance.'

'I'm not exaggerating. The doctor said you nearly broke it. She asked me if I wanted to press charges for assault, actually.'

My mother stopped what she was doing and turned to face me. My heart sank.

'So, let me get this right,' she said slowly. 'You told someone that I hit you? That I actually hit you? It was a slap, Pippa O'Shea! Did you give them my name? How dare you! That's the reputation of the alpaca farm down the drain, you stupid child!'

A daughter like me looks for the weapon, that comes after words like that. My eyes saw the cup of tea, filled to the brim with scalding liquid. I watched as her eyes saw it, recognising it as appropriate. I followed the motion of her hand, reaching for it. A daughter like me is fast, though, in our reaction, and we know how fast we must react. The cup hurtled towards my head, as if in slow motion, and I could see every twist and turn it made. I turned to one side and waited for impact. It missed my head, instead, hitting the doorframe with such force that it shattered into shards. Hot liquid scalded my arm, and brown liquid covered my clothes.

I looked up at her. Her face was still angry. She was not horrified by her impulsive action. Not guilty. Just satisfied and brimming with more rage.

'Okay. You need to leave.' I told her, moving the ice pack onto my scalded arm, sounding eerily calm. My emotions were now packed away. I needed to maintain tight control. My emotions were never relevant in situations like this. My logic was what counted when survival was aimed for.

'Now you are throwing me out? Into a strange city? You are the worst daughter, Pippa! If anything happens to me, it will be your fault.'

'Yeah. I know,' I said, looking at my arm and wondering if it was going to blister. I needed to get it under cold water quickly.

She then packed. The zips on her suitcases emitted more anger in my direction, and then she stormed out, slamming the door behind her muttering that she was taking the emergency key with her for the next time I messed my life up.

'JESUS PIPPA. Your face is as bruised as hell.' Brad shook his head, looking shocked. He plugged his computer into the charger on the table and then sat, facing me.

'Yeah, she got me good.'

He stared at me and then shook his head. 'How's your arm?'

'Just a bit of a scald. Not too bad, considering. Just a couple of places where it blistered. It could have been worse. She might have got my face.'

'I don't know what to say, Pippa.'

'Neither do I. Oh, she took my diary on her way out.'

'What diary?'

'She gave me a diary when I was fourteen. I wrote in it every day at the time. She's taken it from my wardrobe.'

'Shit. Who does that?'

'She does.' There was a lengthy silence.

'They usually photocopy the pages they don't like and then file them.'

'Sorry? Who does that?'

'My parents.'

'They photocopy them? Have they done this before?'

'Yeah.'

'Do they have any concept of boundaries?'

'I don't think so.'

'Do you want coffee? I can get you a flat white, the Columbian blend?'

'Yeah. Just need a straw though, thanks.'

'Sure. I'll het them to make it luke warm too.'

I sucked my coffee through a straw, which was difficult, given the pain.

'So, Pippa,' said Brad.

'I know what you're going to say.'

'Hear me out anyway.'

'Okay.'

'This isn't normal. You do know that.'

'Yeah. I get it. It's my normal, though. That's the problem.'

'So, she's never been like, standard normal?'

'Not really. At least I don't think so. How would I know what normal is, though? The alpacas think she's normal, I assume. She can appear normal to people in short bursts, put it that way. Everyone who meets her says how nice she is.'

'You need to get away from her. She's dangerous.'

'I know. The thing is, I am away from her Brad. I live in Sydney, and she lives in Tasmania. Here comes the choice again. Cut off from my entire family and go through life alone.'

'It might be easier?'

'Have you ever thought of cutting off your entire family?'

'No.'

'Exactly. It's not a matter of just saying 'see ya all later.'

'I get that.'

'You know what though? Want to hear some irony?'

'I think so?'

'She cut off from her own family. Never spoke to any of them ever again one day. Even when they all died, she didn't give a shit. She is forcing me to do the same. Only she did it because she didn't stop to work through any issues.'

SAM LOOKED AT ME APOLOGETICALLY. I knew what was coming next.

'I think we're over, Pippa. Your Mum blamed me for pushing her down the stairs. I didn't do it.'

'Yeah. I know you didn't. I'm sorry she accused you.'

'It was nice… us. You're a good person and all, but I never knew that mothers hit their daughters like that.'

'Yeah, I know.'

'I wish you all the best in the future, and I'm not a paedophile either. The whole block of flats heard that, and people are starting to ask questions.' Sam walked up the stairs quickly, not looking back at me. He honestly couldn't get away from me fast enough.

JOSEPHINE THE THERAPIST

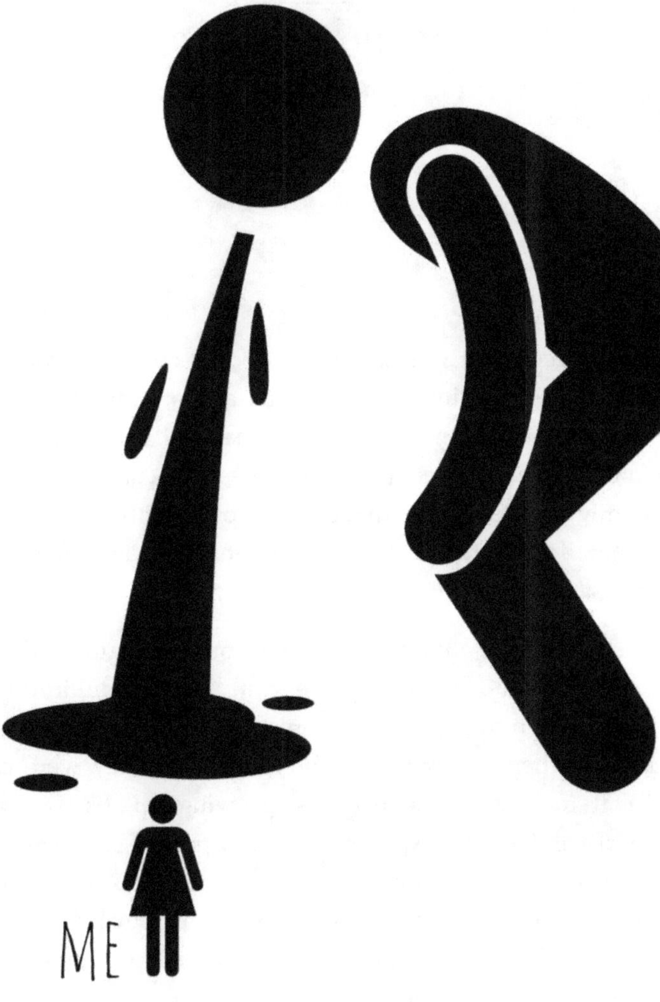

9

VERBAL VOMIT
YOU LYING

I t was a secret that was as dirty as secrets could be. A mother and father who loved in the wrong way and an adult child who was still being controlled and berated as if a small child. There wasn't a place in the world for such gloom and misery. Social norms dictate that your family should be an image of happy, healthy and functioning. Those that aren't are quickly vilified and avoided as if somehow contagious.

My parents used the alpaca farm as their public disguise. It seems that long eyelashes and quality fleece can hide a multitude of sins, especially if worn by an alpaca. People projected their adoration of the alpacas onto them. A free ride, and one which they were careful to nurture. It meant that none of us, growing up, had anywhere or anyone to validate our experiences. What people saw was a farm of cuteness, big eyes and long lashes, not the festering truth, hidden behind closed doors. My parents would run hour-long tours of the farm and remain so cheerful and sweet, and visitors would walk away saying how lovely they both were.

Early on, I learned that people would dismiss my accounts of the truth as being over-zealous and, at times, fermenting within a sick imagination. I was labelled quickly as a bit odd and as a liar in most instances. Even bruises and red marks were looked at, with a bias that overlooked their distinct shapes. How can a handprint on a child's leg, not be seen as such? How can a riding crop's lash not be identified correctly when leaking from a sibling's school shorts? Even when my mother threw a purple stain over my brother's hands to teach him a lesson, and he went to school looking purple-bizarre, no-one dared to speak up. I waited for the day that someone would stop long enough to say, 'that's not right. I wonder what's going on there?'

They didn't. We were fed and watered as adequately as the alpacas. We had our clothes washed, and our hair was brushed. We had extras given to us, which made us look like we had every opportunity at our feet. We weren't going to die from it all, so no-one said anything. Their choice was simple in hindsight. Ignore what was plain to see or be potentially brought down themselves, by speaking out.

Only it was the invisible that was doing harm, like when I was ten and closed the fridge door too hard. A bottle of my father's whiskey, precariously balancing on the top, fell and smashed. Fists aimed in my face, seething anger and mother in-between us. What does a ten-year-old do with that? There were no marks to show, just the internal shock from a father that valued his alcohol more than the sacred image of his own daughter in that moment. The next moment was fine, so no damage done, right?

Going to school during a period of constant tensions in which instability at home had featured every day meant that I often arrived crying. On one day, I arrived with marks on my legs where the vacuum cleaner hose had been used to punish me. Why? I hadn't cleaned my room well enough, and my mother had again looked for the nearest object to help her unleash her rage. My tears and explanation for the marks weren't enough for anyone to offer comfort. Instead, my teachers ignored my explanation, labelling me as 'overly emotional,' a label that I still can't shake off today. Children are easier to deal with if the problem lies with them. They can be told to 'go and wash your face and hurry to class.' You hid the secrets, or you were abandoned for life, just like that.

The dynamic inside the house was one of educated anger, always seething as a pan of water might simmer. Any excuse was used to unleash the rage, the boiling, the volcanic explosion. Any hint of stepping from what was expected, even if having dusted something the wrong way, not made a bed or said the wrong word was an *excuse* for detonation. If I met a boy, boundaries would be violated, mail opened, read and shredded and always the shouting. The arguments that would go for hours. Over what? Over nothing. Just a form of communication that was co-dependent, in the sense that two people had found a fellow sounding board, to unleash whatever the fuck was bothering them both inside.

Navigating my teen years was akin to avoiding active landmines whilst trying to hide all sense of growing up. When I shaved my legs at thirteen because I was being teased at school, I was screamed at for not having sought permission. I wasn't allowed to pluck my eyebrows, despite having an embarrassing mono-brow. I was forced to wear a school tie when no-one else did. Sexuality was banned, and my own emerging sense of self was being suffocated. I was an extension of her, there to prove her with a vicarious way to seek pleasure from life. That was my purpose. I towed the family line, or I could be thrown out on the spot. A lesson I learned early on.

At fourteen, I first got thrown out for daring to report a particularly unsettling experience with my mother to my father. I tried to step discreetly over the landmines, and my words were chosen carefully from a place of love. It was a mistake, as although her behaviour warranted further investigation, even if only to see if she was okay, I was thrown from the house after having been raged at and ordered to pack a suitcase. It was dark and cold walking from the farm that night. My mother found me and brought me back, later that night, and I had to go to school the next day as if nothing had happened. Again, my sullen face and apparent seeping despair made me look as if I was emotionally fragile, a loner or maladjusted. No-one ever asked me if I was okay.

I became a top student excelling wherever I could. I learned that academic excellence and achievement earned millions of parental brownie points. I was a machine, churning through different activities and always reaching the top, searching for that excellence which would internally make me feel like I had 'arrived.' It never found me love though and my constant facial expression of exhaustion and confusion was again always attributed to some sort of internal freak feature, rather than a weight that I was finding difficult to carry. I was exhausted by the end of school and chose to work full-time rather than attend university. Work provided money and thus, independence.

I didn't need enemies, even as an adult. I had my mother and father. In times of rage, mother would pick the phone up and find my contacts. I don't know what she said to them, or my neighbours or my school teachers. I just remember seeing someone I knew in the supermarket one day, who turned upon seeing me and ran the other way. I would have friends phone me in tears, accusing me of betraying them, neighbours explaining random visits from her, accusing me of saying things about them, only to discover that my own mother had provided the information.

Boundaries were violated and even as an adult when I was living and dating in the city close to the farm, they would drive around and around my house, to see if I had a visitor parked in my car-space, suggesting that I had started a relationship that they disapproved of. I was a toy for them to play with that allowed them disapproval, condemnation and an excuse to make themselves feel better about themselves.

My family shrank one by one, as my siblings' presence irritated my parents. When it was clear that autonomy was a permanent state, they would be cast out, some deemed dead, just like that. Then the casting aside included extended family and then their friends. Our family tree became smaller and smaller with relatives standing back, as I was seen as an extension of my parents' dysfunction. I became lost in amongst their crap and alone in the world. Not because I had done something to hurt anyone else. I had just followed a typical life trajectory within a context that just didn't want *me.*

My crime was simply, being me. I hadn't robbed a bank, become a drug dealer or had deliberately hurt others. I was leading a normal life path in which my normal actions were seen to be as negative as someone who goes off the rails and opens fire in a shopping mall.

Christmas time consisted of a visit in front of plates of nuked vegetables, mother's hysterics and father and me. My siblings refused to play and weren't ever invited anyway. Such fun. Not. It was as if we played at Christmas, knowing that it felt and appeared all wrong because not doing so would have made the dysfunction obvious. I used to look at the TV ads around Christmas, seeing families sitting around Christmas tables smiling and laughing. It was a joke because none of the ads ever showed families that might want to harm one another at Christmas time. Families that hated sitting around a table with each other. Families that frowned, snarled and bashed each other up.

Presents were an excuse for passive-aggressive anger. My mother took great delight in giving me gifts that were irrelevant and at times, quite hurtful. A book on 'what to say in social situations,' free cloth napkins printed with a logo that she got as an extra for buying something for herself. Wrinkle cream… a music box that played what can only be described as demonic music using the wrong notes from Fur Elise. One year it was a shower cap, then men's socks. It was as if she didn't know me in the first instance and decided to spend the minimum amount on me. Her cards would have *love from, from* or simply her name, depending on how she felt about me in that year. I would buy expensive perfumes for her, some of which she would tell me were awful. The postage cost her more than the gifts she sent my way. My gifts to them sent as a way to try to express daughter-love were at times, scorned, mocked and never spoken about again.

One year I got them gratitude gifts which went down as well as if I had sent them both envelopes of funnel web spiders. There was a look of incredulity, shock and horror when they realised that someone else benefited from the money I had spent. They missed the point completely as I described a woman in India now having a sewing machine and a new business and a man in Kenya who could now raise goats to feed his family. I remember their faces… 'Why?' they had asked me, looking as sad as children who hadn't found presents under the Christmas Tree.

As I got older, my ex-communicated siblings turned on me, as our earlier pact, necessary for protection was no longer needed. They resented my Golden Child status as my mother's protector, not seeing that it was a position I hadn't applied for. They resented that I had been hit less than they had been, not seeing my frantic attempts to be the one to drag her off them, their screams still etched into my memory. Then they glued themselves together as one globby mess and directed their force of disappointment towards me. They would phone me with snippets of gossip about what had been said about me by other siblings, all of whom denied ever saying anything. They would name call me, ridicule my achievements and always say that the only reason I had succeeded in my hobbies was because I'd been given special treatment. Everything I said was examined and deemed as laden in madness by them. Mocking, shaming and ridicule became my norm. I had become the black sheep of the family.

As an adult, the problem presented itself as a huge issue. If told, my truth would act as a form of social leprosy, its weight, ruining the froth on many a morning cappuccino. My truth socially isolated me more and more, until I concluded that creating a false self was the only way to maintain social life semblance. I would need to lie about my truth for people to accept me as anything other than a distasteful object of pity. My truth didn't make people like me, it made people want to distance themselves from me. My very presence and truth forced me into a very lonely place. Why is it when you speak of family dysfunction, not of your own making, that it ruins your social status? What I was craving, was simple. It was connection, and it was dignity. In a truthful space, my soul, bearing to another and being accepted. I was sick of their dysfunction, defining me in the eyes of others.

I felt utterly alone in a world of billions. I felt as if my presence wasn't wanted. I had perhaps, been a mistake, a notion reinforced several times by a mother moaning to me about how her children had ruined her life. I was the wrong egg and sperm joining at the wrong moment, coming into the world, speaking a language that neither of my parents understood, at times. They were without empathy, and I seemed to have been given too much, something that they labelled as me being 'overly-sensitive.' If I got angry at having my boundaries violated, I was 'abusive' and 'hostile.'

If I ever tried to engage in conversations about their behaviour, a rage descended quickly. I was the problem. It was me. Pippa O'Shea, not them. There were a million things wrong with me. I believed them too, because no-one else would listen, to tell me that they were wrong.

None of this would have worked, as in a relationship sustained, if there hadn't been good bits too. That's how you get frozen between the good and the bad. There was as much function as dysfunction, with laughs being exchanged, cups of tea being held and experiences shared. That's what the child in me held on to. The good bits. The moments where I felt, I might have belonged. That's where the wiring starts for someone like me to be able to love a psychopath. The fact that I can love good and evil. I can be patient waiting for good to return, and I can accept evil without batting an eyelid because it always turns back into good.

Yeah, kids like me learn to love both good and evil. We have to. If we complained about the evil, then we would lose the roof over our heads. We lose the love we so badly crave. We wait for the good, which always shows itself because a child has to be taught to trust. Think about that wiring. We can love nice, and we can love bad. That sets us up for so much that is just never going to work.

BRAD WAS CONCERNED. 'So, you've tried proper counselling Pippa?'

'Yes. Many times. It comes down to this. If I want a relationship with either of my parents, then I have to accept them for who they are. They aren't going to change. This will never be a family that can sit down with a counsellor and fix bad habits. It's a one-way street.'

'Even if that means you get hit? She almost broke your jaw, Pippa. That tea? She has no self-control when angry. What about the rest as well? The complete lack of boundaries?'

'The alternative Brad is to walk away from all of them and become a self-proclaimed orphan. It means walking away from my entire family and doing precisely what they do to everyone else. That's not an easy task. I wanted to do my life differently.'

'So, you've tried opening up to friends, and they shut you down?'

'Yeah. Their elderly parents are sweet and kind. They have siblings that they meet with, regularly. They all go home for Christmas and have fun. I remember one woman sounding angry with me. She told me that her parents had died and that I was ungrateful. People automatically assume that I'm doing something wrong, to warrant reactions like that. If someone gets angry enough to hit you, the first inference can sometimes be, 'well, what did you do to provoke them?' It's complicated to explain.'

Brad frowned, thinking. 'The realities of life easily confront people, I think. It's easier for them to shut you up than it is for them to say something that acknowledges that this stuff happens. People are quite lazy when it comes down to it Pippa. They prefer the simplistic - like a family that's kind to each other.'

'Yeah, but I'm so sick of lying, or leaving bits out and not joining in. I feel like I'm always on the outside, hiding, for fear that my truth will upset someone's delicate sense of togetherness.' I shook my head. 'I've never heard one of my friends ever say that their parents behave like mine.'

'I hear you. This is hard. I think you should possibly try another psychologist to be honest. There are layers and layers here that need exploring in a more professional setting. I'm only a life coach, kind of not used to dealing with stuff this serious. I'm also technically not supposed to deal with anything outside of my professional limitations, remember.'

'Yeah, I get it.'

'When are you going to Paris, now that your jaw is better? That's something positive to end this session on.'

'Nah, not feeling it right now. Might leave it a bit.'

'Are you okay, Pippa?'

'Define, okay?'

'Fair point. Although I think we should stay in touch daily, even if only a quick email or message. You've been through a lot.'

I raised my right eyebrow at him, 'You think so?'

'I've never been able to do that,' he said, looking at my eyebrow, before realising his botox faux pas.

'Don't try?' I offered, watching him furiously blink, his eyelid being the only part of the upper portion of his face that still moved.

I LEFT my flat needing fresh and moved. The memories of my mother's meltdown and my broken relationship with Sam were constant reminders that my life was at times, shitty. My neighbours had avoided eye contact with me when I met them on the stairs, in the days after her performance. I'm not surprised. Number eight on my mother's list had been 'Pippa is dangerous when she drinks,' so there wasn't much else to say to them, despite me only drinking on rare occasions and even then, not getting drunk. Sam had moved on, and his awkward, pitying smiles had made me feel even worse. I needed to find a new flat and to start again.

Despite so eagerly praying to her Catholic God for fertility rights, my mother resented having all of us. Our family story was like one of those Aesop's fables, which has a moral attached at the end after personal struggles have been endured. Only our end hasn't been written yet. We're just a bunch of upset, adult-kids who feel miserable. Our despair is so heavy that our family collapsed into a black hole of futility.

On this occasion, however, she and my father decided that my behaviour had been so abhorrent that as soon as my mother had returned to Tasmania, they sent me a list in the mail, via registered post, of my wrongs.

Firstly, I had been in a relationship out of wedlock. Second, I had become an atheist and, therefore, had sinned against the entire Catholic Church.

Third, I was ungrateful as a daughter.

Fourth my boyfriend had 'thrown' my mother down a flight of stairs.

Fifth, I'd told someone my mother's name, in relation to her mild slap, defaming her through exaggeration, and possibly destroying the reputation of the alpaca farm.

Lastly, the stuff I'd written in my diary at the age of fourteen was disgraceful. They had photocopied the relevant parts and placed them in a file for future reference, as predicted.

I was then discarded in true narcissistic style with flaming arrows thrown in my direction for good measure, including writing me out of their wills and forbidding me to see the alpacas ever again.

Brad put me in touch with a psychologist.

'This shit is way beyond my capabilities.'

'So, you're disappearing on me too?'

'Never Pippa. I'm here. Like a piece of chewing gum, stuck to you.'

'So, why ask me to get a referral for a psychologist?'

'Because this shit is big stuff and out of my professional league. If I were going through it, I probably would get stuck too.'

'You think I'm stuck?'

'Yeah, I do. Anyone would be.'

. . .

JOSEPHINE, my new psychologist, was a lady in her late forties and was quite clearly in the wrong profession. Her first response after asking me to summarise things was to vomit-shout at me using a verbal cannonball. Words were flung my way and all I could hear was anger. Who does that? Seriously? What sort of psychologist shouts at a client, especially after spilling their guts out to them? Trusting them with the contents of their damaged soul?

'Where are your emotions, Pippa? I see nothing! You sit there, all dry and wooden. It would be more appropriate to say all of that *with* tears. There is nothing! You dry! You dry!'

What the fuck?

'I don't feel like crying about it right now,' I said, clearly confused by her outburst. What did she want? A drama performance? I contemplated wailing from my chair and decided even I couldn't stoop that low.

'I do not believe you. Nothing you have said rings true. I know of the alpaca farm, and your parents seem like good people. I once visited that farm, and they took me on a tour. They are lovely people! You tell me all this stuff, and yet, I have seen people like you… I have heard stories with far less in them, and it is normal for people to cry, Pippa. A lot of tears! You? You just dry!' She looked over at the box of tissues sitting next to me and shook her head. Then she waited.

What the hell? Was this a test or something? I looked around the room feeling vaguely unsettled. This was not heading in the right direction. What was with her having been to the farm too? That seemed like a bit of an unfortunate coincidence.

'You run too much from it all.' she ventured after a period of awkward as shit silence. 'You say you are always changing things and running. Running, running, running. Sit in the emotions and feel them. Now. Do as I say.'

What? Feel them Now? Just like that? Or what?

'Why would I sit in the moment if you don't believe me in the first instance. Which moment would I sit in? Yours or mine?'

'I did not say I do not believe it. I just said that you aren't convincing. People would cry in your situation. You don't. Therefore, it raises issues of validity for me. Of dryness.'

'Dry validity?' What are we doing, like a research project in here? No. You said you didn't believe me, because the alpacas have big long lashes, and they're cute. You met two smiling, happy people next to the cute alpacas. I didn't cry in front of you because I couldn't find any tears left to cry. Why did my face say liar instead of truth?

'I cannot help you Pippa if cannot be truthful.'

Okay. I'm reporting this woman. This cannot be helpful. This just cannot be helpful. My truth again, has earned me the title of being a liar. Always a liar. I got up and walked out, paying way too many dollars for the exchange.

'WELL, FUCK THAT,' I said to Brad a week later. 'I'm more depressed than I have been in ages. Where did you find her? Great advice that was, for a hundred and eighty bucks. Is she even allowed to shout at me during a session?'

'Sorry. A friend recommended her. I've emailed her and told her not to hand out her name anymore. That was the last thing you needed.'

'Yeah. It was. I reported her actually. She shouldn't be a psychologist. What sort of psychologist accuses a client of being a liar? Seriously?' I sounded and felt angry.

'Look, I know you probably don't want to do this…'

'No.' I said defiantly. 'Not after that. That was not helpful, Brad.'

'You don't know what I was going to say.'

'I do. You're going to recommend someone else.'

'Okay, I am…'

'NO.'

'Pippa, hear me out. This woman… I have known her for ages. She's unconventional but pretty good. Her name is Cynthia. Give her a go? Just once, and if she doesn't do it for you, then we'll start again.'

'Fine. Brad, I'll do this one more time. You do realise that sometimes my dysfunctional background is so brilliantly weird, that no-one believes a word that I say.'

'I believe you.'

'Thank you. However, this one had better be more understanding than the last one.'

CYNTHIA LIVED on a small bush block in the middle of a concrete jungle, three suburbs away. A beige house built in the seventies with a flat roof, surrounded by a garden that was all flowering native.

'Welcome,' she said, smiling, studying my face intensely.

'Hi,' I said with unease, not confident in how the plague had left my skin.

'So, Brad has told me a bit about your situation and thinks I can help. I've got a lot of time for Brad. He's got a heart of gold.'

'Yes. He's been good to me.'

I looked around the pink therapy room and felt strangely relaxed.

Candles, comfy chairs, relaxing music, crystals, and a fragrance I couldn't put my finger on, made me feel safe. Better than crazy cannon-ball Josephine, that was for sure.

'How do you feel?' asked Cynthia.

'Safer than I did seeing my last therapist.'

'Good,' she said, smiling warmly. 'Lonely?' she added.

I was taken aback. 'Sorry?'

'Do you feel lonely?'

'Um, yes. Why?'

'Brad has told me enough to let me know that with your story, it must be lonely, being you.'

'Yeah, very.' I had spoken two words of truth. I already felt better.

I saw Cynthia every week for two months. Her therapy approach was anything other than conventional. The first task she got me to do was get two cushions and call one mother and the other father. I was to sit them down, as they would have been positioned at home in the lounge room. It was where they had sat, throned, and demanded that their children stand before them. Then, they had screamed perceived wrongdoings at them. I was to sit them down and then stand over them. I was to tell them everything that I had been unable to say to them, for all of these years. My truth needed to find a voice.

After each session with my cushions, I was to go and run around the block as fast as I could, and more quickly than a cushion could run.

'Faster than a cushion can run?' I was confused.

'Yes,' Cynthia had said earnestly. 'You have to run faster than they can run. They must never be able to catch you again.'

'Metaphorically, I get that. What about my back?'

'Well, if it's only pain that you will experience, take some pain killers each time.'

'No-one has ever told me to use pain killers in order to run. Up until now, I've just been told to be careful.'

'Be careful, yes, but run as well. You have to run Pippa.'

I went home and chose a big fat cushion, grey with black tassels, and drew a frown on it for a mouth.

'Hello, mother,' I said dryly. 'You're looking mighty fine today.' I stopped, looking around, waiting for some form of retaliation. There was none. I felt awful that I'd sounded condescending. I was hopeless at being cruel.

Father was a brown coloured cushion. 'You look a bit like a loaf of bread,' I said to it. Still no attacks. I made myself a cup of tea and then sat opposite the two cushions. 'So,' I said. 'Lost for words, today are we? Nothing to say to criticise me?'

I went to the window and peered around the netting. What if someone could see me inside my lounge room talking to cushions? I went back to the cushions and sat. I had so many words that needed saying, only I didn't know where to start, or how to start. I realised the significance of the moment. I was going to choose words to express how I was feeling for the first time in my life. I sat quietly, in the silence, the words, however, not becoming obvious. Instead, I ran and raced around the block, my feet pounding on the concrete. I ran until my lungs felt like they were bursting. I pushed myself faster, and by the end, I realised that I was running somewhere new. I was indeed escaping, looking a bit mad as well, I surmised. A young woman, running awkwardly along the pavement, with tears streaming down her face.

This epiphany was short-lived when I ended up back with the cushions at the same point I had started from. My back had handled the run pretty well, better than I had expected. Nothing had fallen off me, and no joints had dislocated. The cushions were just sitting there, and I felt sorry for them, realising that they were a little vulnerable in the scheme of things without arms, legs, and a voice. There was an imbalance of power. I mentioned this to Cynthia when I next saw her.

'It seems like I have an unfair advantage. I don't feel right in hurting them.'

'Really?' she asked me quickly. 'Just as they did when you were a child? Were you allowed to speak? Were you allowed to run or fight back? What happened if you spoke Pippa?'

'They shut me down.'

I was slammed between the eyes with a memory of my mother beating up my brother when he was six, and me, hanging off her, my little hands hitting her, trying to get her to stop. All five years of brave little me, screaming at her. She had physically flung me off, and I had been silenced, listening to his screams as she had hit until her anger had been unleashed. I felt a rage building inside of me.

'What are you feeling?' asked Cynthia, obviously seeing my expression change.

'I'm not sure. Anger, perhaps?'

'Sit with it. Just feel it,' she said.

'Anger. Oh, God. I've found all this anger I didn't know I had. I wasn't ever allowed to criticise their behaviour, no matter what they had done. Any suggestion of condemnation and they would start to justify everything, deny it or accuse me of being a trouble maker for bringing it up.'

'Go back and beat the shit out of those cushions,' Cynthia said, quite matter of factly.

'Like actually hit them?'

'Yes. Hit them, just as they hit others.'

'Won't that make me like them?'

'No. You've already found the process difficult. Hitting doesn't come naturally to you, and it's not as if you are hitting actual people Pippa. It's a way to feel like you are fighting back, rather than attacking.'

I closed my curtains this time and then did precisely that. I was screaming at both of them and punching into their squishiness. I threw them both around the room. Then I sat them up again before kicking them into another room. Then I ran around the block, faster this time. The anger was falling off me as if the running was freeing me from some sort of casing. Guilt coursed through my veins, though. What if I had hurt the cushions? I hurried back and checked on them, just in case.

'Cushions don't feel pain,' reassured Cynthia over the phone. 'Bring them with you next time for some family therapy.'

'INTRODUCE ME, please,' asked Cynthia.

I put the fat grey cushion onto a chair. 'This is my mother, Bridie O'Shea, and this brown cushion, is my father, Callan O'Shea.'

'Welcome, Bridie, and Callan. Pippa has told me all about you. I'm sorry, did you say something, Bridie? No, you both have to be quiet at this point. This is Pippa's turn to speak, not yours.'

I smiled, a little awkwardly.

'Now, Pippa. What's something that your mother did to you?'

I thought through a series of disturbing memories. 'Probably the recent hit. The stairs, poster, diary, cup of tea, and breaking my relationship up with Sam. There's worse, but this is the most recent.'

'Happy to work on this one then?'

'Yeah, sure.' I was intrigued as to what would happen next.

'So, Bridie. Welcome. Now, Pippa here tells me that you almost broke her jaw. No Bridie, it wasn't a slap, otherwise, the doctor wouldn't have done an x-ray, or asked Pippa if she wanted to file assault charges. Pippa wouldn't have gone to the hospital if it had been a slap, would she?'

The cushion sat there.

'So, you must think that hitting Pippa is okay? She decided to leave the Church, as an adult, and so you hit her?'

The cushion pleaded the fifth.

'That's what you call love Bridie?'

I inhaled deeply. Cynthia had got straight to the point.

'In what world is your love acceptable Bridie? What have you taught Pippa about love? That it comes with rules, punishment, compliance and silence? That sometimes you will love her and at other times, choose not to? Do you think that might be confusing for Pippa?'

Ouch. Now it was hurting. 'What do you think, Pippa?'

Oh God, she was speaking to me. 'Um…' Nothing. There was nothing in my head. Blank.

'It's okay, Pippa. You will find your words. In the meantime, I'm going to speak up for you, because I imagine it's the first time in your life that anyone has.'

That got me between the eyes. Yes. It was the first time anyone had stood between them and me, even if they were a pair of cushions right now.

'Callan, my man,' Cynthia said in an overly-friendly tone.

I smiled. My father would object to being spoken to like that. He would have ignited like a match with kerosene on the end.

'What gave you the right to watch Pippa and her siblings suffer, and never look up long enough to see what your dear child-beating wife was doing to them? Oh, of course. You thought chasing Pippa out of the house with your fists in her face was okay. That explains your complacency. No response Callan?'

She stood up and walked over to the cushion. 'How does it feel to be sitting there helpless Callan? Knowing that you can't do anything right now and that I could take dear Bridie here and beat the crap out of her in front of you. Would that be okay? Just as Bridie here, took your children and beat them up because she could. Why could she, Callan? Because you allowed her to. Sorry? Oh, you joined in raging at them? Was it a bit of a comedy act between the two of you? A way to let off your own frustrations? I see.'

Cynthia suddenly stopped. 'Cup of tea time,' she announced. 'Sugar Pippa?'

'Yes, thanks… just one.'

The cushions sat there, looking at me. I could tell they were outraged at how Cynthia was speaking to them. If my parents had been sitting there, there would have been raging, and they would have stormed off. They were good at dishing out criticism but could never take it themselves. If you ever questioned them about their actions, it was always anger and outrage as a response. I couldn't remember a single time when they had shown any insight into their behaviours. They were blinkered into believing it was everyone else who had the problem and not themselves.

'Are you feeling sorry for them, Pippa?' asked Cynthia, sipping her tea from an elegant, blue tea-cup.

'Yeah, I do. Why? Why am I feeling sorry for them? I feel like I want you to stop speaking to them like that.'

'You've been wired to love your abusers. Have you heard of Stockholm Syndrome? To survive, you have to love them. If you hadn't, where would you be? This is important. Compliance was mandatory to stay in the clan.'

'That's true,' I said, thinking deeply. 'I had to always forgive them and move on as if nothing had happened. I always thought their rage was akin to someone who might cut themselves, like a pressure valve release or something. The rages wouldn't stop until they appeared exhausted. My truth was never enough to stop any of it, though.' I added sadly.

'Punished for telling the truth? Go and kick them for that.'

I did. I kicked the grey mother cushion and then stomped on the father cushion. Then I picked it up, screaming words of anger, before throwing it out of Cynthia's front door and onto her driveway. Then I slammed the front door after it. Then I stood in the silence. It was a powerful moment in which there had been no punishment for fighting back.

'Excellent,' she said, sipping her tea. 'Now leave Callan out there for a bit in the rain. We need to have a chat with Bridie. Let's bring her chair a bit closer, and we'll yell at her for a bit. Just like she used to do to you.'

I moved Bridie the cushion, into position. It was two against one and no-one to rescue her, just like it had been when I was growing up.

'I can't do this,' I said, shaking my head.

'You're wired to protect. Even when she hurts you.'

'I can't even leave the other cushion outside, Cynthia.'

'Just try.'

'Okay,' I inhaled deeply, trying to fight off the confusing feelings. Logically I knew that this was a cushion, however, I felt extremely uncomfortable. I never saw people in terms of all good or all bad, and so both sides of them could equally exist for me. I still loved them.

'Try,' said Cynthia. 'Let's replay a situation. That way, you're not thinking on the spot. Pretend that you are your mother right now, Pippa. Your mother can cop whatever it was that she yelled at you. Replay something she said.'

I knew immediately which scene needed to be replayed. It was one that had shredded my dignity and my confidence. I explained the background to Cynthia to set the stage. I'd hemmed my school dress a little, to stop being teased about its length by other students.

'You little whore. That's disgusting' I said to the cushion, a little tentatively.

'How old are you again, Pippa?' asked Cynthia.

'Thirteen.'

'A thirteen-year-old whore Bridie? She hemmed her dress up a little bit so that she could fit in better at school, and you think that makes her a whore?'

I shook my head, remembering that I'd been standing in front of the window, and the light had shone through my school dress. My mother had screamed at me for that too. 'It's see-through!' she had yelled, her face red from the shouting. 'You're disgusting! Pippa.'

I folded my arms instinctively from the memory.

'Pippa. Reply to your mother. Now. As a thirteen-year-old. Say whatever was going through your mind at the time. Speak your truth.'

I took a deep breath, being in the room again. I shook my head because all I could think was that I needed not to show them that I was hurting.

'I can't,' I said, meaning it.

'You've been conditioned into not showing your feelings.' She went and got the cushion in from outside.

The two cushions sat there, and Cynthia looked over at me. 'The problem with childhood abuse Pippa is that it all gets bottled up. Eventually, the sheer weight of it overwhelms, and you get depressed. A lot of the time, the depression stems from a feeling of sheer helplessness. We need you to find your power again and tell your parents all the words that are currently suffocating you. There must have been many unspoken words from your corner, I imagine.'

'Yes, but does it work, if I'm saying this to a pair of cushions and not my actual parents? The two responses are going to be very different. If I tried to say anything to my parents right now, over the phone, they would just tell me I was causing trouble and slam the phone down on me - or call me mad.'

'That's convenient.'

'Yeah. I suppose it is.'

'It's the act of finding the right words. That's the therapeutic part. You gain your voice. That's what matters.'

Cynthia had hit the nail on the head. I was suffocating under the sheer weight of their actions. All those words that hadn't been spoken at the time and nor had they been told as an adult either. As soon as I had ever started to speak, I would be cut off with rage as if my response was redundant in the exchange. My opinion about anything and everything was never invited or valued. I was seen as a trouble maker if I wanted to engage in conversations to explore feelings.

By the end of the week, I had five cushions lined up on my sofa in the flat. It was almost comical. I had my mother and father and my siblings - Margaret, Gareth, Harry and Paul. Harry was given a special part of the sofa, as he'd always been good to me but had been the first to have been thrown out of the house. I hadn't seen him regularly since. Every day, I talked to them for hours, saying all the things that I'd never had an opportunity to say. I explained the hurt that I carried, at being cast aside as if I had meant nothing to any of them. I explained to them that I'd never asked to be labelled as a Golden Child and that I had suffered as a result. I told them that I was lonely too, that not having a family was hard at the best of times. I told them about the rejection I felt. How could I love myself when my own family couldn't love me? How would I ever be able to know what healthy love felt like?

I surprised myself at how much I had to say. None of it was cruel, instead what came out of my mouth was a thoughtful account of events from my own perspective. My truth wasn't to hurt, it was to explain how I was feeling and to work through why situations had always been fraught with anger.

The breakthrough came several weeks into the therapy, during a family session with Cynthia. She had all of them in a circle, and we'd been dealing with issue after issue. The moment had come out of the blue and was completely unexpected. I interrupted her.

'I don't deserve this,' I had said to them all. 'What did I ever do to all of you? Try to love you? Was that my crime in all of this? I just tried to

LOVE YOU! Wow. Shoot me now, for trying to see through all the crap and keep a place in my heart for you all.'

Then the memories had flooded me… so many, and all of them terrible. It was as if I had been forced to live in a house with two people who enjoyed raging for the sake of rage. I wondered where all of their anger had come from. Two people who occasionally, loved and sometimes, enjoyed humiliating the very people they were supposed to protect. Their own children.

Then I had sat, realising that those words were my truth. My only crime was to have tried to love a bunch of people that I had been forced into a family unit with, due to my genes.

Cynthia smiled. 'Now, let's have another cup of tea, and then I want you to organise to go to Paris. You also have a question to answer Pippa, too.'

'A question? About what?'

'I want you to ask yourself, what is it that you want?'

It was a simple question and one that could now be mulled in a new context of separation from all the dysfunction. So I thought, anyway. However, the universe and I have a complicated relationship, and sometimes it likes to complicate my life as a result.

'Nah,' the universe said to me, some weeks later, as I was mulling over what I wanted.

'Nah, what?' I asked.

'Do you think this in your control? Any of this?'

I looked up. 'Yes, I do, actually.'

'Do you think that talking to cushions and running around has solved *all* of that?'

'Yes,' I replied, somewhat defiantly, having worked hard to get to where I was.

'You didn't run fast enough, Pippa.'

'From what?'

'From what happens next.'

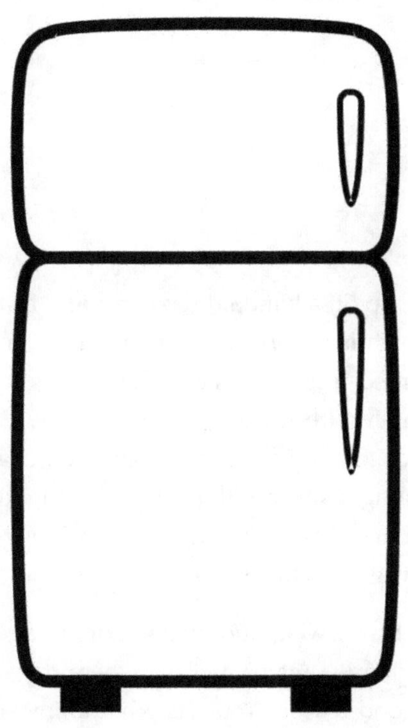
$8K OR HARRY
DOESN'T COME
OUT OF THE
FRIDGE

10

WRESTLING WITH PIGS

THE FAMILY

When you rip off a bandaid too early, any festering mess hidden underneath is unfortunately exposed, assaulting the eye with inevitable, unwanted unpleasantness. Before my great rip, everything had started to shine with the suggestion of new. Cynthia had helped me move forwards, albeit in terms of contained chaos. I was standing within a new healing context with the sun coming up and going down, surprisingly regularly. I was holding on by my fingernails to this new routine, but that was an achievement to be proud of in my world.

Then my brother Harry went and died suddenly, and I was sucked into the black hole of family again. A place where the sun is too scared to shine, and with good reason. You see, what followed the great rip was the great mess. A place of dysfunctional chaos where everyone was suddenly vying for positions within the pecking order hierarchy. Whispers behind backs, blatant bullying, accusations, nasty emails, phone calls, messages, name-calling - you know, the sorts of things that supportive families do to each other behind the scenes when one of their own dies on them.

My family, the one I've been talking about, wreaks a special kind of hell into the world, as you may have guessed by now. There isn't another mob quite like them. They hail from a clan lineage known for being experts in conflict and at times, gruesome murders. Their crest features an axe and scythe - no more needing to be said. My family have an ability to turn the mundane and straightforward into spiralling stuff that is quite impressive if that's the sort of thing that gets your rocks off. They take dysfunction and then turn it into a whole new level of dysfunction, one with too many letters after all of their names. Their weapon of choice is mental agility, using words to crucify white matter and souls. A sort of super-dysfunction that defies the laws of reason and physics. Dr Phil could have done a whole year's worth on those layers of dysfunction and possibly discovered that they were as infinite as the size of our universe. At the end, he may well have decided that he'd run out of advice, too.

Any family dysfunction is bound to amplify by the death of one of its members, but in this case, it was enough to tilt the angle of the planet from the sheer weight of crap that burst forth. It took a matter of moments for the news of Harry's demise to spread quickly throughout ranks and conversations were had for the first time in too many years between family members. At first, it was awkward silences whilst members found their footing and factions and then it was game on. At this point, gravity took over, and the dysfunction spiralled towards a point of no-return singularity. War was declared, and all hell broke loose.

'She's friggin' well abducted him,' I growled.

'Who?' Brad looked confused.

'Her. The ex. The woman he hasn't seen for fifteen years. Cause she's Catholic, she refused him a divorce. He's dated since and she's shacked up with a new partner. It turns out she's still got next-of-kin status. She found out he'd died and has absconded with his body and all of his Estate.'

Brad looked up from his coffee. 'Okay, start at the beginning. By the way, you look terrible. Have you been sleeping?' Brad asked, noting the heavy, black rings under my eyes.

'No. I can't sleep properly. My brain is fried from them all. This situation beats all others that have come before. The dysfunction is exquisite, even for them. I thought my family had been as dysfunctional as was humanly possibly. But no, I find there are further and darker layers to investigate. We're approaching the core of the planet at this stage.'

'I don't know if I want to hear,' said Brad. 'I already thought all of this history sounded bad enough.'

'Okay.' I took a deep breath. 'I'm trying to remember how this mother of all messes evolved. So, Harry died, and it took her two weeks to tell us that there had been an online police appeal to find his family - us. This gave her time to run in and take anything of value from his flat and take control of his funeral.'

'But she knows how to contact you. Facebook?'

'Yeah. She has our numbers and contact details on messenger. She wanted to make sure she could go and take his personal belongings without us being involved.'

'Lovely.'

'She went in the next day and cleared his flat out apparently, telling the Coroner that his family had abandoned him.'

'Ouch.'

'Then, two weeks later, she announces to us that he's died but then won't tell us how. Says he was found on the floor, many days after he died.'

'He's in the UK, yeah?'

'Yup. Living alone. Then she says she handed his body over to the State.'

'What?' Brad sounded incredulous. 'What does that even mean?'

'No idea. I contacted the police, but they told me to contact the Coroner. I'm not next-of-kin so they won't tell me anything.'

'How do you give a body away? Can you even give a body away?' Brad asked, perplexed by the thought.

'No idea. The first thing she said to me? I need eight grand for his funeral. Not, I'm sorry your brother has died. No compassion. Just a demand for money, with no paperwork,' I added, gulping in the air because I was so furious with it all. 'As if I'm going to hand eight thousand dollars over to her.'

'Did you give her any money?'

'Not at this stage. I don't even know how much she's taken out of his bank account. She even asked me for his banking pin.'

'Would you even have his banking pin?'

'No. Why would I?'

'So, has she give you any details?'

'Nope. Why would I even have his pin?' I said, reiterating the absurdity of her question. 'She's been gaslighting me the whole time. At one point she said she'd handed his body away and that he may have already been cremated.'

'I thought you said she needed eight grand for the funeral?'

'Yeah, she does. Even though in the next breath she says she has found a charity to cover the funeral and that he's already been cremated. My head is spinning from her.'

Brad shook his head. 'None of that makes any sense. How did Harry die?'

'No idea. Coroner won't release the information to me at this stage. Forty-four days and he's still in the fridge.'

'Not her fridge I'm presuming?'

'Wouldn't surprise me.'

'So, are you able to plan a funeral?'

'Nope. The truth of the matter is that there is no funeral I just found out. It's called direct cremation according to the funeral director who is providing the fridge. It should be called body disposal. No speeches, no time with his body, no music. Just a transfer from the fridge to the crematorium.'

'Is that even allowed? What about what your family wants?'

'In the eyes of the law, she is his only family. She has even banned me from a picture of his casket with my flowers on it. That's her latest insult towards me.'

'How do you know that?'

'I wrote to the crematorium and asked if I could get a photo of his casket when it arrived with my flowers on top. They wrote back saying that Harry's *family* had said no.'

'Jesus. That's bitchy.'

'Yup. She's abducted him. Literally.'

'Is this even allowed?'

'Apparently. That ancient marriage certificate allows her to do this. Even his friends aren't allowed near the crematorium to see him off.'

'Jesus, Pippa.'

'Yeah. Then she wrote to me saying she didn't want his ashes and I could have them. Then, she asked me what sort of flowers I would be buying for his casket. When she found out how much money I was willing to spend on the flowers, as opposed to giving it to her, she attacked me and said I couldn't have his ashes either.'

'Wow. So, there's no funeral?'

'Nope.'

'No service?'

'Nope.'

'I've never heard of this before… and… you have no idea how Harry died?'

'No idea at this stage. Can't follow most of what she is saying. Just online messages of mystery. The woman has the ability to put sentences into paragraphs and then throw them up into the air, and when they land on the page, they are nonsensical. Well, unless she's insulting me. Then her language is remarkably sensical and straight to the point. She loves insulting me for some reason.'

'Why, what did you do?'

'Nothing. That's just it. I've never even met her. It seems she didn't like being told I wasn't going to hand over eight grand.'

'Wow. Okay. So, you don't even know how your brother died, and it's like weeks later?'

'Literally, no idea. I may as well have been trying to read hieroglyphics.'

'He wasn't very well at the end, was he?'

'Not really. Again though, I'm not exactly sure. Communication wasn't great over the past couple of years. I believe he was slightly pickled at the end, although not enough to kill him. Alcohol would preserve, though, wouldn't it?'

Brad shook his head. 'This is confusing.'

'Yup. It is. My father said he deserved to die given some of it was self-inflicted. We're just charming, aren't we? A real, sweet clan, even in death.'

'Um… Yeah?'

'He fell over a few times too,' I offered. 'Maybe that had something to do with it all?'

Brad took a sip of his coffee. 'Christ Pippa. Did you ask your parents and siblings to help with all of this?'

'With the supposed funeral costs and perhaps a few kind words? Yeah, of course.' I sipped the sweetened coffee, glad for the sugar hit. 'Their reactions varied from outright rage to silence. My family doesn't do kind words about each other, I've discovered, even in death.'

'Wow. So who's paying for the funeral? A charity you said?'

'Some charity? Although calling body disposal a funeral is a bit rich. She's gone for the no-frills option. Don't know which charity, because as I said. I'm not next of kin. Can't find much out right now. No-one will answer my emails. Although the eight grand was excessive, given he's simply being cremated. It turns out the actual cost of this funeral is five hundred pounds, not eight grand. I think she just wanted me to give her a wad of money for a holiday. Hard to get your head around it all. Cause I'm not next of kin, I'm not allowed to get involved either.'

'Petty at best. So, what did your parents say about all of this?'

'It was like detonating an atomic bomb. I'm surprised my neighbours didn't put in a noise complaint. That was just when I was breaking the news to them. It didn't go down well.'

'Upset?'

'No. Angry. They were angry - and they didn't *say* anything. It was mostly shouted. I seemed to have insulted their peace with the news that one of their children had died. Let's see. I wrote it down.' I searched in my bag for the piece of tattered paper.

'You wrote it down? Why?'

'I wanted to try to get my head around it. Want to read it?'

'I suppose? Is it going to traumatise me?'

I laughed. 'My family traumatise you? Oh,' I said, seeing that Brad was serious. 'It shouldn't do. You've heard and seen worse, I imagine? Come to think of it I got a message from one family member that was far worse than what's on this piece of paper. I'll ease you in, with this, though.'

'Traumatise me? Maybe this will? I'm only a life-coach, not a psychiatrist. I'm an expert in goal-setting and motivational stuff Pippa, not in health and safety.'

'Want to give it a go?' I held out the ragged piece of paper. 'It's from memory, but hopefully, it's close to exact.'

Brad took it and took a deep breath. 'Alright. Set the scene for me. Is this where you're breaking the news to them or what?'

'No, I broke the news to them in the morning and spoke to my father. He said he would call me back after speaking to my mother. They never phoned back. So I sat there crying all day and then called them seven hours later. I wanted to share my grief, having just lost my favourite brother and offer support to them. It can't be easy losing your own child. Let me re-phrase that. It shouldn't be easy losing an adult child.'

'That seems fair enough.' Brad started reading, inhaling heavily at times.

'In your head, you have this idea as to how people will react,' I explained. 'In my family, they manage to do the complete opposite. They live in a parallel universe of opposites.'

Brad shook his head. 'Pippa. I don't know what to say. He actually said this shit in response to his son, dying? He seems to be completely oblivious to social conventions, as well as to how you might be feeling.'

'Yeah, I know. I made him angry, not sad. All I said was, *are you okay?* He took that as an insult.'

Brad read some of the statements out. '*Why have you phoned now?*' He shook his head. 'It should have been fairly obvious as to why you were phoning. Here's another one. *I'm really quite angry about this.* Was he angry? Why? Why would someone be angry?'

'Yeah, he was shouting at me. He said I had made him angry with the news. Not sad.'

'So he says here that Harry had been dead to him for thirty years?'

'Only because he refused to take his calls and filed all of his letters when he got them. My father keeps files on all of us, not just for my diary entries.'

'Sorry? What? Files, as in actual files? Why?'

'Why the files or why was Harry already dead to him? Harry was a disappointment. We all were. The minute we showed independent thought, it was seen as deliberate confrontation. Independent thought and action was a disturbance to their carefully crafted, control measures. Disturbances were eliminated. Permanently.'

'So, they cut people off who went against them?'

'Yeah, even their own kids.'

'This is sad Pippa. In this bit, he bites your head off and asks you if you are sad? He's daring you to say yes. This can't be right. Then he slams the phone down on you? Wow. Gees, I'm really sorry.'

'Thanks,' I nodded. 'I'm so shocked by two people not seeming to be even slightly sad at the death of their firstborn child. It's hard to process. The worst thing is that I was close to Harry, so I feel like I'm reaching out and somehow, my grief is deemed unacceptable. Oh yeah, Harry hated me according to my sister's new partner, whom I've never actually met.'

Brad shook his head. 'I'm honestly finding it difficult to keep up with this crap.'

'Yeah, I got this sent to me.' I rummaged back through my bag. 'Take a look at this.' I handed him a print-out of the email.

'So has this guy ever met Harry or you?'

'Nope.'

Brad read in silence. 'Shit Pippa. Who writes this to someone they don't even know? It's like a raging page of insults.'

'My family does.'

'Why are you pretending to be sad over someone who hated you? You are a sad, pathetic jerk-stroking boner dick. Charming.'

'Aren't they just the sweetest?' I said sarcastically. 'I don't even have a dick,' I added. 'Idiots.'

'You need to run Pippa. This is shitty.' Brad handed the piece of paper back to her. 'I don't know what to say. Your family, Pippa. There's just no sadness and no empathy, is there? One of their own dies and they can't reach out. Instead, they are trying to crucify you. Why? It's like your normal emotions and grief are seen as some sort of threat to them all.'

'I don't know? I honestly feel like I'm in the mud wrestling with pigs. Not a shred of dignity amongst them. No empathy. No warmth. Just fighting.' I held my hand out in front of me, noting the wrinkling skin. 'I'm shrivelling up from dehydration, from all the crying too, I think.'

'This is so confusing.' Brad tried to think of something else to say. 'How are you feeling? Do you think you should have some water?' He poured a glass and pushed it across the table.

'You're the first person to ask. I appreciate that.' I sculled the water in one go. 'I think my parents forget that their son is also my brother. They assume that any grief reaction is for them to state only. I literally don't count. I feel terrible. Like my soul is spilling out of my chest. I'm exhausted from grieving. Can't eat... didn't shower yesterday and I just want to stay in bed. Grief hurts, and it hits in relentless waves. You either let it out or crumple into a heap, and both options are so awful... I just feel so...' I paused and looked out of the window. 'Heavy. It's as if Harry and my relationship has suddenly landed in my chest, all in one go.'

'What about friends to help you through this?'

I laughed. 'Try maintaining genuine friendships in amongst all of this? I have people sending condolences and then asking me when the funeral is? It's such an innocuous question. I have two choices - lie or tell them the truth.'

'Have you tried telling the truth?'

'Can you imagine landing all of that on to someone's lap? Who doesn't have a funeral? Most people run in the other direction, Brad. My association with this crap coats me in unacceptable dysfunction. I look like I'm part of some mad cult. If I lie, to protect myself, then what sort of friendship is that supposed to be? One in which I have to be fake.'

'So are they all talking to you yet? Did your siblings phone to check on you? Has anyone asked how you are dealing with this? You and Harry were close, yeah?'

'Yeah, we were.' My eyes filled with tears. 'It's painful and complicated grief, Brad. Not even just his death. It's the history. Most of our relationship had to be hidden from sight. The very mention of his name was a deal-breaker. The fighting, the discards - him reaching out to be heard. The weight of the family despise just suffocated him. My siblings wanted it that way too. If he was the black sheep then it meant they had a chance to work their way up to golden status - at least some of them played it out that way. Others walked away and never looked back. I'm not surprised. It's been a giant chess game with my parents moving their children around squares of love and rejection.'

Brad nodded. 'Good analogy.'

'Even on the *actual* day of death, points were being scored. Instead of Harry being remembered and our collective grief being shared, I was being told by one of my siblings about all the stuff that had been bitched about me over the years by my mother. I'm an alcoholic, I'm a liar, I've never worked… I'm on drugs, and I'm mentally unbalanced. I was thinking - who is this person that I'm supposed to be? No wonder my siblings refuse to speak to me - although they love the scandal.'

'You've never worked?' Brad asked incredulously. 'Why do they think that?'

'Yeah. I know, right. That's what she *supposedly* told them.'

'Do you even drink?' asked Brad.

'Hardly. It's pretty insulting to be called an alcoholic when I hardly drink. As well as being mentally unbalanced. Although trying to deal with this lot, is driving me nuts.'

'So, they chose to attack you with silence and accusations on the day you all needed to come together to grieve?'

'Yup. That's my family. One of us dies, and it's an opportunity to bitch. Not grieve, not reach out, not contribute and not hold a funeral. I mean, what the hell?'

'I'm really sorry, Pippa.'

'I mean it's probably way more complicated than that. Who knows what people think has been said. What's real and what isn't. It's a mess. Just a giant mess, and one that's now too big to be fixed. I just discovered that my voice can't be heard and that my truth is unnecessary. So I blocked the lot of them.'

'Wow. That's a step forward.'

'Yeah. Things went from crazy to dead quiet, pardon the pun.'

There was a silence as things were mulled.

'So, what is definitely happening about his funeral?'

I sighed. 'So yeah, apparently a charity is organising it, and she pockets his Estate. I don't have control to change that. It's horribly undignified.'

'So she wanted eight grand from you and had already palmed him off to a charity organisation?'

'Yeah.'

'Surely, between all of you, you could pay for the funeral of a family member?'

'Yes, we could have done.'

'So… what is going to happen then?' Brad sounded concerned. 'This is a mess, Pippa. You can't just leave Harry in a fridge. I'm presuming it's definitely a morgue fridge and she hasn't got him in an actual fridge?' He appeared hesitant to hear the answer.

'Really, Brad?' I raised my eyebrows at him.

'I'm just checking. Nothing would surprise me in this story.'

'Yesterday she said the funeral had already happened and he'd already been cremated. Makes no sense. That's why I contacted the police and then spoke to the funeral director. He's still in the fridge apparently. I've organised for a private investigator to take the photos I want.'

'What?' Brad looked up. 'You serious? You've hired a private investigator?'

'Yup. Drastic times call for drastic measures. No-one tells me that I can't have a photo of my brother's casket arriving at the crematorium. It's a public space. Psycho bitch can't stop someone else from shooting a few happy snaps. Anyway, you're the expert. Do you have an answer to this crap?'

'No. Your family Pippa. They are…' he paused. 'I can't find the right words. I don't even know if there is a collective term that suits. This could be a world first. They're just…' he stopped and thought hard. 'Arseholes.'

'Yup,' I said, sculling another glass of water.

'As your coach, I'm supposed to have something constructive to say. I don't.' Brad looked panicked. 'I'm supposed to have comforting words and guidance for you. There's nothing. This is a first for me.' Brad was experiencing a life-coaching crisis. 'You should definitely run. Change your phone number, move house and disappear from sight?'

'I told you when I first phoned and asked if you could work with me that there were going to be times where you just wouldn't have the words. This is one of those times.'

'How did this get so bad?' Brad asked. How can you even call them family? They seem to go out of their way to be cruel and the blame they throw at you for everything? I mean, they seem to think that their own shit doesn't stink.'

'I know. You don't get another family either. You either stick with the one you have or go and face the world by yourself. It's a rough deal, and no-one wins.'

'No-one is looking out for each other though in yours, not even in death.'

'We were like a bowl of fruit. We looked great on the outside, but nobody checked on the fruit pieces in the bottom of the bowl. The quiet ones, just lurking away… and now one of them got squishy and well…'

Brad interrupted her. 'That's a terrible analogy Pippa, given how Harry was found.'

'Yeah, I suppose it is. It's true though. How did we manage to leave one of our own on a floor for days on end in the first place without checking on him? How did my parents manage to kill him off before he even died? How have we justified leaving him inside a fridge and putting him through a charity funeral? We could have done a bit better. He needs some dignity, Brad.'

'He does. So do you Pippa.'

'Yeah, it's weird grieving alone.'

'I can imagine.'

'Dignity. I wonder what that feels like. To be completely honest and retain your dignity?'

'Again, Pippa. I'm really sorry. Usually, a family comes together in death. Yours has obliterated itself.'

'Maybe that's a good thing?'

'Well, with everything else that's been going on, it might be a good thing. Can I suggest that you take this time to go to Paris, perhaps? Run in the other direction as fast as you can and don't look back.'

'That might be a good idea. I'm quite fit already from Cynthia's program. I've changed my phone number by the way. Nothing is going to be able to mend all of that. There's a protocol to be followed in death, and they just insulted every aspect of it. Running sounds good.'

'Just make it fast. You need to get away from this clan.'

'Yeah, I do.'

'Forever Pippa. Don't ever look back.'

we just hung out together

11

LISA WAS COOL
THE SKULLS WERE NOT

B rad was proud of me some weeks later.

'Progress has been made, it appears.'

We were sipping a hot chocolate, catching up for another coaching session.

'I've got my airline tickets rebooked, and all the accommodation sorted. Work is giving me two weeks off. It would have been nice to have been given the original four, but my new boss said two was all she could find for me as it's a busy time of year.'

'Two is enough, for now, Pippa. You deserve it. You did well with Cynthia, you know, and processing Harry's death.'

'It was an interesting way to approach it all, cushion therapy. I had no idea that I had so much to say to be honest. I mean, it was kind of ironic that right at the end, just as I thought I was free, I was thrown back into all of it again.'

'Yeah, but it gave you some closure too, didn't it?'

'For now. Until the next crisis comes along. Hopefully, I'll be able to deal with them more effectively next time? I miss Harry, though. It's been a very solitary grieving process.'

'Yeah, I can imagine. We need to maintain this new, good place. What's the plan for Paris? Still going to try and find decent cheese and wine?'

'Well.' I smiled. 'I'm going to live the fantasy, albeit for two weeks. Rustic apartment, red wine, cheese and art. I've been practising my French, although apparently, they all speak English, when they want to, that is.'

'Yes, they can be quite selective about speaking English.'

'We'll see. I've got an open mind, an open heart, and I've been putting this adventure off for far too long. It's time to be brave and just do it.'

'I agree. You deserve this Pippa.'

'Thanks, Brad.'

FLYING IS a form of torture for people who hate flying. Some individuals get onto a plane and find the thought of hurtling through the air at phenomenal speeds so dull, that they fall asleep before take-off. I am not one of those people, and even with twice the amount of prescribed Valium in my system, I was praying out aloud to my no-name God on take-off. A God that I don't believe in, but one that I need for the flight duration. Does that make me opportunistic? He refused to speak to me, in any case, still miffed that I'd had him on ice for so long.

Turbulence over India was met with muffled screaming into my clothes, and I spent most of the night-time walking in and out of the toilet because it gave me a sense of routine. I'd flown before, many times, but it had never got any better, no matter what measures had been taken. For me, when the plane lands, it's a feeling of wanting to fall to the floor and kiss it. It's an act of survival, a form of rebirth. I walk from a plane, as a survivor. Everyone else walks off looking for their luggage.

However, here I am, standing in Paris, in the Jardin Des Tuileries, gazing up at a giant Ferris wheel and hearing the laughter from those above. I pinched my arm. I had done it. I was standing in a place I had dreamed of visiting for years. I sipped my way through my second water bottle. The temperature was already 28 degrees in the shade, my arrival coinciding with a once-in-a-hundred-year heatwave. Australia was hot in summer, but for some reason, Paris felt even hotter.

I walked to the Louvre and stood in a queue for two hours, waiting for opening time. It wasn't exactly a romantic start to my holiday, standing on hot paving with people whinging and moaning all around, in a hundred different languages. More and more people kept arriving, the line weaving its way further and further away from the entrance. Body heat, mixed with the heat from the searing sun, made the experience feel like I was being simmered, French style to be precise.

I looked at the Louvre map and realised that the visit would have to be thought through. Perhaps a strategic run from exhibit to exhibit and hopefully not get crushed in the process? I decided to visit the Mona Lisa first, just to get my anticipated disappointment over with, as soon as I could. Everyone I knew, had told me that she was smaller and not as impressive, as made out to be.

Once in, I ran through corridors of exquisite art, ignoring everything until I found her. Then we were alone, in a room, together. Just me, her and a bemused security guard. Lisa smiled at me, a kind of wry smile, and I smiled back. My cushion running had made me fast on my feet, and I had beaten the hoards to it. I wasn't disappointed at all. I thought her to be elegant, thoughtful, and understated. She was beautiful and obviously keeping secrets from us all with an expression like that. Three minutes later, I was being jostled by too many over-eager tourists and it was then that I realised that everything I was going to see was now a competition to get there first. Any visit to something popular would require cunning planning and defiance, not to be pushed out of the way before I had finished looking at something.

My rental apartment was small but cute. French cute, in fact. From its white-washed kitchen, natural floorboards, and mural-painted walls, it made me feel French just by association. It sat across from a formal public garden, complete with a pond where ducks quacked with a distinct French accent, and birds sang chansons. I discovered a wooden seat under an oak tree and immediately thought of Alan. I took a moment to pause and reflect on what our life might have looked like if he had survived. I could see a sprawling home, children, and a gravel drive. Alan was sitting in our rose garden, sipping wine... I smiled. Perhaps the romanticism of Paris was already working its magic on me? I decided that this would be my anchor spot in Paris, where I could come to reflect, if I needed to.

The burning heat made most activities impossible for the next seven days. After eleven in the morning, the temperature would soar, with tightly packed streets absorbing any hint of a cool breeze. Instead, I started my days with the dawn, walking down near-deserted streets, imagining all the history layered underfoot. I wish I could say that Paris fulfilled my dream, only it didn't. The Paris I had always imagined, was magnificent in its architecture, generous with its food and was full of poodles and ladies in wide-brimmed hats, posing near the Eiffel Tower. A bit like when someone asks you about all the kangaroos that bound around Australian cities. My Paris was an illusion of love, perfumes and romanticism. The reality was a little different.

I was sharing Paris with thousands of pilgrims, all of whom were seeking out their own Parisian fantasy. Hoards of people trying to squeeze into one space is a legitimate physical problem and one that was dealt with in France by being forced to stand under a searing sun, slowly winding yourself around in endless snake coils around rope. Inching forward towards any entrance felt like a small achievement, and I would get a small dopamine hit each time my feet moved in the right direction. When I did manage to get into anything, it was like playing moving sardines and being relatively short, I rarely got to see more than someone else's camera or sniff anything other than a sweaty armpit.

I had arrived at the Catacombs in the late afternoon, hoping to meet the dwindling sun and fewer competitors, only to find that everyone else had done the same. After that, it was a game of maths, with everyone counting everyone else in the line, working out how many were allowed in, and then splitting it all, with the time left for opening hours. No toilets and water made for an irritable three-hour wait. Once in, pods of people were urged to 'keep moving,' otherwise, the next pod would catch up to them. I felt like I was in the Hunger Games, running past millions of skulls and wondering how many of them were heart attack victims, made to run too fast in the cold, underground tunnels, in the months before.

However, the evenings were quiet and relaxed, the disadvantage being that all the museums and attractions were shut. I ate out twice, but it was more expensive than my budget would allow. Instead, I found a local supermarket and bought supplies, taking them down to the edge of the Seine. I sat with the sparkling Eiffel Tower as a backdrop. It sounds perfect, and it was close to my fantasy. I ignored the countless hawkers annoying me, trying to get me to buy plastic Eiffel Towers, the homeless, resting on their patch-stained mattresses, and the rubbish being tossed on the ground by the drunken crowds. Somewhere in all of that, I had found a small piece of my Paris.

I raced from one attraction to the next, power-walking through Montmartre, imagining forgotten artists and eager prostitutes. I climbed up the Sacré-Cœur Basilica and saw Paris as an eagle might. I paid my respects to Poulenc, Oscar Wilde, and Edith Piaf at the Pere Lachaise Cemetery. This visit made me catch my breath, for as famous as these individuals had been, death was an apparent equaliser in this contemplative space. As I stood amongst the mighty tombs with the broken stones of others, at their feet, I realised that everyone dies and that the future marches relentlessly forward, catching the fallen as it goes. I thought again about Alan, his slaying forcing me through a sliding door, and into a different reality. I wondered about Harry and what death had felt like when he had breathed his last breath.

The heat was relentless in Paris and worse outside of it. The temperatures in France were hitting forty-six degrees, hotter than I had ever experienced in Australia. It wasn't possible to walk anywhere or do anything without risking heatstroke. Therefore, on this particular day, I decided to stay indoors and visit the Palais Garnier, an opulent Opera House built at Napoleon the Third's behest.

I bought tickets for a modern ballet performance, strung my pearls around my décolletage, and wore my only-packed evening dress. I'd arrived an hour early, too eager not to be late, and the building was shut. There was a traffic jam of quite spectacular proportions at my feet as I waited on the steps, wishing I could find somewhere to hide from the burning sun.

My makeup was running, and sweat was dripping down my expensive evening dress. The cars were gridlocked, and French people can be very impatient, I discovered. Horns honked louder and more frequently than in Delhi's streets, and some people drove over pavements to get further forward, only making the gridlock worse.

Then the Police Nationale arrived, their sirens adding to this mad cacophony, and the noise became unbearable. It was mayhem. It was loud, and it was hot. Just so, so hot. Then the doors opened, and as I entered the building, the noise turned to exquisite opulence. The building was a place of such exquisite beauty that it is hard to find the appropriate adjectives to do it justice. It was beautiful from floor to ceiling, dazzling with chandeliers, art, and magnificence. I took my seat in a small theatre box, facing directly towards the stage, and felt stupendously *posh*. I was about to watch French Ballet in the grandest theatre in the world. I felt like I may just have made it - as what I wasn't sure, but somewhere elegant, at the very least. The lights dimmed, and there was silence. I held my breath waiting for tulle, tiaras and pointed feet.

A pod of barefoot dancers, came galumphing onto the stage, looking more like flamingos might, if distracted, and not sure where they wanted to run. This pod thumped and stomped from left to right and then stopped, heads going right and left, hands clasped behind. Then they swayed, all the way over to the left and then to the right. Then they collapsed into a heap onto the floor. They then moaned, rocking and flailing around. Thunderous applause followed, and the French people murmured and clapped effusively. Had I missed something? I strained my neck, looking around, hoping I might have done. What followed is hard to describe. Dancers were randomly kicking their heels and running off stage, to the back of the stage, and some right off the front of the stage. There was a fight scene, a knife scene, and a strange scene where one of them rolled himself up in a red rug.

Then it was over, and everyone was speaking excitedly in French. Someone turned to me, their eyes searching for my artistic response. 'Ahhhhh' I said, waving my hands around earnestly. They nodded and repeated my 'Ahhhh' to the next person, who nodded and passed the response on. It was a French-Mexican wave which made no sense, no matter how you looked at it. I left feeling like I'd missed something, wondering if my lack of exposure to culture had made me ignorant of the real thing. I promised myself I would go and experience more dance when I got back home.

For two weeks, I tried to find the Paris I had expected, to no avail. I ate a lot of cheese, though, stacking on a fair amount of Parisian weight, an affliction that only affects non-French women. You see, real French women, for some reason, are just gorgeous sticks of long limbs, artistic noses, fine lines and sophistication. For some reason, injections of cheese didn't make them all soft and squishy like I was now. However, it was definitely worth my new softness. Cheese is cheese, and I would happily eat cheese and only cheese until the end of my life. I also tried as many red wines as was possible, and ate freshly baked baguettes, sighing every time the white fluff melted on my tongue.

Then it was over, and I was back on the plane, flying back to Australia. I'd had two weeks of escapism in an unfamiliar Paris, one that I now knew bore little resemblance to my fantasy. It was time to go back to my real world. My suitcase was filled with tea-towels with prints of women standing next to pink poodles under the Eiffel tower. I had three bottles of real French perfume and copious amounts of Le Chat Noir merchandise in the form of tea towels, a t-shirt, a music box, several notebooks, and an apron. I would take the fantasy back with me to remind me that I had not found it. I was hoping and praying that Cynthia's work with me had longevity and that I could return to

Australia with a new sense of purpose, and feel like the past was rightfully behind me.

'So, this is where it all the psychopath stuff now starts?' Brad asked, looking hopeful.

'Yes. Do you think I've explained it right?'

'The lead-up?'

'Yeah. Will this next bit… the psychopath bit, make sense now?'

'I think it will Pippa. I think it's obvious that your understanding of love wasn't exactly ideal to start with.'

I laughed. 'I could have just written that one sentence. Might have saved a hundred pages of words.'

'Do you ever wish that you could turn back time, knowing what you now know?' asked Brad.

'Interesting thought. Yeah, I suppose. I might not have joined the art class that I'm about to join.'

'Now, tell everyone to hold on Pippa. This next bit is going to start the rollercoaster.'

those etchings look nice

12

ARTY-FART
INTRODUCING MR PSYCHOPATH

After returning from Paris, I decided to join a local art class, burning with the desire to paint again. I had studied art at school, finding that I'd had a bit of a talent for it, but had never pursued anything seriously as an adult. Paris had ignited the artist in me again. My art class met on a Tuesday evening at seven and was advertised as a beginner class, a good place to start. All I had to do was show up and express my inner artist. Stuart, my teacher, enthusiastically explained everything to me over the phone.

'Have you ever painted before?' he asked hopefully.

'Back during school. I just went to Paris though, and got inspired by all the art.'

'You went to Paris? Lucky you! I've always wanted to visit.'

'You should,' I said, keeping his fantasy alive, just like everyone had done for me. No-one should be responsible, ever, for shattering the illusion of fantasy Paris to another.

'I'll look forward to meeting you, Pippa. It's a lovely class you'll be joining. Everyone is at a beginner level with acrylics, and the main thing is that you have fun.'

'Sounds good. Do I need to bring anything?'

'Just the weekly fee, and of course, yourself. Everything else is provided.'

I arrived to find nine other people already set up. Easels, tubes of paint, canvases, paintbrushes, and aprons were scattered everywhere. They smiled and welcomed me, and then it was time to paint. I hadn't been interrogated about anything during any welcomes, and right at that point, all that mattered was the canvas in front of me.

Stuart was fantastic, a young guy in his twenties, full of boundless energy, and brimming with kindness and motivation.

'I really don't care what you paint, Pippa. Just get the colours onto the canvas and see what happens.'

I looked around me at the others. They were a couple of weeks ahead, and their art ranged from the good to the exceptionally bad. That reassured me that no matter what ended up on my canvas, that it would be warmly spoken about, even if utter crap.

Matisse was on my mind with vivid yellows, blues, and reds. I wanted simple outlines, filled with colour. I wanted the eye drawn to shapes that had meaning. Lines drawn with charcoal, an image forming. Then paint on my palette, mixing with whites and blacks. The world became small, just me, and this vision that needed to come alive. For the next two hours, nothing else mattered. Not the others in the class, my past, my present, and nor my future. Just the artwork that was being crafted in front of me. Then it was over, and Stuart was asking me to wash my brushes. Had that been two hours? I had been somewhere else, speaking to Matisse and asking him which colours I should choose.

I had painted the Paris that I had wanted to visit. A couple sitting on the bench in the park that had been opposite my apartment. Two people in love, in companionship, sharing this small place, as it should have been. Not one woman alone, trying to find artificial happiness in her solitude. In the background was a gaudy Eiffel Tower with people clambering all over it. I'd drawn the bird, singing its chansons, perched in a brilliant blue tree.

'Anything is possible in my Paris.' I had told Stuart as he had stood back to appreciate my efforts.

'I like this, Pippa. I do. It's really interesting. Not what I expected from you.'

'What did you expect?' I asked with curiosity.

'Not this.' He said, turning his head to one side. 'This couple? They seem to fit well together. In a kind of separate existence to everyone else. It's a nice juxtaposition of ideas.'

'Yes,' I replied. Alan and I did now exist in a separate existence, one that was in between life and death. However, never again, could we be somewhere together, other than in my mind.

BRAD LOOKED CONCERNED, however. 'I love the fact that you went to the art class, Pippa. Great job. However, Alan's memory should have faded by now.'

'That's a bit un-life coaching, isn't it?' I asked. 'As well as being highly judgemental.'

'I'm stating it now because it needs to be brought up. You only knew Alan for a few weeks, and yet Nigel, whom you were married to, never gets a mention. It's always Alan.'

'True,' I said, understanding that Brad was right.

'So, any thoughts?' asked Brad.

I pondered for a bit until I found the right words.

'Alan was my safe place. A fantasy that could never be tarnished by reality. As if I'd never gone to the real Paris and only ever believed that Paris was full of pink poodles, croissants and women with broad hats. There was no time for the illusion of Alan to be ruined. He remains a fantasy, a relationship that will always be perfect.'

'Do you think it's time you put him to rest so that you can let someone else in?'

ALAN HAD BEEN a fantasy that I had been holding onto, and perhaps it was time that I did lay him to rest. I travelled to the cemetery where he was buried and sat by his grave. It was a modest tombstone, new looking, with a photo of him inserted into the granite. I had almost forgotten what he had looked like, but his smile made me wince. He shouldn't be smiling given the condition he was in down there. Instead, he should be looking more concerned.

'Hi,' I said quietly.

Silence.

'Just thought I'd stop by and see how things are. Probs not so great?'

I looked around to make sure no-one else was close by. I didn't need a live audience for what I had to say.

'I'm sorry you died, Alan. That wasn't fair.'

Silence.

I rearranged myself in the grass, which was slightly damp. 'I went to Paris, you know. To that cemetery, you once told me about. There were all sorts of famous people there, but they were dead too. Like you, really. You would have liked it though I think. Not too many people, nice trees and some of the tombstones were like works of art.'

I wasn't expecting a reply, but still, the conversation felt one-sided and stilted. In reality, I didn't have much to say, and I realised that most of the relationship had been played out in my head. Brad was right. I'd jumped in and cleaned, been easy to bed, and the whole thing had been a fantasy - a part that I thought I should play. How much of the real me had been involved in it, I wondered? I looked at the dried flowers on his grave, realising that Alan had a family that had only ever met me at his funeral and knew nothing else about me.

'Anyways,' I said, standing. 'I want you to know that I appreciated our time together. Again, I'm sorry that you died, but to be honest, it's time that I get on with living and meet someone else. I hope wherever you are that you're doing okay too. Goodbye Alan. Goodbye, Alan Parker.'

I placed a small heart-shaped stone onto his grave. It was done. I had relegated Alan into my past, allowing someone new to take his place.

CYNTHIA WAS IMPRESSED. 'That took guts, Pippa. How do you feel?'

There was that question again. One that always felt so alien when it was asked of me. I couldn't remember a time when either of my parents had ever asked me how I felt, as my answer was inconsequential in the scheme of things. As a result, I always struggled to find the right way to describe often, complicated feelings.

'Take your time,' she reminded me.

'I feel relieved to have put him to rest. Although having said that, it's a little contrived to decide to move on suddenly.'

'True. The action, however, is symbolic,' she smiled.

'Time to move on?'

'Yes. Baby steps. One small step in the right direction. That's all you have to do. So, how can I help you today?' she asked.

'Brad thinks I need to learn what real love feels like, so I don't go in and start cleaning up after people again. When I say that, I literally mean it. I don rubber gloves and open a bottle of disinfectant, as a way to demonstrate love.'

She laughed. 'I've heard stranger things, but at some point, you were loved for cleaning I'm guessing? As for finding love again? That's complicated and yet simple, Pippa. You will know when love first finds you because it's demanding and all-consuming. After the find though, you need to learn to stand back and be willing to lose that feeling.'

'Lose the feeling?' I was confused.

'Yes. Our brains have us addicted to the feeling of love. It stops us from eating, sleeping, we obsess, we plan, chemicals take over, and we 'fall in love' - only that side of things is the easy bit. It's effortless to enjoy the 'falling in' component of love.'

'Okay,' I said.

'After that initial burst, we need to be able to read people. Tell who is a good egg from a bad egg. In your case Pippa, you've been wired differently. You jump in, and if things go bad, you think it's normal.'

'I think I understand?'

'Think of the rules you have grown up with. Not your rules, were they? What happened if you broke a rule? You were punished. If you followed the rules, you were loved.'

'True,' I said, nodding.

'That's not love, though. That's simply learning to comply. You were taught that love is both good and bad. It's not.'

'No. It's not, is it? Love should be good, whereas actions can be both good and bad.' I paused. There was a lot to process in my mind.

Cynthia got up to make the tea, as she always did when something big had been said. It gave me time to ponder it.

'So, we need to re-wire you to learn what unconditional love… real love feels like,' she said, bringing in her posh tea set, that always made me feel so regal when sipping from the delicate cups. 'Then, when you meet someone who genuinely likes you and not just your compliance to them, you'll have a chance to form a proper relationship.'

'So, I've learned to be compliant, to gain love?'

'Absolutely. Although to be clear about all of this - to gain a proper diagnosis for your parents, I'd have to meet them myself. In-person and not just cushion form,' she smiled.

'So, I've grown up essentially moulded into a person that conformed to someone else's rules?'

'Yes, Pippa. You had to in order to survive.'

'That freaks me out a bit.'

'Why?'

'Is this the real me then? Or is there another form of me that hasn't been expressed yet?' I started sweating. This posed an important question. 'What would have happened if I'd grown up unfolding to a different set of rules?'

'Interesting question,' said Cynthia, nodding. 'Probably you would have turned out a bit differently. It's a bit nature vs nurture if you're interested in reading up on more of it. We are all a product of upbringing and genes, although in your case, I think there was an imbalance on the nurture side.'

I went home having a mild existential crisis. What if the person I was supposed to have been, had been suppressed and replaced by someone who had been moulded by a set of someone else's rules? More to the point, how would I ever know?

ART CLASS PROVIDED RELIEF, with a new canvas and a unique opportunity to paint something. I stood, gazing at the canvas as if waiting for inspiration to hit.

'Sometimes nothing pops into my head either,' a well-spoken voice said. I turned and saw white-blonde hair, vivid blue eyes and a soft, smiling mouth. A man who looked a little older had spoken to me. A man who had made me smile and blush at the same time, catching me off-guard.

'Hi, I'm Noah.'

'I'm Pippa.' I held my arm out, awkwardly to shake his hand.

'Nice to meet you. You just started art classes today?'

'I did art at school, but this is my second week here. You?'

'I was away last week. I've been painting for a while now. Love it. This class is great. Really warm and supportive. Welcome.'

'Thanks.' Then I didn't know what to say. I looked at him, then dropped my gaze.

'Well, I'll leave you to find your painting,' he said, collecting an art apron on the way past.

Stuart hurried into the art room. He was incredibly tall and his charcoal-black hair was pulled back into a shoulder-length pony-tail. 'Welcome, everyone,' he said, raising his paint-splotched hands into the air to get attention. 'I have exciting news. Everyone listen up.'

The class stopped what they were doing. 'There's a local art exhibition coming up. I want you all to submit something. Let's see if we can all get a work included. The entry forms are on the table near the door. Pick one up as you leave later. This is a great opportunity to produce your best work. Now, get painting!'

How on earth could I produce anything that might be at a standard to enter into an art exhibition? Stuart must have sensed my unease and headed straight towards me.

'Don't worry, Pippa, given it's only your second week, just try your best. You never know what the organisers are looking for. Your painting last week was a great start. Maybe keep working along the lines of Matisse and try another one?'

I loved this, whatever this was. I was just Pippa, who likes Matisse, and no-one wanted to know anything more about me. I stood back and looked at my canvas and then down at the acrylic paints. I had every colour to choose from and an infinite number of combinations after that. I picked up a tube of paint, and instead of carefully allocating an amount onto the palette, I squeezed a massive blob of the paint into my hand. It was cold, soft, and promised to lose its form into a state of creamy. I placed my hand with the palm onto the canvas and then dragged my hand down, noting how it felt as it was pressed onto the textured surface.

Next, I picked up a different tube, and as I squeezed, I dragged the tube downwards, the paint forming onto the canvas like a line of toothpaste from a tube. I picked up a metal paint stripper and then flattened the paint under the edge. It formed random shapes with thickened tips that reached upwards. I watered some paint down into a jar and then flicked the paintbrush towards the canvas. Small droplets fell as they were supposed to, and then I stood back. It was as if I had painted a scene of wildflowers, as one might find near a stream that never sees footprints. I continued painting without rules, layering long lines of colour and building shapes that emerged outwards, upwards and towards me.

Stuart clapped his hands as he approached. 'Wow. Pippa? Seriously? This is great!' His enthusiasm stopped the class, and they all came over to see what had excited him.

'Nice use of the paint,' agreed Noah, nodding in appreciation. 'Very creative.'

'Uses too much paint up,' mumbled Louise. 'I prefer oil paints.'

I looked over at her and raised an eyebrow. Charming.

'Classy work,' Noah said, as we cleaned up after class. 'I like your style, Pippa.'

'I was just experimenting with what the paint could do.'

'A bit like taking a car out for a test drive?' he suggested, washing his brushes into the sink. 'See how far you can push it, before crashing and burning?'

'Yeah. Something like that. Although what I'm going to paint for this exhibition evades me right now. Have you thought of something?'

'I'm thinking of continuing to work on the one I'm doing for the time being. Come and see it before Stuart puts it away. Anyway, let the painting find you. Don't force it all too much. Then it's authentic. Yeah?'

I stopped in my tracks and stared at him. He had said exactly the right words to get my attention. If I allowed the painting to find me, not forcing any ideas, I could be authentic in what I was doing. I stood back and looked at his artwork.

'I love Whiteley,' he said eagerly. 'Just the range of vivid blues he would use, with strokes of white leaping out. So, my work is in his style, without the talent,' he added, smiling.

'I know Whiteley,' I said. 'I love his art. I have a print of, what's it called again? 'Interior, With Time Past'? Lots of orange.'

'The one with the people having sex in the background?'

'Yeah,' I laughed. 'That's the one.'

'So, in this work, I wanted to capture the harbour and my boat. Sailing is a passion of mine and I like to go out on the weekends sometimes.'

'Then, you must have heard of Slessor,' I said enthusiastically.

'Sorry, who's Slessor?' he asked me, looking confused.

'Oh, sorry. He's an Australian war poet. He wrote a poem that depicts the harbour, that's all. For some reason, I assume everyone has heard of him.'

'Ah, I'm from Brisbane.'

I laughed. 'Sorry. Sometimes I assume everyone shares my passion for Australian War Poets.' I inwardly cringed. I sounded like an idiot.

'Anyone coming for hot chocolate? Speak now,' called out Jo, a middle-aged woman with curly red hair. She seemed in love with life, bouncing around the studio in her vintage purple overalls, constant humming and beaming smiles for free.

'Want to come? We all go for hot chocolates and coffees at the cafe next door. It's nothing much. You don't have to speak, just be there,' he added.

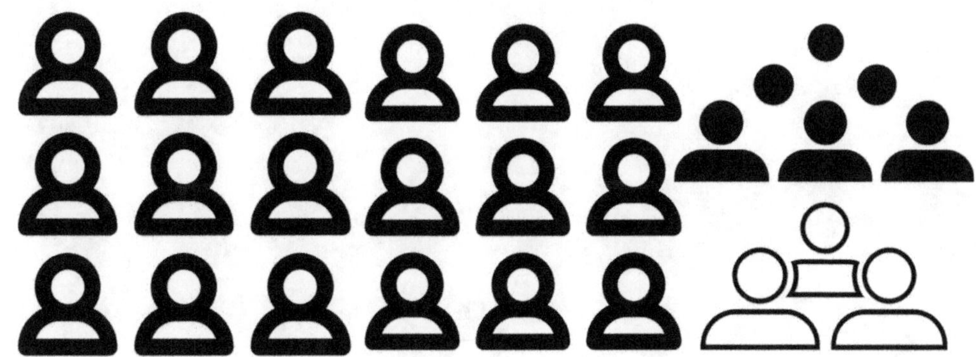

in nature and serenity with the rare parrot

13

WHAT'S YOUR NUMBER?

OH MR HART!

I walked to the cafe with Noah, who felt a bit like my protector in a way. I felt painfully shy around the group and a bit wary of Louise, who seemed to have taken an instant dislike to me. Stuart didn't follow us to the cafe, preferring to clean up the art studio, ready for his early Wednesday morning class. I followed the group to their regular Tuesday evening table, situated near the window, overlooking the busy suburban street. The warm cafe was chattering, bursting with people, and snippets of discussed mundane wafted through the air. Our small talk as drinks were ordered was mainly about painting.

'So, how long have you been painting?' asked Jo, smiling warmly towards me.

'I studied art at high school, but haven't picked up a brush since. I'm glad I have though, I'm loving these classes.'

I was. I loved the spontaneity. I loved the fact that I could express myself without fear. That thought was thwarted somewhat by Louise.

'Yeah, everyone makes mistakes when they go back to it. You'll soon get the hang of how paint is supposed to be used.'

'Steady on,' said Jo, coming to my defence. 'Have you ever seen a Pro Hart, Louise?'

'Yeah,' said a few others, nodding in agreement.

'Didn't he throw himself on a floor covered in spaghetti in an ad?' Jo asked.

'Never heard of him,' snapped Louise.

'Oh Mr Hart,' Noah imitated the woman from the ad, making everyone laugh, except for Louise.

'There's no right or wrong, Louise,' said Jo. 'Painting can be an expression of whatever which feels right.'

Louise simmered in silence, and I wasn't exactly sure why she had taken such a disliking to me, given she knew so little about me. I was going to ask Louise more about herself, to break the tension between us, when the frothy hot chocolates brimming with floating marshmallows were brought to the table and conversations turned to the small stuff that was going down in everyone's lives.

Jo was having issues with her teenage daughter, Bill was getting sick of his neighbours throwing rubbish over the fence. Noah told a story about arriving at work, having put on different coloured socks in the morning in the dark. It was the small, silly stuff that they were sharing. No-one asked me to say anything that might make me uncomfortable. Maybe this was a lesson that I was learning? That I didn't have to throw anything serious onto the table. I could stay being Pippa Matisse in this context, and that might just be enough for now.

Noah walked me to where my car was parked. 'So, taking a small risk here, but if you ever wanted to text me, say if you need some inspiration about your art, then I wondered if I could offer you my number?'

I said yes without hesitation, and we exchanged numbers in the dark, with the rain starting to spit at us.

. . .

I SAT STARING at the number on my phone. It was now a waiting game as to who would text first. I googled the issue. How long was long enough, before texting someone? The internet suggested two to three days so that you didn't look too eager. In terms of actually meeting, it said another two to three days so that you could find out as much information as you could about the person. It was all about pacing and safety. I didn't have Noah's last name though, so I couldn't google him. All I could do was sit and wonder what to do next.

'HE GAVE me his phone number,' I told Brad, excitedly at our coaching session, which was in a new cafe in the city. Grey, metallic and minimalist had greeted us and we had been placed into an all-metal coffee pod to drink our coffees. I felt like I was sitting in a space ship.

'Excellent. So, what now?'

'That's why I'm meeting with you.'

'Oh, you want me to tell you what to do? Nope. This one is under your direction.'

'Yeah, I get that. I just want to make sure I'm doing it all properly. Learning to look for the right signals and all that.'

'Okay. So, what are your first impressions, and why?'

'Of Noah?'

'Yes, of Noah. Gut intuition?'

I smiled. That was my intuition. A smile.

Brad laughed. 'Well, that's a good start. Now speak.'

'He seems kind. He approached me during the class and made me feel welcome. Then he encouraged me to meet the group after class at the cafe and made sure to walk me through the process.'

'That's a good start. What about chemistry?'

I smiled again. 'I like him. I like his hair.'

'He has nice hair?' Brad looked as if he was waiting for more.

'Yeah. This kind of mangled blonde nest. It's cute. He's from Brisbane.'

'Remember that cute hair is just that… hair. Like him for who he is, and not just on how he looks.'

'Yeah. Fair point. Alan had nice hair too, come to think of it.'

'I remember. How are the memories of Alan now?'

'Gone. Faded. After I went to visit him, he seemed to merge into his rightful place.'

'Progress again, Pippa. You're doing great. Slowly does it with Noah. Let him text you first. Don't run after him and don't offer anything to him. Not yet.'

'Okay. I'll sit tight and not text.'

MY PHONE BEEPED with a text from Noah, three days later.

N: Hi, Pippa. Just wondering how u were going with ideas for yr painting?

I stared at the message. He'd made the first move. Both Nigel and Alan had made the first move too, and look at how they had turned out. I needed to remain calm and not respond too quickly. I googled how long I should wait before responding to a first text. The internet told me one to three hours, as leaving it later could feel crushing for someone and be interpreted as a form of *cruel mind game*. I didn't want to be cruel, so I left it dead-set in the middle and texted him back two hours later.

P: Haven't got very far as of yet, but thanks 4 asking.

Three minutes and twenty-four seconds later, he replied.

N: Let me know if u need any ideas. I am always here to help!

I lasted nineteen seconds.

P: Will do Noah, thanks :-)

Then the exchange was over. I wondered if it was enough? Had the smiley face seemed a bit immature? Had I fobbed him off a bit, I wondered? I didn't want to seem too keen, so I left it at that. I thought about him though, and each time I did, I found myself smiling. This had to be a good start. Yeah?

I DECIDED to free form my next artwork, just as I had done the week before. I painted the canvas a bright yellow this time and then stood back.

'So, what are you going to do this week?' asked Louise as she strode past to grab an apron. 'Throw spaghetti at it?'

'Sorry?' I was taken aback by her tone.

'You know, like that Pro Hart. I looked him up. Anything goes apparently, so it won't matter what you do.' She added a false laugh at the end of her comment and then walked off, shaking her head.

'Seriously?' I called after her, feeling my anger building. She turned around, now smiling because I had taken her bait.

'Pippa!' Noah appeared and stood, blocking my vision of Louise. 'Don't. She's not worth it. She's only been in the group for a couple of months, and she's a bad apple. Ignore her. How are you anyway?'

I took a deep breath. He was right. Louise was spoiling for a fight, and engaging would be stupid, no matter what her issues were.

'I'm good. You?'

'Fine. How did you go with it all? Got an idea?'

'Yeah. I've decided to free form until something feels right.'

'Sounds good. I like the yellow. It suggests hope.'

I played with the yellow background, adding highlights and depth and then built up the thickness of the paint on the canvas by allowing large globules of blue paint to slide their own way down, from top to bottom. Then I built them up carefully, layering different hues of blues, creating a painting that seemed to leap outwards from the canvas. By the end of the class, I had created a canvas of blue streaks on a bright, yellow background. In my own way, there was a juxtaposition of ideas within it. The sun was so hot that you could never see her tears. I was showing a side of the sun that she could never show herself.

'They do look like the tears of the sun,' commented Stuart, doing his end of class appraisals. 'I like the intensity of the yellow, suggesting searing heat, and yet it hasn't turned the tears to steam. That's neat, Pippa. I like your ideas.'

'Thanks. I haven't given it a title yet, but I think I'll combine something Noah said earlier and your comment. I'll call it 'Tears of Hope.' I think that's an excellent description.'

'Deep,' said Stuart, nodding. 'Tears of Hope,' he repeated, standing back, head cocked to one side. 'You know Pippa, this would be one to enter into the art exhibition. It's simple but has a really compelling message. What do you think?'

'Really? Something like that might make it in?'

'Yeah. I think so. Why not put it in and give it a try?'

Louise was less than impressed at the cafe afterwards.

'It looks unfinished to me,' she said. 'I think you need to add more.'

'Like what?' asked Noah, 'chickens?'

I looked perplexed. Jo giggled. 'Louise paints chickens in everything.'

'Oh,' I said, aware that Louise was looking at me with a strained expression. I wasn't sure what to say.

The conversation continued with Barry explaining that his mother had been admitted into the hospital after suffering a stroke.

'How is she?' asked Jo with kindness in her voice.

'Not great,' he said, a look of seriousness falling over his face. 'She's eighty-one though, so she's at an age where this stuff happens. The best thing the doctors say is that she passes in her sleep. She won't recover from it though, too much damage.'

'That bad? Sorry, Barry, I hadn't realised…' Jo stopped.

Barry shook his head. 'It's okay, Jo. Really. She's been in very poor health for many years, so it wasn't unexpected.'

There were sad murmurs around the table. This triggered me, and my thoughts soon started racing in my mind. I wondered if Barry's mother had been a good mother and deserved the sad agreement about her predicament. There was also a thought percolating that was so socially unacceptable that it should remain unspoken. However, there must be lots of older people who have been spiteful and abusive to their children. Did they have anyone feeling sad when their time came? It sat uncomfortably with me until Noah interrupted my ruminations.

'So, where are your parents, Pippa?' he asked.

I stared at him, probably looking bewildered. 'They live in Tasmania, on an alpaca farm,' I finally managed to say.

'Wow… nice. I love alpacas, they're the cute animals with the long eyelashes. Yeah?'

'Yeah.' I said, hoping he wouldn't start gushing about alpacas.

'Brothers? Sisters?' he asked. I could be an only child. I toyed with the idea, rolling the words around in my mind. How easy would that be?

'There's four…' I paused. Now there was one less. 'There are three of us. Kids that is. Plus my parents.'

'Three kids?'

'My brother recently died.'

'I'm sorry.'

I wanted him to stop asking. This was precisely the precipice I always found myself standing on. Yes, both my parents are alive, and yes, I come from a relatively large family. Now what? What comes after that? Changing the subject, running from the table or explaining that my family was a disjointed mess of crap? Then I would watch his face fall slightly, and the spark disappear from his eyes.

'You?' I jumped in quickly just as more words were forming on his lips.

'My mum passed away when I was six. Sudden brain aneurysm. My Dad lives in Brisbane.'

'I'm sorry, Noah. Do you get to see your Dad often?'

'Yeah, about twice a year. I go up in winter, and he comes down in summer. Means we don't get too cold or too hot.' He changed the subject. 'How often do you see your family?' he asked.

I went to say something, but nothing came out. I started to feel angry that my family couldn't at least pretend to be nice to each other so that in social situations there was something to say that didn't relegate me to some sort of crazy. When asked about their family of origin, most people feel that they are in a safe space, like asking if you own a cat. They don't expect to hear that you own a tiger that bit someone's face off and that has everyone terrified to move out of corners when negotiating their way around the house.

'Brothers? Sisters?' I asked. Our conversation wasn't making a lot of sense, continuity wise.

'Three brothers, all older. Biggish family, so snap on that one. Growing up, my mum... until she died, used to call it a house full of testosterone. My brothers are now scattered around the place. One in Finland, one in Spain and the other is in Darwin. We don't see each other much now, but we try to Skype now and again, which is good. I miss them.'

'Cool,' I said, wanting to shut down the conversation. I would appear unfriendly as if I didn't want to get any deeper. I turned and asked Jo something instead.

I phoned Brad as soon as I got home.

'This is the same problem, over and over. Where's the manual for stuff like this? Their dysfunction somehow always becomes my dysfunction.'

'Pippa… breathe…'

'No, Brad. Nothing helps! What am I supposed to say?'

'Breathe.'

'Brad. I'm serious.'

'I know you are, and you also sound like you've wound yourself up.'

'Why does everyone ask me those questions?'

'Because they are normal questions to ask someone.'

'I suppose…'

'Okay, let's just anchor here, Pippa. Take one deep breath. Let's get your cortisol down a bit here. You'll be able to think more clearly.'

I breathed in deeply. Brad was right. I'd got flustered, and my thinking was scattered.

'I do feel better after breathing' I said, sounding calmer.

'Good. Now we can talk. So, he was asking you some personal questions? What's the situation with Noah's family?'

'Close with his Dad. His mum though, died when he was only six. A brain aneurysm. He and his Dad visit each other, twice a year, and he has three brothers who stay in contact through Skype.'

'Just see how it goes, Pippa. That's all you can do. If Noah pulls back because you come from a shitty family, then he's a superficial git.

You'll know soon enough. Just try to keep stories simple whilst he's getting to know you.'

That night I went to bed, angry and frustrated. I was angry with Louise. She knew nothing about me and yet was spoiling aspects of the art class for me. Then I thought of Noah. I felt terrible for him, losing his mum like that, especially at only six. That had to have hurt. I was angry too with my history, knowing that it was one that made me look weak, dysfunctional and chaotic. I wondered about the fairness in it all, immediately resenting people who had a strong family background to wave in people's faces. I wondered why no-one ever spoke about any of this too. There must be countless people in the same position as I was in, so why all the pressure to play happy families out there? Why were people like me always made to feel inadequate because other people couldn't get it right?

MY ANGER continued through the night and into the next morning, affecting my workday. It turned out to be one of the worst I'd had in a long time. I started the day booking a lengthy and complicated tour of Europe with a middle-aged couple who seemed to be in the middle of a domestic. I say this because somewhere between Rome and Budapest, the man suddenly got up from out of his seat and announced that he was going off to get a coffee. He didn't come back. That meant that the woman lost confidence in the process and then told me to cancel everything - two hours of work down the drain and nothing to show for it.

My next client was a woman wanting to go and photograph a rare breed of parrot in Thailand. She spoke at length about them, but it reminded me of my Paris fantasy. I'd already been told several long stories about how the whole place had now become crowded and disappointing. How too many people with cameras had resulted in an abundance of new hotels being built in the area, scaring the birds away. I told her not to bother.

'Really?' She sounded a bit deflated.

'Yeah. I went to Paris recently. I wish someone had warned me too.'

'You mean it's not worth the money?'

'It depends on how well you can adapt your fantasy with reality. It's worth what you are willing to spend on it, knowing the realities of it, I guess.' I shook my head before catching the eye of my supervisor. She looked like she was going to throw something at me. She shook her head back at me, disappointed that I was telling the truth to my client.

'Why don't you try going to Greece for photography instead? There are hundreds of options, and for the same price, you could go and visit quite a few places.'

The woman thought for a moment, and then her face lit up. 'It's funny you say that because before I'd found out about the blue-ring parrot, I'd always wanted to go and photograph Greece. There's something about those clean white lines against the backdrop of Greek blue.'

'Let's do it then,' I said, started to type earnestly into my computer. I handed her a brochure as well, and she grinned at me.

Over lunch, Adele, my supervisor, pulled me to one side. 'For God's sake, Pippa, stop telling them the truth.'

'Really? You want me to lie to my clients?'

'Yes, really. We don't pay you to shatter dreams. We pay you to book the damned flights and hotels to take people to their dreams. It's up to them to adjust to the reality of it all when they get there. What's gotten into you today anyway? You look pissed off with the world.'

'Nothing. However, those parrots? Have you seen the blogs online about the reality of the place vs that 4K video that everyone watches online? That's why everyone wants to go. They think it's the same as in the video. That they will find serenity and nature - not a thousand people who stand ready, cameras shoved in each other's faces. The reality is bleak.'

'It's up to the client to gauge all of that. Not you. Imagine if we told everyone who walks through the door that their idea of a place will never meet with their fantasy. Imagine if we warned them that thousands of other tourists are photoshopped out of every single picture they see in the travel magazines? They would never travel anywhere if they knew the reality. We'd be out of business.'

'Whatever.' I turned away from her. I wasn't in the mood to be told off.

'Pippa. Look a bit happier, at least for the rest of the day, please?'

I went into the toilet and then stuck a finger up at her, which was childish at best. The position really should have been mine when it had become vacant. Jane, who had made her way to being supervisor, had left to have a baby and had decided not to come back. Adele had been holding down the job in a temporary capacity, but the position really should have been advertised and not just converted into a full-time position like that. Adele was always nitpicking at me, and everyone else, making her an unpopular team leader.

The afternoon dragged on, minutes feeling like hours. The office's air conditioning was set too high, and I felt hot and stuffy, which made my mood worse. My next client was a retired gentleman booking his fourteenth holiday to Bangkok in seven years. It made me wonder what kept him going back to the same place every six months.

'Shirts actually,' he said confidently.

'Shirts?'

'Yes, I found an amazing tailor. He hand-sews the most amazing cotton shirts. I get people measured up, send the orders over, and then fly over and bring the shirts back.'

'Couldn't you just get him to post them over when he's made them?' I asked innocently. The man's face reddened.

Adele pounced. 'Would you like a glass of water, sir?' she asked, glaring at me for the thousandth time that afternoon. It was an unspoken rule never to ask a client *why* they wanted to visit a destination.

There was the usual lull between three and four, and then it got busy again, as if clients panicked, knowing we would be closing at five. On hold for forty-five minutes, I was stuck trying to book a first-class flight between Sydney and London for my last client of the day. A woman too young to be flying first class, who also glared at me, as if it were my fault that I couldn't get through.

'Did you like phone the right number?' she asked me, in an affected accent.

'Yes, of course.' I said through gritted teeth.

'I could have phoned myself, I suppose,' she said, 'I thought getting you to do it would save me time. Don't you have like a special number to call, being an agent and all that?'

'No, sometimes we have to wait, just as long as the public, unfortunately.'

She whined that she would be late for her pedicure, and all within earshot of Adele, who kept shaking her head at me. I wondered what it was that she wanted me to do? Tell the kid to shut up? I played out telling her to SHUT UP in my mind a hundred times, and then all of a sudden, I had got through. I handed the documentation to her.

'Thank you so much,' she beamed sweetly at me, now having got what she wanted.

Then the day from hell was over, and I was back in my flat. Tonight, it felt like a haven. I poured myself a large wine and then jumped under a hot shower. The action did the trick, and the heat washed off my horrible day, and the wine mellowed my anger. Then my phone beeped. It was Noah.

N: Hey Pippa this may be too forward, but how would you like dinner sometime?

I stared at the message and then re-read it again. Noah wanted a date! My mind started to race with permutations of too many questions being asked, not enough information being shared, or perhaps Noah might get run over too, just like Alan had?

Brad laughed over the phone. 'Just go out on a casual date with him and expect nothing. Don't build this into something bigger. It's just a date, Pippa. It can go either way at the end of the night. You either arrange another date or part ways. Treat it as flexible and non-permanent.'

'Okay,' I squeaked back.

'Enjoy someone else's company just for a few hours. That's all it is. A chance for the two of you to get to know each other a bit better and find out if you are compatible.'

do you want some
dessert?

14

———

AMPUTATION

IS IMMINENT

I completely understood the rules that had been set in place by both Brad and Cynthia. I was to get to know Noah on a superficial level and look out for red flags. These are things that might indicate that all is not well and should provoke me into taking a step back. In hindsight given how all of this eventually played out, I wish I had been more… whatever. Despite this list of red flags, I couldn't have gotten things more wrong, than if I had tried.

Cynthia had listed ten flags and made me promise that if Noah exhibited any one of them, I would disengage with him, see the date out, and then go home to think about things. Here's her list.

He should not divulge too much about his previous partners.

Language should be respectful.

He should at least offer to go halves with the bill.

Personal hygiene should be at a satisfactory level.

Avoid a criminal background.

If he asks too many personal questions, change the subject.

He should not be pressing for sex on the first date.

Weird topics should be avoided.

If there is evidence of him being cruel to an animal, then I shouldn't pursue things.

If my gut tells me to leave, then leave.

Noah texted me before our date.

N: What's yr fav food? Getting ideas.

P: LOVE anything French?

N: French it is. I'll book us a table at 'Table Piaf' Saturday at 8.

I chose my outfit, wanting to keep it simple yet elegant. Black dress, arty red necklace, and a red bag. Three days until date night. I texted him.

P: Looking forward to dinner, Noah.

N: Me too, Pippa.

Noah's face lit up as I saw him outside the front of the restaurant.

'Pippa. Lovely to see you. You look beautiful this evening.' He then kissed me, politely on the cheek. That was respectful, so that got a tick.

'Thanks, Noah. You too. You look nice too.' Awkward, but not completely incompetent. He did look nice, dressed in a black t-shirt, slim leg jeans and black dress jacket, a sophisticated casual look, that took the formality out of our date.

'Shall we?' He indicated with his arm towards the door and opened it for me. That got a tick. I like good old fashioned chivalry.

'Yes, thank you.' Still awkward, but I was surviving. I felt physically sick though, from a combination of nerves and excitement. French music created the backdrop for a beautiful interior to the restaurant. Black velvet seats sitting at tables with crisp white table cloths, flickering candles in the centre. Crystal chandeliers dazzled above our heads, and long-stemmed red roses had been placed on the window ledges, framing the magnificence of the harbour view. I felt as if I had been transported back into an opulent time of long ago. I half expected to see Les Six sitting in animated discussion in a corner.

The staff seated us at a large bay window, allowing us to appreciate the expansive views across the harbour and towards the city lights. I immediately thought of Slessor, which triggered thoughts of Alan, leading me back to his tombstone. I stopped my mind from following this lateral trail and concentrated instead on ordering a drink, hoping to subdue my nerves. I chose a sparkling wine and then fussed a bit with the food menu, trying to coax my nerves into hibernation for a bit.

'Weird seeing you in this context and not covered in paint.' He beamed at me, his blue eyes searching in the candlelight for something, and I was glad that he was finding so much happiness at the moment. Optimism and whole sentences deserved a tick.

'Yes.' I needed to find more words. He was making an effort, and I was letting him down. 'So, what do you think you will submit for the exhibition. The boat painting?' I asked, sounding enthusiastic all of a sudden.

'Yeah. I'd almost completed it during the class, so took it home to finish off. I've got a small art studio in my garden. After I'd been going to Stuart's art class for a while, I wanted to take it more seriously, so I built one. Helps me to unwind after work.'

'What do you do for work by the way?' I asked, hoping it sounded more like a conversation starter rather than sounding like I was trying to gauge his worth.

'I'm in advertising, here in Sydney. I work for 'APPI AD'. Have you heard of them? They do all the big brands around the place. They're the best advertising agency in Australia. It's the reason I moved down from Brisbane. They wanted me to lead the Creative Design Team. How could I refuse an offer like that?'

'Sorry I haven't heard of them. So, you're extremely busy then, I imagine?' That was awkward, not ever having heard of them, and I had no idea why I had admitted the fact.

'Yeah, it can get a bit crazy. I was supposed to be at a launch party tonight, but got someone else to fill in for me.'

'Oh, really? That was sweet.' That got an instant tick.

'So, what do you do, Pippa?' I internally cringed and momentarily considered saying I was something that had more status. I decided to be truthful instead. 'Travel. I work in a travel agency. I sell dreams and adventures.' I smiled, realising how crass that sounded.

'You sell people their dreams too? We have much in common. You must have travelled all over the place then, I imagine?'

'I went to Paris recently...'

The waiter interrupted us, and we ordered. The conversation flowed about the inconsequential, and then, after the wine had settled our nerves, and we had finished our main course, Noah mentioned his previous relationship. I felt a small knot form in the pit of my stomach. This was number one on Cynthia's list. Was I to walk from the table and end things or hear him out? It depended on how much he stalled on the topic and how detailed he wanted to be.

His previous relationship had been complicated, and I was trying to keep up. There were three children, two boys aged fourteen and eight and his daughter, who had just turned twelve. His ex-wife, also from Brisbane, had become depressed, shortly after their move to Sydney, but no matter what he had tried, she just wasn't engaging in their relationship. She'd slept in a different bed for the past eight years. In the end, Noah had left and now shared the children with equal custody. Given his daughter was twelve, I guessed he was in his mid-thirties?

'Well, I certainly wouldn't have slept in a different bed,' I said, without thinking.

'Sorry?' he asked.

'If I was married, that is… seems a shame to be in a different bed.' Good save, I thought to myself. I needed to change the subject and fast. 'That must be hard, having the kids, if you are working in such a demanding role.'

'Yeah. I tried to shuffle my hours a bit, but in the end, I hired a nanny. She's great. By the time I get home, the kids are fed, homework is done, and they are bathed. This means that I get some decent, quality time with them each evening. Do you have kids?'

'No. I… not yet.' Then I started to panic internally. What if he was looking for someone to look after his kids, instead of a nanny?

'Yeah, so the problem at the moment is that she wants to return to Brisbane, because her parents are there, and take the kids with her. That's not possible with the existing parenting plan, and I don't want to move back to Brisbane, now that I've lived in Sydney. Messy, hey?'

'Yes, that would be hard.' I didn't know what else to say.

That was a cross. He was portraying his previous partner in a negative light.

'Would you like some dessert?' He looked down at the menu, and I wondered if he knew he'd said too much, too soon.

'You know what? I could fit that in.' I smiled, wanting to lighten the mood a little.

He leaned forward to pass me the desserts menu and then winced, grabbing onto his shoulder.

'Are you okay?' I asked, alarmed at his expression. I wondered if he was having a heart attack.

'Yeah, all good. I have this darn shoulder injury. I tried to lift something too heavy when we were unpacking our things in the move down here. I tore my rotator cuff.'

'Do you need surgery?' I asked, not understanding too much about rotator cuffs, but understanding that many people tore them.

'I did have surgery, then I went to a physio and did rehab, then had steroid injections, pain killers, the lot, really.' He paused, looking serious. 'Unfortunately, the next step is amputation.'

My eyebrows shot up in surprise. 'What? Amputation for a rotator cuff injury?' I was alarmed. My mind started racing. Maybe he wanted someone to be there for him after the amputation? This certainly wasn't on Cynthia's list.

'Yeah, I saw a specialist, and the only way to stop the pain I'm experiencing is to amputate completely. Do you think you could date someone with one arm?' he asked, smiling.

'Yeah, of course,' I replied, trying not to look alarmed. 'When?' I added gingerly, imagining a bloodied stump and a jacket arm that now swayed in the wind.

'When the pain gets too much. I think I'll have the sticky date pudding. It looks rather nice.'

I stared at the menu, not seeing the words. My mind was racing. His arm seemed to function just as well as the other though. It seemed almost reckless for anyone to suggest cutting it off. I could understand if it were hanging dead as a doornail off his shoulder, but it looked just fine.

'I'll have the strawberry ice-cream,' I said eventually. 'How will you paint?' I added, wanting to sound more compassionate than my internal dialogue was sounding.

'With my other arm, of course,' he grinned. Luckily I'm right-handed. 'If I had to have both cut-off, I would use my teeth or my feet to paint. I've already thought that through.'

I stared at him. Now I was dealing with two stumps in my mind.

He laughed. 'Just kidding.'

'For both?'

'No. It's just one.'

He paid for the bill, insisting that he cover it, and I was trying to recollect if the rule was that we were supposed to share the bill? I couldn't remember what Cynthia's list had advised, as I was still obsessing over his impending arm amputation.

'Want to go for a walk?' he asked after dinner. 'We've got ourselves a perfect evening, I have great company, and look at that view. It seems too good not to stop and enjoy it for a while.'

We walked along the harbour foreshore for a while, watching the ferries hurrying to and fro from the suburban wharves, into the city. Dark folds of water lapped against the stone sea wall, and his silhouette was framed in the city lights, the street lamp illuminating the side of his face.

He turned to me, 'Ferry the falls of moonshine down,' he said in a softly spoken voice.

'Wait. That's Slessor, isn't it?' I asked, surprised. I was sure he had said that he hadn't known who Slessor was. He smiled.

'Yes. I was intrigued by this poet you had asked me about. I read some of his work. Five Bells is brilliant. Captures exactly the feel of this.' He looked out. 'It's so beautiful. The sound the boats make, the ferries… the lapping of the water. I wouldn't want to be anywhere else at this moment. In Brisbane, we have the river, but it's just not like this. It's such a beautiful harbour. It captures my attention, every time I look at it.'

'I agree. I fell in love with this harbour as soon as I moved here. It sometimes makes me feel as if I'm the only one standing at its edge. I always get a sense that my story is personal with it, despite there being millions of other people here as well.'

'Yeah, I understand that feeling,' he said, nodding. 'Hey.' He turned and faced me. 'I've had a lovely evening Pippa. Thank you for agreeing to meet for dinner. It's been delightful.' He walked towards me.

I knew what was coming. I knew that I was about to break the rules for one of Cynthia's red flags, but the moment indicated for rebellion. There was a slight change in the pace of his body movements and a difference in the rhythm of his speech. His breathing sounded louder and more intense. Then his head tilted to his right slightly and he gave his lips to me. It was an exquisite kiss, soft lips on mine, and then his arms were around me, and he was drawing me in closer. I didn't resist. I felt like I had found home amongst his earthy aftershave and warm skin. All I knew at that moment, was that the feeling he gave me was one that I didn't ever want to lose.

He texted me later that evening.

N: I haven't laughed like that in ages. Thank u for an evening shaped by so much beauty and finesse. Let me know if u would like to do that again.

P: Yes. Thank you for a lovely evening, Noah. I'd love to.

I had texted back immediately, forgetting to wait a bit. I'm sure that I had just broken unspoken rules again. I was jumping in. My ticks from the evening had easily surpassed my crosses, though. Anyway, if the water is warm, comforting, inviting, and feels that darn good, then why not jump… both feet first? If I was totally candid, I didn't ever want to come out of it again.

15

ZIP

WITH RED BOWS

We planned to spend the night together at a hotel, the following Tuesday. This went against everything that Brad and Cynthia had advised, aside from the fact I wasn't rushing over to invade his home and meet his kids. That was a tick, whilst the hotel was a definite cross. I knew I was rushing it. I knew that I should wait. I didn't, though. I couldn't. Three days after our date, every atom in my body was now burning with insatiable desire. I'd forgotten how lust invaded and steered one's mind down a one-way street. My brain was a cauldron of bubbling chemicals, designed to lead me to just one act. This man, with the white-blonde hair, standing so nonchalantly on the harbour's edge, had invited me to partake in a night of deadly sins. Lust, greed and wanting… so much longing, it drove me into an aching of desperate desire, and a determination to sin.

ADELE KEPT LOOKING over at me, oddly, at work.

'You look different?' she said after staring for a bit, trying to work it out.

'Do I?' I smiled.

'Let me know what your secret is?' she had asked.

'If I told you, then it wouldn't be a secret, would it?'

'I suppose not.'

I BOUGHT champagne and chocolates and placed them in the room, reserved in his name. The hotel room was posh-nice, with a king bed, spa, and thick, comfy robes. It seemed almost too dignified a place to act out our dirty desires, but Noah had agreed to pay for such a luxurious stage. He'd said that we weren't ready to visit each other's personal spaces just yet, and I had agreed. I didn't want his kids dampening this promise of raw, sexual encounter and I didn't want my flat to disappoint him. I had a sense of purity about this upcoming experience, despite my mother's voice in my head, telling me that the devil would also be present along side of me. I wanted this, and I was an adult, after all. There was no shame in laying bare, next to a man that wanted me for all the right reasons.

I wasn't worried about ghosting afterwards, as there had been nothing to suggest that Noah was simply after sex. The worst he had confided, had to do with his ex-wife and how they had issues with their current parenting plan. Hardly anything serious to worry about. Anyway, he had to see me again at art class which would make ghosting a bit difficult. I went over what Brad and Cynthia had told me though, and then felt tinges of guilt. There was no way that they would approve of any of this, but then I wasn't searching for their approval.

I was a complicated mess of needing and wanting pleasure, and now guilt was creeping in before I'd even done anything. It was as if feeling that sense of home when I was near him was everything I had been craving… *needing* all of my life. I tried to self-analyse the situation, justify what was about to happen and failed miserably. My logic was drowning in my surge of hormones. God, the *needing*.

I had gone shopping and had bought black lingerie in anticipation. The devil costume that I paraded in my hands grandly to the cash register was all crazy black lace. A one-piece number with small red bows on the neckline, and a provocative zip travelling down the front. I imagined Noah slowly pulling the zip down, my breasts now understanding why Jane had attracted both sailors to her cleavage that night. I was a woman driven solely by animal instinct and a need to have my thirst quenched. I had waited a long time to feel loved, be needed, and touch another. If I'm brutally honest and wanting to stop describing this lust in polite, colourful and descriptive terms if I'm truthful here? I really just *needed* a good fuck, thanks to Mother Nature and a thing called desire.

Brad phoned me as I was paying for my red-bowed secret.

'Good time to call, or are you busy?'

No, not a good time. I'm currently planning to go against everything you told me to do, actually. 'I'm just in the shops, it's fine. Go ahead.'

'Well, I'm just touching base. How did your date go?'

He has messed with my head and hormones. All I want to do now is be naked, in his arms. 'Perfect.'

'Like really perfect?'

Yes. It was exactly what I've been looking for. 'Well, not like perfect, perfect… but it went well.'

'How did the red flags go?'

Red flags? Yeah… there were a few, but this feeling I have? Bugger the red flags. 'Well, to be honest, he spoke a little about his previous relationship, but on the whole, we kept it light, and he never asked me more about my family.'

'Good work. When are you seeing him again?'

We're planning to fuck each other's brains out as soon as we can. I took a deep breath. 'Tuesday.'

'That's quick?'

Yup. The sooner the better. 'Art class.'

'Of course.'

I had lied to Brad. The one person whom I had promised never to lie to. Our deal had been clear from the start. Unlimited life coaching in return for a monthly fee. His honesty in return for my honesty. I had just broken the back of that promise. Tuesday was indeed, art class night, that much was true, only Noah and I weren't going to be in the class. We were going to be in a hotel room instead, where we would undress each other and, hopefully, if our plan went well, we would share our bodies until the sun came up.

WE DIDN'T WASTE any time once the hotel door was shut. We ran a hot spa, poured the champagne, and I asked that I get in first. I wasn't overly confident with my appearance, despite my attempts to tidy myself up, but then Noah wasn't exactly young and fit himself. He told me with a frown that he had put on a bit of weight, now that he was in his early-thirties, which had made him feel a bit insecure. I needed to allow Noah to see me unclothed gradually, and so was up to my neck in bubbles when he returned to the bathroom. He undressed behind me and then gently sank into the tub. I could feel the coarse hairs on his legs brushing up against me and felt hardness pushing against my lower back.

'Let's get some music happening and more bubbles,' he said, gently kissing the back of my neck.

'More?' I asked, imagining an immediate avalanche of too many bubbles sliding down the side of the spa and onto the floor.

'Yes, let's live dangerously and bubble the place out? More champagne too, and then we can just relax Pippa. How does that sound?'

It sounded pretty good. It also sounded tame, a tad awkward, and it sounded like he was trying to put me at ease. A polite rest before we jumped into the bed. He took control of how he wanted things to unfold, and I allowed him to take charge. He would be the ebb, and I would respond, as the flow.

He laid me naked onto the bed and then looked at me. Properly looked at me. Our eyes met for a fleeting second and then paused. We were looking intently at each other, *into* each other. His blue eyes meeting my green eyes. I smiled. He smiled. This was something different, a proper connection. I usually found eye contact difficult. Not now. Not with Noah. I didn't move my gaze away as his face drew near, and his lips hovered above mine. I lifted my head, eager to feel his kiss, and then it happened. It was so easy - as if this was how it was supposed to feel. Our connection was made.

We made love. Slowly and thoughtfully. It wasn't sex. It was something else. Maybe it was how sex was supposed to be? I didn't know. All I knew was that I was present and responding to his touch. I was not planning my next move, hoping for him to react in a pre-determined way. I touched him and felt him, all of him, and we responded to each other, naturally and lovingly. He took his time, and I took mine, no pressure, and no haste.

I began to trust what I was doing, testing out touch in a new way. There was no wrong, right being a sigh or a smile. Then I allowed him in. His touch melted a thousand layers of protection, and he saw me. I allowed him to see me, raw and vulnerable, and I trusted that he would love me and not reject me in the process. That level of connection is the most potent force in the universe. It stops time. It prevents thought. It erases everything other than the moment. It transcends from this plane to another, although where I do not know. It was a private place, only known to Noah and myself, that night.

We stopped to sip champagne, chatting about nothing, and everything, naked in amongst the softness of the sheets, and attraction drew our eyes back together.

'You are a beautiful woman Pippa,' he said, his head leaning to one side, studying me, with a slight smile on his lips. His mop of hair was ruffled into an after-sex shape, and I smiled because I believed him. I smiled because, at that moment, nothing was forced. I smiled, because at that moment, I *was* beautiful. No more words were needed, and I leaned forward and kissed him again. Champagne lips on champagne lips, softness, and then urgency. I couldn't wait any longer to feel him again. I pulled him onto me and then grabbed his waist. Pulling him, pushing him, and he, leaning forward to kiss me over and over and over. We stopped only as the sun awoke, seven hours having melted into our limbs, our kisses, and our connection. I realised that I hadn't even worn the lingerie.

Saying goodbye was more practical, and the magic of the night before vanished with the reminder of commitment. Noah had to get to work early, so he raced into the shower, got dressed, and then was gone, promising to settle the account on the way out. I was on his heels, having to get home, change, and then go to work. The night was over, but it was replayed a hundred times in my mind during the day.

N: *Amazing night. You have ignited my passion. Words fail me*, he texted mid-morning.

P: *Just *sigh, amazing yes, Noah.*

N: *I cannot wait to fuck you again, Pippa.*

I drew a breath. Had that been a fuck or a making love, kind of night? I wondered if men didn't use the term 'making love,' anymore, as it did sound a bit sentimental. I could say something that asked him for more details in his text, but that would complicate everything. It would show my vulnerability, my neediness for this to be *more* than casual. I wanted to know that he had felt what I had felt. Real connection. I would agree to keep the air clear of disagreement.

P: *Me too.*

I was in love, no matter what words he chose. I was captured in his web, silk threads that promised kindness, warmth, and a future. There would be no need to escape.

I AWOKE TO A TEXT, asking me to take a drive with him at the weekend. Just a half-day trip after he finished work Saturday morning.

N: *Wear a headscarf. Like they used to in the old movies.*

P: Why?

N: Because my lady of beauty. Just because.

I was perplexed until there was the sound of a hearty engine outside my flat. Noah was behind the wheel of a fast, expensive car, and the roof was down to allow the sunshine in.

'Perfect day, just as we had a perfect evening. The weather is being kind to us, Pips,' he said, accelerating onto the northern beach road. His car happily purred from the touch of the bitumen.

'Yes,' I agreed, relaxing into the warm breeze, reassuring me that I was in the right place at the right time, with the right man. I had no doubts that this was where I had always meant to be.

We drove up the ocean road along the cliff tops, his car now roaring from the attention of the two happy humans inside. I could smell the sea in the air and hear sunny snippets of laughter from people playing in the sand. I could see the random patterns of dots of surfers riding the waves, and the combination made me want to sing with happiness. It was as if I had finally been given a key, that had unlocked what everyone else already had. Normal felt like paradise.

We drove until we could drive no further, the end of the peninsular in sight. Instead of turning into the carpark however, Noah slowed the car, turned to me and smiled.

'I know a discreet little parcel of bush further up the hill? Want to see it?'

'What, a bit like, do I want to see your etchings?' I laughed a nervous laugh. What was he suggesting? Maybe a nice view from the top?

He drove into a densely wooded area and then turned off down a side road. Then he stopped the engine. It was quiet, aside from a few birds chatting in the trees.

'So, what do you think? Private enough?' He looked keen for something.

'For what?' I asked, looking around.

'For a bit of mucking around?'

'Here?' I sounded surprised.

'Yeah, why not?'

'Aren't we a bit old to be doing stuff like this, and what if we get caught?'

'We won't. Trust me. You just need to trust me.'

'Okay.'

I didn't think. I just decided to go with it all. I'd never done anything like this before. It felt as exciting as if I'd been sixteen and had climbed out of my bedroom window to meet a clandestine boyfriend. I think I even giggled as I got out of the car.

'Now, all you have to do is just bend over,' he said, leading me onto the front of his car.

I did as he asked, which looking back, makes me shake my head with mature, nearly-thirty, disbelief. I was yellow skirt against red bonnet, keen to create orange lust. He reached up under my skirt and pulled my pants down. I worried that my noticeable cellulite might look bad against the badge of his car, but yeah, people think weird thoughts at strange times, hey. He said nothing. Then he simply pushed himself into me, no kissing, no holding, just raw sexual desire. He thrust harder, grunting, and I was looking around, hoping to god that no-one was watching.

My mind started to race… what if this was a setup and someone was filming us? A weird person, quietly hiding, with a lens pointed our way? I thought TikTok, Snapchat, Youtube, porn sites and then blackmail. I could see Adele at work sniggering as she viewed my cellulite online. As I was thinking of someone hiding behind a tree, I thought of Oak and Alan and his tombstone. An image of a decaying body filled my mind, and then suddenly, Noah let out a lengthy moan. Oh, God. Protection! I hadn't asked! Shit! Stupid! Brad and Cynthia would be appalled. I am appalled. I am genuinely appalled. Not only at my negligence but also with the quality of my own thoughts at a time like that.

Noah pulled his pants up and left me to do the same with mine. I was relieved to finally cover my orange-peel dented skin, which had seemed more average, than porn star, clashing surely against the newly waxed, expensive sheen of his car.

'Again, Pips. Utterly amazing,' he said, smiling. 'I am, indeed, a lucky man.'

I smiled at his grinning face. 'I just had to stand there,' I said. 'I got the easy bit.' I was a bit disappointed that my head had been in another place for the duration, but he seemed happy, so I just went with being comfortable too. It wasn't how I usually did things, but perhaps I had helped him play out one of his fantasies? It was nice to think that I might have helped him in some way. Then I wondered how he knew about the parcel of land, and if he brought every date to this place? That then spiralled me into dark thoughts about sexually transmitted diseases. Why hadn't I remembered protection?

'Lunch?' he asked, interrupting my ruminating. 'I know a very nice cafe not far from here. They do this amazing salmon salad with fresh green beans. Completely delicious. Want to try them with some Chardonnay, perhaps?'

'Sure,' I said. 'Sounds good.' He seemed to know what he wanted and when. I liked that. A bit of direction.

We drove down from the peninsular, and he was humming in the car. I smiled, looking out of the window, wanting to shout to everyone that I'd just had sex in a wood with a man who thought *I* was beautiful! I felt that I made Noah happy and that I'd discovered a new power within me. I was finally a woman deeply desired, a woman of great courage, just as Jane had been all those years ago when she had walked off with a sailor on each arm. I felt great, aside from the niggles that I'd forgotten protection and that I had to trust that someone hadn't been watching. I'd set off for a beach drive, not a casual meet-up in a wood though, so I forgave myself for my mistake in not bringing protection. I suppose I could have said no, but I didn't want to if the truth be told.

After lunch, we perused old bookstores, gift shops, and antique dealers. We were two people, meandering in new love, enjoying each other's company, and sharing a forbidden experience in the wood. We stopped to sit by the beach, late afternoon, watching the sun settle towards the horizon. Our ice creams dripped in the warm evening air. An older lady, out for an evening walk, stopped in front of us.

'I do enjoy seeing two people in love,' she said, smiling at us before shuffling off. We laughed, like two teenagers might, at her words.

'I'm so glad I met you, Pips,' Noah said. 'I'm not sure where you came from, maybe heaven?'

I beamed. Now he was likening me to an angel? I could get used to this. 'Me too, Noah. I've been waiting for you for a long time.'

I knew it sounded as contrived as it gets, but it was nice too. My mind remembered a poem my mother had once told me as a small child. It was about being given a box, tied with ribbons. Inside this box, were things saved for later on, when you finally met the person you were destined to be with. At that moment, I realised that I had been waiting for Noah. Lots had happened to me on my journey to him, but I just knew that Noah had been the man that the box had been intended for.

He then reached over and pulled me closer, and the smell of him and his warmth made me feel more content than I had done, in years.

I WENT to bed that night, feeling peaceful as if everything had fallen into place. A smile formed on my lips as if I'd gone back fifteen years and was back in a youth which still promised everything. I replayed the scene at the hotel over and over, the moment when our eyes had met, how his lips had felt, and how time had lost all meaning. I was turned on again, regenerated, and wanting Noah. So much wanting. I replayed out our tryst in the woods and how Noah had led me there, and then had taken me, with such certainty in his actions. Then panic interrupted me. Protection. How the hell had I allowed that to happen? I comforted myself by replaying the scene. He'd said we were going for a drive, not that. I wasn't prepared because I wasn't supposed to have been prepared. Maybe I should have stopped him?

I did some slow breathing, finally relaxing enough for sleep to take me. It gently took the happy veil from off my body, replacing it with a cloak of something else. I'm little, now that I'm dreaming, only I don't know how small. I'm back at the farm, looking for something. I can't find it, and nor do I know what it is. I go from room to room, trying to remember what each room used to look like, where the furniture was placed, and I know at my side, is this thing. It's a phone, I realise. I hear it ring, only I can't turn my head in order to answer it.

I awake from the dream, breathing heavily, in a pool of sweat. I put the bedside lamp on, and the instant light comforts me, illuminating authentic surroundings. I look at my phone, seeing that the dream has woken me too early. There are eleven missed calls, all from my mother. Something must be wrong.

The phone rang again.

'Pippa, where the hell have you been? I've been trying to ring you all night. Why on earth won't you pick your phone up when I call!' My mother sounded panicked. I felt sick. 'It's your father. He's in the hospital. He collapsed. You'll need to come.'

'What? When?' It was the first time I had spoken to my mother since Harry had died. I wondered if I should mention his death.

'No. You just need to come now. Don't ask me anything. Now is not the time for questions. He may be going to be flown over to Melbourne for surgery.'

'Then why don't I fly there?'

'No. You know I can't drive anymore, and I need help with the alpacas.'

My heart sank. It wilted, then shrivelled, fell out of my body, and then made its way down the street.

I waited for some reference to Harry, but there wasn't any. Her child had died - my brother, and yet the fact was to remain silent. There would be no allowance for grief or acknowledgement. My heart winced with pain, both for Harry and for the truth having been deemed, unacceptable for discussion.

'What can I do, other than go?' I asked Brad once it was respectable to call and I was on the way to the airport in a taxi.

'You probably need to go. If he is that sick, then you have to see him or get some social services in place for your mother.'

'Yeah, good point.'

'Well, is anyone else in your family going to do it?'

'No, probably not. No-one else has gone back to the farm in years.'

'Pippa. Do what has to be done, and then come back.'

'Okay. I'll stop off at the hospital first and see him before going to the farm.'

'Is your mother going to visit him this time do you think?'

'Probably not. Says she doesn't want to cry in public.'

'You know Pippa, in all the years that I've been seeing clients, I have never heard of a woman, refusing to see her seriously ill partner, because she doesn't want to be seen crying in public. Where are you staying, by the way?'

'Not there. Not at the farm. I haven't been invited. Last time, she had me out the back in the old caravan, infested with spiders, and made me use a bucket for a toilet.'

'Why?'

'She said it was easier if I had my own personal space.'

'How big is their farmhouse again?'

'Four bedrooms.'

'Lovely. Have you got a hotel booked?'

'Yeah. I managed to get one, although it isn't cheap.'

'Stay in touch, Pippa.'

I texted Noah.

P: My father has been admitted into the hospital, so I'm going to be away for a bit. I need to fly down to Tasmania.

He responded immediately.

N: Let me know if there is anything I can do, Pips xx

P: Thanks Noah, x

N: I'll be here for you, my angel.

I smiled at being called *'angel.'* It was cute. I arrived at the airport, the place milling with people keen to fly out to somewhere early. I'd managed to secure a seat on the dawn flight out of Sydney. Although I was white-knuckled the whole way, a tailwind nicely knocked off twenty minutes from the flight time. I hired a car and then drove the short distance from the airport to the hospital. I headed straight to the front inquiry desk and was given instructions to find the ICU ward. I would need to provide my name at the ward door, and then one of the nurses would buzz me in. It sounded complicated for so early on in the day.

I didn't know what to expect, indeed not my father sitting up looking more bewildered than anything else.

'Oh, hello, it's you,' he said, sounding surprised to see me.

'Hi, I got a call from Mum. I flew straight here.'

'Yes, I collapsed. They think I've got a misbehaving ulcer. They're a bit concerned by a few tests they have run as well.'

'That's no good?' I said, asking a question, as well as making a statement. There was the sound of machines beeping, and then his blood pressure cuff did an automatic measurement. 'So, have you heard from everyone?' I asked, trying not to be nosey to see what his measurement had been on the monitor.

'Yes, all of them. Although those conversations are private.'

'Oh.' There was a pause. I realised *everyone* was minus Harry, only he didn't want to mention that fact either.

Exit stage left real Pippa. Entrance stage right, fake daughter Pippa. The one that he wants me to be right now. Leave all emotion off in the wings and be perfunctory, minimalist and formal. Anyone who has grown up this way knows exactly what I mean.

'Do you have a prognosis?' I asked, stepping into the new role, as he had just let me know that this was all he would accept in this space.

'Might die, might not apparently. They haven't determined my outcome yet.'

'Oh.' I was surprised at his matter-of-fact tone and that he was suggesting that his condition could go either way. I checked the monitor to look at his vitals. They seemed okay?

'Yes, not that I care particularly. I've had a good life.'

I was surprised at his bluntness. I thought people fought hard to stay alive. Not just fall over the line with such nonchalance and haste. 'Don't you want to live, though?' I was surprised at his no-fuss attitude towards a possible, imminent demise.

'Well, you know how it is.'

'Not really,' I said. 'What about Mum?'

'She's fine,' he replied, missing the point.

A nurse, neatly dressed as if he'd just started his shift came in. 'Hello,' he smiled brightly, 'and you are?'

'Hi, I'm Pippa. I'm Callan's daughter.'

'Nice to meet you, Pippa. I'm Darrin, looking after your Dad today. Let me know if you have any questions.'

'Thanks, Darrin. I might just leave you to do all of this. I've just taken an early flight from Sydney, and I'm a bit knackered, to be honest.'

'Oh, you poor thing, in this heat as well. One in a hundred-year heatwave they are saying for today. I imagine you'll be wanting to get some rest. Are you staying at your Mum and Dad's alpaca farm? Such a lovely place, so your Dad has been telling me. Alpacas are just the cutest animals, aren't they?' He was still smiling.

'Yes,' I said, embarrassed by the fact that I hadn't been invited to stay at the farm. Instead, I was paying $260 a night to stay at the local hotel.

'Okay, Dad, well, I'll just head up to the farm then, and check in on Mum. Make sure she's got food and water.'

'She's not an alpaca,' he said, looking annoyed.

Darrin laughed and then stopped, seeing that he was the only one who had found that funny.

'What?' I asked.

'Food and water,' added my father, somewhat curtly.

'Oh. Yeah, sure, no, of course not.'

I left feeling confused. My instinct had been to greet him with a hug, maybe even share a concerned tear. It was an instinct deeply embedded in compassion, driven by an innate desire to be a caring, kind, and worried daughter. Instead, he had insisted that I play a role that he had determined, the script precise, cold, and factual. I felt like a stranger, having walked into the wrong room, finding a few words to say to the bemused patient in the bed. I had wanted to thank him too, for being my Dad, because those words were the appropriate words, the ones needed to be said at that moment. If it were true, and there was a chance that he could die, why couldn't I speak them? I'd been someone else standing there. Someone, in fact, so *unlike* me.

I drove slowly up to the farm, my soul sighing ever so slightly when I saw the familiar white gates. This was the territory I'd grown up in, witnessing so much that had gone on, behind the veil of felting, yarn, and potential. Now I had to walk back in and not let it suffocate me with memories that had yet to be fully processed. The farmhouse itself was traditional in style with cream brickwork, a grey metal roof, and a small rose garden. I parked in the allocated visitor area, sinking into the newly laid gravel and gingerly walked towards the front door, deeply embedded in the generous, wrap-around verandah.

I peered through the lounge room window, and mother was sitting in her chair, watching television. I tapped on the glass, and she jumped. The last time I'd seen her was when she had thrown the tea at me. Luckily it looked as if her cup was empty, which gave me hope that it would be a safe welcome. She greeted me by forgetting to greet me at all.

'Pippa. I've got a bag here that I want you to take to your father. It's got his fresh clothes in it, the newspaper, three books and some samples of the new felting packaging for him to look at.'

'What? Now? You don't have many alpacas left? Why are you still doing the felting? Should he be working when he's in the ICU?'

'Yes, he needs the samples. The company wants us to decide on the packaging. I just said that.' She looked at me as if I'd asked a peculiar question.

I looked back, at her peculiar answer. The air hung heavy as it sorted itself back to normal.

'Well, would you like to come with me and see him, perhaps?'

'Why would I want to do that? I can't leave the alpacas alone.'

'There are only four alpacas, and they are easily taken care of. I could have you there and back in a couple of hours each way.'

'No. I can't leave the farm, Pippa. It's not safe. Some people rob empty houses over here, you know. I'll pray for him instead.'

'Really?' I was surprised that the area had suddenly become crime-ridden.

'Why do I pray, Pippa? You might well ask that given you've given up the faith yourself. Do you always need to ask so many stupid questions?'

I paused. Here we go. Another conversation to navigate my way through.

'I'll just pretend he's out the back with the alpacas for a while,' she said confidently, hands on hips as if that solved everything.

'Sorry?' Had my mother just said she was going to pretend that my father was out the back, with the alpacas, when he was apparently balancing between life and death in an ICU ward?

'It's easier to think that he's out the back than thinking he is in a hospital,' she said, looking at me as if I hadn't understood her. I got that it was easier to think that, not that it was appropriate.

'He isn't that well. Don't you want to come and be there for him? He might be feeling a bit lost with everything that's going on? The ICU can be quite intimidating.'

She laughed. 'Lost? Callan? Never. No, he said he would phone me this evening.'

'He can phone you from the ICU?'

'Yes, they hand him a phone, and he dials, and then we speak.'

I took a deep breath, trying to remain calm.

'Okay, so in terms of food. What would you like me to go and get for you? I can pick up some groceries on the way back?'

She shuffled off and then handed me a list and some cash. I looked down the list, and it seemed straight forward. Nothing on the list that wouldn't be readily available.

'Is it hot out there then?' she asked me.

'Yeah, apparently it's going to be thirty-nine degrees. It's going to be quite difficult to run around in this sort of heat.'

'I'm glad I have the air-conditioning in the house,' she said. 'Although, I never had a problem running around in the heat myself.' She looked me up and down, her gaze ending on my hips.

I ignored her gaze. 'Yes. The air-conditioning must be lovely.' God, the conversation was painful. It was like two strangers trying to make small talk.

Five hours later, I'd returned from the hospital where my father had changed mood, now being grumpy and rude to me. I'd handed him the fresh bag of items and suggested that I bring Mother in for a visit. I told him that she was pretending that he was out the back with the alpacas. The truthful statement was seen as apparently offensive and unleashed his anger. Here was my elderly father, in an ICU bed, raging at me. It would have been comical if I hadn't cracked and run out of his room, crying. I felt like I was still a child, being told off, yet again.

I HANDED her the bags of groceries, and she started to lift them out of the bags, wincing in pain, each time she moved.

'Would you like me to put things away for you?' I asked.

'No,' she snapped. 'You don't know where anything goes.'

She held up a can of soup. 'This brand of soup tastes like toilet water Pippa. I didn't want that one. I wanted the one specifically on the list I gave you.'

'Yeah, they didn't have any, unfortunately. I quite like that brand, though. Have you tried it? It's quite creamy. You like creamy.'

'I hate creamy, Pippa. I have hated creamy for the past twenty years. I won't be eating it. You got me the wrong water too.'

'What, the plain water? What's wrong with the water?'

'It tastes awful, compared to the other brand. The one that I like. The one that was on *my* list.' She shook her head at me as if I was a lost cause.

'Really? Aren't they both spring waters?'

'Yes.'

She didn't appear to want to discuss things further, so I asked her to make sure she had the phone on her at all times.

'In case you fall, because you can't get up when you fall, from memory, can you?' I remembered several stories of broken ankles and legs and hours on the floor as my father had tried to get her up. They were a lousy comedy act, choosing to fight with old age instead of just calling an ambulance. They had recounted stories of six hours lapsing, as my father tried to get her upright. I did know that if she fell and no-one was there, she could die from it - something about kidneys failing.

'I'll put the phone in my dressing gown pocket,' she said adamantly. 'I'll make sure it's on me at all times. Now, make sure you padlock the farm gates on your way out for security. The padlocks are down under the big rock, near the gates.'

'Are you sure you want to be locked in? Can I have a key, at least? What if you need the fire brigade or something?'

'They have a key to get in, it's fine. They are special padlocks, designed to let the police and ambulance in too.'

So, the police and ambulance were allowed in, but not me? I left, locking the gates behind me and wondering if it were sensible to do so. After all, how would I get back in tomorrow? I imagined that she would make me park out on the road and walk all the way up the farm driveway, in the heat.

I was right. The next day, I climbed over the double white gates, greeting the inquisitive alpacas in the front paddock on my way past. They seemed to remember me, allowing me to scratch under their chins. However, there was an urgency to my walking because my mother hadn't answered the phone when I had rung two hours ago. I was hoping that she hadn't had a fall, not wanting to find her half-dead on the floor somewhere. She wasn't. Instead, she insisted she had slept well, had eaten breakfast, and had showered, having decided that the phone was a stupid idea and had put it down somewhere.

'I thought you said you couldn't shower by yourself? That Dad had to help you in and out?'

'No. I'm fine.' She stared at me, daring me to challenge her shower comment.

'Can you keep the phone on you please? If you do fall, you need to be able to contact me... or the hospital. Especially if you're in the shower.'

'No. I've decided not to carry the phone.' Then she burst into tears. I instinctively walked over to comfort her, understanding that suddenly being left on her own with the thought that she may lose my father was overwhelming. When my arms went around her, she froze though. Stiff as a board, she went, and it was awkward. I didn't know how to respond to her sudden rigor mortis. Was I supposed to hold on and wait for her to soften, or release my grip? In the end, the silence and the fact I think she was also holding her breath became too much, and I released her.

'I think I'll take a nap in my chair,' she said with a perfunctory tone.

'How about I make you a cup of tea?' She seemed to like that idea and got into her electric massage chair. I was just putting the milk into her tea when the power went out.

'Pippa!' she called from the lounge room with urgency. 'I'm stuck!' She was. In the middle of an intense deep-massage cycle, her electric massage chair had stalled, along with the power. All fifteen airbags had remained fully inflated, however, effectively trapping her into the chair. Her arms were pinned as well as her legs.

'Does it hurt?' I asked, staring at what looked like an impossible situation.

'No!' She snapped crossly at me, as if I was tiresome in asking.

'Okay, do you have the instruction booklet? There must be a way to deflate it all?' I looked around the room not quite knowing what to do, to help.

'No, Pippa!' She raised her voice at me.

There was a stalemate. She, puffy and trapped, and me, staring and wondering what to do.

My phone rang. It was Brad. 'How's it all going?' he asked cheerily. I left the room to take his call.

'Well, I'm at the farm, but my mother is stuck in her massage chair right now.'

'Your mother is stuck?'

'Yes, literally. The power has gone out, and she is one of those electric massage chairs with all the airbags.'

'Really?'

'Yes. What should I do?'

Brad started laughing. 'I'm sorry, Pippa… but the image… oh my god…' The sight was indeed ridiculous, and his laughter was infectious.

'I'll have to call you back,' I said, laughing. 'You've set me off now. I don't know what to do, though.'

'You could stab the airbags? Maybe deflate them? Just don't stab your mother as well.'

'Brad! I'll call you back. I'd better see if her circulation has been cut off.'

It hadn't been. She just sat there, and I sat opposite to her, not knowing what to say. I played the role of her daughter, but my performance was going down like a lead balloon. I ended up not knowing what role she wanted from me. So, we just sat in silence, avoiding eye contact.

'I read somewhere that if you are tied up, you shouldn't move,' I offered. 'Something to do with muscle swelling, I think?' It was a paltry offer of conversation. 'Try wiggling your toes and fingers?'

'Well, you're bloody helpful,' she said. 'You're just sitting there, doing nothing.'

'Should I call the fire brigade?' I suggested, hopefully.

'No!' she snarled loudly. 'Stop being so bloody stupid, Pippa.'

'Okay.' I decided to play the role of mute instead, looking around the room and occasionally towards her.

The power came on much to my relief an hour later, and she continued the massage cycle to the end, asking me to make her a fresh cup of tea before I left.

'Don't forget to keep the phone on you,' I called out, heading back down the driveway to my melted hire car. My phone rang, half-way home.

'Pippa, it's Stuart. How are you? I missed you in class.'

'Yeah, sorry Stuart, I've got a few things happening right now.'

'I've got to get the artworks onto the list for the exhibition. They want to start weeding out which ones they want to include. Are you still thinking of putting in 'Tears of Hope?' Is that what you are still naming it?'

'What do you think?'

'It's simple, but says a lot.'

'Okay, well, it can't hurt to be hopeful, can it? Send it in.'

'Are you back next week?'

'Hope so. I'm down in Tassie right now, though. My Dad got sick and is in the hospital, so I'm just sorting a few things out.'

'Shit, sorry to hear that, Pippa. Look, I'll see you whenever you can get back, okay? Take care.'

The next morning, I repeated the climb over the padlocked white, wooden farm gates and trudged in the heat up the long, winding driveway. On this day, large wasps were hovering near the security door frame, and as my mother opened the front door to me, she sprayed me in the face with industrial-strength fly spray.

'Sorry, I was just getting the wasps out of the way for you,' she said, sweetly.

I rinsed the chemicals from my burning eyes and started the back and forth between the hospital and the house. All day, to and fro as she remembered more and more items she wanted to give him.

'Are you sure you don't want to go up and visit him before he flies off? The surgery carries a fifty percent risk the doctor was saying. I asked about a wheelchair for you, if it's too much… the walk from the car to the ward that is?'

'You expect me to sit in a wheelchair? In front of other people? Have you wheeling me around? No Pippa. I won't do it. It's embarrassing, sitting in a wheelchair. I'd like to keep my dignity, thank you very much.'

'Lots of people sit in wheelchairs at the hospital, Mum. The doctor said it would be ideal as a way to help you to get in and see him.'

'You spoke to a doctor, Pippa? Who said you could do that?'

'Sorry?' I was taken aback. I was the one in the ICU room and was family. Of course, the doctor wanted to discuss the surgical options and other matters with me. 'The doctor updated me after his ward round.'

'Well, the doctor shouldn't be telling you anything,' she said. 'This is between your father and me.'

'I didn't ask to be told. I'm the only family who is in there, though. If you were in there, they would be speaking to you.'

'Pippa. It is completely inappropriate for you to be involved like this. You don't speak to the doctors. Do you understand that? This has nothing to do with you.'

I felt like a thirteen-year-old being told off. I felt anger welling in me. I was nothing more than a courier for them. I was asked to fly down at my own expense and then stay in a hotel. What… so that she could get me to do the jobs she was supposed to be doing? My anger started to grow. Anger too at myself, for standing there, partaking in this stupid charade.

'He also said that Dad could be in the hospital for a few weeks, and I will need to get back to work. I'll need to organise some services for you in the meantime.'

'Over my dead body,' she snorted at me.

'Well, it will be your dead body if you don't carry the phone around with you. I tried to call last night, and again, got no response.'

'That's because I don't need it. I fell out of my chair last night. I did. On the floor I was, and I had no problem getting up by myself. Just for the record,' she added defiantly. 'You seem to think I'm helpless for some reason.'

'How did you get up?'

'Well, the chair was tipped on top of me…'

'Which chair?' I asked, looking around the room.

'The… the massage chair.'

'What? That heavy chair… you what?… just fell out, and then it tipped on top of you, and you got back up? How?' I was trying to imagine the physics of it.

'I used my arms to lift myself.'

'And the chair? You lifted that heavy chair off yourself as well? It's got to weigh close to a hundred kilos.'

'Yes,' she said, squarely looking at me. I felt like we'd just done our ten paces and pistols were aimed.

'So, why have you not been able to get up off the ground for years, sometimes for eight hours at a time, and all of a sudden, you can get up, and lift a hundred kilos off you as well?'

'I can. That's why. I've been doing my arm exercises.'

'What arm exercises?'

'With… with the baked bean cans.'

'What?'

She rudimentarily demonstrated her arms lifting small cans of baked beans. I gave up. I left with another set of clothes for my father and made an appointment to see our family GP, urgently.

'So, she's got the alpaca farm gates padlocked, can't get up if she falls, said she couldn't shower on her own and can't drive?' Dr Brown asked me, looking concerned. 'Does she have the ability to get food in for herself?'

'Not at this stage. Some of the food in the fridge is a couple of years out of date too. She said it tastes just fine, however. I'm concerned about what to do with her… I have to get back to work.'

'I'll call her myself,' he said, 'while you are in the room.'

My mother repeated the story and told him that he could visit if he wanted to, but he would also need to climb over the farm gates and walk up to the house because she would not unlock the gates for anybody.

'Can you not give Pippa a set of keys?' he asked, shaking his head at me in disbelief.

'Nope.'

'I might find it a bit difficult climbing over the gates though Bridie. I'm sixty-three, and my knees are bad.' He paused, hoping to hear something promising.

'Well then, you shouldn't visit, if that's the case, Dr Brown. I'm just fine.'

'Okay, Bridie. Just make sure that you call if you need anything.'

'Pippa, you'd better organise for a food delivery service and have a word with one of the social workers at the hospital,' he said afterwards. 'She's acting like a petulant child.'

'Sorry, Pippa,' he added, as I was leaving.

'Thanks for trying, Dr Brown.'

It was seven days before I could get a flight home. Seven days at $260 a night. My bank account was groaning. My father had stabilised enough for them to do some emergency surgery at the local hospital and had survived. It looked like he would be able to return home in a couple of weeks. I offered to organise someone to do some necessary cleaning, but my mother refused.

'I'm not having a stranger coming onto the farm, cleaning. They may take my stuff, and they might steal the alpacas.'

'But they could help. Is a cleaner likely to steal an elderly alpaca? I mean you couldn't exactly fit it in a car, could you?'

'Yes, absolutely! They make excellent pets. No. The answer is no. Stop interfering, Pippa.'

'I'm not. Look, I've flown all the way here. Taken time off work…'

'And?' She looked at me, as if confused by what I was alluding to.

'Do you want a hand clearing up the house before I go, perhaps?' I looked around at my mother's hoard, which was getting out of control. She found it hard to negotiate her way around all the mess and falls were getting more frequent because stuff was forming narrow passageways along the corridors.

'Why would I need help?' she asked, looking perplexed.

I gave up again. 'Well, I'll probably go home then.'

'Okay. Have a lovely flight home. Let me know when you get back safely.' She had already turned to do something else.

I drove to the airport, feeling confused. I'd done everything I was supposed to do. I wanted to be a good daughter and look after my elderly parents, yet everything I did, seemed to go wrong... or was taken in the wrong way. It was like fault could be found in every step I took. Had I failed? Had I monumentally failed at being their daughter? Maybe I had? I didn't know what it was that they wanted from me.

All I wanted to do was to see Noah, fall back into his arms, and find that place called home.

HIS KIDS
WERE SO SWEET

16

HI KIDS
BYE KIDS

Being away from Noah had started to feel like pain, as if a small piece of me was missing, each time we parted. I had become accustomed to his arms being around me at night-time, his soothing, calming voice, lulling me into sleep. He felt the same, sending me a late-night text.

N: God, I miss you, Pips. I so want to be wrapped up with you now.

P: Yeah, me too x

I had quickly replied, lying in bed, about to drift into sleep.

N: Can I call?

P: Of course.

I was eager to hear his voice again, despite being exhausted.

He had then phoned me, and we had talked about nothing and everything until three in the morning. He described his life growing up in Brisbane, relaying funny stories about his brothers and sharing painful moments around his mother's death. I listened to his memories, which sounded almost as if he were reading from a book to me, such was his eloquence. I never wanted our conversations to stop.

Then our words had become slower, each of us drifting off into sleep, our phones still on, our eyes now shut. It was as if we were becoming fused, having found our other half.

IN AMONGST ALL OF THIS, I did need to find some solitude and start asking myself some pertinent questions. I could see Cynthia's point. I was indeed merely replaying the same patterns over and over with my parents. Each time, I would head back in, playing this disfigured role of daughter, only to be spat out. Round and round, the three of us went, two against one. I had been born from people who had no sense of connection with their emotions, and yet here I was, brimming with too many. I think they saw my range of emotions as dangerous to them. They wanted to keep me at a distance, and I wanted to be close. I knew that the relationship was abusive, but if they refused to acknowledge this pattern, then it was up to me to break the cycle. Somehow.

I found a spot in the gardens near the Conservatorium of Music after work and could hear students practising, from within its sandy walls. There was a flute, playing repetitive scales, up and down, then a bit higher, over and over. A piano-playing something classical. It sounded Russian. The music created a beautiful backdrop in which for me to mull and ponder this tiring dilemma. I kept going back, again and again, only to be hurt, time, and time again. A predicament that had resulted in me self-flagellating all my life, the scars hidden, concealed, and ones that generated shame. It was as if I drank dysfunction in secret, not knowing why I did it, hiding the empty bottles from people, not wanting to feel accused, and shameful for my actions.

There were so many people online who told others to simply go 'no contact' as if it were easy to relegate your family into nothingness. I doubted if any of them had gone through a smilier experience. It wasn't what I wanted anyway. I wanted to be a daughter and a sister, not a self-relegated orphan. There had to be some compromise, surely? Was the real cost of belonging to a dysfunctional family going to be walking alone through life, without my clan there for support? I would lose my title as daughter and sister, to become what? What was the term for someone like me? An aloner?

I watched people jog past and realised that none of us really knew what another person was grappling with. We rarely see inside someone else's world. Instead, we judge people on their external appearance. If someone is clean, well dressed and articulate, we assume them to be well put together. Someone else, dressed poorly with dishevelled hair, may be deemed to be less-than. It is superficial, rapid, and unfair judgement. No-one would have guessed the complexity of the question that I was working through right there, at that moment. I would just have looked like a woman approaching thirty who had stopped to rest for a while, perhaps watching shadows lengthening over the harbour.

What I wanted from my parents and family did indeed prove to be a hard one to figure out. I just didn't know anymore. I wondered if I had been ruminating for so long, that I had created neural pathways in my mind, which forced me around in circles. I remembered back to Karen Maclaren's perfectly made salad sandwich. I'd wanted that instead of tomato sauce. I had wanted my parents to meet Nigel too, only my mother had refused ever to allow my partners onto their farmland. Being hit by my mother hadn't been pleasant either. When I started to think about what I did want, all that sprang to mind was mostly what I hadn't wanted. In the end, I gave up. It was like trying to imagine something I knew I needed, but couldn't define, because I'd never experienced it.

'THAT'S THE PROBLEM, Pippa. She's right.' said Brad adamantly over the phone. 'Until you define it, you'll be chasing everything that it isn't.'

'It's like I go to say it, and there's nothing there.'

'I hear you. Hey, you've been quiet for a bit. How's Noah?'

'Good.'

'Just good?'

'I'm not expecting anything, just going with the flow.' That much was true.

'So, he might be a keeper?'

'That's a trick question, Brad.'

'You know me too well, Pippa. You don't know him well enough to be able to answer that yet.'

'Of course,' I said, smiling.

THE WEEKEND CAME QUICKLY, and Noah had arranged for me to meet his kids. I felt apprehensive as I'd not had a lot of experience around children. I wanted kids, but not on my own. I didn't see myself as a single mother, being inseminated with random sperm. I wanted more than that. Two people to raise a child together, in some sort of family unit. I saw it as my opportunity to create a loving family and not repeat the same mistakes my parents had made. I didn't know a lot about Noah's children, other than their ages and names, and that I was the first woman, other than their mother, whom he was introducing them to.

N: This is a big deal for them, Noah texted me. *So, let's keep PDAs to a minimum.*

P: PDAs?

N: Personal Displays of Affection. It might be uncomfortable for them.

P: Ok

N: Careful with yr language too.

P: My language?

N: Yeah, yr swearing + stuff.

P: Oh, yeah, sure.

N: Also, don't let them know we sleep in the same bed. I haven't told Emma yet.

P: Ok

N: Best not 2 say you r my girlfriend, either.

P: Ok

I was getting nervous, trying to remember all the things I wasn't supposed to do, in front of his kids. What if I did swear or something? Would I damage them for life? We'd arranged to meet at a child-friendly museum, a hands-on place where the kids could amuse themselves, and I could follow them around. It took the pressure off me, relegating me to glorified nanny for the afternoon, given Noah had said that their nanny wasn't coming too.

Noah greeted me with his children outside the front of the museum. 'Seb, Rose and Steve,' he said proudly. 'This is Pippa.'

'Hi,' Rose and Seb both smiled, but Steve stared at the ground in silence.

'Are you Daddy's new girlfriend?' Seb asked immediately. I laughed, quickly changing the subject, as instructed.

'Happy Birthday, Seb. I hear you've just turned the big nine.'

'Yup and I got a remote-controlled car for my birthday. It's really, really fast!' He ran around in circles, showing me how fast his car went.

'Mummy bought it for him,' added Rose quietly. 'She saved up for ages.'

Noah ushered us in. 'Who wants to go and see some dinosaurs?' he asked enthusiastically.

'Me, me, me!' Seb and Rose were eager to get the show on the road. Steve walked in, his head down.

Noah purchased a family ticket, including me in it. 'That bit went well,' he said after they had headed off towards the dinosaurs.

'I hope so,' I said, wanting to wrap my arms around him, as was usual.

He kept his physical distance. 'Yeah, that was good. I think they like you.'

'I'm glad… relieved.'

It was then that things went a bit odd. At first, I couldn't put my finger on what was going on. Seb seemed to be running in the wrong direction, away from the dinosaurs, and Steve was shouting in the distance.

'Daddy, I think you need to come and help.' Rose ran up, out of breath.

'Sorry, Pippa,' said Noah, turning quickly and starting to run off. 'I need to go and sort this out.'

I walked around the precious rocks collection for a while and then went to try and find out what had happened to them all. I could see Noah kneeling, with his hand on Steve's arm. He was speaking to him, quite seriously, judging by the look on his face. There was no sign of Rose or Seb.

'I want to GO!' shouted Steve, trying to get away from Noah.

'No!' said Noah firmly.

'I said, LET ME GO!' shouted Steve. He punched Noah hard in the stomach. Noah reeled backwards, and Steve kicked him in the leg while he was down. I winced. Noah reached up, to rub his shin.

'Do NOT kick me, Steve!' He reached into his backpack and pulled out a bottle of water.

'Drink this and calm down.'

I wasn't sure what was going on.

'Steve is having some issues at the moment, Pippa. Some of it relates to all the changes in our family situation. He'll be fine when he calms.'

Rose came running up, looking panicked. 'Daddy, Seb has run outside. Says he wants to throw himself under a truck.'

'Shit! Pippa, can you stay with Rose and Steve for a bit? I need to go and find Seb.'

'Sure,' I said, wondering what had just happened to make a nine-year-old want to throw himself under a truck.

Rose sat quietly with me. 'They are always like this,' she sighed. 'They just fight, *all* the time.' She folded her arms crossly.

'Really? That can't be too much fun.'

'No,' she said sadly. 'I wish I had a sister.'

My heart sank a bit. It was like someone had popped my bubble. Here was my perfect man, with a ready-made family, only everything now seemed a bit more complicated than it had a few moments before. I felt like I was entirely out of my depth. I didn't know how to help.

Steve sat on the floor in front of me, playing on his phone. However, I was beginning to think that there was more to his behavioural issues than not liking change. He avoided eye contact with me and was saying stuff to himself, that I didn't understand. He at least seemed more relaxed, which was a relief, as I wasn't sure what I was going to do if he started to lash out again. Noah returned thirty minutes later, dragging in Seb.

'He'd got quite far. Must have run quite fast,' he panted. 'Steve, are you hungry?'

'Yes. Finally. I am starving.'

It was chaos. Noah spent much of the time trying to contain Steve, who had multiple meltdowns every time he didn't get his own way, and Rose was left to deal with Seb, who took great delight in explaining how, if he used one of the sharp rocks from the gem collection, he could make his leg bleed so much, that he might die.

'There would be red blood, pouring everywhere,' he said with a dramatic tone.

'Yes, I can imagine,' I said, lost for words that seemed more appropriate.

'I would bleeeed out… I could put holes in me everywhere. Punch! Punch! Punch!'

Rose shook her head. 'It's okay. He says that stuff a lot. He never means it.'

Seb than ran off again, with Noah in pursuit, and I was left to look after Rose and Steve. Steve started to make a dash for it, but Rose grabbed him by the arm.

'Get off ME!' shouted Steve and slapped Rose in the face. Hard enough to make her nose bleed, making her cry.

'Oh shit… I mean… Rose… are you hurt?'

Crying and clutching at her nose, she let out a muffled, 'Yes, I think so. There's blood!' I gave her a tissue and got her to hold her nose tightly.

'Steve, please don't hit your sister.'

'Please be quiet,' he told me. 'Can you just be quiet? Quiet. Just be quiet. Quiet. Shut up.' Then he stood up and ran back and forth between two points in the room.

Wow. Now I didn't know what was going on. I had no idea what to say that would appease him, and so instead just sat back down, watching him until Noah came back.

Noah eventually returned and managed to get the children onto the same page for the rest of the afternoon. There was no room for any affection between us, and I understood why he might be single. I got why he had needed to employ a nanny and why his wife might have been depressed at times. I understood that if I continued in the relationship, it would be Noah, myself, and his three children.

I needed a bit of time to process the afternoon when I got home. I wished that Noah had mentioned Steve's issues earlier because his behaviour seemed to indicate a significant problem. What? I wasn't sure. It seemed a bit more than a simple adjustment problem, especially given their separation had been several years ago. However, I'd not raised a teenage boy myself, so honestly didn't know what it all meant.

Seb was possibly trying to get attention from Noah, I deduced, with all the acting out, as Steve took up most of Noah's time. However, the constant threats to hurt himself had been confronting from someone who had only just turned nine. I didn't know how serious they were. Rose, I figured, was lost somewhere in amongst all of that. She seemed sad. The afternoon had been exhausting and not at all what I had imagined.

N: Did you have a good afternoon? Noah texted, later that evening.

I wanted to text back and say *No, not really. Your children are complicated.* I would lie, however, to protect Noah.

P: I had a wonderful time. I hope the kids enjoyed themselves.

N: They did :-) he texted, adding a smiley face. *They really liked you. I love you for the way you handled them.*

Love? I re-read his text over and over. Should I text, *I love you too?* No. I didn't want to, but the exchange felt unbalanced if I didn't send something.

P: I love the way you parent them.

I meant it. He did handle Steve beautifully, despite the judgmental stares from other parents. I sat with my lie for the evening. It gnawed away at me. I hadn't had a great time at all, but it would appear politically incorrect to admit that, even to myself. If I did, I might ruin my fantasy.

BRAD CALLED.

'How's it all going?'

'I met his kids.'

'Noah's?'

'Who else's kids?'

'Fair point. Is everything okay? You sound a bit off.'

'Yes and no.'

'Explain? I know that tone.'

'Well, there's just a lot more to it. His son, Steve, has quite serious behavioural issues. I didn't know… I wasn't prepared, and his other son keeps threatening to kill himself.'

'How old?'

'Steve, the one with the behavioural issues is fourteen, and Seb is nine. He threatened to throw himself under a truck.'

'Okay, that's young to be threatening stuff like that. Had Noah mentioned any of this? Are the issues with Steve serious?'

'Yeah, they are. Here's the problem. It kind of unfolded in my face with no warning. I was blindsided.'

'That was a bit unfair, you have to agree.'

'I'm trying to work out if he thought I might run if he had mentioned it? Maybe he doesn't see it as an issue? Maybe the kids don't behave like that around other people? Could just have been 'new girlfriend' syndrome?'

'There you go again, Pippa. Always trying to give people the benefit of the doubt.'

'I know. There's Rose too. She's twelve and trying hard to stay alive in the middle of all of that.'

'That's a lot to deal with in a new relationship.' Brad sighed.

'Yeah. I'm feeling a bit overwhelmed.'

'It's burst your bubble a bit, I imagine?'

'Yeah, I was just thinking the same.'

'How do you feel about dealing with a fourteen-year-old with significant behavioural issues?'

'It's complicated when I don't know what's going on.'

'Fair enough. How's the problem solving going?'

'Oh, the question about my parents? I need to set aside some more time, I think.'

'Do Pippa. I don't want you to lose momentum with this. Cynthia has given you an important question to mull over.'

'I agree. I'll try to do something this coming weekend.'

ART CLASS came and went, with Louise deciding that speaking to me was now off-limits. Our paintings had been returned from the selection process, with the news that three of us had made it in. My painting had made it, as had Noah's and Jo's. Stuart was ecstatic. I was a little bewildered given the lack of technique in my painting but figured they needed balance with their chosen works.

It was now up to us to frame them and write a brief blurb which would be stuck on the wall next to our paintings. Stuart brought in boxes of recycled frames for us to choose from. I chose a black frame, figuring that hope arises from despair, indicated by a black frame. Noah wasn't there, as he'd had to finalise some accounts back at work. I was glad in a way because I was still feeling guilty about my lie. It wasn't that I wanted Noah all to myself, as I understood that people came with children. It was just the intense difference between Noah with his children, and Noah without his children, and the levels of stress that Steve and Seb generated. I needed to decide if I could cope with that or had the skills to know how to cope. More to the point, could I give up the fantasy of perfect Noah.

. . .

I DECIDED to go away for a weekend retreat to think about everything. I needed to sit in the quiet and sort out my relationship with my parents and how I was going to cope with Noah's kids. It was a perfect relationship between the two of us, but certainly, when the five of us were together, it was going to be challenging. Brad and Cynthia would have been proud of me. This was a moment where I was genuinely stepping back and making an attempt to evaluate where things were at.

I booked in at a Buddhist monastery that allowed short stays, north of the city. I figured that going somewhere that promoted silence as an activity might help me work through things. I smiled at my irony, assuming that something as complicated as my life, could be sorted out by being silent. My mind, when sensing silence usually went into over-drive.

'Welcome,' smiled the fully-robed monk as I checked in. 'Your room is down the corridor, second on the left. Number eight. We rise at five to meditate, and lights go out at ten. You will make your meals in the communal kitchen, which is in the centre of the building. We have a vow of silence between nine and six. If you have any questions, please come to me, and ask. Thank you, and may your retreat enable you to find the answers you are seeking.' He smiled and nodded, then sent me on my way with my key.

My room was stark, just as I had expected, given its mission. I had a single bed, a small wooden desk, and a wardrobe, squashed into the corner. There was a poster on the wall of a small kitten sitting in front of a mirror. In the reflection was a lion, staring back. Underneath was a statement. *'Find yourself, be yourself.'*

I nodded at it, realising that part of my work was just that, to find myself and perhaps feel comfortable to be myself without feeling the need to change. Right now, though, if I did look into such a mirror, I imagined seeing a stranger staring back. Someone who had tried too hard to be loved by family, that they were now a facade. It wasn't that I couldn't see how bad things were either. It was that I didn't know how to fix them.

Given the clock had now reached twelve, the monastery was now in silent mode. People, just like me with burdens to unpack, silently nodded to me, as they passed me in the corridors. I made my way out into the monastic gardens, which were beautifully landscaped. The monks had created small pockets of courtyards, in which people could sit in solitude without bothering each other's musings. I wandered until the right space leapt out at me, a small area of manicured green, with a statue of an angel in the middle. I smiled and grabbed a picture on my phone, intending to send it to Noah later. My courtyard had four, tall, box hedged walls and a small wooden seat on which to sit. I chose to sit on the grass instead and took my sandals off. I reminded myself of the question that I had been asked to ponder. *What did I want?*

I sat with the question, at times forcing potential answers to present themselves. These weren't the right answers, though. I had to be patient and wait for the right answer to come to me, the one that resonated with me. I knew that my own needs were unfulfilled in my family. I felt as if I was always swimming upstream, trying to fight against an image of me that didn't fit. I had tried to explain who I was after Harry had died, only no-one wanted to know - to take the time to hear me out. It was easier for them to believe the gossip-based image of me than find out for themselves. I was hurting, that much I knew.

How could I ever fit into a society obsessed with the notion that happiness was tied to family? Would I always remain 'unhappy' because my family had given up? My head was a ruminating, rambling mess of thoughts, unrelated to the question I was supposed to be finding an answer to. I gave up, instead choosing to replay scenes of making love with Noah. I sat until the sun started to set and then went back inside. End of day one. Fail. Sex addiction? Certified.

A clue came to me in the night, during a particularly vivid dream. I was again in the family home. I was standing in a room, and my parents were shouting. I told them that I was there, but they couldn't see or hear me, being too involved in their arguing. I looked down at my arms and could see them myself. I screamed to prove that I was there, hearing myself, but again unable to get my parents' attention. I was invisible to them and yet visible to myself. I stood for what felt like hours in the dream, with the light around me transforming from light to dark. I remained inconspicuous and occasionally screaming out for help.

I woke feeling heavy and despondent at five, for the early-morning meditation. Sitting cross-legged, I looked around and counted seven others, all of whom looked equally as tired and uncomfortable on the cold, hard floor. A red-robed monk entered and then sat in front of us. We were first encouraged to do several rounds of deep breathing. Then the monk gave a short talk about the necessity of self-love and that today, during the meditation, we would imagine that love was pouring into us from a higher source.

I was a bit cynical when I started the meditation, but then something shifted in me. I felt an emotion rising and tried to suppress it. Not here, not in front of all of these people I told myself. I thought of something else and tried distraction, but it was useless. There was an image in my mind, and it wouldn't go away. Me as a child, just standing there, alone. Always alone. Then the accompanying emotion roared up as if fighting for its own life and threw itself out of me. Tears streamed down my face, and my whole body shook. The monk put his hand onto my shoulder. 'Just accept it,' he said quietly. 'Accept the love.'

That made me cry even more because it wasn't love I was feeling at all. It was the feeling of *not* having been loved that had hit me between the eyes. I left the meditation to sit quietly in my room acknowledging that something had shifted. I spent the day walking around the grounds before settling back into my courtyard later in the afternoon. Why was I always little in these dreams, for instance? Why was I always invisible? Then insight hit. I was only ever praised for my achievements, and never the fact that *little me* just existed. I was not a miracle of life to my parents, someone they could look at, and go *wow, look what we made.* No, instead, I was invisible unless I made them *feel* proud. In a sense, I was their drug of choice, sustenance for when they craved pride and attention themselves. In later years, I had become convenient as well. A role of daughter who helped out, but gained no rights of character, from doing so. A daughter always waiting off stage, whilst an impersonator played her role.

This small insight allowed me to move further forward within the question. *What did I want?* The answer didn't come to me, complete with fanfare or rustling from the box-hedge. It was just a quiet realisation that started small and then grew bigger. It was simple.

I wanted to feel loved *just as me,* with all of my good bits and bad bits. It was as simple as that. I wanted to be seen to have grown from *little me* to *big me* with continuity and consistency as a daughter. I wanted my parents to recognise their traits in me so that I belonged as part of a lineage. I wanted them to feel joy from my existence. I wanted them to allow me to fail and that it wouldn't lessen the love they felt for me. I wanted to know that I was loved by the two people who had made me and the siblings around me.

The flip side was that I wanted to reciprocate love. I wanted to be able to look after them when they needed help. I wanted to phone them about the small stuff in their lives, such as how the alpacas were doing. I wanted them to allow me to see their vulnerabilities too. That's what I wanted. To be a part of the family that had made me.

There was anger welling too. Harry. The elephant in the room. I was angry that his name had been forgotten before it had been mentioned. I was perplexed as to how, two people could birth a child and then not feel anything in death. Nothing. Two cold, grey rocks.

I thought of my reality and how they would mock and shame me if they read these words of insight. They would laugh and then perhaps chew my show of feelings for days. Displays of vulnerability and emotional insight were banned, seen as signs of weakness. My words would be analysed to prove mental instability or perhaps indicate a form of self-loathing that might accompany a medical diagnosis.

I was invisible as a child and now as an adult. All I thought, was how much they would mock me for the insight that I had found. They were lost in amongst their endless raging about the world, and their blindness as to what stood at their feet. Their disappointment at life, and in life, was palpable. Their constant rejection of the real me was appalling. The minute I deviated from the version of me that suited them, I was punished, silenced and ignored. Fists, hands, words, doors slamming, silence and shaming. All for having been lucky enough to have been created by them.

I had chased their love, exhaustingly, mainly through phone calls and occasional visits during my adult life, but the conversations were bizarre at best. One-sided stories from their pasts that merged, and I, required only to be their audience. Maybe if they had an audience to listen to them, it provided them with a sense of existence? If I complained that they never dialled my number unless in an emergency, I was told that it was my responsibility to phone them. I couldn't remember the last time they had worried about me, every conversation centering around them. It was a mixed-up relationship with confusing rules and endless punishments. I admitted to myself that I was exhausted from trying. We just didn't speak the same language.

Why didn't I stop chasing their love, though? Was it a lack of courage? Was I too scared to see the truth, perhaps? Maybe it was because the little girl in me needed to hear something specific before she moved on? I started to cry there and then in the monastery garden, my mind opening like a lotus might, during a period of enlightenment.

Then I understood what the little girl needed. She knew she had been born, but now stood, alone, waiting off stage. What role was she supposed to play if she didn't know that she was 'enough' as she was? Where was the script for her? Instead, she would run onto the stage and get it wrong, only to be booed at, mocked, shamed and hit for getting it wrong. Every time she ventured onto the stage, she was hissed off. No wonder she felt so alone. She was waiting in the wings for something to change.

She needed to stand on the stage, alone. A spotlight just on her. There should be applause. Just because *she* was standing there. That's what she was waiting for. That was her script. It was a script that every human being was handed when souls were created. A right to stand on the earth feel as though you belonged and would be loved unconditionally by the people who had created you.

I articulated the thought aloud in that small garden, the sun shining on me, my skin warm, the angel as my witness.

'I am enough.'

I wanted to sit with the notion of *little me* for the afternoon. Metaphorically, the two of us could make a daisy chain perhaps. There would be no right or wrong, no pass or fail, and her daisy chain would be perfect because she was perfect. She could stand in the sun, and she would know that she was loved, as she was. At the end of the day, if my parents wanted to mock such innocence and purity, then what did it say about them?

I had been seeking love from people that didn't know what love was. It wasn't about control and hurt. Love was about belonging. Only they didn't know how to recognise it, and so I was on stage and off stage all the time, getting it wrong in their eyes. I needed to resign from their play and create my own, one in which there was just one part for me to play, *as me.* I smiled. I think I'd worked out what I wanted.

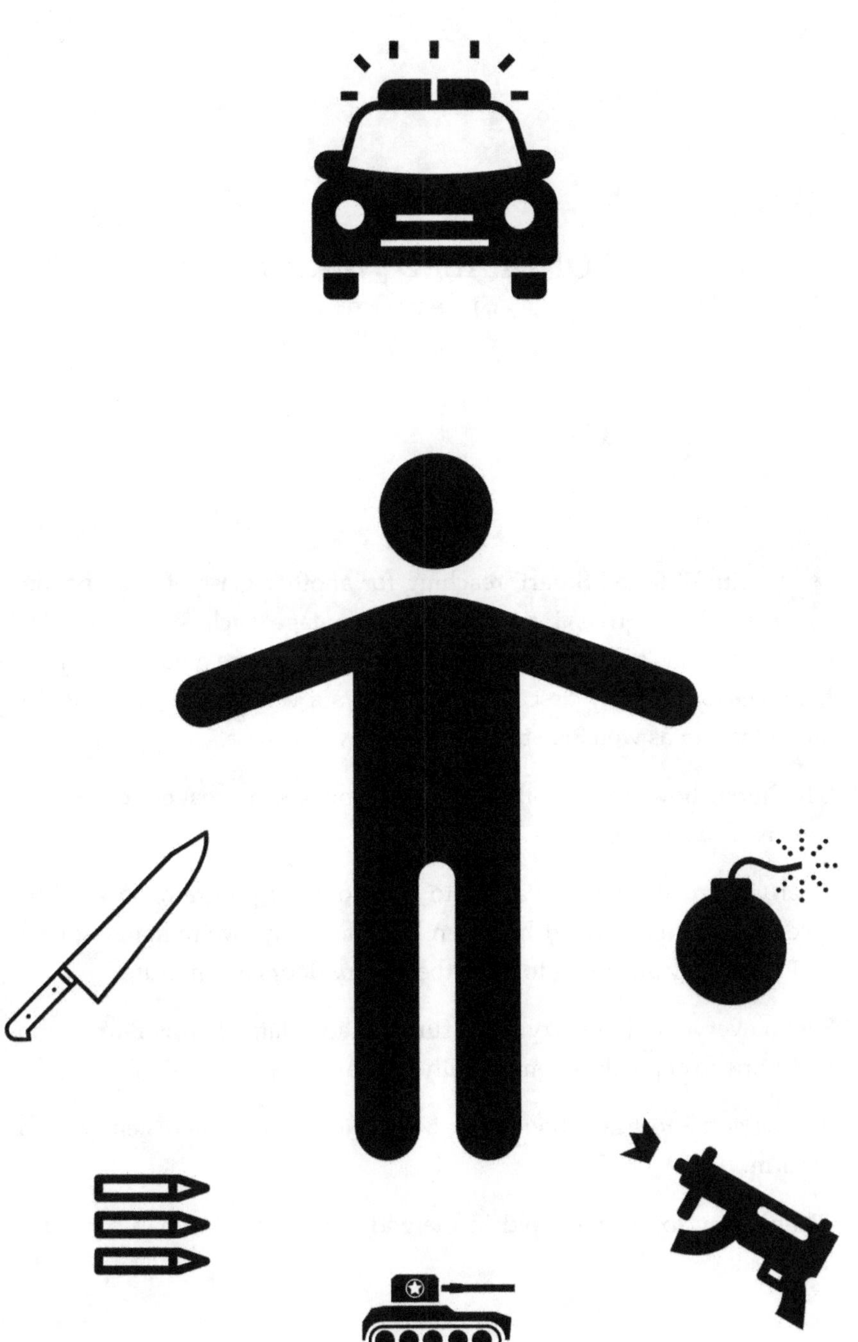

17

———

CONCEALED WEAPON

IN MY PANTS

'Excited?' asked Stuart, reaching for another glass of champagne. 'While it's free, I try to take advantage such situations.' He smiled a tipsy smile at me. 'You are about to see your art Pippa, hanging, for the very first time. It's always a very proud moment, for an art teacher as well.' He took a small bow.

'Hi Pippa, how good is this?' Jo had bounced in, eager to see her contribution, *Still life. Door*.

'Yeah, it's great. They are about to hand out the program, so we'll be able to see where our art has been hung and who we're hanging next to. I think they are going to open the gallery doors in a minute.'

'Hello everyone, I'm sorry to be running a bit late.' It was Barry, who had come to enjoy the evening with the class.

'I'm so sorry to hear about your Mum.' Jo put her hand gently onto his arm.

'Thank you, Jo. It was rapid in the end, thankfully. We had a service last week.'

'Oh, I'm sorry, Barry. Did your Mum not pull through her stroke?' I asked, feeling like I'd missed out on something important.

'No, she died last week. How's your Dad by the way?'

I didn't really know. The last conversation with my mother had been about home-delivered groceries from the local supermarket. When I had asked them if that was the same service that I'd recommended to her, my mother had laughed and said no. She had thought of it, not me. I presumed because I hadn't heard anything else, that everything was okay. I made up my reply to Barry because not knowing how my father was, seemed negligent.

I sipped my champagne, waiting for Noah. The past week had been confusing for me. Although we'd seen each other alone, I'd finally been able to see where he lived without his kids. It had been disappointing and a little confusing, as what I thought I knew, wasn't matching up with what Noah had been telling me.

'This isn't home exactly, my ex-wife is in that,' he said sadly. 'For now, though, this will have to do. We're still finalising the property settlement, but she's made it complicated, and it's been dragging on for longer than it should.'

'I thought you were already divorced?' I was surprised. He was still separated and not divorced?

'In every other aspect, we are. Won't be long, and then I can get out of this dump and back into a real family home again,' he said hopefully.

The moment reminded me of the day when I had stepped into Alan's flat. Instead of style, I had found a mess and a level of disorganisation that was begging to be sorted out. This was the same. How did Noah expect his children to live in a mess like this? What had happened to his nanny?

'Where do all the kids fit, when they are here?' I asked, looking around at the unpacked boxes, over-filled washing baskets and piles of rubbish with a sinking feeling.

'The boys have a bunk in the second bedroom. Double on the bottom for Steve, Seb on top, and Rose is in the other bedroom.'

'Does she mind having to sleep in a storeroom?'

I wondered if I should have called it that, but it was. Boxes and boxes of stuff up against the walls that hadn't been unpacked and little room for Rose to put her belongings anywhere. Her bed didn't have sheets on it either, and the mattress was filthy.

'It's only every second weekend, remember.'

'Oh,' I said, sounding confused. 'I thought you said you had them fifty percent of the time?'

He smiled. 'I used to. However, it just got too expensive with the nanny in the end, as I had so many launches in the evenings to attend, and Steve wasn't coping with all the changes. So, I decided that they would probably be better off with their mother during school time. No need for the nanny anymore either.'

'This must have happened recently?' I asked, not having heard about these changes. I was sure that when we'd met, he'd said that he had them fifty percent of the time.

'After I met you actually,' he said. 'Gives me a bit more time, just with you, and its calmed Steve down, a lot.'

I wasn't sure how I felt about that. I certainly didn't want to come in between Noah and his children, and nor did I want Emma to be overwhelmed on her own, with the kids.

'So...' I said, not knowing what else to say, and where to sit. The chairs and sofa were covered in papers, clothes and old pizza boxes. 'Hey, show me your art studio. I'd love to see it.' I'd remembered that he'd said he'd built one especially for his art.

Noah led me out into a small back garden. In one corner was a small garden shed. He slid the doors open and shone his phone light in. There was an easel in one corner on a concrete base and some paints in a small cardboard box in another. Down the other end was a lawnmower and some power tools.

'This is the art studio you built? Or is that over at the family home?' I was sure he'd said that he had built one and I had imagined a quaint studio at the bottom of a garden. My mistake at running away with a romantic imagination.

'This is the one I built.' he said proudly.

'Oh, okay. So, your boat? Do you keep that here on a trailer or is it moored somewhere?'

'My boat?' Noah sounded confused.

'The red one. That's in your painting.'

He smiled. 'Unfortunately, I had to let it go. Sold it recently. The cost of the mooring increased too much Pips.'

I made another small adjustment, understanding that Noah was unfolding into the person he was, and not the one I may have perceived him to be. If I had taken Brad and Cynthia's advice, then perhaps I wouldn't have to be adjusting. However, now wasn't the time to dwell on my mistakes, because Noah told me that we were going out for a 'romantic dinner' and that he had a surprise for dessert.

'I cannot wait to undress you later,' he said, drawing me in closer and placing delicate kisses onto my neck.

'Me too,' I said, starting to undo his buttons.

'No. Be good for now. I'll allow you to do what you want, later.'

Dinner was in a noisy pizza place. Not quite what I had imagined, but the food was good, and Noah was smiling, as if he had a secret to tell me.

'I cannot wait to show you the dessert,' he said beaming.

In my head, I was wondering what he'd lined up. I was hoping for a theatre show, a movie... maybe some live music somewhere? I'd mentioned that I liked live jazz, so perhaps we were heading into the city for that?

He slowed the car and parked.

'So, where are we going?' I asked, looking around. This wasn't a part of the city that I knew very well.

'Wait and see Miss Impatience.'

He walked up to a shop. 'XXX Delights' in hot pink lettering, was flashing in the window and plastic mannequins wore badly fitted lace outfits, with untidy wigs falling over their blank faces.

'Come on. I told you this would be good.'

I stared, making a quick mental adjustment. Was Noah taking me to a sex shop for dessert?

'So, how would you feel if I tied you up later?'

Jesus. He said that loud enough for a few people to look up at me. Was he serious? How would I feel being tied up? I suppose it depended on why he wanted to tie me up. I imagined industrial ropes, stockings, binder twine and razor wire.

'Pain or pleasure?' he asked.

Now I was imagining electrified, barbed wire. I must have changed my expression because he quickly added, 'pleasure Pippa. I'm joking.'

He put his arm around me and squeezed. 'Seriously, I would never hurt you, Pippa.'

'Yeah,' I said, relieved. I *could* be tied up for pleasure, but certainly not for pain.

Noah walked over to the bondage section, picking up toys that did this and that. It wasn't that I was uncomfortable in that sense, I just felt like the subject had never really been discussed between us. I'd imagined an evening of jazz, and he'd been imagining… well… to be honest, given some of the stuff he was holding up… I wasn't really sure.

'Electrified nipple clamps,' he grinned, holding them up. 'Now they would hurt.'

'Yeah,' I said, not wanting my nipples to experience pain at that moment. I imagined the voltage being too high and smoke coming from them. I could see myself arriving at emergency with smoking nipples and having to explain why.

'Are you comfortable here?' Noah asked, holding up some sort of strange medieval contraption.

No, I wasn't. This had come out of the blue. I had wanted to go and hear some jazz, not this. Was I boring? Maybe? However, Noah had never even hinted that he was into all of this. I was mentally trying to catch up.

'Yeah, this is cool, Noah,' I said lying, trying to find the positive.

'Sorry, Pips, I must have misread things. Look, I'll just buy a few things for myself then, shall I?'

'No, it's fine.' I had upset him with my prudish reaction, and now I was saying things to make him feel better because he looked devastated that he had missed the mark.

'It's fine. It's honestly fine.'

There was a bit of awkward silence in the car on the way back.

'Did I shock you with what I bought or something?' he asked. 'You seem a bit quiet.'

'No, of course not. I just wasn't expecting that for dessert. It's fine, really Noah. I was just… surprised.'

He placed his new toys onto the kitchen counter and poured some wine.

'You seem a little out of sorts, Pips. Anything wrong? How's your Dad, by the way?'

'Do you want the long version or the short version?' I said, suddenly feeling the need to be upfront about everything. The toys on the counter seemed a worse option than my truth at that moment, so the extended version might be the better choice.

'The long version, angel. Let's sit down, drink some wine and just chill. You talk, and I'll listen. How does that sound?'

The wine allowed my truth to flow, and I opened up. I told him everything about my family, and after I had finished, he just nodded and then held his arms out for me to fall into, reassuring me that everything was going to be okay. I loved him even more at that moment because he'd accepted my truth, and had loved me for it. We had sex that night, that was still as passionate and time-bending as the first time, although I insisted that the toys stay on the counter, for the time being.

'I'm sorry, Pippa. I'll put them away and leave them in a dark cupboard. Okay?' He laughed at his own mistake.

There was no denying that when I was in Noah's arms, I was where I was supposed to be.

'PIPPA… SERIOUSLY?'

'What now, Brad?'

'This is reading like one of those dreadful romance novels that you can buy for $1.99 on Amazon. Did he have a white stallion tethered in the garden too? Near his art studio?'

'Haha. It *was* like that, though. It was lovely when it was just the two of us. Really lovely.'

'Yeah, but what about his kids? You weren't just two. You were five.'

'I know. I made a line down the middle though. The half with the two of us was perfect.'

'Perfect? If you say so. So, you told him all of that stuff about your family after he's just decided that a sex shop was dessert and you discover his house is filthy, he isn't divorced, his kids have all-but disappeared, as has his nanny and his boat? He holds his arms out, and you then fall into them?'

'Why? What's wrong with that?'

'Everything, including that last paragraph. Vomit Pippa. Vomit.'

'Harsh.'

STUART HURRIED towards me. 'Oh my god, Pippa. You're not going to believe this. Guess who they have put your painting next to? Guess! Guess!' Stuart was bursting with excitement.

'Who?' I asked.

'Ken Done. I'm not joking! I'm so, not bull shitting you!'

'For real? Ken Done! Really?'

'Yes, follow.' He ran off, slightly lopsided from all the champagne.

I stood there, along with other milling arty-farts, and there was my painting. Yellow canvas with streaks of blue, 'Tears of Hope.' It looked good next to the Ken Done artwork, as our colour palettes seemed to understand each other.

'Goodness,' I said, thinking that anything could be called art if framed and hung from a hook. Even if only yellow with blue streaks.

'You must be so proud,' Jo said, standing next to me. 'This is the main section of the gallery, and you're next to a Ken Done. You've officially made it.'

I laughed. 'Where, though? Where have I made it to? Where's your work, Jo?'

'Over in the far-left corner, near the door. Noah got next to a Blankley in the back section.'

'Is he here then?'

'Yeah, he's stuck though, discussing art with the exhibition organiser.'

'I might go and catch up with him,' I said, as innocently as I could.

Noah looked at me, begging to be released from the organiser's grip, a man vividly describing the artistic processes involved in creating the exhibition poster.

'Hi… Noah, excuse me,' I said, smiling. 'I'm so sorry to interrupt, but Stuart needs some help.'

'Sorry, Bob, I'll catch you later,' Noah said, hurrying away from him. 'Thank you. I was beginning to feel like I was passing out. The man just wouldn't stop talking.'

'So, you're next to a Blankley? Show me.'

Noah stood proudly in front of his painting and asked me to take a photo. 'I have to tell you something, by the way,' he said, 'after you take the pic.'

'What?' I asked, pressing send on my phone. 'You should get that in a sec. Tell me if you want another one done.'

'I had to buy a new pair of pants for this evening, right?'

'Nice' I said, looking at them.

'Okay, this is super weird. See the bottom of them?' He pointed to the bottom of his trousers.

'Yeah?' I wasn't sure where this was going.

'I needed to hem them, so popped out to get some pins. So, I parked at the main centre, then walked across the road to that park, you know, near that school? I bought them, and then I was putting the pins in, innocently enough, and the next minute, this police car pulls up.'

'Why?' I asked, concerned.

'They got out, and two officers walked towards me. I was shitting myself.'

'Why?' I still wasn't clear as to where his story was going.

'They saw me messing with my trouser legs and then asked - are you ready for this? They asked if I had a concealed weapon up there.'

'What? Up where?'

'A concealed weapon up my pants! Is this America now or what?'

'So, they were just driving along and saw you were pinning the bottoms of your pants up, and then they stopped? Thinking that you had… what up there?' I was confused.

'A knife, I suppose, or a gun perhaps?'

'Really? Why would they do that? You don't look like the type of person to be doing that? Wasn't it obvious you were pinning your trousers?'

'Yeah. It's bizarre, isn't it?'

'Yes, Noah. Weird.' I shook my head. That was strange behaviour from the police. I felt sorry for Noah as the humiliation of being searched like that must have been awful. I'd never heard of it happening to anyone else.

'So where are you?' he asked, looking around towards the back of the gallery.

'This way,' I said, pointing to the front. I led him to my work, which had a small crowd of people in front of it, as everyone wanted to admire the original Ken Done next to it.

'Wow,' he said. 'A few weeks into an art class and you got next to Ken Done?'

'I think art is very subjective, I mean, Done's work is brilliant. Mine well… isn't quite at the same standard.'

'I bet Louise is here,' he said, looking around. 'Just to see where they put your work. She will be livid seeing this.'

'I doubt it.' I said. 'She would only have come if her chickens had made it in.'

Jo ran up. 'Want a photo next to a Ken Done, Pippa?'

'Yes, thanks.' I liked Jo. She was one of the warmest people I'd met in a long time and the only person who would wear a red set of overalls to a gallery opening night.

'WHO WOULD DO THIS?' I asked, running my hand down the side of my car. 'It's been keyed.' I looked in dismay at my car. I'd bought it new the year before, on a lease and I had looked after it so carefully. Now it had two broken headlights, and someone had walked around the outside of it, dragging something sharp into it.

Noah shook his head. 'Look, there's a note on the windscreen.'

'What does it say?'

'Be warned, move your fucking car next time, or I'll ram it. You parked way too close to mine.'

'So, the person who parked next to me wrote that?' I looked around. 'That makes no sense. The only other car was yours, Noah, when I arrived. Have you moved yours?' I looked around, wondering where his car had gone.

'Yeah, I had to pop out to get the pins for my pants, remember? I parked around the front on the way back. That's pretty low, Pips. Are you insured?' Noah put his hand onto my shoulder, comforting me.

'Yeah, luckily, although there is the excess to pay. I think it's about $500.' I inwardly groaned. I didn't have $500 lying around, to waste.

'They must have done it while we were all inside looking at the art,' said Jo, shaking her head at the damage.

'Are there any cameras around?' I asked.

'There's one over there,' said Noah looking around, 'but it would have to have night vision. I can go in and ask Bob if he knows.'

Bob was concerned. 'In all the years we've been running the art show, this has never happened. It must have been done by someone jealous that you got your painting next to Ken Done, Pippa. Or maybe it was just random? Someone who felt angry and took it out on you?'

'What about the camera, Bob. Does it work?' Noah looked up at it. 'It was facing in the right direction.'

'No, remember I was telling you about the graffiti issues we were having at night? This is the camera. Day vision only, I'm afraid. We thought it might act as a deterrent, obviously not. It gets switched off at 5 pm each day.'

'I can't believe someone would have done that' I said to Noah, 'and without any cameras, I'll never know who it was.'

'It was a low act, that's for sure,' he said, scrunching up the note angrily and putting it in the bin. 'Sometimes, people just make me so pissed off, Pippa.'

'Yeah' I said. 'Me too.'

Go to jail. Here are some flowers. I love you. I hate you.

18

EGNASSA

AND TERRORISTS

We were enjoying a Friday night discourse over dessert, at my flat. The sort that rambles and jumps from one topic to another. Sometimes friendly and at other times we would be talking over each other, trying to make our points heard. I had roasted a chicken, some baked potatoes and had poured a mellow Cabernet Sauvignon. The table was lit with candle light. Noah had melted into the atmosphere, his blue eyes reflecting the candle flame back to me. I enjoyed spoiling him, not minding the effort after a long day at work. Somehow, it helped me to unwind too.

As I'd placed the steaming, hot apple pie dessert onto the table, the conversation had fallen onto the topic of Egnassa, a man being held in jail, awaiting trial for releasing Government secrets to the public.

'I think if the intention was transparency, for the good of the people, then releasing them should be seen as a service.' I ventured.

'You think that? For real?' Noah had asked defiantly, sculling back his wine and pouring another.

'Yeah, I mean, this information was about the murder of innocent men, and a government cover-up, wasn't it? Who is at fault at the end of the day? Not Egnassa, surely.'

'Depends on his motives. Stupid to release data that puts operatives at risk don't you think?'

'I agree on that part,' I said, nodding, thoughtfully.

'He's a terrorist though, Pippa.'

'Who is a terrorist?' I looked at Noah to see if he was taking the piss. He seemed angry.

'Egnassa.'

'How can Egnassa be the terrorist? He's the one exposing pissy behaviours.' I poured myself another glass of wine. 'I once belonged to an Egnassa support group. Didn't do much with it from memory. They never actually sent me any emails. Thought was there, though.'

'Well, that makes you a terrorist as well.'

I laughed. 'Yeah, I'm really a terrorist, Noah. I make bombs in my garage for fun.' I paused, lowering my voice. 'I can't say the word bomb, can I? Isn't that against sedition laws? I think I can be locked up for a month with no legal representation for doing that?'

'It's not funny, Pippa. There are laws for terrorists. You should be reported to the Federal Police for that.'

I stopped and stared at Noah. 'For what? For making bombs in my garage, or saying the word bomb?' I laughed again, at the thought.

'No. For supporting a known terrorist.'

'Are you being serious?' I stared at him.

'Yes. Of course. Why wouldn't I be being serious?' He stared at me without blinking.

'You would report me for being a terrorist, because I joined an email support group for Egnassa, and then happily see me go to actual jail?'

'Absolutely. The man is a terrorist, and anyone who supports him is also a terrorist.'

'Noah… I'm confused. Are you taking the piss right now?' He was talking matter of factly, and his tone was cold - like he was speaking in a straight line. 'It's not illegal to support him. That's called free speech. Why would you want me to go to jail anyway?'

'Well, if you are supporting him, then you deserve to go to jail.'

I stopped and stared. Noah was being serious and not mucking around. The problem was his tone. It hadn't changed. I couldn't read him. Was he trying to be deadpan funny, perhaps?

'I'm going to go for a shower before bed.' I said, trying to diffuse the apparent tension.

I stood under the hot running water, trying to get my head around what had just transpired. What was that? I had no idea how to process it. Was he genuinely being serious? Maybe he'd had too much to drink? We had managed to get through a bottle and a half of wine between us, and he'd drunk most of it. It had to be the alcohol talking. There had been the story about the concealed weapon the other day, too though. Both had thrown me off-kilter.

'Bed?' I suggested, returning to the table, lightly touching him on the arm.

He winced and rubbed it as if I'd banged into him. 'Sure,' he said. 'That hurt.'

'Sorry.'

'Tell me you weren't serious, Noah?' I snuggled up against him in the bed.

'I was serious. I should report you to the Federal Police.'

'You're not making sense,' I said, sounding frustrated.

'Nor do you sometimes,' he retorted back, his tone still as even as wire. 'I'm entitled to my opinion,' he stated. He rolled over, facing the other way from me as if we'd argued.

'I think we need to discuss this,' I said quietly.

'No, we don't,' he snapped. 'I'm tired, and I need to sleep Pippa.'

'Noah, this isn't making any sense.'

'What? That I actually have a different opinion to you for once? No, you aren't making sense. I think you need to be quiet for a bit.'

I hugged myself tightly and held my breath. The sudden coldness of his tone was scaring me. What had just happened? How could I now be a terrorist? I made no sound, silent tears trickling onto my pillow. I didn't want Noah to hear how upset he had made me feel. Who was this Noah in my bed?

THE NEXT MORNING, he woke me with bacon, eggs, and freshly brewed coffee.

'We should go for another drive,' he said, smiling. 'There's a lake walk that might be nice to do? Just the two of us. It's beautiful weather out there today.'

I stared at him. This was the same man who had wanted to have me arrested for being a terrorist the night before.

'Okay,' I said quietly. 'Do you want to talk about what happened last night?' The air needed clearing.

'Why? It was nothing. You're not still going on about that, are you?'

'No. Of course not.' I heard myself utter those words, and they felt false. I was appeasing him, hoping that he wouldn't get angry again. Maybe he'd just had too much to drink, I reassured myself? There was a little daisy that he had picked from the flats' front garden, on the breakfast tray, after all. It was a sweet gesture.

'Let's just go and have a great day. How does that sound?' he suggested, sounding as if he just wanted to move on from it all.

I chatted as we drove, about nothing in particular, until Noah interrupted me.

'You talk too much, Pippa. I just timed you. A hundred and ninety seconds without taking a break in fact.'

'Sorry?' I was taken aback. Was he joking?

'You need to allow for silence in the car.'

His words stung me, and I retreated into silence, staring out of the car window. He pulled up to a large home and beeped.

'Where are we?' I asked.

'We're taking the kids for the weekend. It's my turn, remember? I mentioned it earlier. We'll take them to the lake with us, and hopefully, get them to burn off some energy. Then we can go back to my place. How does that sound as a plan?'

Had I wholly misheard him? Was it his turn for the kids?

'Sorry, I thought *we* were just going for a drive.'

'No, I said it was all of us.'

I shook my head. I felt like I was going mad. Then I heard myself say 'No worries. That sounds good.'

The kids were sent out of the front door with their backpacks while a woman, whom I'm presuming was Emma, hid herself behind the door. The kids ran to the car with Seb and Steve having their usual fight about who would sit next to the window.

'Hiya, everyone. How are we today?' I asked, smiling.

'I'm okay, Pippa,' said Rose, smiling back, before looking out of the window.

'Get off me!' shouted Seb from the back. Steve punched him hard on the leg.

'OW!' screamed Seb, starting to sob. 'Steve punched me.'

'I did NOT punch you. You touched my leg!' shouted Steve, now dragging Seb out of the car.

'I want the window SEAT!' Seb got back into the car, and Steve pulled on his legs. Seb fell out of the car, and Steve quickly jumped in. Seb then jumped on top of Steve.

'I was there, FIRST!' Seb yelled. Steve punched Seb hard on the arm, resulting in Seb screaming in pain. Noah reached around and grabbed Steve's arm, hard.

'Stop it!' he shouted through gritted teeth. 'Just fucking stop it!'

The children went quiet. Steve sat in the middle, refusing to speak and Seb calmed and did up his seatbelt next to the window. Then he sat looking out, smiling.

Noah seemed stressed, breathing heavily as we drove away. I started to speak to lighten the mood.

'You need to shut up,' said Seb from the back.

'Excuse me?' I asked in surprise. I turned around to look at him, and he was grinning. I smiled back, wanting to diffuse the tension in the car. 'That's not a very nice thing to say, Seb.'

'I know,' he said in a little sing-song voice, 'but it's true. Daddy said so. He says that you talk, talk, talk, talk, talk, too much!'

I turned to Noah, waiting for him to say something. He stared straight ahead. 'Noah, your son just told me to shut up.'

'… and why would he have done that, Pippa?'

'It's a bit rude.'

'Maybe you needed to shut up for once?'

I looked out of the window, humiliated. What the hell was going on?

'We'll stop off by the house for a bit before we go to the lake,' he said.

The house was even messier than it had been on previous visits. The boys took over the sofa and played noisy video games. Noah joined them. I was left to entertain Rose, and I sat and braided her hair. Several hours passed, with Noah refusing to speak to me. I didn't know what I had done to anger him so much, my mind replaying the dinner from the night before. It had been fine until I'd mentioned Egnassa. Maybe the subject of Egnassa had a history with him? He was certainly acting as if it did.

I left early, realising that there would be no walk at the lake, and made my way back home by bus. I didn't feel welcome and didn't know why everything had changed so much. Right now, I needed to get some advice from Brad, but I already knew what he would say. He would say that Noah had overstepped the line between what is acceptable and what isn't. I decided to leave Brad out of it all. I would need to work through this myself. Something was wrong with Noah, that much I understood. I curled up in bed, just after dinner and had just put the light off when my phone beeped. Noah had sent a text.

N: Sometimes, the boys are so hard. I want to drive into a tree.

P: ??? Are you okay? Where are you?

N: It's just so hard, Pippa… my life with Steve. I can't ever go anywhere and just have a typical day. He's always so angry about everything, especially now that I'm seeing you.

P: Are you in the car now?

N: No. I have the kids remember. I'm at home.

P: What do you need me to do right now, Noah?

N: Stay in touch tonight? Can we talk later? It would be nice to know that you are at the end of the phone for me.

P: Yes, of course, xxx

N: I love you, Pips.

He had said it. He loved me. In the middle of all of this, he loved me. Despite everything he had said about terrorists and me talking too much, he loved me, after all. I felt a weight lifting, reassured that everything was going to be okay.

P: I love you too, Noah.

He phoned at midnight, waking me from a deep sleep.

'I feel depressed, to be honest, Pippa.'

'What's happened? You're not in the car, are you?'

'No. It's just life Pips. Sometimes I just feel suffocated. Take Steve. He's not doing well at school. I'm constantly being contacted about behavioural issues that he's having. Seb is acting out, and Rose just seems to have disappeared into herself. I want to divorce my wife, but it means selling our investment property. We've got a block of flats in Brisbane, and the market is complicated at the moment. Not the best time to sell. That's why we're arguing so much.'

I didn't know what to say. Maybe this is why he'd been so impatient with me? Perhaps the stress had got to him? I should allow people to be imperfect, I thought. After all, he was brutally honest with me. If I rejected him, then I was no better than my parents, wasn't I? Surely, everyone has the right to mess up occasionally? I decided to take a deep breath and help him work through whatever was bothering him.

'So, she wants to sell the block of flats and the Sydney house?'

'Yeah. Then she wants to head back to Brisbane with the kids. I feel guilty that I didn't do more to help with her depression, but I'm not having her taking the kids away.'

'There's a lot on your plate, Noah. Do you think you should see someone… a professional perhaps?'

'Maybe?'

'I think you should. I can do my best to help, but some of the stuff you are talking about sounds pretty serious.'

'I'm sorry that I'm such a fuck-up Pips. I don't mean to be a disappointment.'

'You aren't a fuck-up Noah.'

'Yes, I am. I've completely fucked up my life. Look at me. Getting overweight and unhappy… and ruining us. I don't want to ruin us Pips. You're everything that I've been looking for. Attractive, intelligent and creative. The kids love you.'

'Look, I love the way you deal with the kids, aside from in the car earlier. That wasn't your proudest moment. You're good with them. Don't beat yourself up too much. I think you are a terrific father. I really do, Noah.'

'I appreciate you saying that Pips. I don't often get told that.'

He started to cry, sobbing into the phone. I could feel his pain as if it were my own. I just wanted to bundle him up in my arms. I wanted his pain to stop. This man was confiding in me, baring his soul and allowing me to see him at his most vulnerable. I wasn't capable of rejecting him in such circumstances. He kept telling me that he didn't feel safe around himself. I would stay awake to ensure that he was safe too. Eventually, he calmed and fell asleep, and I could hear him snoring on the other end of the phone. I managed to follow him at around four.

I PHONED him the next morning after I awoke.

'Just checking in. How are you feeling?'

'Still depressed, surprisingly enough. Still wanting to kill myself. Steve was up at five playing video games, so I only got a couple of hours sleep.'

'Yeah, I'm a bit tired too. Hey, I was doing some thinking. Maybe you should go on a course of antidepressants if you are like, really depressed?'

'Really?' he said, in a tone that made the hairs on the back of my neck stand up.

'Yeah, you mentioned feeling suicidal. That's kind of serious.' I said quietly, knowing that I'd said the wrong thing, yet again.

'Look, with respect Pippa, you're not a doctor. You are a travel agent who knows nothing about medicine. You don't know what you're talking about, so don't get involved with that side of things.'

I was surprised that he was telling me not to get involved after staying on the phone with me half the night, telling me he'd been suicidal and saying that he needed me.

'Don't get involved like that? I'm sorry.' I wanted his anger to go away. I would apologise until his voice sounded normal again.

'Just don't interfere. Okay?' He still sounded annoyed with me.

'Sure. I hope you have a better day.'

I felt physically sick coming off the phone and confused. He'd spent hours on the phone discussing how suicidal he'd felt. I felt involved… hadn't he made me involved already? How was suggesting a course of antidepressants the wrong thing to do? However, I wasn't medically trained, so perhaps he was right? I felt like I was being spun around a bit by what he was saying and doing, though.

That evening, after he'd dropped the kids back off with Emma, he phoned. I felt relief seeing his number appear, as he'd been quiet all day and I'd been concerned about how he was feeling. I didn't know how much contact he wanted, especially given the threats about driving into the tree.

'I had the weirdest experience today,' he said, chuckling and sounding much happier.

'Tell me all,' I said, glad to hear him feeling better and speaking with a more positive tone.

'The kids and I were just in the grocery store, and we were trying to get up the aisle and past this woman. She was massive. Anyway, I stood there for a while, and she just wouldn't move. I tapped her heels with the trolley, disgusting they were too… cracked and yellow. She had these filthy thongs on.'

'Gross,' I said, imagining the heels he was portraying.

'Anyway, she wouldn't move, and so I knocked her over with the trolley.' He started laughing as if he'd just told me the punch line to a joke.

'Sorry?' I was shocked. 'You knocked her over, as in… onto the ground?'

'Yeah, it was so funny because she couldn't get up.' He was laughing.

'What? Did you leave her on the ground? Noah, what were the kids doing?' I was appalled.

'Laughing, it was hilarious. Anyway, I was then standing in the cashier line when the store manager came up to me and said he was calling the police on me. I explained what had happened, told them I could cause more trouble if they wanted to go down that route, and he backed down. I intimidated him, right? Then, they said they would let it go.'

'Noah, that just sounds odd.' I was concerned.

'Odd? How is that odd? She wouldn't get out of the way!'

'So, you literally knocked her to the ground? Was she hurt?'

'No idea. Too funny, isn't it.'

I paused as my head was spinning. Noah had knocked someone to the ground, and he thought it was funny? There was nothing funny about assaulting someone, especially in front of his kids.

'So, did I tell you about when I used to fish at the beach?' He asked, changing the subject.

'Sorry, Noah, I've got something on tonight, I have to go.'

'Oh,' he sounded disappointed. There was that tone in his voice again. I panicked. 'Later then?' he asked hopefully.

'Yeah, sure. It was nice to hear from you, I'm glad you're feeling happier.'

I winced from my own words. I just wanted Noah to stay as nice Noah, the one I had met initially.

'I'll check in on you later. Bye, Pips. I love you.'

'I love you too, Noah.' I heard the words coming from my mouth. It seemed more comfortable to say them than to explain why I wasn't saying them.

I went to bed and curled up. I didn't believe the story he had told me. It didn't sound real. However, why would he tell me something like that? It made no sense. I googled the issue and didn't find anything helpful. What was going on? What was I supposed to do? Just walk? I felt my heart sinking at the thought of having to end things so abruptly. Surely there was a way to fix this? I expected him to check in on me before he went to bed, as he'd promised, but he must have been exhausted himself, as my phone remained silent.

THE NEXT EVENING, there was a knock on my door. It was Noah, hiding behind a massive bunch of yellow gerberas.

'I thought I'd pop in and surprise my beautiful girlfriend.'

'These are gorgeous, my favourite colour,' I said, putting the flowers into some water. 'A surprise visit in the middle of the week? I feel honoured. Are you feeling a bit better then?'

I could tell he was, by the tone of his voice. 'Yeah, fine. I thought we could just snuggle and watch a movie, perhaps? Then, if it's okay, I might stay the night? If you'll have me? I've been a bit of an arse lately, and this is my effort to make it up to you.'

I wondered what to say. This was unfamiliar territory. He was apologising for being unkind. I was supposed to forgive him, I think?

Isn't that what you are supposed to do if someone shows enough insight to apologise? No-one had ever apologised to me for being unkind before.

'No Pippa.' It was Brad again.

'You can't keep jumping in Brad. I told you before. I just need the story to unfold.

'Yeah… but Pippa. This was *the* moment.'

'What moment?'

'The one that counted in all of this.'

'Why?'

'If someone abuses you, you walk away. That's why.'

'Yeah, but I didn't know that, at this moment in time.'

'I know what you're going to do.'

'Do you?'

'Yeah. This was your sliding door moment with Noah.'

Noah walked towards me and kissed me. I sighed. There was something about his kisses that made me feel reassured. It was as if the anxiety I felt about our relationship falling apart, and his nasty tone, silenced when I was in that space. I wanted that feeling again. To be loved, to be held…

'Selling one's soul.'

'I didn't say that?' Brad sounded surprised that someone had spoken.

'No, that was me, speaking out aloud.'

'Thank god for that. It seemed a bit harsh for a life coach.'

'It's true. I sold my soul to feel loved. I can see that. It's pathetic. I am pathetic.'

We settled down on the sofa to watch a French movie with subtitles. I sat, and he lay with his head on my lap, obviously needing some attention. I stroked his head gently and felt him relaxing into me, and soon heard the familiar sound of his snoring. Carefully, I raised myself, so as not to disturb him, and laid the throw rug over him. He looked cute, I thought, all snuggled up. He looked safe. I felt like I had done the right thing to look after him. He was a human being in need of a safe harbour, and I was able to provide that for him.

I went around, getting everything sorted for the night, washing up, locking windows and closing blinds. Then I got my clothes ready for the morning. I tiptoed around, not wanting to wake him. He must be exhausted from all the recent depression, I surmised.

He tapped me on the shoulder in the kitchen, making me jump.

'Well, thanks for ruining the movie,' he said with a fake smile.

'Ruining the movie? Sorry? I don't follow.'

'I was enjoying it. Why did you switch it off?'

'You were asleep, Noah… snoring.' I laughed.

'Only for a moment. Why would you switch it off?' He wasn't laughing.

'It wasn't a moment.' I looked up at the kitchen clock, working it out. 'It was for forty minutes.' My smile faded from my face.

'Pippa. Lying doesn't suit you.' There was that voice again. One etched in disappointment and reeking of scathing.

'Sorry, Noah. Honestly, I thought you had been asleep. I put the throw on you… how about we watch it again sometime?' I asked, hopefully.

'No. I don't want to watch that one now. You've ruined it.'

'I'm sorry,' I said, hugging him. I felt him soften, slightly.

That night in bed, he was more attentive than he had been in weeks.

'You smell like heaven,' he said, kissing my neck. 'I love every part of you, Pippa O'Shea. Every single bit of you. You are my everything.' Then he wrapped me in his arms and held me all night, exactly how I liked.

'Huh? I'm confused,' says Brad.

'So am I.'

DURING THE FOLLOWING WEEKS, I became alarmed at the stories that Noah was telling me each evening over the phone. I was becoming exhausted from his late-night phone calls that often went until three in the morning. Some days he claimed to be depressed and wanted to drive into a tree, and on others, he was sick and needed to see a doctor.

He went onto depression meds and then came off them, the withdrawals causing more issues for him. I couldn't keep up with each crisis. However, there were now strict rules I had to follow. I wasn't allowed to offer any medical advice, the sort of stuff I might have searched online, to help him with. I was starting to say less and less and only say things that I thought he might approve of. I was afraid of disappointing him, and I was scared of the cold tone he used, when angry with me.

As he recounted all of his untrue recounts, I started to notice that the pitch of his voice went up slightly, and he would speak more quickly than usual. I wonder why he was telling me so many lies.

The previous evening he'd been telling me about his childhood and how his neighbour had popped over to give them some leftovers from a BBQ. She had brought their dog with them, the same breed of dog as one I'd had when I was a kid. That was unusual, as we'd had a relatively rare crossbreed of Labrador and Husky that had chased the alpacas all the time. The Labsky had lunged at Noah, and the woman had panicked. She picked up a vase that had been nearby and then had repeatedly hit the dog on the head until it had died.

'Until it died?' I asked, shocked. 'She killed her own dog?'

'Yeah, I've had a fear of dogs ever since,' he said.

This evening, he'd claimed that a woman had accused him of looking like a terrorist in the department store, earlier on in the day, because of his beard, in the toy section.

'But you only have a small beard… you don't look anything like a terrorist.' I'd said, wondering what a terrorist was supposed to be doing in the toy section of a department store in Australia, and what they were supposed to look like.

'I do look like a terrorist. To her, anyway. I was so embarrassed standing there while she was making all of those accusations, though. Everyone was watching.'

On Saturday, he claimed to have been given a phone number by one of the store's young, female cashiers.

'Really? Why? I've never heard of that. Why would the cashier write their number down onto the receipt?' I asked, surprised.

'Well, she asked me if I was single.'

'At the checkout?'

'Yeah. She was looking for a ring on my hand, I could tell.'

'So, what did you say?'

'The truth. I told her I was separated from my wife.'

My mind started racing. 'You didn't say you were in a relationship with me?'

'No. Why?'

'So, what did she do then?'

'Got out a pen and wrote down her number on the receipt.'

'Did you have the kids with you?'

'Yeah.'

'So, you had three kids with you, including Steve, and she gave you her number?' I wondered if she'd been a social worker, working a second job? Maybe she saw three kids with issues in front of her? 'So, why, Noah? Why would she have written down her number?'

'Sex, I imagine. Yeah, sex,' he said confidently.

'Can I see the receipt with the number?'

'I threw it away, of course!' he said. 'I'm with you, Pips. I'm happy with you.'

Then he said that two colleagues had approached him for group sex at work.

'How old were they?' I asked. I thought he would say in their seventies, and that it had been a joke.

'Fifteen and Sixteen. Work experience girls.'

'What? How did you get around to talking about sex at work in front of kids?'

'It happens,' he said. 'I didn't agree to it, though. Obviously.'

'I would hope not, it's illegal' I said.

I began to have serious niggles about Noah. These stories were getting more and more bizarre, and they didn't ring true. When I asked for details, though, he seemed convincing. He always maintained eye contact with me when speaking in person, and that was one of the signs that someone was telling the truth, wasn't it?

A RANDOM
PIC OF A
NAKED TRUCK
DRIVER WAS
SENT TO ME

19

PICS AND TRUCK DRIVERS
IT'S JUST NOT RIGHT

The one thing I hadn't yet done was google Noah. Maybe it was time to see what was out there? I punched in his name, and a few of the usual sites came up such as Facebook, Linkedin and Twitter… nothing too exciting. There were a few pics of the kids, and some tweets about his advertising campaigns from the company website, but nothing that seemed out of the ordinary. He was the same character online, as he was in real life. I felt reassured and even a bit silly. Perhaps I was reading too much into things and needed to 'calm my farm?'

Later in the week, a text came through from Noah with a pic.

N: What do you think of this?

I had to stop and take a second look at the image confronting my face. It was a photo of another man's genitals. No face, no name, just a full frontal.

P: What is this???

N: I've got us a threesome.

P: What??????????

N: This dude is a truck driver. He's passing through Sydney this weekend. He liked my pic.

P: What pic???

Another photo came through of Noah's privates.

P: Why are you sending dick pics to a truck driver?

N: Remember? Want to be a part of something amazing?

P: ????????

N: Why so surprised? You said you wanted to have a threesome.

P: No?? I didn't? That dude is like sixty-five!

N: You did. Maybe you were drunk. Look, I haven't mentioned this before, but check out my private Instagram. It might get you inspired, Ad80dude. Password. Flow4069.

I was shocked. Had I been drunk and not known what I was saying? I didn't think I even had been drunk in front of him, as I rarely drank enough to get drunk. I had never wanted group sex, aside from a fleeting thought years ago, as Jane had gone off with those sailors. I'd certainly never hinted at wanting group sex with some random truck driver! I typed in the username and password for Noah's Instagram account and then held my breath. A page appeared with pictures of women. Most of them were pretty graphic and unpleasant as if the women were in pain. It didn't take a brain surgeon to see what he'd wanted in the sex shop that evening. Maybe I'd sent out the wrong signals, I wasn't sure.

I googled the name Ad80dude, and another site came up. Ad80dude was a member of this site, but I couldn't gain access and gain more information unless I joined as well. I created a fake ID, calling myself '3not2girl' and logged in. Whomever Ad80dude was, they had been writing a lot of posts in one of the forums. For what though? I opened one of them, called *'Break me'* and started reading. My stomach heaved. These posts were reviews for experiences with prostitutes, male and female.

Was this Noah? Had Noah been sleeping with all of these prostitutes and leaving reviews? I read through some of them but wasn't convinced it was him. This guy was violent in the reviews… degrading even. Maybe there was another Ad80dude out there? I sat back, feeling overwhelmed and confused. There was the group sex issue to deal with right now, as well as the fact that he was waiting to see what I thought of his Instagram. I sent him a text, not wanting to inflame the situation, but my mind was scrambling.

P: Yeah, saw your stuff. Interesting. I'm sorry we got our wires crossed. I don't want to have group sex right now.

N: It's okay, Pippa, honestly. Must have been a communication issue. You should start your own Instagram account. Show me what you like. Yeah? You can do it and be anon.

P: Maybe? Glad we sorted that out.

I was relieved he had taken my rejection so well. He hadn't got angry with me, or seemed humiliated that he'd sent his own pic out there to a stranger. It must have been a simple misunderstanding between us, although I couldn't figure out when the mistake had been made. As for the reviews of the prostitutes? That couldn't be him, I was certain. Judging by the dates, he would have been sneaking out of the family home with his kids asleep in their beds, to sleep with prostitutes, right under Emma's nose. I say sleep, but that's not what was happening. The reviews were way too nasty to be Noah. It made no sense.

BRAD WAS CONCERNED. He put his coffee down and lowered his voice so that the people at the next table didn't hear him.

'Pippa, come on. Red flags are flapping in the wind… in your face here.'

I'd only told him a slice of it… how Noah had become angry with me. I was too worried as to what he would say if I told him the rest.

'None of those times are times where anger was even remotely appropriate. Telling you to shut up? Allowing his nine-year-old son to tell you to shut up? Charming.' Brad shook his head.

'He was suicidal on that day… so…'

'So what? If he was suicidal, then he should have been speaking to a professional. Not dumping that onto you.'

'I know Brad. Just for once, though, I want to be able to work this out.'

'You aren't qualified to sort something that complicated out. This guy is layered with dysfunction from what you've told me.'

'I'll speak to him.'

'Can you not see what's happening Pippa?'

'No.' I looked up at Brad and bit my lower lip. Something I hadn't done in years. 'I'm not sure it's that serious, is it?'

'Look at your own words. You're scared that Noah will get angry, and so you are choosing alternative words, so as not to inflame him. Think Pippa! Think!' Brad sounded frustrated.

I reflected for a moment. 'Yeah, okay, Brad. I can see that. I'll not do that… yeah, you're right.'

'Think about how you are wired, Pippa. Your family? How did you manage to stay in the house and not get kicked out? You had to forgive behaviour that was unacceptable… constantly. This is what you're doing now. For what? To feel loved?' Brad sounded plain old angry, and the people at the next table had stopped chatting, to watch.

'I know, I know. I don't know how to stop,' I said with a lowered voice.

'You do.'

'I can't. I can't do that yet. I'm not ready. I'd have to end this.' It would be another failure. Another rejection. I would be losing love, yet again. Just after having found how pure it tasted.

'Pippa. Just don't get yourself hurt.'

'I won't.'

'Yes, you will, if you don't get this under control.'

I FELT a bit angry with Brad after our conversation, although angry was harsh under the circumstances. Brad didn't know that I'd found *home* with Noah, a man who fitted into me like we had been made to fit together. When I'd made love to Noah, it was as if we became one. I'd never felt that way before, about anyone. It was like oxygen to me, and I felt panicked every time I thought it might be slipping away. No, not oxygen, it had gone further than that. I felt like an addict, getting my needs met after so, so long. It was like finding the answer to everything, and that's not making it sound more than it was. I'd had plenty of sex with guys over the years, but making love to Noah was completely different. It was a genuine connection and one that I had been craving for my whole life. I would have to give up the one thing that I'd been looking for and go back to feeling unloved again. How? How was I supposed to do that?

At the same time, Noah's stories were concerning me, as well as the misunderstanding we'd had with the group sex and the accusation of me being a terrorist. I couldn't put my finger on what was wrong? I knew *something* was wrong but was it worth ending the relationship over? A few miscommunications and cross words were my usual, having grown up in a home where that was the norm, not the exception. It felt familiar, and so it made me want to work it through rather than obliterate it. Noah still felt just as warm and loving when we were wrapped up in each other's arms. How do you reconcile a conversation where someone has accused you of being a terrorist with being held so warmly, only days afterwards?

I decided to investigate it further and bought a book on 'How to spot a liar' and had read it cover to cover. I learned what to look out for when someone was lying. Eyes that didn't look at you square, or perhaps were too square. Changes in pitch and rhythm of voice, amendments over time, concerning small details of a story. When Noah was asked about his stories, face to face, he was text-book convincing. His pitch changed over the phone as he recounted them, and he rushed his words a bit. I wondered if I was the one who hadn't placed enough trust into Noah? Was he lying if I couldn't prove he was?

He was also struggling with difficult issues, mostly to do with suicide. He needed help from me to sort himself out a bit, not condemnation. If I pushed him too far, he might drive into the tree instead of merely threatening to. Would it be my fault if he did? Would I have failed him? I was helping Noah at a time where he needed obvious and critical help. What sort of person would I be if I turned him away now?

However, seeing it all from Brad's perspective, I could also see why Brad felt concerned. I was glad he was looking out for me, even if I had to pay him for the honour. Then I felt immense guilt. Why was I paying Brad to be invested in my wellbeing when I was blatantly ignoring the very unrest that he was warning me about? I could not deny that something was flapping in the wind that didn't feel quite right.

Noah texted me early the next morning.

N: Pippa, come to dinner. My place. 7.30. I want to cook something special for you. I know I've been an arse. I want to make it up to you. I'm so sorry Pips.

P: Sure… what about our art class, though?

N: Thought you might want to see my etchings instead?

P: Haha…

N: So, you coming?

P: Yeah, xxx

I arrived right on the dot, and he greeted me at the door. The old Noah. The one who resembled the Noah I had first met. He was smiling, relaxed and squishy when he pulled me close to him. His rigidity had softened, and his anger had diffused.

'I'm sorry. It's just been a stressful time,' he said, pulling me in close. 'I apologise for being such an arse Pips. I can do better than that. I just hope you'll let me try.'

'It's okay. We all go through stress.' I cringed inside when I said that. I'd just given him a get out of jail free, pass. It meant that I was allowing him to mistreat me by putting it all down to stress. I knew only too well how stressed my parents had been with the farm and how quickly they could rage, blaming it on the stressful demands of the alpacas. However, right now, why would I rock a settled boat? Wasn't the outcome to be in a boat on glass level water?

'Want some wine? I got your favourite.' He held up a bottle of Cotes-du-Rhone.

'Lovely,' I said, smiling. That was nice of him to have gone and got my special wine. I looked around and noticed a new, framed photograph on the wall.

'Where is this?' I asked.

'A few hours north of my parent's place. My Mum just sent it down to me.'

I paused. 'Didn't your Mum die when you were six from a brain aneurysm?'

'No… we had a friend of the family who died, but not my Mum. She's actually in excellent health for her age. You've got confused Pips.'

I was indeed confused, clearly remembering him telling me on several occasions. Where had we been? In the cafe after art class. I remembered the moment clearly. I took a deep breath. There had been other conversations since, never mentioning her. Was it the time to confront him about the lies? I looked over at the bottle of wine he had bought me and felt guilty. Why ruin the moment? The lies could wait.

'It's beautiful,' I said, ignoring the issue and studying the photograph instead. 'I love the house here,' I said, pointing to the centre house, which was a vast, sandstone colonial home built near the waterfront.

'I was hoping you would say you liked it.'

'Why?'

He was smiling at me. 'Because we are going to go there for a holiday.'

'Are we?'

'My parents own it and have invited us up for a few days.'

'Sorry?'

'Yeah, my parents own it. It's their holiday home.'

'Own that? Really?' My heart sank. Was this another lie?

'Yeah. They built it about fifteen years ago. They own the four houses either side, as well. Dad bought the block years ago. Always had a dream to develop it, despite knowing nothing about developing... he used to be in bespoke landscaping. Once he retired, he hired an architect, and that's what they came up with.'

'It's stunning' I said again, noting the address, written on the bottom left of the photo. As soon as I could, I went straight to the toilet with my phone and googled the address. Sure enough, there was the information with his parents as current owners in a local paper article about the development.

'I don't like to tell too many people about the development Pippa. My Dad inherited a heap of money from his father who provided the money for it all, although I'm not sure that he knew it would increase in value as it has. It's worth twenty-five million now.'

'Twenty-five million?'

'Yeah, he sold off half of it - thus the funding for the buildings. Made a small fortune, to be honest. Sold the eight homes just out of the pic at over a mil each. It's one of the reasons my parents never really got on too well with Emma. They thought she was after my money. I'll inherit the title to the development when I turn forty.'

'So, all this worry about finances right now, will be resolved in a few years?'

'Not necessarily. I don't plan on selling it soon.'

'Oh.'

'I do have a trust, though, which I can also access in a few years. My grandfather set it up for me in his will, saying that I could only access it when I had gained enough wisdom to be sensible with it. It's been sitting there for years just accruing interest. He left it up to my parents to decide when I could get my hands on it when I wouldn't blow it on women and fast cars.' Noah laughed. 'Then, I'll be truly financially stable. It's one of the reasons my parents are annoyed with me. The longer I delay the divorce process with Emma, the more worried they get that she would be entitled to a larger portion. It's valued at around thirty million right now.'

'That's a lot.' I tried not to look impressed. So, he was rich? It didn't change how I felt about him. I couldn't understand why he was stopping Emma selling the investment property in Brisbane, and the family home, if he was going to be financially wealthy soon? Surely if he divorced her, then the matter would be sorted? Again, I felt confused about the details. After I'd judged he was remaining in a good mood, I broached the subject of the reviews that I'd found online.

'I've got a question, Noah. It's an awkward one to ask.'

That got his attention, and he stopped what he was doing in the kitchen.

'Okay. Fire away. I have no secrets with you, Pips.'

'I was googling you, as in Ad80dude, and found a site where someone had reviewed prostitutes online, using that name. Was that you?' The question was bleak at best.

Noah shook his head and then laughed. 'Pippa, sweetheart. No… no… no. I pretended to write them to get to gold class status within the organisation. You earn points if you do the reviews. The juicier the review, the more points you get. I just wanted the status with the other guys. You know how it is. It's all fiction.'

Again, another riddle of an answer that required more questions to be asked, for any of it to make sense.

'I don't fully understand.' I said. How could he have pretended to write the reviews if the reviews were there for everyone to see?

'It's nothing to worry about. You must have been going nuts! Thinking I was doing all of that? How did you find it all again?' He cocked his head slightly to one side and made direct eye contact.

'As I said. I just typed in your Instagram name into Google. The one you texted to me.'

'It's okay. I haven't slept with prostitutes. I promise you.' He was chuckling, finding the thought amusing. 'In fact, I tried it once - actually booked one when I was going through a rough patch with Emma and ended up just chatting on the end of the bed with her. No sex. I would never have had sex while I was still living with Emma.'

'That's a relief.' I said, wondering who pays for a prostitute when married and then sits on the bed talking to them. Probably heaps of people, I surmised.

'You must have been concerned?' he suggested.

'I am… I was. The reviews were a bit… well… not like you?'

'No, I had to make them like that though, so that I would get the points. I got extra for both men and women,' he said matter of factly.

'So, what did you get with these points?' I asked, not liking the nonchalant tone in his voice. It was as if we were discussing the weather.

'I got status.'

'That's it? Status? What kind of status?'

'Yeah. Just the normal type, I guess. It's what I wanted.'

More riddles. However, his tone was level, and he'd made direct eye contact. I believed him. His surprise at my angst had been convincing, and his story seemed odd but genuine. Status though? What did that mean? I had more questions, but he interrupted me.

'I've made you dinner, so please, take a seat,' he said, indicating to the clean table, now complete with a tablecloth, candles, and fresh flowers, again one of my favourites - pink peonies.

He then spoiled me with one of my favourite mains. Brown mushroom and chicken ravioli, followed by a home-made pavlova, topped with fresh cream and strawberries. Then he reached forward and gently pulled my head towards his.

'When to those Venusbergs, thy breasts, By wars of love and moonlight batteries,

My lips have stormed, O pout thy mouth above,

Lean down those culverins twain, and bid me spike.'

'Slessor…' I started to say… as his mouth gently brushed mine, pressing and releasing, I could feel the warmth of his breath, and then he was kissing me, needing me, and finally having me. I had my old Noah back, and as I was lying next to him that night, his arms were once again tucked around me.

'I never want to let you go, Pips. Not ever. I don't tell you often enough how much I love you and appreciate you. I do with all of my heart. I know things have been a bit down lately, and I didn't intend things to be like this. I don't want to let you down Pips. I'm going to do better, I promise.'

I PHONED Brad the next day.

'I've sorted it, Brad. Everything is okay again.'

'Really?'

'Yes. I went over to his place, we chatted and sorted it all, and I stayed the night. He was fine.'

'Are you fine?'

'Yes. He seems to be back to normal.'

'I asked you if you were fine, Pippa, not him.'

'I'm fine, Brad, really.'

'The fact that he wasn't normal for a while concerns me though Pippa. Can you see that?'

'Yes. I think so. Put it this way. Intellectually, I can see that it wasn't right, but my heart is with this man.'

'I have alarm bells ringing at my end Pippa. I really do. I don't like this.'

'I don't hear the same bells,' I said. 'He seems fine. Like the old Noah.'

'Pippa, there shouldn't be two Noah's. There should just be the one.'

I MET THE OTHER SIDE OF HIM

AND I TROD BAREFOOT ON A LARGE SPIDER

20

TORN SOUL
SHREDDED

He invited me to go away with him for a few days at the end of the month. To a cabin in the hills, he sold it to me as if it were a fairytale holiday. We would be hiking during the day through the highland forest, maybe playing golf and snuggling in front of a campfire in the evenings. Later on, in the week, the kids would meet us for two days to go kayaking in the nearby lake.

'It's a perfect place, Pips,' he said excitedly. 'You'll love it. I promise.'

'I thought with your arm, that you couldn't play golf anymore?' I asked.

'It's been a lot better lately, even managed some push-ups with it. You never know, I might be able to keep it, after all.'

BRAD WAS WORRIED. 'For God's sake, Pippa, take your phone. If you don't feel safe, then phone me. Okay?'

'Yes, Brad. I know. However, he seems to be trying to put everything right again. He deserves a chance, doesn't he? Anyway, his kids will be there too.'

'Just promise you will call if you need me. I can't stop you from going, but I can advise against this.'

'I promise I will call.' I knew I probably wouldn't call Brad, though, because I was an addict. I just wanted to lie in Noah's arms and feel loved. The cost of business was hurting me, that much I knew, but *how* was I supposed to stop?

Hi, I'm Pippa, and I'm addicted to lying in Noah's arms.

Even I knew that I had a problem, but like a runaway addiction, I didn't know how to stop doing it.

LATER THAT WEEK, I felt Noah pull away from me as if a chasm had developed between us. It was hard to put my finger on what had caused it, though. It started with him reducing the number of texts he sent me. Since meeting, our ritual had been to send each other a wake-up text with a silly emoji. Then one day, they stopped without a reason. My message would go unread until the afternoon, and then a perfunctory text would be sent back. I texted, asking him about it.

P: Noah, is everything okay between us?

N: Of course, Pips, Why?

P: You just seem to be a bit distant.

N: Just busy. Working hard at my end. Too much work!

P: I miss our texts, though.

N: Well, maybe we were doing too many lol? I mean, it was like twenty a day. Probs best to cut down a bit? What do you think?

I had to agree. Otherwise, I would appear needy. I would sound weak. I would come across as demanding. I needed to let him hear what he wanted.

P: Yeah, sure. All good Noah xx

N: You make me happy Pips. It's like you're the only person on the planet who understands me xx

The next day, I was worried. He'd phoned me the night before, talking about driving into a tree again. I had been texting him for hours all day, and my phone calls had been going through to voicemail this morning. I was worried that something had happened and was wondering whether to call his office. I texted him in the early evening for one last try.

P: Hey Noah. Is everything okay? I've been trying to get a hold of you all day. Are you okay? I'm really worried.

He waited two hours, then replied.

N: Yes, Pippa. I'm just busy. You worry too much, xx.

P: Glad you are okay, xx.

It was more mature only to text a couple of times a day, and I had to agree. We were adults, and we were now in a stable relationship. Maybe it was the sudden way in which he had reduced the number though? Maybe it was the way in which I was now organising myself around him? What about when I was feeling vulnerable or needy and needed a return text? Everything seemed to be organised around his timetable.

I remembered someone once telling me that people had different love languages, and it was good to know what yours was. I read up on it and discovered that my love was demonstrated mostly through words, with love actions and gestures coming in second. Thus, it made sense as to why I felt unloved when Noah forgot to text me. I texted him through the info, hoping for a couple of extra texts to reassure me. I needed his sentiments to match his actions. He responded immediately.

N: Of course, Pips. Messaged received. More texts coming your way, for sure! Yes, of course, I love you xx

He then ignored my texts for the next five days, and I became terrified that he was breaking up with me. There was no reason for his silence.

How could someone proclaim to love me, and then blatantly ignore me for days on end? I was getting confused by what seemed to be blatant contradictions. I became tearful on the phone to him.

'Noah, I'm so confused, what's going on?' I sobbed.

'Nothing Pips. Why? I've been busy at work. I've already explained all of that.'

'You always used to call, that's all. I miss talking to you, that's all.' I sounded apprehensive. 'I just need some consistency,' I added, quietly.

'Pippa, you sound a bit controlling. That's how you are coming across. Do you want to push me away? Then keep going like this. Right now, though? Chill, everything is fine. Look, I've got a meeting I need to get to. Talk later.' The phone went dead.

Controlling? How was I being controlling? The Noah I'd met was disappearing into thin air. I felt as if I were flailing between fantasy and reality. I phoned him back again, sounding tearful. He sounded frustrated with me.

'Pippa, seriously, I'm late for my meeting. Have you heard yourself lately? You are the one that sounds like you need to go on antidepressants. You sound like you are mood cycling! I told you I have this meeting and I need to go to it!' The call cut out.

I had made everything worse. I shouldn't have called back. I was an idiot. I googled mood cycling. Was he suggesting that I was now bipolar? I was upset, for sure, but suggesting I was unstable? The more he ignored me though, the more upset I was getting. If he loved me, then why did he ignore me for days on end? I just wanted to hear his voice again, the voice he'd used at the beginning - not the cold one that seemed to be my new normal. I didn't know where I stood because he said that he loved me… but this didn't *feel* like love. He said he would text more often and then ignored me for days on end.

He made a few attempts to contact me over the next couple of weeks, and I was continually jumpy and teary. There was no consistency with his communication anymore, and the more spartan his texts, the more anxious I became. I was sending long texts asking too many questions, and he was replying with anger. In the end, my neediness aggravated him to the point where he phoned me, shouting.

'Pippa, for fuck's sake! What the hell is your problem? What do you want from me?'

'I want the old Noah back,' I replied quietly.

'Are you implying there are two of me? You need to get some help, Pippa. You're all over the place. You sound like you have serious depression or something! Go get some fucking help! You're just... demanding.'

I did feel depressed. I couldn't stop crying. The love that had been given to me so freely, with so much hope, was dwindling. If he didn't want to be in the relationship, then fine. I could deal with that. I would be devastated, but so be it. What I wasn't dealing with, was the sudden pulling away and contradictory messages. He was saying one thing and doing the opposite. I went to see a GP at my local medical centre, hoping for some comfort, maybe some pills or a magic wand to make me feel better.

'I'm feeling upset,' I said, tears streaming down my face. 'I'm so sorry,' I said, apologising for my distressed state, 'I'm generally not like this.' I felt mortified. I had gone in ready to explain how I was feeling, but more emotions than I knew how to handle had suddenly bubbled out of me. I was a crying, mess of a woman sitting in front of the cool, composed, doctor.

She asked if something had happened, looking at me with a look of distaste, more than empathy.

'My boyfriend has stopped speaking to me... as much as he used to. He's pulled back a bit... a lot actually.' The tears were now falling in a silent cascade down my face.

'Is that it?' she asked, insensitive to my distress. She appeared overworked, and that she would rather be anywhere else, than sit there, listening to me.

I felt like an idiot. 'I'm fine,' I said, pulling myself together. 'I must just be hormonal or something.'

She gave me a script for some antidepressants, as that was her easiest option, and I took them. They made me desperately nauseous and sleepy. I struggled through my work week, feeling confused and then decided to ask him outright. I texted.

P: Noah, are we still together?

N: Yes, of course, Pips, why?

P: You haven't seen me for three weeks. I miss us.

N: I miss us too, babe. I'm just busy. I'll see you at the cabin. Everything is okay. You need to relax. We are going to have a wonderful time. I'm looking forward to it. Just busy at work, yeah, angel?'

P: Sure. xxx

N: xxx

Although he had sent kisses, It didn't feel okay. I felt like my head was being messed with. Noah had planted a seed of self-doubt into my mind which had familiar resonances. I was the one who had apparently messed this up. I was demanding, needy, and overly sensitive. I'd heard all of this so many times before from my parents growing up, as my distress at their raging had been reflected back to me as my weakness and not theirs. Noah had done the same. I was the one who was losing it, not him. This whole dynamic between us was my fault.

THE CABIN WAS in the woods just outside of a National Park. Built by a local couple, Noah told me that he had been visiting it for the past ten years, initially with Emma and the kids. It looked entirely out of place in the forest, with its little red roof, yellow window frames, and bright blue door. It looked like it was intruding into the natural bushland. Noah had seemed happy on the drive there, so I felt like I was back in more familiar territory. I was relieved.

Whatever he had been going through, seemed to be over, for now, at least.

The place was overrun with spiders of all shapes and sizes, though, which made me nervous, especially as during the first evening there, just as I had taken my shoes and socks off, I had put my foot onto something warm and furry in the bedroom. It had cracked under my foot. Looking down, I could see that I had trodden, barefoot onto a giant huntsman that had been crawling around, near the edge of the bed. I instinctively looked up to find a second one glaring at me. Probably its partner, and appearing now, to want revenge.

'SHIT!' I had screamed.

Noah had laughed. 'They eat bugs. It stays. It won't come near you, especially the way you just screamed at it.'

We ate and then spent the night making love, like old times. Although, when the huntsman disappeared, I had one eye scanning the room for it.

'See, we're back,' he sighed into my neck afterwards, snuggling into me. 'I told you everything was good. You didn't believe me, though. See… Noah was right.'

'I love this,' I said to him, meaning just that. I loved being in his arms. 'I never want to lose this, Noah.'

'You're never going to Pips. You can change as much as you want, and I'm never going to stop loving you, not ever.'

'Really?' I asked, wriggling in closer. Those were the words I had been waiting to hear. Ones that showed that Noah loved me unconditionally. There would be no need to try for perfection, and I could just be me. He would allow me to be imperfect.

'Yes, Pippa, really.'

'Not ever? You are going to love me warts and all?'

'Yes, angel. You're mine now.'

I smiled. Those words soothed my soul, and at that moment, I felt complete. I was home again. I was sated.

I WOKE in the night with an old-accident migraine and took some meds for it. I rarely got them now, but when they hit, they knocked me around a bit. There wasn't too much to say about it, other than I felt like someone had hit me over the back of the neck with something. Noah didn't seem too concerned, and only briefly woke up to ask me why the light was on.

The next morning, I got up early and made crispy bacon, eggs, sunny side up, and thick toast, his favourite.

'I'm sorry Pips, I think I must have drunk too much last night. I'm not feeling that great. I drank so much I think I blacked out. Can't remember anything after dinner.'

'Really?' I hadn't seen him drinking that much. Did that mean he didn't remember the night and what he'd said to me? 'Can I get you anything?'

'No. I'll just stay in bed, I think. That's okay with you? Yeah?'

He stayed in bed playing games on his phone while I did a load of washing and kept an eye on him. Luckily, my migraine was short-lived, and I felt great by lunchtime. Mid-afternoon, there was shouting outside the cabin. It sounded like the kids, only they weren't supposed to be arriving for a couple of days. I looked out of the front door, confused. There was no sign of Emma. She must have dumped them with their bags and had sped off, back down the mountain.

'Get off me!' shouted Seb. Steve was on top of him, punching him hard. *Yet again.*

'Steve, please. Get off Seb!' I grabbed at his sleeve to see if I could release his grip.

'Please be quiet,' he said to me, smashing his brother in the face with his fist.

Seb screamed again, 'GET OFF ME!'

'Where's Rose?' I shouted at Seb.

'In the cupboard.'

'What cupboard? Is she already inside?' I hadn't heard her come in. I pulled at Steve, trying to get him off, Seb.

'What's going on?' Noah had walked out, looking alarmed.

'GET HIM OFF ME!' Seb was screaming.

'She's hurting me!' cried out Steve. I pulled my arm away quickly.

'Where's Rose?' Noah asked, looking around.

'In a cupboard apparently,' I said.

'What cupboard? Steve, GET OFF!' He pulled Steve off and then sat him down inside, on a chair.

'You will NOT hurt your brother. Do you understand?'

'YES!' Steve shouted at him, punching him in the neck.

'I'll take them out onto the lake I think,' Noah said, coughing and rubbing his neck. 'There are some paddle boats in the shed. Want to come?'

'Yeah, okay. I'll find Rose first.'

I found her in the wardrobe of the second bedroom. She'd made herself comfortable, taking in a packet of biscuits and a rug. She was reading a book using her torch.

'Want to come out onto the lake. Might be fun? We can paddle together, away from the boys?'

'Sure,' she said. She tried smiling, but her face looked more tired than it should have, for someone of twelve.

Noah was paddling with Steve and had asked that Seb paddle behind, keeping a close distance. Being by himself in the kayak gave him more freedom than he should have had, though. I watched him paddle furiously towards one of the embankments as soon as Noah and Steve were a few metres ahead. Then he ran, barefoot into the forest. I yelled out to Noah, but he couldn't hear me.

'Rose, we're going to have to go after Seb.'

Sharing a kayak, we paddled as fast as we could to the same embankment, Noah finally turned around and saw that Seb, was gone.

'WHERE'S SEB?' he shouted, looking panicked.

'I saw him run into the forest!' I pointed in the right direction.

He paddled in and dropped Steve off. 'You look after Rose and Steve. I'll go and find Seb.'

I got the kids to paddle back to the shore, and Steve started to throw mud at Rose. She ran off, back to the hut, refusing to stay, and then Steve started to hit one of the kayaks with a paddle. He sent it off by itself into the lake.

'Steve. Please. Can you not do that?' I asked as calmly as I could.

'Be quiet,' he said.

'I'm just asking that you do the right thing while your Dad is looking for Seb.'

'You should shut up,' he laughed. 'Fuck this,' he added. He then sent five more kayaks off by themselves into the middle of the lake, wading in, to push them further out.

'No. Steve. Don't send them into the water!' I yelled, running towards him. He picked up one of the paddles and came charging at me. I froze.

'Bang! Dead!' he yelled. Then he ran along the small pebbly beach area, shouting something. I kept thinking over and over that all I had to do was keep him safe until Noah got back. I turned around, and then Steve was gone.

Shit! I looked first at the lake. He was wearing a life jacket, though, so he would be floating if he'd gone in. What if he had drowned? No, the life jacket was there to keep him alive, and Noah had tied it in a secure knot so that he couldn't undo it. All I'd had to do was keep an eye on him. I had failed. I ran to Rose, who was back in the cupboard and asked her to help me find Steve. He was out there somewhere. We searched and searched, running along small, dusty bush tracks, calling his name, but couldn't find him.

Rose went back into the cupboard, shrugging her shoulders at me. Noah hadn't taken his phone, and now I didn't know where he and Seb were either. This was a total disaster. I prepared what I needed to say, in preparation for whatever was coming my way.

Two hours later, a tired-looking Noah, with a smiling Seb perched on his shoulders, walked back into the hut, followed by Steve, who was moaning about having to walk so far.

'Steve found us out in the bush. Lucky about that, hey.' Noah said, sounding tired.

'Thank God. I tried to keep him in the one spot Noah. I did.'

'IT'S OKAY. He's difficult. I get it,' he said, pouring two glasses of wine in the bedroom for us. 'One day, of course, they're going to be independently wealthy and won't need me at all. I hate to say that I'm actually looking forward to that day. I shouldn't be. I'm their father.'

'Sorry?' I wasn't following him. The statement had come from nowhere.

'Well, the inheritance in my family skips a generation. I won't get any of it, but these three will be extremely comfortable. They get the development, the trust fund, and any other real estate. Lucky guys. That's why I don't worry too much about the future for them.'

I was confused. Hadn't he just told me that he would be receiving an inheritance or a trust fund or something? Now he had changed it to his kids. I didn't say anything, but it had been an out-of-place comment to have made in the middle of all of this. I felt resentment building with the inconsistency of what he had told me. I felt like he was accusing me of being a gold-digger and was telling me that there was no money coming his way. I felt a burning sense of humiliation encasing me.

We spent the next two hours collecting all the kayaks that had made their way around the meandering lake and brought them back to the shore. Dinner was tacos and ice-cream, then a fight to get the kids all bathed and into bed. We finally climbed into our bed, exhausted, and Noah had just started to kiss my neck when Seb ran into our room.

'I wet the bed,' he said, smiling.

Noah got up, but couldn't find any clean sheets, and the mattress was soaked through. Seb climbed into the bed next to me. By the time Noah had finished trying to sort it all out, Seb was asleep.

'I'll go sleep on the sofa,' I whispered.

'Thanks,' said Noah, climbing in next to Seb. I couldn't find any extra blankets despite searching the hut and nearly froze to death in the chilly, night air.

THE NEXT DAY we went for a bushwalk. Noah spent the whole time running after the boys, who ran off in different directions. Seb would run straight to an edge and then stop as if about to jump, and Steve would then run in the opposite direction. At one point, Seb climbed up a small rocky hill and then threw stones at me. I leapt out of the way and backwards, to avoid them hitting my head.

'STOP!' I yelled at him. 'That's not funny, Seb!'

'WHAT'S NOT FUNNY?' shouted Noah from over near a large boulder that Steve had climbed, but now couldn't get down from.

'SEB IS THROWING STONES AT ME!' I shouted over to him.

'WHY?' Noah shouted back.

My patience was wearing thin, as a stone landed forcefully on my foot.

'HOW THE FUCK SHOULD I KNOW? THIS IS A NIGHTMARE!' It was. Now I had sworn in front of his kids.

'I HATE THIS!' shouted Steve, jumping from off the boulder and crashing down onto his knee. Now he couldn't walk, he claimed, insisting that Noah carry him. Rose walked by herself, saying nothing. We gave up. It was impossible. All the boys wanted to do was play video games back at the hut.

Rose put herself back into the cupboard, and Noah went to bed.

'I'm feeling a bit depressed if you can't tell,' Noah said in a solemn tone before walking into the bedroom and shutting the door after him.

He left me with the boys who had settled down and seemed oblivious to my presence. I looked after them for a few hours, mainly trying to keep them settled, and then took a sandwich up to Noah.

'I'm not hungry, Pips. Have you taken them out for a walk or a drive, or something? You have the car keys. You could have taken them down to the village shop for an ice-cream at least.'

'The kids? No. They've just been playing downstairs. Peacefully, thank goodness.' I smiled, feeling mildly successful that they were all still alive.

'So, you haven't done anything with them?'

'Well, they seem happy enough. I did three loads of washing, though, and made them all lunch.'

'Whatever.' He rolled over in the dark, sounding disappointed in me.

My heart sank. 'Do you want me to open the curtains and let some light in?' I asked, hopefully.

'No. I want to be left alone.'

. . .

'I HATE THIS. IT'S BORING!' shouted Seb, and he started to bang his head against the wall, drawing blood on his forehead.

'STOP!' I yelled at him, horrified at what I was witnessing.

'NO! I WANT TO DIE!'

Noah got up. 'What's all the fucking noise?'

'He's hitting his head against the wall, Noah.'

'Don't yell at him,' he snapped at me. 'SEB. STOP IT! JUST PLAY YOUR DAMNED VIDEO GAMES!' Noah roared.

WE TRIED to watch a family movie that night, but Steve's behaviour was upsetting Rose. I retreated into the toilet, as Noah played a game on his phone, not even watching the movie. I needed some time myself to think this through. The kids were just exhausting with every visit, and every activity was proving to be complicated. There wasn't any laughing or smiling or fun at all. It was just physical violence, escaping and screaming, *all the time.* I felt like I just didn't have the experience I needed, to know how to handle Steve effectively, or Seb, for that matter. I was happy to see the light at the end of the tunnel though, with the kids leaving in the morning. I helped them pack.

Emma arrived. I was hoping to give her a smile or a wave, but she stayed in the car, and Noah told me to stay inside. Once the kids were gone, there was a sudden peace. It was like we had been in the middle of a war zone for two days.

'Right, we've got the place to ourselves for two days. Now, what should we do?' I smiled at Noah.

'Who knows?' he snapped.

'What's up?' I asked. 'You seem a bit irritable? Are you okay?'

'You irritate me,' he said, matter of factly.

'Sorry?'

'I said, you irritate me. I'm going for a walk. By myself. Maybe I should throw myself off a fucking cliff while I'm at it.' He walked out.

'Noah!' I ran after him.

'Fuck off, Pippa.'

He was gone for a couple of hours, and I sat in the quiet which now seemed threatening, more than peaceful. I wasn't sure what was going on. Did I irritate him? How? I sat and mulled over what I'd said and done since arriving.

He returned, still angry. 'I'm going to have to go and have a blood test done, aren't I? Make sure I haven't picked anything nasty up from you?'

'A blood test? For what?' I was confused.

'You fucking tell me, Pippa. HIV? Hep? Name your disease.'

'What?' His anger was scaring me.

'We didn't use protection, that day we went for a drive up to the Peninsular.'

I replayed the day over. It had been months ago. Why was he bringing this up now? I hadn't thought we would be doing that, that's why there was no protection, and luckily, I'd not fallen pregnant. I'd had a blood test since, just in case too. I hadn't told Noah because I hadn't wanted to offend him.

'Noah?'

'What Pippa?'

'Sometimes, you say things that are a bit blunt, and they hurt me.'

'I like to be blunt, and I like to hurt. Deal with it.' He walked into the bedroom and slammed the door.

He stayed in the bedroom all afternoon. I gave him his space. I went for a walk myself, trying to find a deep breath. I couldn't. My stomach muscles were so tight, I felt like I was only getting half breaths in. I really wasn't sure what to do. Noah appeared to have snapped. I was scared that he might decide to suicide, given his mental state, but at the same time, I didn't know what to say to him. My very presence seemed to be setting him off.

I made a simple dinner and called him to the table. We had a stilted dinner exchange, which was better, but not perfect. At least he had calmed down. I didn't ask him any personal questions, though, in case I said the wrong thing. All I wanted to do was to keep the peace, but I felt like a deer in the headlights.

I felt a bit better when he suggested we watch a movie together and was relieved to hear him snoring next to me. If he was asleep, then he couldn't say anything else that might upset me. I felt my muscles beginning to loosen, realising that it was the first time that day, that I had relaxed.

I laid in the bed next to him, later that night, trying to get a bit closer, trying to reconnect the chasm that had appeared between us. One that I wasn't sure how to mend.

'I'd love a cuddle...' I started to say.

'You know, you're a bit of a bitch when you're on meds,' he said.

'What? No, I'm not,' I snapped back at him. What was he going on about now... my meds for the migraine? I'd stopped taking the antidepressants as they just made me feel spaced out. 'Noah, that's not fair...'

'Can you just piss off?' he snapped.

'Sorry?'

'I need quiet, Pippa. Just shut up. You talk too much... still. I thought we had gone over that. Has anyone else ever told you that? Haven't you realised yet why no-one likes you?'

'What?' I said in disbelief.

'I told you to shut up,' he said slowly. 'So, just do it.'

I turned over and went as quiet as I could. I curled up as small as I could. I wasn't going to fight back with him anymore. He had crossed a line, and I just wanted to go home. *I'd had enough.* I was exhausted from whatever all of this was. I was tired from his kids and tired of his criticism that seemed to launch from nowhere. I was going to have to take a break from him, that much I knew.

I woke some hours later to a feeling that the bed was moving. I turned. Noah was watching violent, gay porn on his phone.

'Why are you watching that?' I asked alarmed. It seemed inappropriate, with me lying in bed, next to him.

'Because I fucking well can,' he snarled. 'Why? Do you now have a problem with this as well? Stop criticising me, Pippa! I can't breathe from it all. I can't breathe from any of this! You're the one pushing for all of this, not me. I can't be the person you want me to be. You're driving me to fucking suicide!'

What the hell? Was I driving him to suicide? Me? My mind was racing. Wasn't he the one criticising me? Or had I just criticised him by asking him about the porn? I didn't know anymore. The video stopped, and I was aware that he had put the phone down. Then I felt him moving in the bed.

All of a sudden, with no warning and no sound, I felt his weight on top of me, from behind, forcing my face down into the pillow. He pinned my arms down, putting heavy pressure onto them and then pushed his way inside of me. I yelled out in pain and then tried to dig my fingernails into his hands to stop him. Sweat poured from my body, in reaction to the searing pain. I clenched my fists. He became heavier on my back, forcing me still.

I froze. Not moving and not making a sound. He wasn't making a sound either. It was surreal. This wasn't happening, only it was. Searing pain, relentless and the feeling of his breath on the back of my neck. Then he finished and rolled off. He didn't speak. I didn't speak. I didn't move. I breathed ever so slightly so that there was no evidence of me in the bed. Nothing moved, nothing made a sound. I just lay. Still. Quiet.

I WAITED until I could hear him snoring, then, quietly, so, so, quietly, so as not to wake him, inched my way from the bed. Small movement… another small movement, making sure the sheets and doona didn't move with me. I didn't care how long it took for me to get out of the bed, so long as I didn't wake him. I made it to the edge, one foot out of bed… reaching to the floor… so, so slowly. Then the other, making sure that the doona never moved. I crept from the room, one footstep and then another. I felt naked, was naked and cold. The cold had seeped into my bones, making me feel brittle and numb. I made my way quietly into the bathroom and closed the door. It took forever, making sure that the handle was released in silence to not click into place. I locked the door and sat on the toilet, my body shaking. I was numb but also in pain. What had just happened? Should I call Brad?

I sat for a long time, now not feeling the cold. How should I be reacting? There wasn't anything inside of me, though. Just emptiness. Then a voice, calling me. I knew the voice.

'Pips, where are you?'

I was jolted back. It was Noah, calling out from the bedroom.

'Just in the loo.' I tried to sound as normal as possible, but fear was racing around my body. If he knew I sounded angry or hurt, what would he do? Dear God. What had I done in agreeing to come here? I was alone in a hut with a madman who had just told me that he liked to hurt people. One who had just assaulted me… had he just assaulted me? Had I consented to that? I was confused. I felt like I had just been attacked, but he was acting as if nothing had happened. My mind was trying to piece together what had just transpired, but all I felt was confusion and this awful emptiness.

'Hurry back. I'm cold,' he called out. I need to get close to your beautiful body.'

'Sure.' I waited a few minutes, deciding that walking back in appearing as normal as I could was the safest option. I didn't want to provoke him further. I was also scared. Why had he brought me out to the forest? There was no-one out there. Nowhere to run.

The bedside lamp was on, and he smiled at my nakedness. 'All good angel?'

I studied his face for a hint of an acknowledgement as to what he had just done. There was none. How could he not have any expression after doing that to me? Did it mean I had got it all wrong, perhaps? I didn't know. I couldn't tell. His messages to me were confused. One minute he was swearing at me, the next, he was kind. That action hadn't been kind though. Maybe his words had been kind? Only there hadn't been any words. He was smiling kindly now. How could he be smiling kindly, though? He'd forced himself into me, and now he was smiling. What he had just done had been monumentally wrong, I was sure.

'Can you just not tell me to piss off again? It hurts me,' I said quietly, immediately regretting throwing the comment out there. It would provoke him.

'What do you mean?' he asked, sounding perplexed.

'Nothing,' I muttered, knowing that the damage was done.

'No, seriously. Tell me.'

'It just hurts when you tell me to piss off and to shut up.' I avoided any mention of him having just physically hurt me and had tried to make my voice sound non-threatening.

'Let's just go to sleep,' he said, rolling over. 'We can talk in the morning.' He put the light off.

'Why can't you ever just shut up?' he then added into the blackness. 'Do you think you could just keep it shut, that mouth of yours until the morning?'

'I think I need to speak now, actually,' I said, feeling brave. 'You can't just tell me to piss off.' I had wanted to add *and assault me,* or whatever that had been, but decided against it. I still hadn't been able to work out what had just happened. I continued to speak, explaining that I did love him, but he had recently become abusive. I felt that finally, my truth was speaking and he rolled away from me. He was finally listening, and not raging at me, I thought, relieved.

'I'm sleeping on the fucking couch,' he said suddenly, and got up with his pillow and stormed out of the room. I lay in the dark and wrapped my arms around my body, mulling over what was unfolding. Noah was acting if I was doing something wrong. Asking him not to call me derogatory names was me just being assertive. Wasn't it? As for insulting him? Was asking someone not to watch violent porn next to you in the bed, wrong? He barged back into the room a few hours later and put the light on again.

'We're leaving a day early, Pippa. I want you out of my life. I'll drive you home, and then I never want to fucking hear from you again.'

'What? What are you talking about?' I was confused. I sat up in bed. Noah's face was angry, and his stare penetrated right through me. This Noah, the one standing in front of me, I didn't recognise. I felt like I were in a horror movie with a mad man standing at the end of the bed - only there was no scary music... just an eerie silence. His stare though was intense and unrelenting.

'What you just did, Pippa,' he said slowly, without a hint of emotion in his voice, 'was domestic violence. I had a pillow over my ears, Pippa, trying to drown your voice out. I was crying for God's sake! You made me cry, and you didn't even fucking notice! WHO FUCKING DOES THAT?' He was shouting now, his eyes still drilling through me. It was as if he could see inside of me, scanning me for weakness.

'What? When?'

'All fucking night Pippa.'

I didn't raise my voice, Noah… I… I was just trying to ask you not to keep name-calling me.' I could still feel pain where he had violated me. I heard my own voice. It sounded pitiful.

'Shut the fuck up, Pippa! You need help. You do. You fucking create drama wherever you go.'

'Noah. I don't get this. What's happening? When did you have a pillow over your ears? I didn't hear you crying.' I was bewildered. My reality and his reality weren't matching up. 'I would have stopped speaking if you'd been crying… I…'

'I need to protect my children from you. You're sick.'

I did feel sick from his abuse. Protect his children, though? From me? What had I done? Ask him not to tell me to piss off?

'Why? What have I done?'

'You swore in front of my nine-year-old.'

I stared at him. I had sworn, but it was after Seb had thrown a rock, which had hit my foot, hard enough to leave my foot badly bruised.

Noah went silent and refused to speak to me, going back into the lounge room. Fear, cold, and alarm ran through my veins. I started to shake. I needed Brad. Where was my phone? Next to the sofa in the lounge room. I could wait until Noah had fallen asleep again and then grab it. I listened for the sound of his snoring, only he didn't sleep. He sat, staring at the blank screen of the TV.

I was terrified that he was going to lose control and do something else to me. He was behaving irrationally, and I needed to get out of there. Running was no good, though, because I'd be running without a phone into a dark forest. I didn't even know which way to run. I looked around the bedroom for a weapon. Something that I could use in case he came back in. I unplugged the bedside lamp, figuring that I could perhaps use that. Then I sat in the bed for the rest of the night, holding my breath and listening for footsteps.

He packed the car in the morning, banging things, breaking things, and storming in and out of the hut. Now and again, he would come into the bedroom and hurl more abuse at me. Then he told me to get into the car and keep my mouth shut.

The ride home was a tirade against me. He brought up my parents.

'I'm not surprised they hate you, Pippa. You should listen to yourself go on and on about them sometimes. You are scathing towards them, No wonder they make you piss into a bucket and won't let you stay in the house with them.' He laughed. 'You are scathing towards everyone. Look at how you treated Louise in art class. No wonder she damaged your car.'

Louise? She wasn't the one who had damaged my car, was she? The person who had smashed my headlights and scratched my car? Hadn't she refused to attend the opening? What was he talking about?

'The way you treated Steve - grabbing his arm like that? He's a fucking teenager with serious behavioural issues. Who does that to someone who has issues? It's abuse, Pippa. Abuse!'

Had I grabbed his arm too hard when he was punching Seb? I didn't know anymore. His kids. The three elephants in the room. Rose, tired of her brothers and tired from always being in chaos. Steve, who needed more help than he was getting, and Seb, who was acting out from living with Steve. I thought I'd been kind with his children and very supportive in the way I'd handled it all. I'd told Noah repeatedly that I thought he was a good Dad and had coped well with all the stress from Steve. He was good with him, but it was clear that he needed more help.

'This isn't love Pippa. You need obvious help. Your problems with your family? They have made you fucking weird. You are one fucked up bitch, and I can't love a fucked up bitch.'

Did I need help? I wasn't the one who had been claiming to want to drive into a tree for months on end. I wasn't the one who had forced themselves onto someone else. I could not begin to understand his anger towards me. I smarted from him, as he mocked my secrets, ones that I had shared with him. I begged him in the car not to do this, not this way.

'Noah. This is ridiculous. Let's just talk. I don't know what you are doing. It doesn't have to be like this.'

'No, Pippa. We are *over*. I never want to fucking see you again. What you do is unbelievable, and then you sit there and constantly blame me for everything? Remember that day I came to visit you and had to leave in the afternoon?'

'When?'

'The day I lost my glasses, and you found them?'

'Yes…'

'You encouraged me to leave. Didn't you?'

'What?' I was confused, trying to follow his rapid speech.

'You did. You made me drive home when I was suicidal. Who the fuck does that? You forced me into my car, knowing, fucking KNOWING… KNOWING!' He drew breath, his face, red, and he was spitting his words. 'KNOWING that I could drive into a tree!'

'Noah… I didn't…'

'FUCK YOU, Pippa. Yes, you DID!' He was roaring at me.

I was so confused. What was he talking about? I remembered the day he had lost his glasses on our walk in the park. I'd managed to backtrack and find them in the long grass for him. Then he'd said he was leaving, and I'd said it was an excellent time to go because he could have a relaxing evening to himself. He hadn't said anything about feeling suicidal and had seemed calm and happy.

'You need professional help. You were the one that said you wanted group sex. You keep denying it. You were DRUNK Pippa. STOP DRINKING for God's sake. I organised it all and LOOK WHAT YOU DID!' He was beginning to fly into a rage while driving. 'I should have known with the amount you drank on our first date. Gees that was a FUCKING fun night, wasn't it?'

I sat in the car, trapped with him, the doors locked, stunned and shaking.

'Is it TIME, PIPPA? IS IT? TO DRIVE INTO THAT TREE?' He was screaming at me. I gripped the edge of my seat and closed my eyes and prayed. He started to swerve the car slightly to the right and then to the left.

He then laughed. 'Your face!'

I stared out of the window, praying to get home alive.

HE YELLED at me to 'GET OUT!' once we reached my flat, throwing my bag into the front communal garden area. He then drove off, his foot flat to the floor and I stood, silent, my limbs, frozen. It seemed like hours before I could move into the comfort of my flat, and it was as if I was someone else trying to fit in with what had seemed familiar territory, only days before. Two hours later, he sent a text.

N: I want my shampoo and conditioner that I left in your bathroom, returned to me.

21

WHAT NOW?

HOW DO YOU HEAL FROM THAT?

I remained motionless, mute and shocked for days. I had no appetite and no desire to see another human being. I didn't cry. I sat instead, still and silent. I was still in physical pain. My Noah had hurt me. The man that I had trusted my heart with, had stomped on it, pulverising it into oblivion. *My Noah* had done this. The man who had quoted Slessor to me... who had held me... told me I was beautiful, and that I could change as much as I liked and that he would *always* love me. I was numb from the shock. I replayed the incident over and over and over. The brutality... yes, brutal... it *had* been brutal. Its silence hadn't needed words, as its action had said everything.

The lack of Noah stopping when I had called out, just the once, in excruciating pain. How he'd not flinched as my fingernails had dug hard into his heavy palms? He had used his size to physically pin me down, an unfair advantage in a sick, conquest. I hadn't fought back, though. Not hard enough. Did that make it assault if I had gone as still as the night? Why hadn't I kicked and screamed more, and forced him off me?

Why had I just gone inwards, hoping to disappear into nothing? Was it assault if I had allowed him to finish by not fighting hard enough? I punished myself for the incident. My conclusion was bleak. I hadn't fought hard enough to make him stop, therefore, it had been consensual. I had *allowed* him to hurt me. He hadn't presumed that he'd hurt me, because he had said nothing - not at the time and not afterwards. That fact and every other fact made me feel as if my life had now reached a new normal, one in which I didn't want to exist within.

I phoned work and told them I would be away for the rest of the week. I texted Brad and told him I was back and that I had gastro, and I would catch up in a few days when recovered. Then I sat. To an outsider, it would have looked as if time had stopped where I was. I made no movements and uttered no sound. I remained in a strange, motionless place, my companion, an awful truth.

I was apparently unlovable. Just as Noah had said.

I considered ending my own life. Nothingness would take away the pain of being violated, raged at and then discarded, by the man I had once called home.

I was unloveable to my family too. My siblings and my parents. My home, it seemed, would always be a place where I found punishment instead of safety. Rejection instead of love. I didn't know if I had the strength or desire even to keep going. What was this life that I had been born into? I knew that I should have ended things with Noah sooner. However, something in me, wanted to help him, to fix him. To mend us, when things had started to disintegrate.

I couldn't find any tears inside of me, just a big space where I had used to reside. Noah had done something to me, far worse than violate my body. He'd taken *me* somewhere else and had then crushed *me* into nothing. When I thought about the assault, I remembered its deadly silence. Far from shouting and screaming, as would have been appropriate for a display of seething anger such as that, all I remembered was movement, weight and searing pain. In my grieving, in my shock, I concluded that having remained quiet perhaps had been the safest option at the time.

It was a few days before my mind healed enough to start processing what had happened. I was left with a confusing number of questions. Who was that man in the hut? I went back onto Noah's Instagram, searching for clues that might enlighten me. None of his behaviour in recent weeks had made much sense to me. I could see he had been busy, with several new pictures having been posted, none tasteful. Then I saw it. A colourful cartoon strip, posted during the past few hours. Two people, a man, and a woman driving in a convertible car, just like his. Several scenarios had been typed up underneath the pics, which looked like they were summarising the trip we had made to the peninsula when we had first met. I read the dialogue, and as I read, I felt myself being swallowed up.

Crystal. *Jerry, I love our drives together. It's a beautiful day, and the weather is perfect, darling. Just the two of us.*

Jerry. *Crystal, instead of driving, we could pull over. I want to fuck you against the car, just like the cheap slut you are.*

Crystal. *Oh, Jerry. I just love it when you take me on a romantic drive away from the city. I love you so much!*

Jerry. *Well, Crystal, I don't love you. Why don't you just put your head into my lap like a good girl? You know, deep down, that you're just a whore.*

Crystal. *Maybe after that, we could find a lovely beach and go for a stroll?*

Jerry. *Or Crystal, I could strip you, stuff your panties into your mouth and just fuck you against this tree.*

Crystal. *Oh, Jerry. I want to stay in your arms. I love you and want to spend the rest of my life with you.*

Jerry. *Do you ever really listen to me, Crystal? I don't love you. I'm just using you and you're so slow to figure it out. You're just an ugly whore who needs someone like me. When I'm finished with you, you'll know.*

I didn't cry. I sat and remained motionless for the evening, staring at the cartoon strip. One which had publicly mocked and shamed me. What was left of my dignity was now gone. Was I a whore and a slut in Noah's eyes? The day trip, the exchange in the bushland, the same day the old lady had told us she could see our love. In his mind, I'd been something else, a slut and a whore.

I searched online, knowing that there would be more, eventually finding him on several dating sites where he'd written that he wanted someone to *'help him play out his fantasies and that looks weren't important.'* I finally vomited, my stomach glad to have released the pressure. He'd had been playing out some sort of sick fantasy, right from the beginning. All I could conclude was that Noah had been biding his time to hurt me, as some sort of final power play.

I phoned a sexual assault hotline and asked the woman if she thought I'd been assaulted, simply because my own sense of accuracy with events was now a mess. Before she could answer, I started to sob. Deep, guttural sobs that shook through my entire body. The woman was kind, though, and allowed me time to express the pain that had surfaced. Then she asked me *what exactly* I had consented to? I knew it wasn't that. I certainly hadn't given Noah the right to hurt me... to dominate me without permission. I was clearer after speaking with her, understanding that silence isn't consent. She explained that often it's how women like me, who sense danger, save themselves. Going mute is smart, *not a yes*. She said that men like Noah have the intention to hurt, right from the beginning. Going motionless was a way in which to minimise further pain, that he would most likely would have inflicted if I'd refused him. Her kindness allowed me to cry, and I did, for days on end, releasing honest grief and hurt. I thought about pressing charges and, then, texted Noah,

P: Why did you physically hurt me?

He texted back only two words.

N: Me bad.

It was only when I took offence to his juvenile admission, that his tone changed. His return email portrayed himself as the victim. Instead, he denied everything, saying I was sick and twisted and that he had done nothing wrong. I was at fault, he said. 'Do I need a lawyer?' he demanded.

I confronted him over his story about the obese woman in the supermarket and how he'd claimed to have assaulted her in broad daylight with his kids watching. He wrote a lengthy email back saying that it was clear that the story was an analogy as to how he felt about his position at work. If I continued to accuse him of assaulting someone, he would take the matter further. He wrote how hard it had been, some nights, to even try to see me, that he had been tired after work, but had pushed through for me. He'd been so tired that he'd become suicidal, he wrote.

He listed every weakness that I had confided to him, in moments where my guard had been dropped. He wrote that he hoped he hadn't caught HIV from me. He tore me down piece by piece until there was nothing left to tear down. In his eyes, he'd had to get away from me. *I was the problem.* When I got angry at his accusations, sending angry emails back to him, he called me mentally unstable and accused me of being Borderline. He mocked me, saying that I was a woman who didn't even know if I loved or hated him. My emails became confused, trying to reason why I was missing the Noah I'd met, whilst hurting from his cruelty and wanting him never to come near me again.

I resorted to emailing him something that would hurt him back. I knew it wasn't right, but I wanted him to hurt too. Maybe if he knew how hurt could feel, he would stop doing it to me. Then he accused me of being emotionally abusive, and I felt guilty for having been nasty. In hindsight, all I had done is point out his lies back to him. When I started unravelling, as facts became distorted and my mind scrambled from having my reality skewered, he told me that he had shown my emails to a third party and that his message was clear. He wanted me to stop all contact. He wrote that I had now ruined any good feelings that he'd ever had about me, with my attacks on him. Then he blocked me. Completely. He had done what I should have done to him. It was the final insult.

I knew that if I took Noah to court that I would be fighting for my truth. I wanted to though, to make him pay in some way. I had trusted him, and he had chosen to be sexually gratified by hurting me. I wondered how many other women he'd done the same thing to? I wondered about all the prostitutes in the reviews and whether anyone would care or believe them if they had mentioned Noah abusing them? Maybe Noah had learned how to slip through the cracks?

Then I beat myself up, remembering that he'd told me that he *liked to hurt people* before it had happened. The truth was painful. I had fallen in love with someone who wanted to dominate other people, and in hindsight, it was now all staring at me in the face. Once he had hurt me, his quest was over. I meant nothing to him after that. Nothing. I had trusted Noah to the core, and so when he emailed me that I meant nothing to him and that he had moved on, I believed I was worthless in a matter of weeks. There must be something so wrong with me that men like Noah proclaim love, want to dominate me and then leave me. Then I beat myself up for caring if a man like Noah did that to me. My head was now screwed on the wrong way, life was upside down, and I couldn't find north.

I CRAWLED my way through the next six months, not returning to art class and merely going to and from work, encased in self-loathing. I was mechanical in my actions and dull in spirit. I cried every night, not knowing what to do with the whole experience. I had lost home, and my version of reality would always be associated with pain. Night after night, painful and raw grief would rip and tear through me, and I would succumb to it, the depths of my tears convulsing out of my body. I thought I had finally found my safe place, and ironically, it had turned out to be the most dangerous. I had done all of that to myself, I concluded. I hadn't trusted my intuition when it was telling me that there was something wrong. It was all my own fault.

I analysed the relationship from start to finish, applying what I knew from my endless online searches. The first bit, including his supposed, sudden admiration for Slessor, was the love-bombing phase I assumed. He'd reeled me in, allowing me to feel safe enough to divulge my vulnerabilities… my secrets to him. Those would be stored as ammunition for later on. He discovered I loved being held, and so he had held me. Then he'd started to devalue me, saying things that were bizarre to me… I talked too much, I was a terrorist… I irritated him… and the lies! All of those bizarre stories that he'd told me, including his arm needing to be amputated, his mother dying, the dog being killed with the vase, the obese lady, the phone number on the receipt and the police stopping him asking about a concealed weapon… all told with that strange smile on his face. He'd been smiling because he had been playing with me. He must have been laughing on the inside at how I'd responded to such bizarre stories. He'd marked me as someone trusting, and I had been.

There was increasing control as well, which had got to the point where I was fearful of saying anything to him. He would dump all of his problems onto me… some heavy, like suicidal thoughts, and then criticise me if I tried to reflect them, or offer insight. I was walking on eggshells, which were exploding into my face. Then he had gas-lit me, by assaulting me and calling it reasonable… telling me that I'd been yelling at him and that he'd been crying with a pillow over his head. I knew he'd not cried with a pillow over his head, and yet he claimed it had. It was a deflection from having assaulted me minutes earlier.

Then he had thrown me away, in public, outside my flat and had discarded me as if I had never existed. He didn't stop there, though. He then posted the cartoon online as a way to mock whatever had been left and made sure to tell me that he had to get away from me. Then he moved on, letting me know that I meant nothing to him. Nothing. I had been relegated to nothing.

I didn't have the vocabulary to describe the emotional pain I was experiencing. I just knew that I felt awful. I eventually went to see Cynthia afterwards and not Brad. I was too ashamed of myself to confide in Brad. This was all my fault, and they had tried to warn me.

Only I was too busy chasing the feeling of home to care. I was too busy wanting to feel Noah's arms around me to listen. I had been an idiot, an addict… and now I had been assaulted and discarded by the man I had been telling them was near perfect.

'I am a failure.' I told Cynthia, crying, mostly out of shame.

'No Pippa. You're not.'

'Yes, I am. You told me everything I needed to NOT get into trouble, and I blatantly ignored it.'

'Life isn't that easy. If it were, none of us would get ourselves into trouble. Remember your wiring. When you see or feel discomfort in love, you feel normal. When you see people in trouble, you race in to fix. Noah played this out in a manipulative and deceitful manner. Most people wouldn't have seen that disgusting discard coming either.'

'Yeah, well, I could see that he was becoming more aggressive and nasty… but to deliberately hurt me? That's the bit I will never understand. I just can't believe that he hurt me.' I shook my head. 'It's my fault, though. I should have left the first time he went weird. I don't know why I didn't.'

'Unfortunately, by the sounds of it, Noah knew exactly what he was doing. He had you conned. You were hanging on for the good bits to happen again. Look at his online presence anyway. He's not innocent in what he has done. It sounds like he planned the assault as part of the discard. He's mocked you blatantly too, in those awful cartoons.'

'I wrote to him and asked him about the cartoons.'

'What did he say?'

'He said I was confused and that they weren't related to me at all.'

'He's brazen, even with the truth. How could he even deny that they weren't about the two of you?'

'Yeah, he told me all of those reviews were fake too. Maybe he *was* leaving his family to go and sleep with prostitutes? I pity Emma.' I paused. 'Also, who did damage my car that night at the art exhibition? Do you think that might have been Noah? It was his car parked next to mine, and then for some reason, he moved his, and he knew about the dummy camera.'

'I honestly don't know, Pippa.' Cynthia got up to make the tea, this time, bringing in large, comfy mugs.

'How are you feeling in all of this?' she asked, curling her feet up and underneath her in the huge recliner. She sat back, wanting me to feel comfortable and relaxed.

'Violated. It's affected me deeply. It's like I don't have the words to describe the emotion I'm feeling, Cynthia. When a man does that to you, it changes every cell in your body.'

'Are you sure you won't press charges?'

'After what he said to me? He could make me look like a fruitcake in court with all the stuff he knows about my family. He accused me of drinking too… being drunk and wanting group sex. I feel like he's set me up. If I did go to court, the truth would be lost in amongst all of that. He would throw everything at me and distort it all. No-one would know who was telling the truth.'

'The truth. You must keep your version of your reality as the truth. Don't ever second guess yourself. This man was clever and highly dangerous. Extremely manipulative. I've been doing this a long time Pippa, and this Noah is one of the worst I've seen.'

'Yes. He played me well.' I shook my head and sipped my tea. Sweet and hot, it hit the right spot somewhere close to where I needed it to go.

'He did. To him, this was a game, I believe. He led you into what you thought was a stable and loving relationship. Then he dominated your time and your attention with his issues. He involved you quickly into his life, reflecting what you needed to see so that you felt safe enough to open up to him. Think about your first date. He took you to the water's edge and recited a poet that he'd never heard of until you mentioned it was your favourite. He was always phoning, needing you… creating a strong connection between the two of you. He told you that he would love you always, no matter how much you changed. This was the fake Noah, Pippa. From what you've told me, the real Noah then emerged. A man who lied, cheated and bent the truth as far as it could go. A man who swore at you and allowed his kids to abuse you. Then, to discard you, he had to find faults, or make them up. He did that, including assaulting you, his final power play. When you finally stood up to him, he flew into a rage. Once he realised you had seen through the pretend version of him, he discarded you. Brutally too. They all do the same. There is never an easy discard.'

'Who is all?'

'Narcissists and psychopaths.'

'Do you think he is one of those?'

'I think you've met a psychopath, Pippa.'

'Really?'

'Yes. This was a man without a conscience, empathy or guilt and who systematically lied from what I can see. He was also very manipulative.'

'What's the difference?'

'Between narcissists and psychopaths? It's contentious. Some believe it boils down to the predatory nature of the psychopath. They hunt for their victims, whereas narcissists accidentally come across their victims. There's less hunting.'

'Why me?'

'They choose their prey carefully. They want the vulnerable. They seek out people who come from homes where they have been starved of healthy love. They know that these individuals won't spot the red flags early on. It's easy for them to chew through their victims… abusing them and then chucking them away because they don't feel any guilt for doing so. From what you've told me about his blank tone, his coldness, wanting to hurt, and the lies? He sounds almost textbook psychopath. It makes my skin crawl. I think you have had a lucky escape, all things considered, Pippa.'

'Yeah. I'm thinking that too.'

'When you meet real cruelty Pippa, it hits you here.' She banged on her chest. 'You know when you've met the real deal.'

'Yes,' I said, instinctively reaching for my chest. 'I can still feel him in there.'

IT TOOK me a bit longer to reconnect with Brad. We arranged to meet at our cafe.

'So,' he said, looking at me intently. 'What the hell happened, Pippa? Every time I've tried to connect with you, you've pushed me away.'

'Everything happened. I failed you. Cynthia said I didn't, because I'm human, but I did. I wasn't honest with you.'

'Pippa. We all make mistakes, and we all cherry-pick advice that other people give us.'

'Well, I paid the price of not listening.'

'I'm sitting opposite you now, not as your life coach anymore, but as someone who knows you pretty well. I have the time right now to listen and to hear you. Want to give it a try?'

I took a deep breath. This was going to be hard. Brad would realise how much I had left out and how I had manipulated my truth, solely to be in Noah's arms. I started from the beginning and left nothing out. Brad shook his head at the end.

'Pippa,' he said quietly.

'Yeah?

'That's fucked up.'

'Yeah, I know. I'm sorry.'

'Why are you, sorry? That man was a psychopath. Worse than I had imagined if I'm honest.'

'Oh, really?' Brad wasn't telling me off.

'Yeah. Smooth operator. He's probably already replaying the whole scenario with someone else.'

My heart sank. I felt like I'd been stabbed. My Noah, with some other woman lying in his arms.

'Sorry, Pippa. The Noah you met wasn't real. Remember that.'

'Yeah, although that doesn't help, you know.'

'What? That he wasn't real?'

'No. He was still real to me. Cynthia said he was a psychopath as well by the way.'

'Exactly. Noah looked at you and then moulded himself into the man of your dreams. Of course, you were going to hold on to that tightly. Of course, you were going to tell me to go to hell if I tried to take that away from you. You've been searching for that feeling all of your life. I wasn't going to be the one to get in your way.'

'I've been feeling guilty, Brad, to be honest. I lied to you. It didn't sit well with me.'

'Under these circumstances, I forgive you. Are you sure you don't want to press charges, though? He deserves to be punished, not walk away, pretending to be the victim.'

'I keep thinking though, if I were in court, the whole exchange could be seen as just a rough encounter, and what's your problem, woman?'

'Even that has to be consented to, Pippa. Do you understand? You didn't give him permission to hurt you.'

'He could say it was accidental, and how he'd been distraught afterwards. He's sent enough emails about that stupid bloody pillow he claims was over his face, as he was crying. It would be his word against mine, aside from the *'Me Bad'* text. I expect though, he would be able to twist that as well.'

Brad sighed. 'The system is stupid. I can see your dilemma.'

'I think about pressing charges every day, I do. I don't see why he should be able to go around assaulting people - but, he's manipulative. I can see how he might defend himself. That's probably why he picked me. He knows that my background is unstable enough for the assault to disappear under masses of dysfunction. How can I prove now that I wasn't some drunk woman, demanding a rough encounter? He would use the sex shop as evidence that I was looking for stuff too. Finally, Brad, how do I ever prove to someone that I didn't ask for that? How well did I try to fight him off? I didn't try hard enough. I wouldn't stand a chance in a courtroom.'

'The law is complicated' Brad admitted. 'I mean you might convince a jury, but I can see where he might twist stuff.'

'I wondered about reporting him to his work? I was uncomfortable when he started telling me stories about young women wanting to have group sex with him. Then, I think that I would just sound like a bitter ex. It probably never happened, and they would tell me that they don't even have work experience girls there. I might end up looking like I exaggerate everything.

'He's already got a third party lined up though, hasn't he? He's shown your emails around, telling his side of the truth and labelled you as a borderline fruitcake.'

'Yeah,' I said, sounding defeated.

'You met a psychopath. A man who had everything stitched up from the beginning. He makes my skin crawl.' Brad looked upset. 'I wanted it to work out for you, Pippa. All that work you put in concerning your family. Then you finally met someone that you fell in love with.'

'I know.'

'You should buy a plane ticket and go back to Paris.'

'What? That's a bit random. A bit impulsive?'

'I'm serious. Pick up that bit of your life again. Go back and replay it, only differently. Then come back and not meet Noah.'

I thought about it. I'd just returned from Paris when I'd met him. I felt like my time with Noah had been swallowed up. A relationship that never was and never had been. A value that I'd thought I'd had with someone, only to find out that I had been deemed worthless. A relationship with a man who had never truly existed. Even my memories weren't ones I could rely on.

'How are your finances looking? Could you do it?'

'Yeah. I've spent next to nothing recently. I've been like a wounded animal, hiding at home and just going to and from work. I could buy a ticket and go back to Paris. However, don't you remember our conversations after I'd been? Paris was a fantasy. Well, my version of it anyway. I don't need to mingle with any more fantasies right now.'

'What if you went back to Paris and found your version of it?'

'Why, though? Why would I?'

'To heal Pippa. You're damaged. Badly, and that's not your fault. Paris would be like a re-set and a challenge. Go and find the Paris you dreamed about.'

'It's not there though, Brad.'

'It's winter now, and the crowds will be less and no one-in-a-hundred-year heat waves to deal with.'

'It's an idea, Brad. I'll think about it.'

'Do, please.'

'I promise I will.'

PARIS SEEMED
LIKE A
GOOD ESCAPE

22

TO BE OR NOT TO BE

THAT IS MY CURRENT QUESTION

I'm sitting in my flat, and I'm the birthday girl, now thirty. Brad says I'm a bit melancholy for a birthday girl and that thirty is hardly old. You reckon I'm a bit low? I wonder why? Harry dying and my experience with Noah has made me feel like ending this. I'm tired. I'm fed up, and I can't see how I'm ever going to learn to be more sensible in this world. I had all the tools I needed, courtesy of Cynthia and Brad, and I blew it. I sacrificed common sense to lie in someone's arms. In summary, I loved feeling loved, and I loved, loving him. I had believed in my own fairy tale.

Looking at all the lies that Noah told me, I just feel stupid. Idiotic if the truth is told. Reading them back on paper has allowed me to see that I must have been under some stupid spell. I'll call it the *Noah Influence.* I keep thinking back, wondering how he had me so duped? Was it the way he looked straight into my eyes as he was lying? Was it the way he kept reeling me back in after he'd spat me out? Was I just a gullible idiot? Probably. Maybe he figured out right back at the start that I just wanted to lie in those warm arms and feel safe.

I think about Hamlet's words, which is a bit random, even for me. I had learned them at school. I say them out aloud.

'To be, or not to be, that is the question… Whether 'tis nobler in the mind to suffer the slings and arrows of outrageous fortune, Or to take arms against a sea of troubles, and by opposing end them. To die… to sleep, No more, and by a sleep to say we end…'

To date, my life had indeed been a story based around a lack of power, at the mercy of a script often written by someone else, with me playing an unfamiliar character. I had indeed suffered a series of misfortunes, some of which had felt like arrows, piercing my heart. My choice in continuing my life does now come down to a decision of life or death. That much, in those words spoken so eloquently by Hamlet, is true. If I chose not to be, on today, of all days, there would be neatness in my life and death dates, similar to the balance in those first six words of his most famous utterances. 'To be or not to be.'

So, right now, it all comes down to the fact that I messed up, and I *cannot* forgive myself. Noah hurt me, and I did nothing to fight for myself at that moment. I'll sit with that thought for a while. I keep going back to the fact that love feels so good when you find it. When you haven't felt it very much, it feels like you have tapped it to something so special. Losing it is hard.

Am I unloveable? I sit with the question. If I am indeed unloveable, then I should end it all because otherwise, life will always be a series of painful endings.

OKAY, so thinking has been done. It's several hours later. Maybe I shouldn't punish myself for messing up? What I should be doing is looking into the future and not messing it up again in the same way. That would be the sensible option right now. A little more optimistic than trying to work out, how not, to be. I think that honesty seems to have cleansed me somewhat, just a little. I've admitted to my mistakes at least, and maybe there is hope in such an action?

Maybe Hamlet's words are limited? He believed that we only have a choice to be, or not to be. Perhaps, there is a third option? An option that opens up when the truth is spoken. I am no longer imprisoned in a sense, by holding onto my misery. Instead, the speaking of my truth has allowed space for something different to form. Yes, I will be, but differently to before. I imagine the opening to the soliloquy with this new perspective.

'To be, or not to be, that is not the whole question, for there may be a third way of being, once your truth is uncovered and spoken. Stand in your power and speak it with confidence, for it is yours to speak and yours only. The evil in others, and that in circumstance, must never cloud the right for another to live within the certainty of their own self.'

I think it's rather good and phone Brad to read it out. It's so good that Brad asks me if I wrote it myself. I'll take that as a compliment. Why should I end my own life because of the limitations of others, though? It is not their right to push me into eternal blackness, while they continue on, finding joy in hurting others. No. I won't do it. I want to live. I want to start again on my terms and live. I text Brad.

P: I want to live Brad, so I'll go back to Paris.

B: I'm glad, Pippa. I'm concerned that you thought you might not want to? Go to Paris. Find your way.

P: Thank you.

B: Be safe.

I sold my car and terminated the lease on my flat. I sold my shares and applied for my work visa. Then I resigned from my job.

'So, you're actually moving to Paris and not just visiting?' asked a surprised Adele.

'Yes. I'm moving there.'

'Why?'

'Why not?' I replied, not wanting to spoil my plans by having someone like Adele find fault with them.

'For how long?'

'As long as it takes.'

'For what?' She raised inquisitive eyebrows.

'For all of it.'

'Wow. That's brave.' She looked at me with a definite hint of admiration.

'Thank you, Adele.'

I THEN SOLD my furniture and put a few boxes of personal items into storage, knowing that I could have them sent over once I was settled. I'd found a flat in Montmartre to live, with the Sacré-Coeur framed by my front window. I had no plans to do anything, with the sale of my shares able to support me comfortably, for the first year. Last time I had visited, I had run around in searing heat, trying to do the Paris that everyone else was telling me to do. This time, I was going to allow Paris to discover me. If I weren't looking for pink poodles and women wearing broad-brimmed hats in front of the Eiffel Tower, I wouldn't be disappointed if I didn't find any.

One of the first things I did was to join an art class. It didn't matter that my French was basic, art was a universal language, and the still-life class I had joined didn't require any understanding of the language. I wanted to study the human form from the outside, taking my time to look at what it meant to translate vision into meaning. My teacher, a retired art professor, named Pierre, who looked uncannily like Monet, encouraged me, in English with intense hues of French.

'Only draw what you see, Pippa. Not what you think you see, remember that. Allow the art to unfold itself to you. It will start to speak in a language that you will understand.'

'Yes, Pierre. I understand,' I would say, rubbing out another charcoal line that had been placed into the wrong position on my paper. My first few classes were awkward. I wasn't as liberal as the French in being around nudity. Sometimes I was worried that the model was getting cold or cramping from having to stay in the same position for so long, not that they ever seemed to mind.

The other students in my class were an interesting mix of young and old, from Aimee, a business student, with her bright pink hair, to Andre, a retired teacher in his seventies. They had been respectful towards me, as an outsider, and had allowed me just to be, and to draw. Sometimes, just as had been the case in my classes with Stuart, we would go to the local café after the class.

'Un café au lait, s'il vous plait,' I asked slowly, for fear of getting my words mixed up.

'Your French, it is improving. I may mistake you for the real deal one day soon.' Raphael smiled at me from behind the counter, his English disguised in a thick French accent.

'Merci,' I said, returning the smile. 'Comment etait ta journee?'

'Pretty good, thank you, Pippa. Nice pronunciation too. Yours?'

'Lovely. I took a stroll up to the top of the Sacré-Coeur and had a picnic. La vue était parfait. I love the view of Paris from up there.'

'And the crowd? Yes? Many less at this time of the year? The cold, it scares them all away, I think so.'

'I came here in the summer last time, and it was packed… très bondé… very bad. Now, I can move around and see everything. I'm cold… très froid… but that is okay.' I smiled.

'I bring your drink to you when I make it. Yes?'

'Merci, Raphael.'

'Merci, Pippa.'

I sat with the others from the class and listened to them speak. They spoke earnestly about things I could only speculate about, their hands used to emphasise points of passion in their speech. I didn't care that I couldn't understand them, I just enjoyed being with them. They were kind in that when they saw me being left out, they often changed to English, to include me, and somehow we all related to one another, being a mixed bag, united in our passion for art.

I spent the first couple of months in Paris strolling around it, with a paper map tucked into my pocket. I would leave my flat mid-morning, wrapped up against the winter chills, and simply choose a direction to walk in. I would stop in and say *bonjour* to the shop keepers, some of whom, now knew me by name, and none of it was rushed. That was my one rule. I wanted to unfold Paris slowly. The universe and I now had a new understanding between us. I promised to live only in pure truth, and it promised to not shit on me anymore. I thought this was a pretty good deal, hoping for a period of Parisian stability that might lie in front of me. The memories of Noah, however, invaded my mind at every opportunity. It was as if I was now trapped in his web of *after*. His actions and words had permeated into every cell in my body, and I was scared that the labels he had ascribed to me, were in fact, true.

It wasn't a matter of just 'putting it all behind me.' I had arrived in Paris with the same memories and the same sense of self which had been shattered. To have fallen in love that genuinely and then been spat out in an act of such calculated violence had destroyed a part of me that I didn't know how to rebuild. I would have to start again and rebuild a new me, set in Paris, and with no preconceived notions as to what would be the outcome. For now, though, Paris provided a buffer between me and the physical locality of Noah. Even if I was unlovable, I could love Paris.

The cold winter wind, transformed into a warmer one, and one afternoon, as I was strolling through the Tuileries Gardens' spring colour pallet, in the centre of Paris, I stumbled across the Musée de l'Orangerie, a gallery containing both impressionist and post-impressionist art. Due to the heatwave during my previous holiday, I hadn't managed to visit, but now, it was nearly empty out of high season. Monet wrapped around the sensual curves of the inside of the building in blues, pinks, and whites, allowing the viewer to immerse themselves in images that would reveal themselves only from an appropriate distance. Then downstairs, I stumbled upon Matisse. So many of his works, one after the other.

Tears sprang into my eyes as I remembered *Pippa, who had liked Matisse from Sydney*, a form of myself from when I had first met Noah. Now I was with Matisse, and it made a difference not just imagining him, but being alongside him. I feasted on his works, walking from one to another and grieved for the Pippa I had been.

I took the train out to Giverny that weekend and visited Monet's home and gardens, mostly out of curiosity. I hadn't expected to be captivated and spellbound by the artistry in the garden itself. It wasn't hard to imagine a white-bearded Monet, dressed in white with his Panama hat, a piece of art himself against the midday backdrop of carefully planted colours and shapes. As I walked around, I remembered what Cynthia had said to me.

'Remain in the moment you are in. Don't ruminate. Look around you, as a child might. Be in awe of everything you see. Wonder about everything.'

I did, stopping to appreciate the wall of colourful flowers, green weeping branches, and lilac wisteria that insisted that I stop on several occasions to inhale its perfume. I didn't know the names for all of the flowers that I saw, choosing only to focus on their shapes, myriad of bouquets, and hues. I found small sections of the garden where there were fewer people, and I sat, *as I am*. Each time I was present in the moment, I was creating Pippa of now. Not fighting in my mind with whom Pippa should be.

I took the train out to Monet's gardens again, later that week, with my art pad and some pencils. I wanted to try to capture my interpretation of Monet's garden, in my style, perhaps with a hint of Matisse. I wanted to discover how I might interpret the walls of colour, the numerous ponds, bridges, and the endless lily pads. I had Pierre's voice in my head,

'Draw what you see, Pippa.'

It wasn't about what Monet had seen when he had stood in front of the same vista, it was now about how I interpreted his world, and there would be no wrong, and no punishment for my effort. My task was to truly connect to the beauty around me and capture it somehow into my heart. I did, producing work after work, each getting better in technique, until one day, I dared to share my efforts with Pierre.

'Pippa, ce sont magnifiques et beaux! I must show the others.'

The rest of the class gave my art more time than they should have, and everyone had something positive to say. Later that evening at the café, one of them told Raphael about my art.

'You must get her to show you. They are beautiful, quite exquisite,' said Gabriel, paying for his coffee.

'So, Pippa, I hear you are an artist of magnificence!' Raphael sounded enthusiastic.

'Really?' I laughed. 'I've been going to Monet's gardens and drawing the beautiful spring flowers. Have you been?'

'Yes, of course. Everyone in Paris has been to his gardens at least once. It is beautiful, yes. Now, can I see this art for myself?'

I dug around into my bag for my phone. 'Here,' I said, taking a deep breath, as he flicked through the photos of my sketches.

'Yes, superb. I love the colours. You are a… which artist am I thinking of? Matisse! You draw like Matisse!'

I laughed. 'He's my favourite artist, Raphael.'

'One day, you can take me to the gardens and let me see them through your eyes?'

I must have looked a bit shocked at how forward he had been, because he quickly added, 'if you like Pippa.'

Would I like? Hell yes! Raphael was perhaps a couple of years younger than me, and he was a good-looking Frenchman, who had caught my eye. However, I'd learned my lesson with Noah. People were like books. You had to read through all of them before you could decide whether to keep them and put them on your shelf. Well, not on a shelf per se, but you get my drift.

'Really?' I asked him.

'Yes, Pippa. Really. When are you free next?'

'I'm fairly flexible, Raphael. I'll work in with you.'

'I can be free on Tuesday, this next one. Yes? I will drive you.'

My stomach lurched. I didn't want to be driven. I still felt uncomfortable in cars, after Noah's raging.

'Is it okay if we take the train, Raphael?' I didn't explain why.

'Yes, Pippa. Of course, we can take the train. I like the trains very much too.'

I smiled. It felt right to be saying, yes.

SKETCHING
MONET'S
GARDEN WAS
BEAUTIFUL

23

PARIS

WITH MONET

I took Raphael to Monet's Gardens the following Tuesday. He was enthusiastic about returning to a place he hadn't seen since he was a child.

'Let me see,' he said, as we walked from the station at Giverny to the gardens, 'I was seven when last here, and now I'm twenty-eight, so it's been what? Twenty-one years since I last saw this. That's the time for… hang on for a moment. I think that's around six hundred and fifty million seconds. Give or take one or two.'

'How did you manage to work that out?' I asked him, rather impressed that he'd done that in his head.

'I understand the maths very well, Pippa. I graduated in astronomy here in Paris, and then I undertook research at the observatory. Then, sadly, I lost my passion, and well,' he said, holding his hands into the air, 'now I work in the café to find it again.'

'I'm sorry,' I said. 'What happened to make you lose your passion?'

'Life happened, Pippa. I just had too much on my plate and then, how you say it? Kaput! It all fell down into many little pieces, taking my passion with it. I hope to find it again one day, though. Maybe it will be here, in amongst the flowers, and I can stick all the little pieces of it back together again? Yes?'

So Raph also had felt shattered. I wondered what had happened to him. 'I hope you can. What was your research about?'

'You may not like it. A bit boring perhaps for you? It is fascinating, to me, anyway. I studied a black hole and how it would feast on material, but it's not the same menu like you think. Some days mine eats more, and some days it eats less. A little like my own appetite!'

I laughed. Raphael had a way with words. 'I hadn't really thought that black holes had days where they didn't rip everything apart.'

'It is true. I am doing a PhD at the time, researching this, but my mother and brother, they died in a terrible car crash. I got the stuffing knocked out of my sails.' He hung his head.

'I'm so sorry, Raphael. That's awful.'

'Oui. I lost my two best friends in the whole world in that moment and I've not recovered. Not yet. Some tell me it will happen and so I wait for the right day.'

'What about your Dad?'

'He left when I was small with the woman he worked with. My mother was devastated beyond her mind.'

'So, do you have other family Raphael?'

'No. I am alone, Pippa. Alone in this bigness of the world.' He smiled despite the sadness in his story. 'It's not as bad as you may think. Most of the time I am a happy person. Just not right now.'

'Well, let's hope today, we can find you some happiness. It's a beautiful day.' I hoped that hadn't come across as flippant. I also remembered that just because the weather is kind, doesn't mean that the person next to you, is too. My mind fleetingly revisited the night that Noah had told me the weather was perfect, as he recited Slessor at the harbour's edge. It was as if a shroud had slowly descended over me. I shook it off. I needed to remain in the moment. Raphael had been brave to tell me something personal, and I appreciated his gesture of trust. Then I wondered about the onion of trust and how a top layer could be deceiving. Noah had told me that his mother had died, then I had discovered it had been a lie. I hoped that Raph was telling the truth.

'I know Pippa, that you too, are here to find your happiness back. I can tell even in the past few months, your smile is getting bigger and there is more hope inside of you.'

I smiled. 'You can tell all of that, without really knowing me?'

'Yes, I see you each week, and now you seem almost happy. So today, we will be two nearly happy people going to find hope in amongst Monet's garden.'

'Agreed. We have a plan!'

We walked around the gardens, commenting on the sheer feast of colour and scent.

'You know, I have this sudden memory in my mind, Pippa. When I was little, all I could think of was eating lunch when I was here.' He laughed at the memory. 'My mother got trés annoyed with me. I remember her saying to me, very angry too. We are here to regard the beauty, not the food in the café Raphael!'

'Well, to be honest, I wouldn't mind a cup of tea right now and something to eat? Shall we go to the café?'

'Let's do that. Then we should find somewhere a little quieter, and maybe you can show me how to sketch something?'

'Okay, Raphael.'

WE HAD FOUND A SOFT patch of grassy lawn with a vista that looked down a winding path, bordered with colourful tulips and towards Monet's house.

'Can you imagine living in such a grand house and looking out from windows in the mornings? My mother would have cherished the house, although she would have cut all the flowers to place them in vases everywhere! She loved the fresh flowers.' He smiled, remembering something private and sweet.

'I think I would do the same. I've never seen so many flowers in a private garden before! No wonder Monet was so inspired to keep painting here. We could do a tour of the house later so that we can see the garden from the house. I agree, waking every morning and looking out over all of this? No wonder he wanted to come out and paint so much.'

'He had many of the children too, despite he and his wife sleeping in different bedrooms, did you know? However, his second wife brought lots of children to this house, with her. I think also, maybe it was his mother who passed on her passion of the arts to him? She was a singer originally and very good too, I hear.'

'You are full of information, Raphael.'

'I try to be, because otherwise, you know, I would make for very boring companionship.'

I handed him a sketch pad and a pencil. 'Want to try to sketch this?'

'Yes. Let's give this a go. What do I do, in order to start?'

'You only draw what you see, not what you think you see.'

'Very good words Pippa.'

'Not mine, they belong to Pierre, my art teacher. However, the advice works.'

'We will see. Now, did you also know that I am an artist of shit?'

I laughed. 'Do you mean a shit artist? I was too once, but somehow, if you keep trying, you get better.'

We sat in the warm spring sunshine and sketched the path and tulips. I added a woman, sitting on a bench by herself, watching the scene unfolding in front of her.

'So, you can add things to only what you see? You have broken the rules, Pippa!' Noah laughed. 'Is this you Pippa, sitting in this garden alone, thinking?'

'I have broken the rules, I confess. Yes, I think it is me thinking about life. How did you go, anyway?'

'I think my sketch looks like a four-year child did draw it.'

'No, Raphael! It's good! Really good! You've drawn the shape of the tulip flowers very nicely.'

'So, tell me more about Pippa.'

The question had come in the middle of something good. Who was I indeed?

'Well, I'm here for the foreseeable future. I work in travel usually, and I love to paint. That's me.'

'That is part of you, yes? I believe there to be so much more. However, on this beautiful day, you will be Pippa, who is in Paris to paint and smile more. Oui?'

'Oui Raphael.'

ART CLASS HAD MOVED onto watercolours, something I'd never tried before. I liked control in my art, and watercolours were anything other than controlled. However, I soon learned that the surprise of their final form was often better than I had planned.

'Yes, Pippa. I love the layers here. You have captured the forces of the water well. See this? Yes, the turbulence from the wind and approaching storm. I like it.' Pierre was beginning to notice my art more. He gave me art books to look through, and I became familiar with all the French painters. Monet, Manet, Matisse, Cézanne,

Renoir… and the more I looked, the more I fell in love with Paris. I still hadn't found a single poodle on a lead, being walked by some ditzy woman in a broad hat, but I was beginning to find the hidden dignity within the city, in random places not frequented by tourists.

I found a hotel in the city where Marie Antoinette had frequented, which now had a courtyard cafe, set in amongst a beautiful garden. The grey stone walls, green lawn, fountain, and delicious caramel crepes allowed me to plan my day in terms of direction and time. I wanted to stumble across beauty and not deliberately seek it out. There was a surprise in finding something that took my breath away, igniting desire in me and the more I found, the more I wanted.

The warm weather was attracting more tourists, and I often passed long lines of tired and worn out travellers, wanting to tell them that Paris is more than ten places to visit. However, a relationship with Paris, I had concluded, is one that you must define for yourself.

I enrolled in French classes and started at an elementary level class. They were run at the local lyceé, and we would sit in the languages room, on small white chairs, and recite the French alphabet, animals and numbers. Then, our teacher, a greying woman with a French-language degree from the university, would start speaking French.

'Je parle en français à partir de maintenant… veuillez me parler en français.'

I always got nervous when she said this, as I would then only be allowed to speak in my broken French. If I used the wrong word, she would shake her head at me.

'Non… non… mauvis mot… trouver le bon mot Pippa s'il vous plait.'

However, as with my art, I diligently stuck to the classes, and within a few weeks, my French was improving. I was meeting with Raphael more and more, too, exploring the Paris that he had grown up within. He drove me out of the city on a few occasions to show me medieval villages, castles, and places where we could just sit and relax.

'I would love to show you the observatory, Pippa. Would you like to see the stars, and maybe a planet or two? This is my real world, my special world. Up there,' he said, looking upwards. 'The lights in Paris are powerful at night, and so they hide all the stars. When you look through the telescope though, you see everything that is hidden. It's like when you stop and properly look at someone. You see what they have tried to keep hidden.'

That comment hit the nail on the head. It was true. We are all so much more than people often see, simply because they haven't stopped to look properly.

'When were you thinking?'

'We will need a clear night, and I will need to book some time. I am still allowed, you know, to do that. They are waiting for me to start back to finish my work. They were very kind when my family died. They said I should take all the time I needed. Time, however, is relative, and the words have an irony I do not like. How can I ever return to where I was? I am changed now, and I cannot bring my family back to start again with me. My time must be a new time now.'

'Maybe you should pick a new point in time, in the future and start afresh?'

'Yes, Pippa. You give me hope that I could start again.' He stopped as if deep in thought. 'I might speak to some people. Now, I will text you when the night is clear, but not an art class night, and when I have a booking? Yes?'

'Yes, Raphael.'

RAPHAEL DROVE me the following week to the Observatoire de Paris, a large building with a white dome perched on top, at one end.

'This is where I sometimes would come, and I wanted to show you the beauty of this building. If you want to see the sky, however, then we must drive to somewhere else that is not too far. There I have lined up a treat, and hopefully, we will see planets and stars and things of great beauty Pippa. As the weather warms, the sky clears and it is a perfect time to see through the telescope.'

'Now,' he said, opening the door to an observatory on the outskirts of Paris. 'We have three hours to ourselves as part of a special favour. I crank it all up? Yes? Then you will see the real beauty that hides itself so well.'

Raphael looked like he had been switched on. It was nice to see him setting up the telescope so eagerly.

'They saw so much from here. The Martian surface, the issue with the canals there. Mercury and even the moons of Jupiter. It was like the sky gave up its secrets here. Now I can share with you, these secrets.'

'Wow' was my word of choice as I gazed through the telescope for the first time. I had no idea just how much of the night sky was hidden under city lights. 'It's beautiful. So, so beautiful Raphael.'

He spent the next three hours, showing me some of the most spectacular images I had ever seen. I was spellbound. I felt that Paris was beginning to trust me, giving up its invisible secrets to me. I smiled when I saw the face of the universe that had shat on me for so long. I had called it a black shit in the past, but it wasn't anything like that. It was colour and shapes and patterns of such intricate detail. Again, Raph's words popped into my head. It was true even with the universe, you have to look closely and take your time to truly understand what we are a part of.

'Now, if we can find a late café, we will chat,' he said, as we packed up. I liked the fact that he often would come up with a question and answer in the same sentence. He assumed that what he wanted was what I wanted, and to be accurate, most of the time, it was.

I had done everything right with Raphael, reading him like a book, turning each page slowly, and not wanting to rush to the end. In a sense, I was glad that he was working through his own issues because he hadn't pressured me for anything else. He was also respectful, something which I needed after my relationship with Noah. I did have flashbacks to the assault. However, I didn't panic when they happened. I just let them unfold, knowing that eventually, they would fade and disappear with Noah's memory. I didn't know how long that was going to take, maybe years? I hadn't heard from him again, as he had promised, and I wondered if he ever thought about me. I doubted it, and that thought hurt. I was out of sight and most likely, only ever perceived as some of the derogatory names he had called me.

I grieved, however for a Noah that had never existed. Few would understand the grief process after having dealt with such a brutal discard. I was most likely grieving for the fake Noah I had met during the love-bombing phase, where he had portrayed himself as my perfect fit. I was also grieving for potential. The illusion of our relationship, which at first, had seemed to be the one I had been waiting for, all of my life. That in itself felt awkward. It made it difficult for me to savour the good bits that had happened before it all went pear-shaped because it hadn't been real to start with. I felt like I'd lost half of every memory, with me being the only participant. I wondered about Rose and how she was doing, but I mostly felt sad for her. I wondered if she would look back when she was older and think that she might have been born with a short straw in her hand as well.

'So, Pippa. How was all of that?' Raphael was smiling enthusiastically at me from across the table.

'Amazing. I loved it.'

'I am glad. Now, a question. Are you happy now? In this very moment, here with me?'

'Honestly? I can say that I am happier than I have ever been in my entire life.' I didn't tell him it was a relative statement. Compared to most people, I'd probably managed to get to about five percent happiness, but it was better than none.

'That is great to hear! I am too. You have made me find my smile again, Pippa. I thought when I lost my mother and my brother on the same day, that my smile was buried with them.'

'Yeah, I can imagine that it must have been awful. My fiancé was killed by a car, many years ago as he was walking home. His name was Alan Parker.'

'Oh, that is sad too. I am sorry for you. We share some same sadness, it seems.'

I had let him in. I had opened the door to the old Pippa. Alan had been many years ago now, but his death was still a part of me. I could reach out to Raphael right now by letting him know that I too, had lost someone from death, in a car accident.

'I notice you have not mentioned your own mother, Pippa. I won't ask. No. If you want to speak about her and your father, you can. But that can be done in your time and only if you want to.'

'Thank you.' I felt my eyes watering.

'I have made you sad by saying that?' Raphael looked concerned.

'No, you've made me happy.' I laughed at my emotionality, which still bubbled from me, like an over-zealous stream.

'You Australians? You cry when happy and turn into stones when sad. You need to be French. Just let it all out and embrace everything that comes your way.'

I smiled. 'I love it here. One day I may become *real* French, I think. It would suit all of these emotions that I have.'

'I would love it if you stayed Pippa, but you would need to find work, and you will need to find love. A passionate love affair that you can hold close to your heart for eternity.'

'A passionate love affair?' I asked.

'Everyone needs a real, passionate love affair once in their life Pippa, but you have to be ready for it and be prepared to wait. You cannot be sad in order to start. Oui?'

'You're very poetic, you know, Raphael.'

His words had hit my heart a little, for I had thought that my once in a lifetime love affair had been with Noah. Now I looked back on it, not knowing what to call it. A disaster, perhaps? I wondered if it was hard to move on from it because it had disguised itself as my once-in-a-lifetime passionate love affair. It had conned me and lured me in, then hurt me. Maybe Raphael had hope that passion was still out there for me?

He was smiling. 'Now an important question,' he said, looking earnest. 'Do you want coffee or hot chocolate at this late hour?'

Raph's legs just
did not fit into
his plane seat

24

DEATH

SHE DEAD

Nic from my art class told me that a friend of his was seeking a travel guide. Someone who could speak 'good English.'

'It's for wealthy Americans who want to visit the real Paris,' he told me. 'They want someone to show them around. I think there is a bus added in too. It sounds like it might be perfect for you, Pippa.'

My ears had pricked up. It sounded like something I could do. 'How do I apply?' I asked.

'I have the number of the lady. You can call her. Her name is Charlotte.'

I called Charlotte the next morning, and she asked me if I could meet her that afternoon. Luckily, her business was based relatively close to my apartment, so my walk there was quick and easy, despite the Parisian early summer heat. It was another 'record-breaking heatwave' and people were starting to ask questions about climate change.

'Bonjour Pippa. I'm Charlotte. I'm glad you found us so easily. This is Robert, who is our Manager.'

'Bonjour,' I smiled at the young pair who had been savvy in seeing an opening in the market for a business, that escorted affluent Americans around Paris.

'So, we mainly deal with people who don't want to go on the big red bus, or be packed in like sardines into the boats. These are people who want to see something else about Paris that maybe locals see, for instance. However, the demand has been much higher than we expected, and we need an extra person to help look after that side of things. Nicholas said you had been here for a while and that you speak English and a little French.'

'Yes.' I said. 'This is my second time in Paris. The first was a quick visit, whereas this time, I'm discovering the hidden layers of the city.'

'Good,' said Robert. 'Nic says you have experience with inside the travel industry?'

'Yes, that's what I've done all my working life. I worked in a travel agency, specialising in European tours. However, I usually ended up booking everywhere with my regular clients.'

'So, how would you feel if we gave you a small bus with a driver? Could you put together an itinerary for people, do you think?' asked Charlotte.

'Yes, I could. Do you want me to plan an example?'

'That would be fine,' said Charlotte. 'But why don't you just tell us now what you might show people? Saves us some time.'

I thought hard, conjuring up a tour that allowed visitors to feel like they had found some of Paris's heart.

'Perfect,' smiled Charlotte, after I had explained it. 'I like that. We pay award, plus you keep tips. Now, what about your visa?'

'Actually, my current visa allows me to work, and I can extend it if I need to,' I said.

'When can you start then? Tomorrow?' Robert looked at Charlotte, and they smiled. I was surprised at how fast they had reached a decision.

'Fantastic. Thanks,' I said, and stood to shake their hands.

They laughed, and instead, leaned forward and kissed my cheeks.

'We seal the deal the French way,' smiled Charlotte, 'and you can take your employment contract with you now, read it, sign it and bring it back tomorrow.'

RAPHAEL WAS THRILLED. 'Pippa, this is amazing news, and they make it work with your visa? I've heard of this company too. Sometimes you see their buses in places, and then these celebrity people get out. 'Big hats, pink poodles. That sort of thing. Very glamorous.'

I stared at him.

'Did I say something wrong?' he asked, looking worried.

'No,' I said, my heart racing. 'I think I was destined to do this job, that's all.'

It was true. The Americans I met were dressed in the most outrageous fashions, and some were accompanied by ridiculously groomed dogs. These were people who wanted to feel special and show-off their Parisian experiences through their social media accounts. I became good at taking photos on phones, and they would do a quick edit, press send, and we would be off again, for the next pose, somewhere else. I soon realised that my tours really should have been called the 'Instagram Tour of Paris' as most of my job was to simply make my clients look good. Often I planned the day to ensure that we were able to stop off at least ten places where the backdrops were beautiful. I made my clients feel like the most influential people in Paris for the day, and I nearly made more in tips than I did with my regular pay, which was generous to start with. I ran a new idea I had been mulling over, past Charlotte some weeks later.

'You want to start sketching classes? Of Paris?'

'Yes. I think people would love to take home something that they have drawn. I can frame them quickly too. So they would sketch in the morning and by the afternoon, I can have a framed version of their work for them, to take away.'

'It's a great idea, Pippa. We can book you for another day then. Your sketch clients could draw in the mornings and visit two or three attractions in the afternoon? Soon you will be more than full-time with us. I think Robert and I are lucky to have found you.'

MY OWN ART had been progressing well. Pierre had taken me through various techniques, from life drawing, watercolours, and now my favourite, acrylics. He was fascinated with the way I dragged the tubes of paint down my canvas.

'I like the way you demand more from your paint, Pippa. These textures you are creating with the paint are interesting.'

'I love the way acrylic sits upon the canvas. You can shape it.'

'Have you ever been in an exhibition?' he asked me.

'Yes, only once though. I painted a work called *'Tears of Hope.'* It was next to Ken Done,' I said proudly.

'I know of this Done. A colourful man, yes? That's very good. I was wondering if you wanted to paint something for the Paris Exhibition, perhaps?'

I stared at him. The Paris Exhibition was nationally acclaimed. 'Do you think I would have a chance?' I asked, wondering if he had been serious.

'Yes. I think so. You would need to do your best, but give it a try. Paint your best, and we will enter it.'

'THIS IS INDEED AN HONOUR, Pippa. I bow in your presence,'

smiled Raphael, who was sitting in his quaint and very French apartment under piles of papers and books, strewn all over his desk.

'Very funny. How's your work going?' I asked.

'I am four months back in, and I feel better than I have in ages. The break has made me come back to the issues with the black holes with new eagerness. Thanks to you, Pippa.'

'I'm glad for you, Raphael.'

'And I am happy for my friend Pippa. First, a job taking special Americans around the city and being invited to try for the Paris Exhibition? You will soon be zooming around in the stars if you get any more clever.'

'Oh, stop Raphael. You are a man researching something amazing, up there.'

'Now, Pippa. I have something to discuss with you.'

'Okay. Is it serious? Is everything okay?'

'Yes, of course, but we need wine, and we need a fire. To take the chill out of the evening.'

He opened a bottle of wine and then built a small fire in his fireplace.

'Make yourself at home,' he said, then stopped suddenly, looking concerned. 'Something is missing,' he frowned.

'Cheese,' I said.

'Yes. Cheese. We must eat some of our delicious French cheese.'

I smiled. The warmth from the fire and the wine and cheese were perfect. I quietly thanked the universe, having gratitude, and the universe smiled at me, thanking me for having taken the time to see it properly. Since coming to Paris, it had kept up its end of the bargain, not throwing more at me than I could handle and allowing me to get some traction with things. I appreciated the simplicity it was allowing me to live within.

'So, are you ready for our discussion?' Raphael asked me, re-filling our glasses. 'I said a few months ago that you needed to have a passionate love affair while in Paris, but only if two people were ready. Have you thought about that some more?'

I was taken aback. Raphael had made it clear that he needed to find his happiness before taking anything further, and I wasn't even sure that he meant with me, either.

'I think two people need to be ready,' I said, sitting on the fence in case he was being general.

'Are you ready, Pippa? Yes?' There he went again, asking the question and answering it for me.

'Us?' I asked, hoping that he would say yes. If he suggested his cousin's friend right now, I was going to look stupid. I was ready to try again, but only with Raphael, and even then, it was going to be hard to trust anyone in bed again.

'Of course, us! Why? Did you have someone else in mind?' Raph looked worried.

'No, I just wasn't sure.' I smiled at him.

'Pippa. You say silly things sometimes. Yes! I want a passionate love affair with you. You have become my best friend, and now I need you to become my lover.'

I nodded.

'Now we will kiss. To seal our promise to be kind and truthful with one another.' Raphael stood and walked towards me. His deep brown eyes said it all. He had found his happiness, and now he was going to share it with me. I was the one who put my hand on the back of his amber curls and pulled his mouth towards mine. I was ready for this, a new start, a new chapter, and a new love. Then panic hit me like a bolt of lightning. I was fine, and then flashes of Noah invaded my mind. I pulled back.

'Pippa, I can see fear in your eyes,' he said, standing back, looking at me intently.

A cascade of memories came back. Me trusting Noah, thinking that I had found true love. Being in his arms and then the night he'd told me to piss off. I felt his weight on my back and the pain. I froze.

'Pippa, would you like to tell me what happened? I can see in your face that there is something very wrong.'

'You know me too well, Raphael, but if I tell you, then you must be prepared for an ugly truth.'

'I understand that the truth can be painful, Pippa. I promise that when you speak your truth that I will hold it in my hands and be very careful with it.' He held his hands out, cupped.

I looked over at this Frenchman, his amber curls framing his boyish face, wearing a jade woolly jumper, making him look soft and inviting. He was promising me a place to speak my truth that appeared safe. I needed to trust him, so I would tell him. A while later, having sat opposite to me as I recounted Noah, he looked at me with a sadness in his face.

'I cannot believe that this man, this Noah, would hurt you. He's horrible. If I meet him, I will punch him. Seriously, Pippa, I will be very gentle with you and very careful. I want to share passion and love with you, not hurt you. I promise. I cannot imagine why someone would want to treat another like that. You will simply have to trust me. Yes?'

Trust. A notion that was only as good as the intention behind it. Was I willing to risk everything again? Was I healed enough to share myself with someone? Was I prepared to lose the love?'

I stood and walked over to Raphael and held my hand out. He took it and gently steered me into his bedroom.

'Wait,' he said, as we reached his bedroom. 'I'm sorry. I wasn't expecting this, and my bed is trashed. Wait, please. It's full of my research papers.' He cleared them away and then returned to me. 'I want to share my love and feel your love, Pippa. Can we do that?'

'Yes,' I said, my heart opening again.

We made love, an experience that was calm, gentle, and guided. Raphael waited to see when I was ready and never forced anything. He spent a lot of time just holding me and stroking my skin. I spent most of the time trying to get Noah's face out of my mind. I would have loved to have said that it was a perfect experience, but it wasn't. I felt as if Noah was still sitting there mocking me for being so trusting with Raph. I didn't say anything, simply hoping that Noah would gradually fade from my reality as time went on.

'I love your freckles, Pippa. From the Australian sun. I can imagine the beaches there, the blue of the sky and the Aussie accents. Maybe one day I will see your Australia?'

'Maybe you will,' I said, savouring the feeling of being held again, and forcing Noah's memories again, out of my mind. I didn't want him to hijack any more of my life. A notion that in the moment seems hopeful, but in reality, isn't always achievable.

THE PHONE CALL came late one evening. It was my father.

'Your mother has died, Pippa. She had a stroke.'

'Christ. That's awful.' I sat down, the shock of the news reverberating throughout my body.

'The funeral is next week, Wednesday at ten.'

'I'm in Paris, though.'

'Paris? Why?' He seemed surprised, and then I realised that we hadn't spoken in that long. 'I didn't know you were living in Paris.'

'I'm working here. I'll try to fly back.'

'Everyone else has said they will come.'

'Okay, I'm sorry. Are you okay?'

'Yes. I'm fine, why Pippa?'

He'd said exactly the same words the day that Harry had died, appearing confused at my concern for him. There had been no emotion at the news of Harry's death, and there was none, now. My father didn't understand that she was my mother and I, her daughter, and that I would have my own grief to deal with. He forgot to ask me how I was because he was incapable of stepping into my shoes and seeing how I saw the world from my perspective. Even though his manner was expected after my experience when Harry died, it still slammed me between the eyes. Could he not, just for once, get out of his head and ask me how I was and perhaps provide me with a safe place to fall?

I sat for a while, knowing that this day had been coming, as parents don't live forever. Then I felt so sad as if my heart was crying. I felt like a small child who had been abandoned, feeling panic that I would never be able to find my mother again. My emotions swung from relief to utter despair. Most of all, I wondered if I had left anything unsaid? Would I worry in the future that I should have phoned again, and perhaps have told her that I loved her? Did I love her? That was a question that opened up a plethora of ruminations.

I didn't understand love properly and had always assumed it should be a two-way process. She had rarely phoned me over the past few years, mostly only wanting to talk about her childhood, or asking me to help in a crisis. Was that love? I didn't know. Did she love me if she were capable of hitting me or throwing a cup of tea at me? Was it love if she tried to control every aspect of my life for me? Was it love if she spoke to people in a disparaging way about me? Was that all part of love? The fact that she told me that it was my job to phone her and not the other way around. Was that love?

What about when we had laughed together? Gone on river walks together as I had grown up? Was that love? She had been interested in my schooling, paying for my education and yet, the other half of the equation had been such condemnation and criticism. I didn't know what love was supposed to look like, or at this moment, whether love was also part of the process of grief.

Was I supposed to feel guilty for not telling her that I loved her after all the sorrow that had come with this supposed love? The grief process felt almost familiar. There were two of her to grieve, just like Noah and the end of our relationship. The mother who had shown me love and then the mother who had hit me and had lashed out with rage when I deviated from out of her control.

I would need to fly back for the funeral, to show my respect, but the thought of seeing my whole family again was overwhelming. I curled up in bed and grieved instead.

I phoned Raphael the next day, a sorry mess of tangled emotions.

'Pippa, I will come with you? Yes? That way, you can lean on me. I will be your post.'

'Are you sure?'

'Of course. Your problems are my problems now.'

HE WAS a little surprised by the flight over.

'We have been flying for one whole eternity and then another one, on top of that. How far is this place called Australia? My legs - look, they are bent permanently up under my chin. I may not be able to walk when we get there. I will be sliding behind you on my back, my legs in the air.'

We landed four hours later, and I chose to tell Raphael a little about my family, on our approach.

'Your mother should be grateful you are even coming,' he said. 'A mother should never hit their child! I am angry and sad for you. We will do our best now, though, as that is all we can do.'

I felt guilt at his response. My mother had been more than that, and yet her wrongdoings suffocated the good bits. I wondered if she had ever realised that herself? That the violence and the rages would always outweigh any good that she was trying to do? I wondered why she had never tried to seek help to iron out her problems? Her death became more and more complicated for me to deal with. I was swinging between sadness and anger.

Brad was there to meet us. 'Pippa! Nice to see you! How was your flight?'

'Long. You forget until you do it again.'

'You both look shattered, to be honest.'

'Brad, this is Raphael. Raphael - Brad.' Brad shook hands with Raph and then looked at me and smiled again. I smiled back.

'I'm sorry about your news though, Pippa. Are you okay? Look, let's get you to your hotel, and we can talk in the car. Raphael looks like he's about to collapse.'

'I am so tired,' sighed Raph. 'That journey is quite something special.'

'I've booked you both into the Regent overnight, and then you've got your flight down to Tasmania at eight tomorrow. I didn't know if you wanted to go for dinner tonight?'

'You go, Pippa. You go and catch up with your friend Brad. I want to stretch out long and connect my legs to my body properly again.' Raphael looked exhausted enough to fall asleep in the car.

After I had showered, Brad picked me up and drove us to a restaurant not far from our original coaching cafe.

I told him about my apartment in Montmartre, and my job taking Americans around Paris and how I would be painting something that might get into the Paris Exhibition.

'Where did you meet Raphael?'

'At a cafe. I did it properly this time, Brad. Just like you had advised all that time ago. Raph is a good one. Like for real.'

'You two seem very happy.'

'We are. It's a nice happiness too. We got to know each other before jumping in. We allowed a solid friendship to grow.'

'Have you heard from Noah?'

'No. I wouldn't want to either.'

'How's the healing doing?'

'Okay. I have my good days and my bad days. It doesn't just go away very easily.'

'I hear you. I'm proud of you, Pippa. Really proud. If you don't mind, I might let Cynthia know how well you are doing?'

'Yeah, if I had more time, I'd go and see her. I only managed a week off work, though.'

'How do you feel about seeing all of your family again tomorrow?'

'Terrible. It will be like being in a room full of strangers, all of us processing the death of a mother we haven't seen in too long. Hopefully, they can keep their mouths shut long enough not to attack me too. Raph said that we would just make the best of it, and he's right. This is about me saying goodbye to her. That's the only reason I'm here. It's the right thing to do.'

'How sad are you?'

'Very. More than I thought I would be. I will miss her. Not everyone is *all bad*.'

'It's been complicated, that's for sure,' Brad said.

RAPH and I sat in the second row of the funeral room. My mother had insisted that she didn't want a funeral of any kind, but my father had decided to allow family in, and family only. To be honest, I'm not sure that anyone else would have gone to my mother's funeral, given she'd not had any friends for years with most of them, dying before her. She had become stuck in a world of ageing alpacas and sitting at home with my father.

My siblings arrived with their partners and children and sat. I'd not met most of their children, and it was awkward to be sitting there seeing children who partially resembled me, sitting there, staring back. I tried to be friendly, not wanting to cause angst or give my siblings any more fuel in which to throw fire at me. I would be seen, support my father, pay my respects to my mother, and go back to Paris and grieve in private with Raphael.

The ceremony was short with no-one wanting to give a speech, instead, we listened to some of her favourite music. I wrote a speech in my mind, though, and took the opportunity to say my goodbye, a much safer option given my siblings' nastiness.

THERE HADN'T BEEN enough interaction with any of us for a formal speech to have been written, and my father wasn't going to get up and say anything, his grief immobilising him in his seat in the form of a stoic grimace. Afterwards, tea and biscuits had been laid on, but I didn't want to mingle with my siblings, as my exchanges would have been fake with pleasantry. I had attended for my mother, certainly not to parade around, trying to small talk with people who had rejected me for most of my adult life.

Raph was surprised I didn't stay to speak with them for longer, but I told him that I had finished doing my best, and he understood. I wondered what would happen to my father, now alone. His time had been mostly spent with my mother and the farm. I presumed he would just chug along with the farm until he couldn't anymore. Raph excused himself to go to the bathroom while we waited for our taxi to arrive and I walked to the rose garden next to the funeral home. I was inhaling some delicate rose perfumes when I heard a voice.

'Excuse me.'

I looked around, to see a white van and a man reaching into it for something.

'Hi, I'm looking for Pippa O'Shea.'

'Sorry?'

'Pippa O'Shea?'

'Yeah… that's me. Why?'

The man took something from the truck and then brought it over. It was a bunch of flowers. Yellow Gerberas. My heart sank.

'There's a card,' he added.

I looked down at the flowers and saw a small envelope simply addressed to *Pippa O'Shea.*

Raphael came out at that moment and walked towards me.

'They are very nice. Who are they from?'

'I don't know. I haven't looked yet.' I knew. I already knew that they were from Noah. He was the only person who knew that I loved yellow Gerberas.

I opened the envelope.

'Sorry for your loss. Noah.'

I looked around, half expecting to see him lurking somewhere, wanting to see my reaction.

'Pippa. Who are they from?'

'Noah.'

'The man who hurt you?'

'Yes.'

'Why is he sending you flowers?'

'I'm asking myself the same question Raph. He shouldn't even know there is a funeral.'

'Is he here?'

'I hope not. Look, we should go, just in case. I don't want any drama while I'm here. I'll phone Brad as well.'

Brad was worried. 'He sent flowers? Is he there?'

'No, I don't think so.'

'Have you asked the florist if they were ordered in-store or online?'

'Yeah, one of the first things I did. Online apparently. They just deliver them.'

'Well, at least he's not actually there.'

'How did he even know about the funeral?'

'Maybe he read the paper? It seems a bit odd though Pippa. Be careful.'

'Yeah. We're heading back to Sydney now. Our flight leave in forty minutes.'

'Look, come back, and maybe we could sit down with Cynthia and have a chat?'

'Yeah, she might have a bit more insight into all of this.'

'How was the funeral, aside from Noah?'

'Basic, pretty awful.'

'Did you see your family?'

'Yeah, but I didn't speak to them in depth.'

'You good with that?'

'Yeah. I didn't have a choice.'

'HE'S reminding you.'

'Of what?' I asked Cynthia.

'That he exists.'

'Really?'

'Yes. At a time of great sorrow, he wants your mind to be full of him, instead.'

'That's a bit sick.'

'Staying in character, though.'

'Has he been checking up on me do you think? Or did he see the funeral notice by accident?'

'I don't know anyone who accidentally sees funeral notices. You have to be looking for them,' said Brad. 'Do you think that Pippa is in any real danger from him?'

'I don't know,' Cynthia pondered. 'He's got psychopathic tendencies. Would he go to the effort of flying to Paris at any stage, though? I don't know. It depends on what resolution he's after. Remember that psychopaths are predators. He may be looking for fresh meat again.'

'How would he find me?'

'Work? What's on the internet about you?'

'My home address isn't there.'

'Paris is also a big city,' added Brad. 'My honest truth? This was a cheap and nasty way to frighten you. I don't think he will do it anymore. He just couldn't leave it alone, though could he? He's like a child, wanting the last word, and at your mother's funeral? Deplorable taste. He may even have just broken up with someone else and be angry? Who knows?'

'Give him the last word Pippa,' added Cynthia. 'As in, don't say anything. Don't respond and do not contact him. This time, please follow our advice?'

'Of course,' I said, feeling my skin redden.

'Leave him thinking that he's had the final word,' added Brad.

'I can do that. Otherwise, he's going to spin a web around me again.'

. . .

IT HAD BEEN good seeing Brad and Cynthia again, despite the circumstances. Now it was time for me to take Raphael around my Sydney, despite my palpable grief from my mother's death. This was the Sydney that I had remembered from my youth. Raph loved the ferry ride, although when I started quoting Slessor, he shook his head.

'I'm not feeling it, Pippa. I don't understand this man, Slessor. I see this harbour as full of light and fun and energy! More like something your Matisse would paint.'

I took Raph up the hill from the ferry, and Oak was still standing there. 'This cross on the trunk,' I pointed to it. 'This is the cross I drew when Alan was knocked down.'

I looked up at the window and thought better than to tell him about how I had stood next to it, waiting for Alan to return home. However, I did point up to the window and explained how I had once tipped a whole bowl of pasta out of the window.

'It honestly looked like someone's brains on the concrete,' I laughed.

I took Raph into the travel agency, mainly to see Adele's jaw hitting her desk hard.

'This is Raphael. He's a Doctoral student in Paris. He's studying Black Holes.'

Her face hadn't disappointed, and her open mouth had formed a bit of a black hole itself. I felt good returning to the agency because it reminded me of how brave I had been in moving to Paris. If you don't make those great leaps of faith, how do you ever know if they will work out? If I hadn't been brave, I would still be sitting there, helping everyone else plan and fulfil their own dreams.

Raph and I walked past the flat where my mother had fallen down the stairs and had hit me, sending me crashing down, onto the concrete. I didn't mention that, but for some reason, as I explained that I used to live there, Raph gave me a little squeeze. I stood there as if there were two of me. One was looking back at what had been, and the other looking out, wondering what was to come. Somehow, two lines of time had merged into one, meeting in a strange duality. I took Raph to Taronga Zoo and Darling Harbour, and then to the ballet at The Opera House. He was in awe of all of it.

'Australia is beautiful. Not as beautiful as France, of course,' he said, laughing. 'It is Pippa beautiful, though, and I love both.'

Raph's black
hole was full

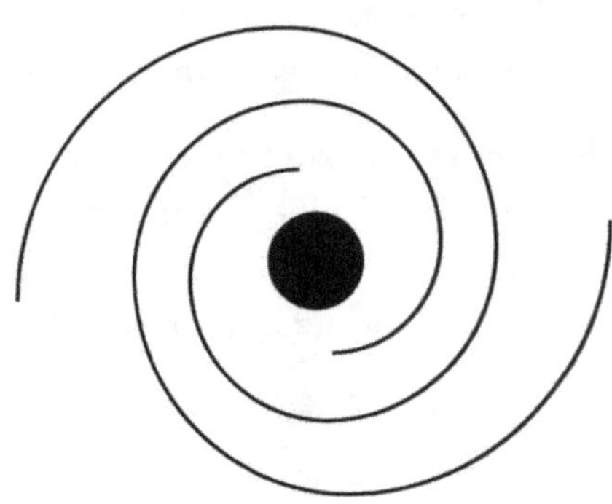

25

BLACK HOLE NOT EATING
OUT OF THE DARKNESS SHONE LIGHT

We returned to Paris, and Raph jumped back into his thesis, and I returned to a busy schedule with my tourists. I also had to start thinking about my artwork.

'Do you have any idea what you might like to paint?' Pierre asked, hopefully.

'Yes. I'm going to paint something close to my heart,' I replied. I sketched out the drawing that evening. I was sure it would work if I got the colours right.

Raph loved the idea when I explained it to him later on in the week. 'Brilliant Pippa. The Paris Exhibition will love it. Now we have another discussion to have. First, I make the wine and cheese, and perhaps you would like to make the fire this evening?'

We then sat, making up a poem that we thought Matisse might have written about Sydney Harbour. It would be glowing but not quite put together right, and vivid and bright. It would be a positive record of the festivity on and always near the water's edge.

'Now, our discussion.' Raph said.

'Yes,' I said, having no idea what Raph wanted to discuss.

'I am thinking that you might want to move in here with me? Yes? With that Noah out there, I don't want you on your own in Paris, and your lease should be almost up?'

I blinked, trying to comprehend what he had just asked me.

'Me, move in here?'

'Oui.'

'Okay,' I said quickly, in case he changed his mind. 'Yes, I agree with Noah out there somewhere… but I'd love to move in with you, just because it's you, Raph.'

'I am happy, Pippa. Cheers to us.' He lifted his glass of red wine and beamed.

It had only been a matter of time before we would take our relationship to this next level, and it felt right. It hadn't felt rushed. I felt that Raph and I had our scaffolding right. He had never raised his voice at me either, which was a good sign. I wouldn't have tolerated it.

I WAS FIGHTING with my artwork and was painting on a canvas much bigger than I was used to. If I could get this right, it would be a feast for the eyes. My idea was to paint Paris, but only include one or two of the usual landmarks. Then I was going to place a little bit of Pippa here and there. It would make the painting a little surreal in places, but I wanted the style to be mine. A combination perhaps of Matisse, Done, Dali, and Hart with a sprinkling of Whiteley? No. Noah had liked him. Not Whiteley. Pierre thought that painting in front of a class might be useful for feedback.

'So, Pippa, I want you to hold a small class for my beginners.'

'Really?'

'Yes, you will be in the centre of the room working on your entry, and they can watch you and ask questions. It will keep you painting on the tips of your toes.'

'Won't that make me self-conscious with what I'm going to paint?'

'Yes, probably, but it will also keep your painting honest.' He nodded, agreeing with himself.

'Okay. I'll give it a go. Have you seen the size of my canvas, though, Pierre? Do you even have enough room for me and anyone else in the studio?'

'Pippa, I will make room if I have to.'

I set up in the middle of the leading teaching studio and felt as sick as if I had been asked to present a masterclass on impressionism. Pierre reassured me that the beginner students wouldn't know right from wrong anyway.

'You could be painting with the wrong end of the brush, and they would think that you are teaching them something special!' he had chuckled.

'I might well be using the wrong end of the brush in this painting. Be prepared Pierre.'

'Then do it with a plumb, my dear woman.'

'Do you mean 'aplomb, Pierre?'

'Oui. I think so.'

It was hard to concentrate with eight other people in the room. I had prepared my canvas and had done a background of white, pink, and sky blue. The rest was going to be painted in layers and textured out from the canvas.

'Everyone, I would like you to see and meet Pippa. She is an Australian artist, and this is her work that will be entered into the Paris Exhibition.'

'Bonsoir,' I said, smiling at the timid group of beginners.

'Bonsoir,' some of them replied, looking more nervous than I felt.

'So, as you can see, I have prepared my canvas, and now I will sketch out my ideas.'

'What is it going to be?' asked a young man at the front.

'It's going to be Paris… my Paris,' I smiled.

I took the rough sketch from my pad and began to transpose it onto the bigger canvas. Pierre added bits of info here and there.

'As you can see, she does not just walk up to the canvas and start making it up. She has thought about what she wants to paint and has done several rough drafts beforehand. This is essential to get what is from here properly,' he tapped his head… 'onto there,' he pointed at the canvas.

It was painstaking, transposing my image from small to large while maintaining the integrity of the artwork. I kept my hand relaxed so that my lines weren't too heavy. My Paris was light and frivolous, not dark and moody. It took most of the art class to do the transposing, and in the meantime, Pierre got the class to do some sketches of me. He gave them to me after class.

'Pierre. I love these! So many different versions of me doing the artwork. I love this one,' I said, holding up a simple line drawing. 'This is definitely my favourite. How can this artist say so much with so little charcoal?'

'She is very talented, I think. Now, when are you coming in to work on the painting next?'

'I'll need to come in every day if that's okay? After work? I'll move the canvas into one of the other studios so that I'm not in the way.'

'You have two weeks Pippa before I have to enter it. I take a photo first of the finished work, and if they like it, you are in. There have only been three of my students who have made it into the Paris Exhibition, plus myself. I managed to come second, which was an incredible experience. If you win a place, they invite you to the ball. It's magical.'

'You think I have a chance of winning something?'

'Maybe Pippa. Paint from the heart, though, don't force it.'

RAPH WAS FRUSTRATED with his black hole when I got home. His desk was under a mountain of papers, photos, and graphs.

'How's it going, Raph? I can hardly distinguish you from all the papers.'

'My hole is misbehaving. It's gone on a hunger strike Pippa. It refuses to do anything, and so my data is becoming illogical. If things don't change soon, then my thesis is on hold. I need more data before analysing it all, and nothing is happening.'

'Maybe it's full?' I asked.

Raph looked up at me and stared for a moment as if thinking. 'Full? Yes! Pippa, you are brilliant. Why did I not think of that myself? My hole might be full. See, sometimes, I need you to step back for me and give me something different. If it is full, then that would be interesting, definitely.'

'That sounds impossible to have a hole that is full, but I'm glad to help,' I said, smiling. I knew he was playing with me. Even with my rudimentary understanding of black holes, I knew that they didn't just stop dragging everything in.

'How did your class go? How has your painting been tonight?'

'Terrifying. I had to paint in the middle of the room with the students around me. No pressure.'

'I would have been scared to death,' smiled Raph. 'I prefer to work with things that are too far away for me to hear them.'

'I was scared to death. However, I've prepared the canvas, and now I'm sketching my image onto it. That's called progress. I think.'

'My Pippa. You are such a clever woman.'

I walked over and put my arms around Raph and squeezed him close.

'I don't know how I managed to be here with you, but I'm so grateful.'

'My beautiful woman. It is me that is a lucky man. You are the first woman ever to appreciate my black holes for a start.'

I HAD ARRANGED to meet with my latest American clients at an old perfumery in the centre of Paris, which had now been transformed into a museum, shop and cafe. They had leapt at the idea of allowing me to run tours in English. I loved taking people around the old building, as at the end, there was always plenty of time to sample the extensive range of perfumes and soaps that were on sale in the shop. Today, I was meeting a group of four, a family from New York. Sisters, who had flown to Paris for a shopping weekend. This was their first port of call.

'Hello, so nice to meet you all,' I said to the four excited young women, 'and welcome to the most romantic, cultured, and beautiful city in the world. I'm Pippa.'

They were all stunning and blonde. They clapped excitedly, obviously happy to be in Paris.

'I'm Anna… and this is Avery, Amelia, and Allegra.'

'Wow, all beginning with A,' I said, smiling at them.

Allegra flashed two rows of perfect, white teeth at me, reminding me of the drag queen, from long ago.

'Today, you're going to have fun. Lots to see and then a whole room full of soaps, perfumes, bubble baths, and handbags to choose from, plus a Parisian lunch to finish off. How does that sound?'

The girls clapped their hands excitedly.

'How was your flight?' I asked them, walking them into the old perfumery.

'It was lovely, thank you. Too much champagne and too much chocolate, though.' said Anna.

It was easy doing this job. My clients were always so happy to be in Paris and were eager to be taken anywhere. Most of the time, I just had to make small-talk and stay enthusiastic - they did the rest.

I led them through several rooms and played a short video about perfume and how it had been made. Then I took them into the bottle room, one of the highlights of the tour. Floor to ceiling shelves with various perfume bottles from various periods of time. It was a stunning display.

'This display highlights all the variations in perfume bottles from over the years. You can see how the colours changed as the fashions did. If I turn the lights down, you'll see all the beautiful detail in the glass bottles.' The room went dark. The girls walked towards the display, oohing and ahhing at everything.

'You do this so well,' said a voice in the near darkness. I jumped.

'Just me.'

I knew that voice… but it wasn't possible… not in the perfumery… not in Paris.

'That's right, Pips. Thought I'd join your tour as a last-minute addition. I've paid upfront, of course. How are you?'

The four girls had turned, wondering who was speaking.

'Sorry, ladies, for being late. My taxi was delayed. So, New York girls I'm guessing from your accents? I'm Noah, from Brisbane originally, now living in Sydney.'

I needed to stay calm. My phone was in my bag at the front counter, so calling Raph wasn't possible. I needed to think and fast. I decided to keep Noah on the regular tour, rather than deal with him in front of the girls. It was safer to keep them around me, anyway.

I took the tour into the history room and then into the chemical processing room. Noah made small talk with the girls and seemed relaxed.

'Over here is the scent room,' I continued. 'This is where ideas were taken from initial concept and then turned into the final product. Feel free to sniff anything that looks like it needs to be sniffed.'

The four girls raced off to start at the number one stand, unaware of the drama that was beginning to unfold. I began to walk towards them, but Noah pulled me off to one side and into a side room, illuminated with the barest of light. He kicked the door shut with his foot.

'You smell good,' Noah said, pinning me against the wall. My body instinctively froze. 'Sandalwood and jasmine, perhaps?' He sniffed near my ear, and I felt his breath, warm on my neck. 'You do a good tour, I hear. Very convincing.'

I felt sick. Sweat was forming on my forehead.

'I could just take you, here and now, in the dark. Would you consent to that Pippa?'

'Stop Noah.'

'She speaks! I'm making progress.' He pressed his body up against me in the dark, grabbing my waist.

'Get your hands off me!'

'No. You liked this on our first date. Do you remember? You pressed your body back into mine, down near the harbour. What are you going to do, Pippa? Call it assault now?'

'What are you even doing here, Noah? There's nothing between us. If you don't go, then I will call the police. How did you even find me?'

'And say what? That I have rightfully joined your tour? I'm not doing anything wrong, and I haven't made a scene. I'm in Paris working with an ad agency right now. There is no crime in doing that, Pippa. Don't think I made a special trip to Paris to stalk you. You would look neurotic and hysterical if you said that, which, of course, you are, and I will use that against you in court.'

I remembered Cynthia's words. Psychopaths were predators. They hunted their victims. Was it accurate in this case, and he was looking for fresh meat?

'We're not going to court, Noah. We were never going to go to court.'

'Oh, I sent you flowers. Did you like them? They were your favourite. I remembered.'

'I got them.'

'Why no court Pips? Because there wasn't anything that happened. You women are all the same.'

'Same?'

'Yeah. The same. You cry foul when nothing has happened.'

'You should be punished, Noah. You should feel guilty for assaulting me. How about sleeping with prostitutes under your wife's nose, while your kids were asleep in their beds? Who writes reviews on prostitutes? Who calls their previous girlfriend, a whore, and a slut Noah? I saw the cartoon. Where the hell is your moral compass?'

Noah stepped back. 'Pippa… I still… love…'

'No. Don't you dare say that you still love me. That wasn't love.'

He laughed. 'I still love ice-cream Pips. That's what I was going to say.'

I took a deep breath. 'Why are you even here?'

'To settle a score and finish a job for an ad agency. I'm in Paris, and you are in Paris. Seems like a good time to do it. So, don't you ever accuse me again of something I didn't do.'

'You did do it.' I remembered what Cynthia and Brad had said. Allow him to think that he's had the last word. I'd just gone and provoked him.

He grabbed me by the arm, pushing me to the ground. I hit the cold stone floor with a thud. Then I felt his foot on my leg.'

'Get off me!' I screamed.

'No. Not until you admit you lied.'

'I didn't lie!'

'Tell the world, Pippa. Tell them that you lied. I want to hear the words.'

'What about all of your lies, Noah? How many other lies were there?'

'I told you the obese lady was an analogy. How dumb can you be? What? You actually thought I'd knocked her down when my kids were with me?'

'You were the one that told me the story, Noah. That's what you said.'

'You're the liar!' He pressed down harder on my leg. I winced.

'I also have your text, Noah. The one you sent me after I'd told you that you'd hurt me. You said, *Me Bad*. You admitted it.'

'Prove it. You can't prove it. Why are you still such a trouble-maker Pippa?'

'Get off me!'

He pressed his weight onto my leg, harder.

'I'm waiting.'

'Noah. Get off me!'

'Pippa. What's happening in here?'

Noah looked up, one of the girls was standing in the doorway, filming with her phone.

'Get away from her,' she said. 'You piece of merde.'

I brought my leg up and kicked Noah, hard. He fell backwards onto the floor.

'I'll get you for assault,' he gasped.

'No you won't,' one of the girls said.

'Look up, Noah.' I pointed upwards.

He looked upwards. In the corner of the room flashed a small camera.

'That's our security system. It's captured every word you said and every action. I can easily plead self-defence.'

I then got up, rubbing my arm where it had hit the stone floor and dialled Raph's number using Amelia's phone.

'Noah is here… yeah, at the perfumery… yeah, the CCTV got it all, as well as one of the girls on her phone.'

The girls circled around Noah.

'Raphael is on his way. You have exactly two minutes to get the hell out of my life. If you EVER come near me again, I will have you charged, and I will find your probable other victims for them to speak up too. Your life will be over. You have three children, depending on you to set an example. What the hell sort of example is this Noah? Really? Do you want Rose to grow up knowing what you do to women? Do you want your sons to go out and do this to women themselves? Go away and do NOT ever come near me again. Go and be the parent that they need you to be!'

Noah backed away into the shadows. He said nothing.

'Don't you ever come near me again, Noah, because next time, I'm not going to be nearly as accommodating. I'm letting you go for Rose, for Seb and Steve. You ever find me again, I will call the police on the spot.'

He backed away. 'You didn't win, Pippa. You are nothing. You mean nothing. Just incase, you had forgotten. No-one will ever love you.'

I heard the exit door shut, and he was gone.

'Shit,' I exhaled and bent forwards, trying to catch my breath. I was aware of pain in my arm and leg.

'Wow, you were amazing,' the girls crowded around.

'So impressed, Pippa,' said Avery, 'and Amelia has it all on film. You could at least get him for common assault. What a maniac!'

Raphael arrived a few minutes later. 'Where he is?' he asked, searching the room.

'He's gone, Raph, hopefully for good this time.'

'Your girlfriend was amazing, by the way,' Anna said, smiling.

RAPH PUT a blanket around me when we got home. 'Here, my love, I have made you a hot chocolate with some cheese. Although I worry that the two will not go well together.'

'Thank you, Raph.' Since I had got home, he had fussed over me. My leg and arm would bruise, but I was in one piece. More emotionally shocked than anything.

'That was a tough day, although I'm glad I could still finish the tour and thank you for waiting for me too. Those girls were so sweet. They bought half the store in the end.'

'And gave most of it to you,' he smiled, looking at the vast number of shopping bags they had gifted, as a thank you.

'I have enough perfume and soaps for a year, at least.'

'So, do we think that this Noah is now gone?'

'Yes. I think so. With the CCTV and video evidence, he wouldn't want to be charged with assault. It's almost a good thing that he did knock me to the floor. It's the first time he's done something that can't be denied.'

'I suppose so. I hope so.'

'Me too. I just want our lives to go back to normal now. I have the Paris Exhibition to concentrate on as well. I don't want to be dragged into a court case right now. I want to move forward.'

'I agree. I have my temperamental black hole to resolve too.'

'Is it eating yet?'

'No. It's too full.' He smiled.

'Can I have some more cheese?'

NOAH HAD THROWN me off course with my art. I needed to get into the zone with the painting but couldn't find my passion. The painting wasn't resonating with me anymore. On the flip side, I felt inside as if a chapter of my life had now closed, hoping that it had been done correctly this time. I phoned Brad.

'He was here, in Paris.'

'Who? Noah?'

'Yeah. He found me at work and confronted me.'

'Are you okay?'

'Yeah, but it was nasty.'

'Has he left? Did you call the police?'

'The CCTV captured everything, including the fact he knocked me to the floor.'

'Are you hurt?'

'Luckily, no. I let him go because his kids need him.'

'Shit Pippa. Do you think it was the wrong advice not to call the police before, when he sent you those flowers?'

'No. He was spoiling for a fight.'

'Ok. I'll let Cynthia know as well. You may hear from her. What an arse, though.'

'I decided to let him go.'

'Why?'

'I don't want to be dragged into all of that again. It's taken me so long to recover to this point. If I try to have him charged, everything is going to be brought up again. I don't want that.'

'Brave decision. Hopefully, he's gone for good this time?'

'I hope so, Brad.'

I STOOD BACK, looking at the canvas. 'I'm not feeling this,' I muttered under my breath.

'What are you not feeling?' asked Pierre, walking into the art studio.

'This work. My heart isn't in it.'

'What you have done so far is good. It's colourful, quirky and alive, so what is wrong, Pippa?'

'I feel like I need to be painting something else.'

'At this late stage? You only have a week to finish.'

'Yeah, I know. It would be madness to start again.'

'Pippa. I ask one thing from you.'

'What's that, Pierre?'

'That you paint with honesty.'

'I hear you, Pierre.'

• • •

I WENT for a walk down by the Seine, looking at the reflections in the water. This was my Paris now, and the colours in the water reminded me of Sydney Harbour. Raphael was my love, and my job was my passion. How easy it was, to now define myself. Getting away from my family was what I had needed to do. Their chaos was infectious and had suffocated me. Here, I could breathe and be seen for who I indeed was.

The painting that I had initially wanted to paint depicted my journey from Sydney to Paris, but there was no conclusion. It was a snippet in time that may not have been fully understood by anyone else. I felt like I had used humour in the painting to cloud the reality of my journey. A bit like what Brad had said about telling my story. Sometimes showing myself as raw was better than hiding in it all. A cheap joke was dishonest.

The truth concerning my journey and its completion was now reflected to me in the water. A woman was looking back at me. Strong, passionate and honest. This was the real end to this chapter, an end without an end in a sense because my experiences now leaned towards a new beginning.

'That's what I need to paint.' I looked out over Paris and smiled.

THE NEXT MORNING, I rushed to the art studio.

'Pierre. I'm starting again. With honesty.'

'Are you sure, Pippa?'

'Yes.'

'You are lucky, Pippa, that it is a Saturday. I can help you to replace the canvas. How big are you going to go?'

'Not as big Pierre. About half the size.'

'Okay. Here you are,' he said, dragging a canvas in from the back storeroom. 'Now, what colours do you need to prepare it all?'

'Black to start with.'

'Just black? You never use black Pippa.'

'Pierre. Trust me.' I prepared the canvas and then painted it a solid black. Then I went and studied my face in the mirror.

'Are you attempting a self-portrait, Pippa? Is this what you hope for?'

'Yes, Pierre.'

I CAREFULLY STUDIED the lines of my face, remembering what Pierre had said to me so often. *Only draw what you see, Pippa.* I saw myself, as a composite of my new life as well as my old. I saw the fine lines that indicated laughter and sadness. I saw how the chickenpox had left its mark, but most of all, I could see into my soul. It had been on a long journey, and the layers of sadness could be seen as pools of green, with infinite depth. My whole story looked back at me, and I understood it.

Green eye to green eye, I gazed back at my reflection and understood that life was always going to be a journey and that happiness could be found in the smallest of places, as well as the largest, as Raph had discovered. There was no real control that we could exert over our lives, other than to live within simple routines, maintaining a sense of hope.

I finished late Sunday night, without having taken a break, other than to go back to the flat to sleep and eat. Raph was also pulling an intensive work shift with his Black Hole, now having fully awoken and burped. It was starting to drag in more matter, and Raph was back in action and spending time over at the observatory.

I stood back and smiled. Yes. This was honesty. This was integrity. This was real.

'Oh, Pippa. Where did this come from?' Pierre had come in from another room to see how I was going. 'I must go and get coffee and just sit in front of this for a while. Then we will talk.'

He did. He brought in a cup of coffee and then sat, looking at the painting, without speaking. I wandered in and out of the art room a few times, hoping for some feedback, but Pierre was leaning back and then tilting his head to the left and the right as if deep in thought. Eventually, he called my name. I stood next to him.

'Pippa. This is magnificent. Well done. I see you… I truly see you.'

My painting was framed, photographed, and submitted. It would be a week before I would hear anything. Instead, I put my energy into my work, now finding that I was almost fully booked each week. The four sisters had told all of their friends about my heroic experience at the perfumery, and now everyone from New York in their circles wanted to meet me. I had tours going out to castles, wineries, and flower farms. My sketching tour was full as well. It was as if the universe had decided I was its number one.

RAPH SEEMED a bit down when I got home from work. Instead of a fire and our regular cheese and wine, he seemed quiet and subdued.

'You okay?' I asked, worried by the fact that he had his head in his hands.

'Not really,' he said.

I tensed. Was he unhappy with me for some reason? He must have seen the look on my face change.

'Pippa. It is not you making me unhappy.'

'No?' Relief swept through me. 'Is it your Black Hole, Raph?'

'No. Today is just the anniversary of when my mother and brother died.'

'Raph. Oh, God. I didn't know. I'm so sorry. I've been so full of work and my painting…'

'It's ok. I didn't tell you so as not to bring you downwards.'

'No. You must tell me these things. That's why I'm here. Yes?' I realised I had spoken like Raph, ending my statement with an answered question.

Raph began to cry. I'd never seen him shed a tear. He looked up at me, his face creasing in pain. 'I miss them so much, Pippa.' He was sobbing. 'My life, it will never recover.'

'It will, Raph. I promise you, and I will be here for you. My poor Raph.' I held him for a while and then lit the fire. Then I cut up cheese and poured him some wine. 'I'm going to be here for you, Raph. Okay? You have a family now. We are a family. Small, but yet, a family.'

Raph sniffed and then wiped his nose on his sleeve. 'You are a beautiful soul Pippa. More than I could ever imagine to meet.'

'I feel the same, Raph. I'm very fortunate to have you in my life.'

'Pippa. We have a discussion to make. Yes?'

'Sure.'

Raph suddenly dropped onto one knee. 'Pippa. Will you and your cheese marry me?'

I felt my knees give a little and held onto Raph's arm for support.

'Really, Raph? For real?'

'Yes, of course, for real. Aside from that blue cheese from the other day, please.' He wiped his nose on his sleeve, his eyes brightening.

'Then, yes. I say yes!'

'Elle a dit oui! Elle a dit oui! Elle a dit oui!' he shouted out of the window to surprised Parisians on the footpath below. I texted Brad.

P: I said, yes!

B: Congratulations, Pippa. You're living a real fairy tale this time xxx.

P: Yes, Brad, I am. Thank you. You're coming to Paris for a wedding, x

B: I have a question…

P: ?

B: Did you think the writing therapy helped?

P: YES! :-)

B: I'm glad.

AN EARLY MORNING phone call broke the silence. It was Pierre speaking at a million miles an hour.

'Je suis très heureux. Vous êtes entré dans l'exposition. Pippa, c'est tellement merveilleux que je peux à peine parler ni respirer.'

'Slowly, Pierre. I didn't catch that.'

'Pippa. You are in!'

'As in?'

'Your painting… ils m'ont appelé ce matin et m'ont annoncé la nouvelle. Vous devez être dans l'exposition.'

I handed the phone to Raph, who listened intently with a serious expression on his face. 'Oui. Je comprends. Je ferai savoir à Pippa.' He gave me the phone back and then his face broke out into an enormous grin.

'Your painting. It seems to have made it into the Paris Exhibition.'

'Oh my God,' I said, sitting down.

THE EXHIBITION OPENING night was a much-celebrated Parisian affair, and we had hired formal clothes for the occasion. I dressed in a pink, dusk coloured, full-length evening dress, and Raph was in a tuxedo. Pierre was sure I had won something, as we had all been formally invited to the private section of the ceremony that started before the public opening, *and* to the ball afterwards.

'I think Pippa, you win something,' he said excitedly when we met him outside the Musée de l'Orangerie.

'I visited here once, right back at the beginning, you know. I found all of these works by Matisse downstairs, and I was spellbound.'

'Now your work is hanging here tonight. It is amazing,' smiled Raph, who couldn't stop telling me how proud he was of me. We were met at the door, and our coats were taken and hung in the coatroom. Then we were offered a glass of champagne from a silver tray, with small slithers of strawberry, dipping their toes into the sparkling bubbles. I was adorned in beautiful fabric, soft makeup, and sparkling jewellery, completely transforming me from Pippa from Sydney, to Pippa in Paris.

I felt beautiful.

The President of the Exhibition gave a short welcoming speech, and then the awards were announced.

'Yours was entered into the 'Self-Portrait' section. It's almost to be announced,' said Pierre, sounding extremely nervous.

Raph gripped my hand tightly as they announced the three paintings that had been Highly Commended. Then third place… second place… I shook my head at Raph and Pierre.

'There's no way…'

'… and the winner of The Self Portrait section for the Paris Exhibition is, Pippa O'Shea with her painting *'To be, or not to be.'*

There was thunderous applause, and I stood, stunned, gripping Raph's hand.

'You did it! My Pippa did it!' he shouted. Then he was kissing me.

'Congratulations, Pippa.' Pierre was nodding and clapping. 'Go… go on up. This is your moment to be shining.'

Raph whispered into my ear, 'I'm so proud of you and so glad we made up an acceptance speech, just in case. Yes? I love you, Pippa

O'Shea.'

CAMERAS STARTED TO FLASH, capturing the moment, and then I was standing in front of a hundred people. I took a deep breath, but the speech that Raph and I had created, seemed less than honest. It had been a little generic, and perhaps I could do more than that right now? Would I dare to show these people who I indeed was? It was now or never… to be as honest as my painting was.

I glanced over to it, now adorned with a banner stating First Prize, and hanging next to a Matisse, who had quietly whispered *'Well done Pippa.'* Taking another deep breath, I smiled and began at the beginning.

My acceptance speech was spoken from my heart, and those standing in front of me nodded, my honesty touching their own, private life experiences.

'I had a choice,' I said, finishing my speech. 'A little while ago, I asked myself. *To be, or not to be?* Right now, everyone? I am so glad that I chose, to be. To be here, to be here now - just to be, me.'

The room broke out in enthusiastic applause, and Raphael looked at me, catching my eye, and smiled… his soul reaching into my soul… and I knew at that moment that I was looking at the man that I would soon marry and love for the rest of my life. This time, I had found my soul-mate, for real. His love felt good, and his love felt honest. There was no other Raph to try to accommodate into the relationship. He was just one, and I loved him. I ran to him, his arms outstretched.

'I am the proudest man in Paris.' Then he kissed me, deeply, passionately, and honestly.

I am Pippa O'Shea. Winner of the Paris Exhibition. Tour guide, living in Paris. *I am happy and most importantly. I am loved.*

THE END.

ABOUT THE AUTHOR

Juliette Cavendish was born in Liverpool, UK and now resides in Australia. She started her career as a classical musician, graduating from the Sydney Conservatorium of Music, University of Sydney, with a Bachelor of Music and Education Degree.

She went on to study in several other disciplines, including holistic counselling, research, life coaching, teaching, photography and metaphysics.
She holds a Masters in Quantitative and Qualitative Research Methodologies as well as a PhD. in Metaphysics.

Juliette was a Life Coach and Holistic Counsellor for many years, working within a medical practice.
She is also a specialist Event Photographer, having been exhibited all over the world, with a passion for circus and rock music.

Juliette enjoys contemplating life, love, philosophy, people, the cosmos, and has been writing stories since the age of seven.

Juliette is married, has two daughters, and lives in Regional Victoria, Australia, along with her Siamese cats, Dotti and Amelia and her Groodle, Paddington.

www.juliettecavendish.com.au

Juliette A H Cavendish

ALSO BY JULIETTE A H CAVENDISH

London Red Publishing

Ziforah: In The Beginning. Book One.

Project IQ. Home Base Mars

The Psychopath Who Nearly Lost His Arm. Love-Bomb. Devalue. Discard.

NEW NOVELS for 2021

Whistle Blower

Consequences

The Third Thought

Ziforah: The Abandoned. Book Two.